RIVER THROUGH TIME

Me ke aloha,
BB Hill

RIVER THROUGH TIME

BB Hill

Aventine Press

© copyright June 2005, BB Hill
First Edition

Published by Aventine Press
1023 4th Ave #204
San Diego CA, 92101
www.aventinepress.com

ISBN: 1-59330-291-6

Library of Congress Control Number: 2005905113
Library of Congress Cataloging-in-Publication Data
River Through Time

Printed in the United States of America

To Atlas,
the one who truly holds up my world.

For my dad, Gus DiPaola.

MAHALO NUI LOA

Deepest gratitude to Atlas Hill, my husband and soul mate. You lived with this project and supported me in a thousand ways. I love you with all my heart.

Love and appreciation to Jay Schwerin, the young man who teaches me so much about optimism and resilience. It is my great, good fortune to be your mom.

Much love to my mom, Grape, for instilling in me a passion for words and the delight of getting lost in a good book.

Marie Zold, you have my profound gratitude and love for our enduring friendship and for being the technical advisor on the operating room scenes.

I'm forever indebted to Carol Houseman for being there every step of the way, asking just the right questions, and helping me believe in myself as a writer. You fill my life with light.

Special thanks to Jerry Bolliger, Amy Matz, and Jane Weyhrauch, the WWW writing group, for thoughtful critiques, enthusiastic support, gentle prodding, and lots of belly laughs.

Thanks to Bobbie Keill, Debbie Sherry, Dr. Jerry Houseman, Frayda Bruton, Joy Dobson Way, Karen Suhr, Renee Dodge, Dr. Karen and Jim Nichols, Ruth Taylor, Mary Tellez, and Laura Kealoha Yardley for reading my work and offering your wisdom and encouragement. You inspired me beyond measure.

Aloha to all my hula sisters and brothers who live the true meaning of aloha. I am joyful and humble in your presence.

To Dr. John Hardaway, Raymond Obstfeld, and Sands Hall for sharing their love of creative writing and teaching me the craft.

Mahalo to Snooky Maikui and Jeanne O'Neal for your warm welcome to Moloka'i. Your reassurance dispelled nagging doubts. I'm thankful the Universe brought us together.

Thanks to my sister, Sue DiPaola, and our WHIM sisters for our walk on the spiritual path. Blessed be.

For help with the glossary, I respectfully acknowledge Mary Kawena Pukui and Samuel H. Elbert for their *Hawaiian Dictionary*, a priceless resource and guide for Hawaiian language and culture.

Mahalo for soul-stirring music to brilliant artists: Keola Beamer, Leilani Rivera Bond, Keali'i Reichel, and Israel Kamakawiwo'ole, lovingly remembered as Iz. When I listen to you, there's never a writer's block.

To the ancient voyagers, whose skill and courage are unmatched in human history, the people of Hawai'i, and their islands of incredible beauty and power. Mahalo nui loa for giving our world the spirit of aloha. May we embrace it without hesitation.

Me ke aloha pumehana,
BB

Ho'omoe wai kāhi ke kāo'o.

Let us travel together like water flowing in one direction.

Hawaiian Proverb

One

Sunny Lyon pushed through the double doors of the surgical suite. The cool air enveloped her, chasing away the warmth of the Hawaiian morning that lingered on her skin. "Hey, Jack."

The day shift charge nurse stood at attention in front of a huge schedule board on the wall. His razor cut hair and properly fitting scrubs shouted ex-army medic. "Sorry you had to come in."

Sunny rubbed the back of her neck, muscles taut from eight ten-hour days in a row. "Three people out sick. What's going on with the schedule?"

Shoulder to shoulder, they studied the board displaying the names of all the patients along with their surgery start times, operating room numbers, surgical procedures, surgeons, anesthesiologists, and nurses. Every slot was full. Sunny felt the familiar adrenalin rush kick in. "You keep a handle on the schedule, Jack. I'll cover Mr. Kamokila's procedure in room five. Lani's scrubbing in there, and I haven't worked with her in ages."

Jack tapped his finger by a name on the board. "David Kaneko's assisting Grace Pukui on that case."

"This will be my first chance to see our brilliant new surgeon in action." She'd missed Kaneko's arrival from the Texas Heart Institute last week.

"Grab your antacid tabs."

"Great." It figured. Now that they finally had a tight team, they'd have to break in a prima donna. Sunny pushed dark curls away from her face.

"Your hair's getting long."

"I'm way overdue for a cut." She knew her blue eyes and fair skin looked better framed with short hair, but she never seemed to have time to make it to the salon. As director of surgical services, she spent most of her waking hours in the maze of green-tiled hallways and precise operating rooms tackling everything from managing a million dollar budget to working in the operating rooms when they were short on staff. Her life resembled a three-ring circus with the ringmaster dozing outside the tent. "As soon as we have Mr. Kamokila in ICU, I'm bolting. This afternoon's my volunteer turn at the village."

"Roger that. We have enough staff on the late shift."

Sunny changed into scrubs and hurried to room five. She shouldered the door open as she adjusted her surgical mask.

Leilani Alamea Lewis organized the sterile equipment on her instrument table. She looked up, dark, almond-shaped eyes crinkling above her mask. "To what do I owe this honor?"

"Jack or me. Take your pick."

"You. Jack's too serious."

"If I'm such a riot, why've we been missing our weekly taco and beer fest at The Wall?"

"You're the one with the out-of-control schedule, girl. How about tonight?"

"Can't. Village duty."

"Tomorrow night?"

"Can I let you know?"

"Sunny, you've got to stop living here."

"Any suggestions?"

"Hire more staff."

"No money in the budget. And I'm betting there are more cuts to come." Sunny grabbed a clipboard. "Ready?"

Lani deftly counted clamps, scissors, forceps, and a myriad of open-heart surgical instruments. Sunny recorded the numbers on the clipboard. It was a treat for the two of them to work together. Most days, the schedule of surgical procedures in ten rooms revved up, roaring on like a juggernaut until early evening, and they rarely caught a glimpse of each other.

"Kaneko's on this one. Easy on the eyes. Porcupine personality." Lani fanned out the packets of gauze squares, thick lap tape sponges, and suture.

Sunny jotted down the totals as Lani counted the packets. "Maybe he just needs to settle in."

"That was a correct administrative response."

Sunny shrugged. "We can handle him."

Lani pulled off her sterile gown and gloves. The smallest size scrub shirt and pants hung loosely on her frame. "I'm going to grab a cup of coffee and a doughnut before we get started."

"How can you eat like that and stay so thin?"

Lani shrugged. "Good genes, great gym. You look exhausted."

"Could you bring me a cup of that espresso roast?"

Sunny scanned the OR, making sure everything from the rolling trash buckets to the anesthesia machine was in place. Sunlight and blue sky glowed through the high windows along one wall. She'd planned a long jog on the beach this morning, a rare chance to get some exercise. She pulled off her mask and tossed it in the trash. It was getting harder to hang onto size eight. No time to worry about that now. John Kamokila and his relatives waited in pre-op.

The room, dimly lit and appointed in soft blues, held the faint scent of lavender. Soothing sounds of water trickling among rocks emanated from a whimsical frog sculpture in one corner. In the center of the room and surrounded by people wearing anxious expressions, an elderly man rested on a gurney, his eyes closed, face serene. Wisps of hair fringed his bald head.

"Hello, Mr. Kamokila. I'm Sunny. I'm going to be with you in the operating room." She placed her hand lightly on his arm.

The man looked up at her, a twinkle in his eyes. "Please call me John. Mr. Kamokila was for my father."

Sunny laughed. "You got it."

John gestured toward the woman holding his hand. "This is my wife, Ruth". He tilted his head back to smile at the people around him. "And my *'ohana*."

"Good morning." Sunny nodded to John's family. "I'm glad you're all here. John, did you enjoy your *lomi lomi* massage?"

"Yes." He burrowed a little deeper into the plush blue blanket.

"Have you been using your breathing and visualization?"

John nodded.

"Good job. I see you have your music tapes. What did you choose?"

"Oh, I've got some Iz, hymns my mother used to sing, and the sound of the ocean."

"Excellent." Sunny checked his chart and identification bracelet. She looked back at John, studied the faces of his family members. "Any questions? Is there anything you need?"

John's wife patted a small bracelet of cowry shells pinned to John's hospital gown. "Can he take this with him?"

"Absolutely." Sunny touched the bracelet. "Who gave you this treasure, John?"

"My granddaughters made that for me. They wanted to give their old *tūtū* something to keep him company."

"You're a fortunate grandpa." Sunny glanced up as the door opened. "Here's Dr. Mike. You saw him last night."

A lanky body and sandy hair made Mike Jansen look more like a surfer than an anesthesiologist. He clasped hands with John. "How're you doing? Ready to go?"

John flashed thumbs up.

Dr. Grace Pukui, John's cardiac surgeon, entered the room. She wore a lab coat printed with whales swimming in deep blue water.

John's smile widened. "Dr. Grace. The question is, are you ready to go?"

The surgeon grinned. "I was born ready."

John winked.

Grace squeezed John's arm. "I'll see you in the operating room."

Loved ones took turns hugging John. His wife paused at the door and smiled back at him. He raised a wrinkled hand to his lips and blew her a kiss.

Sunny guided the foot of the gurney, with Mike at John's head, down the hallway. When they paused at the door of the operating room to adjust their masks, she could hear someone complaining about fee reimbursements. The voice sounded deep and resonant, but a sneer marred the tone. She turned to see him cornering Grace at the scrub sinks. Athletic build, golden-brown skin, striking cleft in his chin. Had to be David Kaneko.

Sunny shot Grace a look. The chief of surgery needed to rein this guy in.

Grace rested a hand on Kaneko's shoulder. "We can continue our discussion another time."

Sunny and Mike helped John slide over onto the operating table as the rest of the surgical team gathered round. They stood quietly while the anesthesiologist administered the fentanyl that would render John unconscious. Sunny held the old man's hand. His fingers felt cold. She pressed them between both of her hands to warm them up.

Mike spoke softly in John's ear. "When you wake up, you'll be comfortable. You won't have pain. You won't have any bleeding. Your healing has already begun. Just picture your healing place and listen to your music." John's deep sigh and relaxed body signaled that the drug had taken effect. Mike looked up. "Let's go."

Sunny checked the volume level on the tape player and adjusted the headset against John's ears. Grace, Mike, Sunny, and the perfusionists who operated the heart-lung pump each placed a hand on John. Lani, her hands wrapped in a sterile towel, stood close by. Kaneko stared down at the floor, hands propped on his hips. After a few moments of silence, Grace spoke. "We have a great team here today. Let's give John and each other our best."

Kaneko shook his head. His reaction reminded Sunny that spending a few quiet moments as a team around their patient before every surgery was an extraordinary practice, one she'd never experienced in any other OR.

The surgeons went out to scrub. Mike scanned monitoring equipment and adjusted medication levels. Sunny inserted a catheter into John's bladder and washed his chest with rust-colored prep solution.

Lani handed the surgeons sterile towels to dry their dripping hands and arms. She tugged them into gowns and snapped gloves over their hands.

Sunny fastened the ties on the back of David Kaneko's gown. "Good morning. I'm Sunny Lyon, the department director. It's good to finally meet you."

He glanced over his shoulder. "I need you to order my special instruments. Wolfram catalogue."

"No problem. We—"

Kaneko walked away and took his place at the operating table across from Grace.

Heat prickled the back of Sunny's neck. She helped Lani push her instrument table into place.

Lani handed Grace a scalpel. Mike turned up the volume on the sound system built into the wall behind him, and the soothing strains of Chopin filled the room. The procedure flowed with the same precision and harmony of a sonata as Grace removed the calcified mitral valve and replaced it with a titanium and Teflon valve.

With the incision in the heart closed, the team prepared the patient to come off bypass. Grace directed the perfusionists to turn the heart-lung pump down gradually to off.

Sunny stood at the foot of the table watching Lani ready clamps and sutures.

"We're removing the aortic cannula," Grace said.

David Kaneko grabbed the suction. "Damn it. We have a tear."

"Suture with a felt patch," Grace said, calm infusing her words.

Lani already had a needle holder ready to snap into Grace's hand.

"No," Kaneko said. "We need a Prolene suture."

Grace opened her hand toward Lani. "I'll use what you've got. Let's keep the field dry, David. "

"This suction is clogged." Kaneko pulled the suction tip out of the tubing and threw it on the floor.

Sunny hurried over to the cabinet, retrieved a sterile package, and peeled it open for Lani.

"Come on, people. Try to keep up here." Kaneko yanked the new tip out of Lani's hand.

Grace put down the needle holder and applied pressure on the bleeder with a gauze sponge. She waited for David to push the tip into the suction tubing. "Okay. Let's give it another try." She finished suturing and handed the needle holder back to Lani. "I think we've got it. Looks pretty dry." The room seemed to breathe a collective sigh.

Lani turned to the instrument table to reload another suture. She looked directly at Sunny and rolled her eyes. Sunny could almost see Lani's lips forming the word "jerk" behind her mask.

"David, now that we have the sternum wired, you can go back to the office," Grace said. "Lani will help me close."

Kaneko stepped back from the operating table and ripped off his gown. He tossed it on the floor. Sunny bent to pick it up. He shot his bloody gloves like a rubber band at the trash bucket. They hit Sunny's arm instead. She straightened up, ready for the confrontation, her neck and face burning. He'd already charged out the door. Damned if she'd tolerate rude behavior from any surgeon let alone from their latest recruit. She'd track him down first thing tomorrow.

An hour later, Sunny wheeled John and his new heart valve into the intensive care unit. She leaned close to his cheek and whispered, "John, your surgery went very well. You've got pain medication on board so you can just rest in your healing place." She squeezed his hand. His fingers felt warm.

Sunny gave report to the ICU nurse and dashed back to the OR, taking the stairs two at a time. She glanced at her watch. An hour's drive from the village. She might just make it before twenty third-graders started climbing all over the wooden tikis.

Sunny coaxed her old Cabriolet into first gear and ticked off the errands she would run after her shift at the village—pick up cat food and bread, call the dive shop about her new wet suit, and spend the rest of the evening doing a mound of laundry. She pressed the accelerator to the floor and navigated the streets to the highway.

Clouds like mounds of sugar frosting floated in a curacao sky. The breeze carried the heavy spice of tropical flowers and a hint of afternoon heat to come. Mynah birds swooped overhead, their raucous calls echoing in the palm trees.

Sunny thought about her volunteer work at Kauhale O Waimea, a restored ancient Hawaiian village. The time she devoted there provided a respite from her long days at UM. She enjoyed conducting history and cultural programs for school children. The village gave her a chance to renew her energy and give back to the community. Sunny grinned as she approached the turn off to Kauhale. Since her move to O'ahu from California more than a decade ago, not a day had passed without a rush of gratitude for her island home.

She squeezed the car into a small patch of shade, wondering at the absence of a school bus in the parking area. A sprint down the gravel path past the first hut brought her into the clearing at the center of the village where Kap was collecting fallen palm branches.

Kapono Hanoa appeared lean and physically fit. His dark skin barely showed a wrinkle. One might have guessed him to be fifty-five instead of seventy-five if it weren't for the white hair combed straight back off his forehead and his white beard.

"Kap, sorry I'm late." Sunny glanced at the scowling tiki statues in the clearing. "Where are the kids?"

"School called. Bus broke." His eyes and mouth narrowed into a tiki frown. "Third time this month." Kap served as curator, gardener, guide for occasional tourists, and coordinator for the volunteer schedule. His family descended from a chief in the court of Kamehameha The Great, the first Hawaiian king. Kapono meant righteous in Hawaiian, and Kap felt righteous about his history. He considered his job a sacred calling, keeping the culture of his ancestors alive.

"Now that I won't be weaving grass mats with a bunch of third-graders, what can I do to help?"

Kap climbed on his riding lawn mower. "Afraid of losing your weaving skills? You can patch up the holes in a couple of *hale*." He jabbed the air with his thumb in the direction of the tool shed. "Load of *pili* grass came in yesterday."

The heat was oppressive inside the thatched structure. Sunny worked steadily, weaving grass into holes worn in the matted roof and walls. Sweat dripped off her chin and turned her hair into ringlets. It had to be 100 degrees. How delicious it would feel to don her scuba gear and descend forty feet below the surface to a cool sea cave. She pictured the cobalt water sparkling in a shaft of sunlight and teeming with a rainbow of fish. She bent over for another handful of grass. Perspiration burned her eyes, jolted her out of her reverie. Her mouth felt sticky and parched. She looked around for her water bottle. Still in the car.

She lurched toward the sunlit doorway, squinting in the bright light. Her legs felt cement heavy. Her head filled with club soda bubbles, rising and popping in her brain. Dehydration? Low blood sugar? She tried to move toward the shade of nearby palms, but her feet remained rooted in the doorway. Her lungs screamed for air. Colors zigzagged in front of her eyes, blinding reds and golds. The colors formed a spiral, whirling faster and faster until they seemed to burst from the top of her head in a shower of sparks that rained down on her body. The sparks coalesced into a brilliant cocoon of light. She covered her face with her hands. Just then a cool breeze brushed her hot skin. The thick sweetness of gardenia scented the air. The blinding light faded and the club soda in her brain evaporated.

She leaned against the doorframe and stared at the clearing in front of her where, moments ago, Kap had been mowing the grass. Little children laughed and chased each other. Brown-skinned women and men worked in the shade around the clearing and stood talking in small groups. The children were naked. The adults wore yellow *kapa* cloth and garlands in their hair. What was going on? She shook her head and closed her eyes, willing the illusion to go away. She looked up. Ancient Hawai'i still wavered in front of her.

Her body sagged. Knees buckling and back pressing the door frame, she collapsed to the ground. She had to get hold of herself. There was a logical explanation for this. Some sort of oasis-like illusion? The *pili* grass. Maybe it had some hallucinogenic substance on it. She knew enough about native and cultivated plants in Hawai'i to know there were substances that could give you a mind-altering experience. If that's what was happening to her, she just needed to stay put and wait for her body to metabolize the stuff out. Deep breaths. Deep breaths.

Sunny blinked open her eyes and stared at her surroundings. Lush foliage ringed the clearing. Flowers glowed against the dark green of ferns shaded by palms—spikes of red ginger, hibiscus in hues of orange red and yellow, and splashes of purple morning glory. Hard-muscled men, using stone tools, hacked and carved on a tree trunk taking the shape of a canoe. A row of small canoes lined the beach along the river. Fishing nets dried on bushes and stake frames. She glimpsed an open-air pavilion with a thatched roof, where an abundance of food covered mats on the ground. A jagged peak resembling a shark's dorsal fin loomed over the village. Frothy clouds encircled it like sea foam. The place looked almost like it did on living history day, but that event had happened two months ago. Besides, there was something different about the clearing.

A huge stone, one-story high with a hole in the center, stood in the middle of the grassy area. The stone's scalloped edges were chiseled into a perfect circle. An extravagant orange flower and fern *lei* and shell necklaces festooned the monolith. The stone didn't exist at Kauhale.

An old woman, her long hair streaked with silver, led a procession out of the jungle into the clearing. A wreath of shells rested on her head. A bright yellow *kapa* robe draped over one shoulder cascaded down her ample body.

The people following her came in two groups. The first group appeared to be adults close to the age of their leader. The women and men marched in proud strides, bodies erect, cloaked in the same golden *kapa*, countenances serene. Each person held a different implement like a scepter—canoe paddle, stone *poi* pounder, wooden bowl. A man carrying a tall drum caught Sunny's attention. His wild hair and strut made her think of the peacocks that roosted in the jungle around the village.

The second group seemed to be younger adults and teenagers, their waists wrapped with yellow cloth that stretched to their knees. Their breasts were bare. Flowers and ferns encircled their heads, and they carried the same kinds of implements. A girl, no more than thirteen with a skip in her step, turned to wave at a boy near the rear of the group. He gave a slight grin, then pushed out his chest and glowered.

The procession circled behind the stone. The old woman took her place before the monolith, closed her eyes, raised her face to the sun, waited. More villagers assembled in front of her, adults gently quieting the children. The woman opened her arms wide. Drums started a steady beat.

A young man at the edge of the gathering scanned the clearing, stretching up on one foot and then the other. He was stocky with the legs of a runner. His skin glistened with sweat. Spiral tattoos swept across his chest and shoulders and down his arms. His hair was pulled into a knot at the back of his head. Suddenly the man started toward Sunny in an easy jog. He waved and shouted, "Mahana!"

She jumped as if a telephone had jangled her from sleep to full alert. He kept shouting at her, moving in her direction. What was she to do? This was crazy. Plain-ass crazy.

Sunny pushed herself to her feet and staggered backwards into the hut, never taking her eyes off the young man. Her heart matched the pounding of the drums. What if he came in after her?

She stumbled, plopped on the ground, and found herself looking down at her bare feet. But they weren't her feet. Thick calluses and mahogany flesh took the place of her fair skin and dolphin tattoo. What in the hell? Panic turned to creeping terror as she realized she no longer wore her shorts. In their place, saffron *kapa* decorated with symbols encircled her waist. She gasped. Her blouse had disappeared and her breasts as well. She looked down at an old man's chest--concave with sparse white hairs.

The club soda bubbles fizzed in her brain again, and she felt the sensation of floating. It was as if she'd left her body and hovered just below the thatched ceiling of the hut. She stared at the old man. White strands of long hair framed his slumbering face. Who was he? What was happening to her?

A scream swelled in her throat. Red and gold flashed before her eyes and swirled into rainbows of color, spiraling wildly. She felt dizzy and icy cold. The colors dissolved to black, and a loud hum filled her ears. Then the darkness in her brain pulled her down into nothingness.

"Sunny! Sunny!"

She forced her heavy eyelids open, tried to focus on the person leaning over her. Kap's face was creased with alarm.

"Are you okay?" Kap frantically patted her arm. "I heard you scream."

Sunny moaned and struggled to sit up. "I don't know. I think I passed out." She rubbed her buzzing head, felt cold to her core. "Something really strange just happened."

"I'll take you over to the emergency room."

"I just need some water."

Kap darted out of the hut and returned with a jug. He held it to her lips. She took a swig. The warm water hit her stomach. She leaned over and heaved.

Wiping spittle from her mouth, she peered through the doorway at the clearing. The round stone and the people had disappeared. The twitter of birds in the trees replaced the pounding drums.

"Kap . . . is there . . . is there a *hula hālau* practicing today?"

He frowned. "Next week."

This time a dry heave doubled her over.

"Come on, Sunny. We're outta here." He crouched, put his arm around her, and propelled her to his Jeep. He clicked the seat belt around her waist. "You look like you've been walking with ghosts. What did you see?"

She pressed the heel of her hand to her forehead. Her temples throbbed. "Mirage?" She cursed herself for not slugging down her bottle of ice water as soon as she arrived at the village.

Kap revved the engine. "Strange things happen here." He steered them out of the Waimea Valley.

The hot interior of the Jeep did little to relieve the chill running through Sunny's body. She closed her eyes and listened to a word echoing in her brain. Mahana. What did it mean?

Two

"I heard you were in the emergency room yesterday. What happened? Why didn't you call me?" Lani stripped off her scrubs in the women's locker room and stuffed them in the dirty linen hamper.

Sunny slipped into her sundress. "No big deal. I wanted the ER doc to look deep into my eyes, tell me to take three months off, and scuba dive until I grow fish scales."

"You wouldn't take time off if Winchester wrote the order on a prescription pad. So?"

"A little episode while I was at the village. Probably dehydration."

Sunny watched Lani draw a brush through her silky black hair, remembered the day they'd become friends. It was ten years ago, and they were both new employees at 'Uhane Māla Wellness Center.

At the end of their shift, Sunny had noticed Lani impatiently tugging on a wig in front of the locker room mirror.

"This thing. I wish I had the guts to go around bald."

"Want to try this?" Sunny retrieved a straw hat from the hook in her locker. "Come on. Let me buy you a drink at The Wall."

Lani threw the wig in her locker, donned the hat, and collected on the offer. She ordered a soda. Chemotherapy and alcohol mixed an evil cocktail.

Sunny munched popcorn while Lani sucked on cinnamon candy to relieve her nausea. They talked for hours. Lani and her brothers had been raised by their grandmother after their mother died of breast cancer. Then Lani quit the first semester of college to care for her grandmother who was diagnosed with the same cancer. Five years later, Lani rolled into surgery for a mastectomy.

Lani raised her glass of soda. "Three's a charm, Sunny. I'm going to be the one to beat this." They clinked glasses, sealing the prediction and their new friendship.

Lani closed her locker and leaned against the door. "What do you mean by little episode?"

"Some kind of hallucination . . . like an acid trip."

"How do you know about dropping acid?"

Sunny threw her scrubs at Lani.

Lani batted them out of the air into the hamper. "Let's go down to The Wall. I'll buy you beer and some mahi tacos, and you can tell me the rest."

"Mystery of the month. Nurse loses her tiny mind." Sunny bent to fasten her sandals, glimpsed an old man's worn foot. Maybe she really was losing her sanity. She blinked to clear the image and followed Lani out the door.

In the hallway, David Kaneko headed toward the OR with a cafeteria tray full of food. "Lani, you go on and order for both of us. I've been trying to get a hold of him all day."

He was already talking before Sunny could proffer a greeting. "We need to get the cases started faster. There's too much time wasted prepping the patient and talking with the family."

"David . . . " Dispensation of titles was part of the closeness of the team at UM. But his first name felt foreign in her mouth, like a bone in a piece of tender fish. "Dr. Kaneko, do you have a minute?"

"Fifteen before my next case."

Sunny motioned him toward an empty conference room.

He slid his tray onto the conference table and dropped into a chair across from her. With a loud sigh, he leaned back and crossed one ankle over the other knee. His jaw was square and chiseled as if he'd spent a lifetime clenching his teeth.

"Dr. Kaneko, sometimes new staff members are a little uncomfortable with the way we do things here. It takes time to get used to our preoperative routine."

"I'm not at all uncomfortable. However, we could drop the knife a little faster if everyone concentrated on getting the patients into the operating rooms instead of making sure they have their massages and music tapes. And no one should be allowed in the surgical suite except staff. Patients can visit with family members up on the units." He hunched forward and wolfed down half of a turkey sandwich.

"Did Grace talk with you during your interview about our procedures?"

"Frankly, I don't recall."

Sunny rested her arms on the table, watched him shovel a forkfull of salad into his mouth. The picture window behind him framed slate clouds and palm fronds, glossed with rain, whipping in the wind. She wanted to make peace. "You have a reputation as an outstanding surgeon, and we're committed to outstanding surgical outcomes. And . . . it takes more than a skillful team in the operating room. It takes caring for the whole person, mind and spirit, as well as the body."

"What patients need is a talented surgeon with a little bit of luck." He devoured the other half of the sandwich.

"You mean a surgeon that presides over an assembly line where bodies get trundled in to have their plumbing repaired."

He seemed to ignore her sarcasm as he attacked a bowl of pineapple and papaya. Why was this guy wound so tight?

Kaneko wiped his mouth with a napkin. His dark eyes locked with hers. "There's constant pressure to do more cases in one day—emergencies, people waiting to get on the schedule, administration demanding that the golden goose produce more eggs. Surgery is the moneymaker. Besides operating, I have office hours and post-op patients to visit. Every single minute counts. I can't stand around waiting while you provide all the comforts of home. This is a hospital for God's sake."

"Making sure our patients are relaxed and unafraid supports a faster, complication-free recovery. That ultimately makes your job easier."

Kaneko sighed, blowing air through his pursed lips. He pushed the food tray aside and jabbed the space between them with his right index finger. "I haven't seen any studies that show this mumbo-jumbo improves patient outcomes."

"The data regarding the positive impact of complementary medicine have been presented in all of the top medical journals. A recent study at Columbia Presbyterian Hospital in New York showed that patients receiving the kind of pre-surgical preparation we provide require fifty percent less post-operative pain medication. The University of Arizona—"

"Small studies and lots of conjecture. Patient outcomes—"

"Our patients are our *hoa hana*—that's Hawaiian for partner. We're here to be their partners in healing. Not just the body, the whole person." Heat rose in her face. She resisted the urge to scream. "You're in Honolulu, not Houston."

In the silence that followed, his face looked serene, almost sympathetic. Maybe she'd gotten her point across.

He checked his watch, pushed up from the table. "I have to run."

Sunny rose from her chair. "One more thing, Dr. Kaneko. The incident in the OR yesterday morning. Your rude behavior has to stop. We have a first-rate staff, and if you haven't already noticed, respect is a big thing around here."

"Ms. Lyon, I will do whatever it takes to get what I need in the OR."

"I can assure you, you'll always get what you need. But not by shouting and throwing equipment."

He arched an eyebrow, his smile more like a smirk. "If everyone's on their toes, I won't have to say a word. Right?"

"I'll schedule an appointment with you during your office hours next Monday to go over our procedures and the patient care data I mentioned."

Kancko gripped the knob on the conference room door. "Sorry. I'm going back to the mainland for a long weekend."

"How about the end of next week?"

"Yeah, sure." He started through the door and turned back. "About those instruments." He retrieved a folded paper from his lab coat pocket and tossed it on the conference table. "I've circled two titanium needle holders and an aortic punch."

"No problem. Have a safe—" The door slammed shut. Sunny looked at the tray of dirty dishes he'd left behind. Lani was wrong. Kaneko acted more like an ass than a porcupine. Some surgeons behaved so predictably, seeing the patient as a heart with clogged blood vessels and calcified valves and acting as though everyone in the world existed only to serve them. She grabbed the tray and headed toward the cafeteria. She'd talk with Grace Pukui. They needed to figure out how to win over Attila the Hun.

As she walked back from the cafeteria, Sunny consciously slowed her pace in an effort to shake off her encounter with Kaneko. She concentrated on the Hawaiian melody playing softly overhead—UM's answer to the personnel paging that went on in other hospitals. Passing through hallways filled with sunshine streaming through skylights and floor to ceiling windows, she felt her irritation drift down a notch.

She paused at the giant aquarium in the center of the lobby. Patients and visitors gathered around the tank all hours of the day and night. Children loved to search for the creatures pictured on the informational plaques displayed around the base.

One night Sunny had been called in for a seven-hour surgery. When she was leaving the Center at three in the morning, she spotted a woman in a wheelchair, her hand resting against the aquarium glass. Probably a patient unable to sleep. Sunny knelt down beside the woman. "Are you okay?"

"Better, now that I'm here," the woman said. "The medication they're giving me doesn't do much. These creatures help me ignore the pain in my leg."

The same butterfly fish, lemon yellow with neon blue stripes, the woman had been watching that night glided by the glass. Sunny smiled. Just what the doctor ordered.

At the front entrance, she stepped out into the apricot light of sunset. She breathed deeply and drew in the sweet scent of plumeria flowers, pungent from the recent shower. 'Uhane Māla meant spirit garden, and it was truly a garden with a profusion of plants and hummingbird feeders outside every first-floor window. Along the path through the grounds, she paused at a waterfall and closed her eyes. The gurgle of water flowing around rocks soothed her. There was magic in this place.

Sunny's growling stomach reminded her of the tacos and Lani waiting at The Wall. She jogged the three blocks to the beach, but the exercise couldn't ace the tennis match of worries bouncing back and forth in her brain. Budget woes and a hotshot surgeon. The image of an ancient man's body.

The Wall, a collection of tin shacks painted in primary colors, sprawled on a small beach frequented by locals and an occasional tourist.

The establishment's namesake was a popular dive site a mile straight out to sea—a coral-covered ridge eighty feet below the surface of the ocean, dropping to a depth of six hundred feet. Although the largest shack sheltered a bandstand and a battered bar, customers preferred to sit outside when none of the local bands were playing. Picnic tables and benches scattered between the shacks were drenched in the same eye-popping colors. Hospital staffers downing a beer before heading home and assorted office types waiting out the traffic, all chitchatted over the sounds of reggae and Hawaiian tunes and the rumble of the surf. The delicious, greasy smell of grilled onions and burgers saturated the air.

Lani waved from a table piled with sushi rolls, tacos, and pitchers of beer and ice water. "Look at this feast, girl. I hope David Kaneko didn't ruin your appetite."

"Not a chance." Sunny plunked down on the bench, crunched a taco and closed her eyes. "Umm. Better than sex."

"Bookmark that topic. First, I want to hear about Kaneko."

Sunny sipped her beer. "Seems like he wants to turn UM into the Texas Heart Institute. I wonder why he left there."

"I hear he grew up in the islands. Maybe he took the position to be near his family."

"I'd hate to see how he is with them." Sunny deepened her voice to a growl. "There won't be any carousing before dinner. Everyone needs to start eating on time."

Lani chuckled. "I used to work with a surgeon who thought it was tough to go home at the end of the day because his wife and kids didn't jump up like the hospital staff when he wanted something."

Sunny finished her beer and poured each of them another mug. "Let's not spend the evening chatting about our new superstar. The day is over, and I don't want to think about Kaneko." She swiveled on the bench to face the ocean. "Just look at that sky."

They sat quietly sipping beer and watching the horizon. Giant clouds, like plumes from a forest fire, arched high into the sky. A patina of peach glazed the sapphire ocean. The profile of a small boat, its sail pregnant with wind, danced against the sunset tapestry. Everyone else in the place had grown silent too. This nightly ritual of reverence honored the main reason for dealing with the drawbacks of island life— the incredible natural beauty.

The horizon faded into a soft glow. Tiny white lights strung between the tin roofs sparkled the night. As if on cue, the hushed vigil ended with a return to loud conversations and laughter.

Lani pushed her plate aside and placed her beer mug squarely in front of her. "What happened at the village?"

Sunny sighed the contentment of a just-full belly. She leaned forward on the bench and described the incident in detail, stopping before she got to the part about seeing an old man's body. "It was like I stepped through the doorway of that hut into another world."

"Were you scared?"

"I've been wracking my brain. An allergic reaction? A native plant like peyote? I don't think I was that dehydrated."

"A brain tumor? Maybe you'd better get a complete physical."

"Jeez, Lani. I just had my yearly. Everything checked out completely normal. I'm not ready to race to radiology for a CT scan, thank you very much."

"I don't think you should let this go."

"It was probably just a freak occurrence."

They were silent for a while. Sunny stared into her beer mug. She could feel Lani's eyes studying her.

"Did something else happen?"

Sunny swirled the last inch of beer around the mug. She remembered how parched her throat had been and gulped it down. "You're going to think I'm crazy. I think I'm crazy. I don't even know how to tell you this."

"I've always thought you were crazy. Try me."

"Something happened to my body. My clothes were gone. Lani, my breasts were gone. My skin was brown as coffee. There were tattoos all over my arms and legs. Suddenly, it was like I was floating in the air, looking down at this old man."

Lani let out a breath in one long whoosh. "No wonder you think you're losing your mind."

Sunny leaned back from the table and tried to shrug off the twinges of fear needling her. "You're the only one I've told about this. Not Kap, not Winchester in the ER. They just think I fainted. What I want to do is try to forget about it. If it happens again, I'll start worrying. I just need some sleep."

"I wish you'd consider getting some tests done."

Sunny held up her hands.

"Okay, okay. I won't nag." Lani put her credit card on top of the check.

"Thanks. I'll get it next time." Sunny tucked a five dollar bill under her beer mug. "With all that's going on at UM, I'm determined not to get sidetracked by what happened at the village."

They walked out to the parking lot. "Want a ride back to the Center?" Lani asked.

"I feel like walking."

They leaned against Lani's car and watched the ocean. The waves, translucent in the silver light of a full moon, rushed row upon row up the beach. After a while, Lani put her arm around Sunny's shoulders. "Could you have fallen asleep in the heat and dreamed the whole thing?"

"I suppose . . . No. I swear I was wide awake right up to the point of my gender transformation."

"Okay, I believe you." Lani spoke softly. "Sunny, you might have gone back to a past life."

"I thought you had to be hypnotized."

"Sometimes it can happen spontaneously if you're in the right place."

Sunny laughed. "My friend, you know I don't believe in that stuff. I used to wish for a time machine so I could live in a medieval castle or rub elbows with the Romans. But they haven't come up with that machine, and I don't think you can go back any other way."

Lani turned toward Sunny. With her long hair and soaring cheekbones, she looked like a priestess on the verge of revealing a mystery. "There's so much more than this physical plane we're on. Even Einstein's work got people thinking about parallel universes and timelines. It could be that sometimes a portal opens up and we get a chance to step through."

"I don't know. I think we all get only one shot on this planet."

"Well, you did see and hear something. If we rule out drugs, dehydration, and brain tumors, maybe we have evidence that you beat us all to these islands."

Sunny shook her head and opened the car door for Lani. "Have a safe drive home."

Lani started the engine. "Skimmer bug."

"What?"

"The skimmer bug bumps into the leg of a human wading in his pond. What he doesn't realize is there's a whole world attached to that leg. He just backs up and goes around. That's you."

Sunny closed the car door and pushed down the lock button. "Maybe that's not so bad."

Three

Lush, earthy-smelling foliage hugged both sides of the road. Driving with all the windows open and the top down, Sunny felt as if she were gliding through a fragrant tunnel. The cool night air revived her like a tonic. She breathed deeply, relaxed into the twists and turns of the highway, felt muscle tension and mental chatter drain away.

A sign loomed out of the darkness indicating the thirty miles to Waimea. What did happen yesterday? If she went back to the village, would she glimpse ancient Hawai'i again? Dehydration sure wasn't a problem tonight. She pressed the accelerator to the floor and flew past the turnoff to her bungalow. The Cabriolet gobbled up the miles of deserted highway. She remembered the young man with spiral tattoos. What if he showed up again?

Sunny swung the car right onto a narrow road and inched along into the valley. She'd negotiated this gravel road every week in the daylight, yet it seemed like unfamiliar terrain. Bushes and jagged volcanic boulders jumped into the headlights out of nowhere. She jerked the wheel from side to side, her heart rate notching up twenty beats. With the stick in neutral she glided into the parking area and cut the engine. She sat straight back in her seat, listening hard to the silence. Gradually the night sounds grew more distinct; the tittering of birds settling in the bushes; the soft whooshing of the Waimea River; a slight breeze rustling the palms. Sunny took a deep breath, felt her pulse gradually slow. She got out of the car and gently closed the door so as not to make a sound. She paused. Who was she afraid to disturb?

The moon silvered the tops of the palm trees and the roofs of the huts. Her footsteps crunched the gravel in the parking lot, becoming silent when she reached the grass. She walked past the first *hale* into the clearing and stood perfectly still. A light breeze, carrying the perfume of gardenias, ruffled her hair. The jungle cast shadows all around the edges of the clearing. The *pili* grass walls of the *hale* shimmered around darkened doorways. Over the whole scene loomed the shark fin peak. Where the point touched the sky, stars glittered like diamonds scattered on black velvet.

Sunny remembered stories told by some of the locals about the marchers. They believed that the spirits of Hawaiian royalty--kings, queens, warriors--marched at night in sacred places all over the islands. People unlucky enough to be in one of those places after dark often lost their lives.

Kap swore he'd heard the marchers at Kauhale O Waimea. He'd lingered by the river until well after sunset on a long work day. Hurrying to put away tools and lock up the maintenance shed, he heard voices. He peered through the gloom to see if late-arriving tourists or local high school students looking for a thrill were coming down the road. He hadn't heard any cars. Suddenly the voices grew louder, merging into a throbbing chant. The trees and undergrowth reverberated with the sound all around him. He ran to his Jeep and gunned it up the road, bouncing back and forth off the rocky shoulders. Kap never missed quitting time again.

Sunny moved into the middle of the clearing. Her foot struck something hard in the soft grass, a large block of stone buried in the ground. She squatted down and ran her hand across the rough surface. She'd never noticed it before. A picture of a huge round stone flashed in her mind, the monolith she'd seen yesterday in her daydream. Maybe a stone like that had stood right here on this base. The archeology report on the village might confirm that. She sighed. She was getting carried away, trying to prove that an illusion really existed.

Something rustled in the bushes at the edge of the jungle. She looked up, but could discern no movement. The breeze picked up, making the palm branches clatter—the sound of a hand running across a wall of vertical blinds. Sunny shivered and felt goose bumps on her arms and legs—chicken skin.

She scanned the jungle around the clearing and saw a patch of light in the foliage directly across from her. The light moved, gradually shifting into the shape of a large, white dog. It emerged from the bushes and sat at the edge of the grassy area. The pale fur glowed in the moonlight. The dog's face appeared serene, even regal. Eyes, chunks of polished obsidian, fixed on her.

Sunny froze. A Rottweiler from her childhood chased through her memory. She pushed down the urge to get up and run. Maybe if she just sat still, the dog would take off.

The dog trotted toward the river. It paused and turned to look at her. A few more steps, pause and another look. The animal was waiting for her to come along. Unable to resist the urge, Sunny rose from the grass and moved in the same direction. The dog resumed its trek, looking back every so often. Sunny followed well behind. The path took them to the sandy beach at the river's edge. The dog stopped, looked directly at her, then disappeared around a clump of bushes near the waterline.

"What the . . . " She walked down to the water and stared upriver. The dog had vanished.

Sunny trudged back up the beach. What in the world was she doing, wandering around out here? She needed to go home and forget all about what happened yesterday. Heading back toward the center of the village, she stopped to take one last look at the river. Dizziness filled her head, made her sway. She veered toward a palm tree, arm outstretched for balance, and plunked down with her back against the trunk. The dizziness subsided. She opened her eyes. Maybe she should get a brain scan after all.

Before the single cell of fear in her gut could multiply, Sunny focused on taking slow deep breaths, forcing herself to relax against the tree. She concentrated on her surroundings. The sand underneath her, warm from the day's heat, felt soothing. She gazed up at the stars. They sparkled, then blurred. Drowsiness clouded her brain as if she'd taken a sleeping pill. She wanted to rest for a few minutes. Just a little while. Then she'd make it back to her car. She yawned and leaned her head against the trunk. The face of the young man with spiral tattoos floated in her mind. She heard his voice.

"Mahana!"

I hear someone calling me, but I don't want to move. I am a healer and seer for my clan, the Anuanua. But as I grow ancient, it takes more effort to summon the *mana*. I find myself wanting only to bask in the sacred beauty of the present—the land, the faces of my people, the laughter of the children. I fill my chest with the misty breath of the river whispering in on the breeze. An old man with flowing white hair and a slack belly should be left to dream in the sun. In my imagination, I see the scarlet flashes of *'i'iwi* birds as I listen to them chirp and twitter in the trees.

I hear the call again. Mahana. Mahana. If I change my name, everyone might leave me in peace. An idle threat. A name is one's most prized possession. As the voice comes closer, I smile. Tanemao, my apprentice, summons his teacher.

"Mahana, the council is starting. Tiare sent me to find you. Come quickly."

I shade my eyes to see his face. Tanemao is an eager young man. He wants everything—his lessons, the people around him, the future—to come quickly. Patience is the lesson we most often review. "Help me up. Tiare will wait. She knows I am slow."

Tanemao reaches down to grasp my arm. Although he is not tall, he is powerfully built. His chest, shoulders, and arms are decorated with the dark spirals of the spirit world. Intricate pictures—the sun, fish in the sea, a turtle—cascade down his legs. His wavy hair flows to his waist. A thin face with sharp nose and chin make him look sullen, but Tanemao's dark eyes dance with enthusiasm. I allow his strength to pull me to my feet. As I lean on his arm, we walk slowly to the long house. I know this is a great effort for him because he would sooner run to the council meeting.

"So, my fine apprentice, what is the urgent matter today?"

"Our lookouts spotted raiding parties closer to the village."

I glance up at the billowing clouds in a sky so bright my eyes water. I worry about our ability to keep the peace. "We thought if we let them take what they need they would leave us alone."

"Some never feel they have enough." Tanemao punches the air with his fist. "We need to protect what we have."

"Ah, the dilemma is how to achieve that. If we believe in abundance, abundance will be ours. If we hold onto what we have too tightly, we will lose it."

I glance up at the peak over our village. Today the Fin of *Mao*, the shark, is ringed with mist. Rain will be here by evening, a good omen for the fruitfulness of our meeting.

We enter the long house, and I pause to let my eyes adjust to the dim light. The *lau hala* mats are rough and cool under my feet. Burning *maile* leaves perfume the air. Tiare's lovely face becomes clear in my sight. I move around the outside of the circle and take my place beside her. She gently pats my arm and leans close to whisper so the others will not hear. "Drowsing in the sun, my beloved?"

We chuckle softly. Tiare and I have been together since we were little children. Now we are in the twilight of our years, and she knows me well. I still cannot take my eyes off her. Her body is ample and soft, long hair streaked with the silver of moonlight. She senses my reverie and clears her throat. When she sees I have turned my attention to the gathering, she calls the council to order.

I look around at my people. They wear the yellow *tapa* cloth of the Anuanua. Seated in the inner circle are the elders of our village, women and men who have seen many seasons, faces etched with experience, hair more the color of bones than rich earth. Each elder is responsible for a craft that ensures our survival—fishing, making clothing, gathering and preparing food, teaching the children, organizing competitions and celebrations, safety, and leading the rituals that keep us connected to the spirit world. In the outer circle are the young women and men. They have come of age, twelve seasons or more, and are apprenticed to the elders, learning the ways of caring for our clan. Mastering a craft will take much of their lifetime.

We begin by simply being quiet and breathing deeply together. Each person makes sure to be in this long house—mind as well as body. We cannot truly listen to each other if someone is thinking about mending the fishing nets or another is worrying about planting a crop. Tiare chants a blessing in her deep, soothing voice. We pass around the bowl of *'awa*. The bitter liquid mixed with milk of the coconut helps the mind to be calm and clear. We are ready to consider what we must do for our clan.

Tiare invites one of the youngest men to speak. Pudgy flesh lingers on his body. He sits erect, face resolute. I know he is determined to show he is worthy of responsibility. His voice breaks in high squeaks.

"We have seen raiding parties hiding in the jungle at the edge of our village three times in the last moon cycle. Before, they would come only with every new moon and stay on the perimeters of our fields."

A woman seated in the inner circle speaks. Aimata, the leader of our safety guild, is big-boned and wears her hair closely cropped. She exudes an air of authority. If she thought it necessary, she would take on the task of defending our village single-handedly. "We think the people of Tauati may be planning to do more than take food and wood."

"What are the levels of our supplies?" Tiare asks.

The elder in charge of our resources answers. He is a vigilant man. Daily, he walks the terraces of taro and squash, talks with our fishing parties, and inspects the materials used to make our canoes and implements. "We have more than enough of everything right now."

A voice booms across the circle. "Thanks be to *Akua*, the Great Spirit." Omo wears a garland of shells that signifies his position as *tahua ori*, master of the dance and ritual priest. His big head is impressive with reddish-brown hair streaming out like ruffled plumage on a great bird. Intricate designs decorate his broad nose and flow across his cheeks.

Tiare nods and turns back to Aimata. "What is it you think the people of Tauati are planning?"

"They may be trying to learn everything they can in order to send warriors here to overtake us. Many such incidents happened between the islands in our old homeland."

Jumping to his feet in the outer circle, Tanemao waves his arms. "We must be ready for them. We should start making weapons. We have none, other than our fishing spears and knives." The long house is silent. A flush glows on his face and he flops back down on the mat.

Tanemao possesses an impetuous nature. If we can help him learn the skill of acting out of knowing rather than urgency, we will have a wise leader for the next generation. I extend my hand. "Tanemao makes an important point. We must be ready for them. Though our way is not the path of fighting, we must plan how we will respond if they send warriors."

Aimata, leader of the safety guild, raises her hand. "I fear we have little time for planning. The wet season will be full upon us by the new moon. Rain muffles sounds and creates the perfect opportunity for attack."

Omo, the ritual guild leader speaks. "Aimata, Tiare, Mahana, and I can make a plan to bring to this council tomorrow."

Tiare looks at each person, waiting for a nod of assent. All are in agreement. "We'll meet after the evening meal."

Tiare begins the closing chant. I study the people around the circle. My eyes come to rest on Tanemao. He is sulking, his face darkened in a scowl.

Four

Māui's grimacing face and hard-muscled body exuded super human strength. Sunny contemplated the mural that covered the entire wall at the front of the empty auditorium. Vibrant colors depicted the Hawaiian demi-god creating the island chain by pulling landmasses up out of the sea with a giant hook and line.

The scene blurred and shifted. Images danced before Sunny's eyes—a circle of people in a dimly lit hut, the chiseled form of a young man reaching down to help her up. No. Help an old man up. Who were they? Her heart started to pound. Was this how a panic attack felt? Sunny forced herself to breathe deeply, hold her breath for a few seconds and then blow it all out. A couple more breaths and her pulse slowed. Maybe this was about low blood sugar. Hormones out of sync? Voices and the shifting of chairs snapped her to attention. As soon as she got out of this meeting, she'd call her doc about some tests.

The UM management team took seats around the large u-shaped conference table. Grace Pukui sat next to Sunny. "I heard this is going to be about cutting costs."

Sunny suppressed the urge to clutch Grace's arm and hang onto an anchor in the real world. "That's the scuttlebutt."

"I can't believe they're having this session while Katherine is away."

"Seeing as how she's the administrator . . ." Sunny swiped at the beads of sweat that had blossomed on her forehead.

Darwin Chang, the UM board chair, tapped on the microphone at the podium. His exquisitely tailored suit and gold wire-rimmed glasses befitted his position as the president of First Islands Bank. "Good morning. I want to thank everyone for taking time to come to this meeting." There was a slight quiver in his voice. "As you probably know, Katherine Nakamura is on vacation. I talked with her on the phone last night, and we decided this announcement couldn't wait."

"How strange," Grace whispered.

Sunny folded her arms against a sudden chill. Strange had become the norm the last few days.

Darwin continued, "A month ago, we let you know that we ran a two percent margin all last year. First quarter figures are in, and the margin is at one percent. Our credit rating has gone down." One of the managers started to ask a question but Darwin stopped him with a raised hand. "We're pursuing a three-prong approach. First, we're embarking on a public relations campaign to get the word out about our services. Second, we're exploring partnerships with other health care organizations. Third, and this is where we're really counting on all of you, we're going to cut our costs by twenty percent."

Team members sat transfixed around the table. No one spoke.

Sunny, her mind now clear and sharply focused, clicked through a mental list of the surgery staff. A twenty percent cut targeted people with more than eight years seniority, people like Lani. She raised her hand but didn't wait to be acknowledged. "Last year, when everyone volunteered to do as much as possible to reduce the budget, we found creative ways to run our programs with fewer staff and equipment upgrades. There's not much left to cut without endangering safe care."

The team erupted. "How soon do these cuts need to be made?" "How much are we paying PR consultants?" "If we cut our costs by twenty percent, you won't have anything significant to market."

Darwin held up two hands. "I know there are a lot of questions. We'll have more answers for you next week. We wanted to give you a chance to start thinking about ways you can achieve the reduction."

Sunny shook her head. Big decisions at UM had always been made by consensus, managers and board members working in concert to identify direction and strategies. This morning it felt like a tank had rolled into the room. "Excuse me, Darwin. Is there any room for discussion here?"

"We want to move quickly. Are there any other questions?" Darwin's eyes swept the room.

Sunny refused to be dismissed. "I bet we could all clear our calendars for a day and put a plan together."

Darwin tapped his fingers on the edge of the podium.

"We need to talk about this when Katherine is here," Sunny said.

The board chair fixed a hard stare on her. "We can take that into consideration. You need to remember that the board has the best interests of UM in mind. We intend to include everyone as we roll out this approach. In fact, there are people on our staff who, with their experience in large health care systems on the mainland, can help us discern the best ways to address these issues."

Sunny stared at the huge fish hook on the end of Māui's line. Was Darwin talking about David Kaneko? She could think of no one else who'd come to UM from the mainland in the last two years. And what exactly did Darwin mean about exploring partnerships with other health care organizations?

Grace touched her shoulder. "Are you okay?"

Sunny glanced around. Nearly everyone had left the auditorium. She hadn't even heard Darwin adjourn the meeting. She looked up at the chief of surgery. "Yeah. Just mulling the twenty percent."

"Do you think Katherine really agreed to this plan?"

"My guess is that Darwin didn't let her know exactly what he planned to announce."

Sunny ripped the tape and cotton from the crook of her arm. A bruise marked the spot where the lab technician had drawn three tubes of blood. She'd been poked, x-rayed, and examined for a battery of tests in the week since her night at the village. She fanned out a sheaf of reports on her desk.

"Anything?" Lani sat in a chair across from Sunny.

"Blood work, urine sample, ophthalmic exam, cerebral CT scan—all normal." She pushed the reports toward Lani. "My doc is mystified."

Lani scanned the pages. "Any more dreams?"

"Nothing. Not even a nightmare." Sunny leaned back in her chair, chucked her pen on the desk.

"God, Sunny, you must feel so frustrated."

"Annoyed is more like it. I don't have time for this."

"Maybe you need to take the time. You could call Steve Winship."

"The psychologist? Guess I don't blame you for thinking I'm crazy."

"Actually, I don't think he's going to be able to give you an answer either. But, you're not ready to hear what I think."

Sunny glanced around her desk—stacks of files covered her calendar, Post-it reminder notes festooned her computer terminal, and lines blinked on the telephone. She had so much catching up to do. "The past life thing again?"

"Have you heard the legends about Pele? Some say they've seen her walking with a white dog. Like a ghost dog. Maybe Pele was there that night."

"I've heard the legends about the volcano goddess. Fire, brimstone, don't take her lava rock home. It makes her very angry. If she was there, I sure didn't see her. I think it was just a stray dog."

"There could be a connection between your dreams at the village and your dog encounter."

"What kind of connection?"

"Maybe a spirit is trying to guide you back to a past life."

"Lani . . . "

"Don't be so stubborn," Lani chided, her voice soft. "We've all lived many lives."

Sunny could hear the creaking of a door closing ever so slowly somewhere in her brain. She didn't even know how to respond to her friend without hurting her feelings.

Lani placed the reports back on the desk. "My grandmother, Alamea Yee, couldn't wear anything—scarves, sweaters, jewelry—around her neck. It caused her great discomfort. She'd lived a past life during the Boxer Rebellion in China and died of a gunshot wound to her throat." Lani leaned forward, eyes narrowed, finger tapping the desk. "My *tūtū* never planted her vegetables until she'd spoken with the spirit in her garden, *pueo*, an owl. The neighbors marveled at her giant crops, year after year."

Sunny wanted to make a crack about Miracle-Gro fertilizer, but she could tell Lani was in true-believer mode. "What does all that have to do with me?"

"I don't know. In each life, we learn things that help us live at a higher level of consciousness. You could find out what you're supposed to learn this time around."

"How?"

"There's a woman on the other side of the island. She was my grandmother's best friend. Marie is a *kahuna*, a seer. She might be able to help you figure out what's going on."

"This is your thing. Why don't you just talk with her and let me know what she has to say? Insight by proxy."

Lani let out an exasperated sigh. "It doesn't work that way." A smile replaced her frown. "What do you have to lose? We enjoy a nice drive to Punalu'u and a visit with a quirky old lady. Not near as expensive as counseling appointments, and she won't stick you for more blood."

Sunny knew her friend wouldn't be easily put off this time. Besides, they hadn't gotten out of the city together in months. She sorely needed a break. They could sample pork *lau lau* from a vendor on the road, stop at a shave-ice stand. The door in her brain squeaked open a few inches. "Okay. Saturday?"

"I'll drive."

"We're on." Sunny grabbed her pager and a manila folder. "Back to work. I have a meeting in ten minutes with David Kaneko."

Sunny walked across the street from the Center to the cardiac surgery office. When Grace Pukui started the group, she and just one other surgeon covered all the cases. Now there were five surgeons. She waited at the reception desk. A young woman with shoe polish black hair and tarantula eye makeup slid open the glass window. "Did you sign in?"

"Hello. I'm Sunny Lyon, director of surgical services at the Center. I have a meeting scheduled with Dr. Kaneko."

The girl closed the window.

Sunny tapped her pen on the counter. Did Grace know the kind of greeting her patients were receiving at the front desk? How long had gothic girl been on the job?

The back office door opened, and a stout woman beckoned to Sunny. "Hi, Sunny. Dr. Kaneko went over to the lab about five minutes ago."

"Hey, Helen. Did he remember our meeting?"

"I reminded him. The pathologist called him to look at tissue samples."

Sunny stepped inside the hallway to the back office and closed the door behind her. "Helen, what can you tell me about Dr. Kaneko? He and I have gotten off to a bad start."

"He's definitely not a Grace Pukui. Everyone here's walking on eggshells." Helen pushed a stray silver hair back over her ear. "But I have a lot of respect for him. His Japanese-Hawaiian family's been on O'ahu for four generations. He was the first one to go to college. Stanford. Hard worker. During his cardiac residency, he once put in so many long hours, he stepped out of the operating room and passed out. Hit the tile floor face first, suffered a broken jaw. Even then, he only missed a half day of work, black eyes, wired chops, and all."

"How do you know all this?"

"His momma and I go to the same church. She's native Hawaiian, tough as nails. Never met him, though. Not until he joined the practice."

"Why did he come back to Honolulu?"

"His folks are getting old. He felt like he was on a treadmill in Houston. Still wants to make a name for himself. Always has his nose in surgical journals and such." Helen propped one hand on her hip. "If you want my opinion, I don't think he's taken too kindly to the slower pace here."

Sunny nodded. The Tasmanian Devil disguised as a surgeon.

"Do you want to reschedule?"

"No thanks, Helen. I'm going over to the lab." Sunny lowered her voice. "By the way, not a real warm welcome at the front desk."

Helen shook her head. "I know. We're working on her. If you don't track down Kaneko, let me know."

Sunny hurried back to the Center with half a mind to leave Kaneko a voice mail saying he'd missed his appointment. Driven physicians with bad attitudes. If she'd realized that dealing with them would be a significant part of her job, would she still have become a nurse?

The moment that sparked her unquenchable passion for nursing resided in her memory as clearly as if it had happened yesterday. A giant red bow and gold paper adorned the box sitting in the middle of the dining room table. She never took her eyes off the package, even while she blew out the candles on her fifth birthday cake. Inside the box nestled a nurse's case, complete with a shiny silver syringe, a thermometer sporting tiny hash marks and numbers, and a stethoscope that made her father's heart sound like a base drum. On Saturday afternoons he became her patient, keeping an eye on the baseball game and obediently munching candy pills.

Her first job as a registered nurse quickly dispelled her idealistic notions. A heavy workload and reams of paperwork cut the time she spent with patients. Nurses under incredible stress possessed little energy or compassion to support each other. Symptoms of their frustration flared in ulcers, burnout, and endless conversations about working as a checker in a grocery store. Clerks made more money back then, and no one ever died in the checkout line. The worst disillusionment was that doctors often treated nurses like handmaidens.

Being a nurse at UM made all those struggles seem like memories from a less civilized era. She'd finally found the health care utopia she long imagined, realizing the dreams locked away in that little nurse's kit. Nurses, physicians, staff, and the people they cared for touched each others' lives in a powerfully healing way.

This time she'd rely on concrete data to enlist Kaneko's support for UM's care model. As partners in their healing process, patients studied their own charts. Along with nurses, physicians, and other members of their care team, they attended conferences to customize their personal care plan. The emphasis always centered on learning how to live a healthy life. Kaneko's visible, if not enthusiastic, participation was key to his patients' complete recovery.

Sunny found him staring into a microscope in a small tissue dissection room at the back of the pathology laboratory. "Excuse me, Dr. Kaneko. We had a meeting at nine."

He continued to peer through the eyepieces as he adjusted knobs on the scope. "Cardiac amyloidosis."

"Excuse me?"

"Stiff heart syndrome." The small muscles along his jaw line flexed. He glanced up at her. "Abnormal protein deposits in the fibers of the cardiac muscle thicken the ventricle and restrict the pumping ability of the heart." He removed the slide and snapped another one onto the base of the scope. "Take a look at this." He stepped back and folded his arms.

Sunny positioned herself in front of the microscope and peered in. She adjusted the focus. The tissue sample, stained pink, revealed long smooth fibers stretching in a uniform direction.

"That's normal cardiac muscle." Kaneko came up beside her, and Sunny moved away. "Stay there." He snapped the original slide on the base. "This is a cross section of tissue showing the amyloid deposits between the cardiac muscle cells."

Sunny examined the slide. Irregularly-shaped red blobs on a bright yellow background made the tissue look like a terrazzo floor. "What's the treatment?"

"Heart transplant."

"Your patient?"

"Never saw him. DOA in the ER. Ventricular tachycardia. We need to start doing transplants here."

Sunny flashed on Darwin's comment about someone from the mainland giving the board advice on how to address UM's financial issues. "Aiming for Texas Heart Institute West?"

Kaneko nudged Sunny out of the way so he could take another look at the slide. "Opportunity knocks."

"Why don't you take some time to learn how things work at UM before trying to change it all up?" He didn't respond. She slapped the manila folder down on the counter. "It's nine thirty. I need to be back in the OR at ten."

He clicked off the scope and glanced at the folder. "What do you have?"

She slid the folder across the counter. "Here's a year's worth of data on our patient outcomes at UM. You'll notice in the summary chart that we have lower infection rates, fewer returns to surgery for post-op bleeding, and faster hospital discharges compared to the national averages."

Kaneko seemed to be only half-listening as his eyes moved down the length of her body. She became aware of every place her blue silk suit clung to her skin. She cleared her throat.

His eyes met hers. "Let me have a look." He hoisted himself up to sit on the counter and grabbed the folder. He leafed through the pages.

"These statistics are impressive, but they could have resulted from any number of factors."

"True. However, we've based our model on research conducted at several large medical centers using control groups. The most critical factors are the time we spend preparing our patients for surgery, teaching them guided imagery and relaxation techniques, and their post-operative care conferences."

He tossed the folder so it slid back down the counter toward her. "My primary focus is doing the best surgical procedure possible and keeping patients on the pump the shortest amount of time. Beyond that, it's all about maintaining a high case load because that's how the Center makes money. That means I need to spend the maximum amount of time in the operating room."

"I got that. As I said in our last meeting, taking time to give complete care, being at those care conferences, means you can spend less time treating complications and dealing with anxious patients after surgery."

Kaneko hopped off the counter and brushed his hands on his lab coat. "As the surgeon, I'm the best judge of how I should be spending my time."

She wanted to leap across the space between them and throttle him. "Dr. Kaneko, the problem is that you think taking care of surgical patients is only about what you do in the OR, not about anything else. Or for that matter, anyone else."

"That is exactly what it's about," he shouted. "In fact, with enough bananas you could probably train a chimpanzee to do what most everyone else in the OR does."

Sunny pictured the techs at the three rows of counters out in the lab looking up from their equipment, ears perked up. She closed the door and leaned against it, struggling to maintain her composure. "We're going over the same ground here and not getting anywhere. Can we call a truce?"

"How do you suggest we do that?"

"Just give our care model a chance. Come to the conferences. Be patient with our pre-surgery routine."

He let out a long sigh.

Before he could speak, she added, "And what we'll do for you is run an absolutely efficient surgical suite so that you can get in and get out."

Kaneko arched an eyebrow. "I'll see what I can do."

"Mondays and Thursdays. Be there."

He grinned. "You don't back down, do you?"

"Never."

"Important quality in an OR nurse."

"Really? I thought we were all just a bunch of chimps."

He looked down. "I apologize for that comment. The staff here is excellent."

"Apology and compliment accepted."

"Like I said, it's about excellent surgical outcomes, time and money. I won't let anything get in the way of that." He held the door open for her. "By the way, I want to add on another case this evening. Fifty-two years old. Left main is ninety-five percent blocked."

Sunny stepped out into the lab. "I'll line up anesthesia and staff."

Behind her, he drew in an audible breath. "Nice perfume."

She kept walking. "Essence of Pit Bull."

Five

Sunny propped her bare feet on the dashboard and drank in the sights as Lani's Corolla zipped around the curves to the north shore. On the right, the road nudged a turquoise ocean. On the left, *pali* vaulted out of lush valleys, the peaks resembling folds of a giant's verdant mantle. Flowering vines festooned weathered wood bungalows, old cars, and anything else left lying around. The air smelled of moist earth and the citrus scent of breadfruit trees.

"How did your meeting go with David Kaneko?" Lani asked.

"Talking with him is like trying to have a conversation with a tornado."

"Bet you won him over."

"We'll see." Sunny watched a grizzled man, cigarette hanging out of his mouth, cast a fishing net out over the swells. "He's totally fixated on efficiency and dollars."

"Not exactly the UM way."

The fisherman tugged the net out of the water. It came up empty.

"I can't shake the feeling that somehow Kaneko has something to do with Darwin Chang's plan to cut twenty percent," Sunny said.

"He just got here. How could he be involved?"

"Maybe the board is terrified of red ink. Someone from the outside with excellent credentials like David Kaneko touts a campaign for financial viability. Instead of looking at all the options to stay in the black, the top dogs start hacking." Sunny spotted a Hawaiian with a craggy face and muscles like anvils in the front yard of a concrete block house. His fists pounded a punching bag hanging from a tree branch.

"UM goes from being a special place to just another pit of frustrated patients and burned-out nurses."

Lani steered the Corolla off the highway onto a rust-colored road. "Brings back memories of the OR in L.A. We cut staff to bare bones and everything went to hell—cancelled cases, delayed procedures, endless overtime hours. Pretty soon everyone started calling in sick."

"That's not going to happen at UM."

The car bumped along as Lani veered to avoid the deep potholes. She slowed near a bungalow nestled in the jungle. Daylight, gathering into a brilliant sunset on the south shore, paled into dusky twilight here.

Lani parked behind an old station wagon pocked with dents and patches of corrosion. *Mu'umu'u* and sheets, billowing on a clothesline, marked a colorful delineation between the red dirt, green grass yard and the dark jungle. Chickens pecked the ground around the front steps.

Sunny followed Lani up onto the *lānai*. A bony black dog with gray around his muzzle stretched out by the front door. Only the dog's thumping tail acknowledged their arrival. At the far end of the *lānai*, a cane rocker and two straight-back chairs huddled around a short, rusty icebox.

Lani tapped on the screen door. She called into the darkness of the front room, "Marie, it's Lani."

Footsteps shuffled across the wood floor. Marie appeared like a beacon in the shadows, wearing a queen-size *mu'umu'u* decked with orange hibiscus flowers. Her black hair was gathered loosely on top of her head. One long strand drooped in front of her ear down to her chin. Her face beamed a toothless smile as she pushed the door open. "*Aloha*, Lani. *E komo mai.* Come in." Her voice rumbled.

They added their sandals to the pairs of flip-flops by the door and stepped in. Sunny grew accustomed to the dim light and spied a jumble of old furniture, stacks of newspapers, shelves covered with books and sea shells, and cartons of empty jars. The wood floor felt cool and smooth on her bare feet.

Marie hugged Lani to her ample bosom. "My beautiful *keiki*."

Lani drew Sunny forward. "I'd like you to meet my honorary *tūtū*, Marie Maikui Kealoha, one of the few full-blooded Hawaiians on these islands."

Marie's laugh sounded like a rattle in her old station wagon. "Not many of us left."

"This is my best friend, Sunny Lyon. She just happens to be my boss too."

Marie bear-hugged Sunny. "*Aloha.* You work her hard?"

"Usually it's the other way around."

The smell of strong coffee and the press of Marie's huge arms across their shoulders urged them toward the kitchen. The room was small but cheerful, its walls painted lemon yellow. Flowered curtains drooped at the window over the sink. A bare light bulb on the ceiling made Sunny feel the need to don sunglasses. Marie bustled around taking out coffee mugs and putting cookies on a plate.

"How's it at the Center?" Center sounded like centah. Sunny found the island patois in the old woman's earthy voice comforting. She relaxed, content to listen to Marie and Lani chat.

"We're busier than usual for this time of year."

Marie shook her head. "Lotta sick people. Need to take better care of ourselves."

"We have classes that teach people all sorts of ways to live a healthy life." Lani accepted a steaming mug of coffee and helped herself to a cookie. "And they don't include your yummy coconut shortbread, *Tūtū.*"

Marie placed another mug of coffee on the table in front of Sunny. "You want sugar or cream?"

"No thank you." Sunny watched a neon-green gecko with red spots and tiny, suction-cup toes scurry across the wall. She smiled. A gecko in the house meant good luck.

Marie took a seat at the table with her own mug and dunked a piece of shortbread in her coffee. Just before the cookie fell apart, she popped it in her mouth. "No teeth. Need to eat soft things. Doctor tried to give me new teeth. They hurt." She shook her head. "Getting tired of bananas."

Lani patted Marie's arm. "How've you been?"

"*Maika'i.* A few aches and pains. Walking with a cane more, but I got plenty time to go slow." After a quiet moment, Marie looked across the table. "How can I help you, Sunny?"

Sunny hesitated, startled by the shift from amiable patter to direct inquiry. "To be honest, I'm really not quite sure why I'm here. It was Lani's idea that we visit you."

Marie smiled. "I think you know in your heart. But your head doesn't want to listen."

Sunny sighed, leaned back in her chair. The stern look on Lani's face spurred her on. "I had a couple of encounters. I'm sure Lani told you all about them."

"You tell me what happened."

Sunny described her experiences at Kauhale O Waimea. The retelling made the events seem even more surreal. She finished by detailing her practical rationalizations, cementing them in her own mind. "Lani thinks there's something supernatural going on. I think there's a logical explanation, and we just haven't discovered it. I guess we're here to ask what you think." Sunny laughed to counter the edgy feeling in her gut and picked up a piece of shortbread. "And to eat all your delicious cookies."

Marie's eyebrows tightened. She pursed her lips. "Could be what you say—not drinking enough water, dreams." She paused. "Could be you getting ready for something big, important in your life."

Sunny shrugged. "I don't know what that means."

"Let's go out on the *lānai*." Marie rose from her chair, one stiff muscle at a time.

The dog watched them come out and went back to sleep. They settled in the chairs, placing their mugs on the top of the icebox. Marie searched in the deep pocket of her *mu'umu'u* and pulled out a pack of Camel filters and a lighter. She lit a cigarette, took a long drag, and blew the smoke up over her head. She finished her coffee and rocked in the cane chair.

Sunny looked around the *lānai*. At the far end stood flowerpots, some brimming with plants and others empty. Conch shells edged the deck like a display of ancient Spanish helmets.

Marie stroked the old hound's back with her bare foot and took another draw on her cigarette. "Hawaiians believe when people die, their energy, part of their spirit stays in the land, the *'āina*. Just by being in the place that holds these spirits, we can connect to them. Sometimes a spirit is our *'aumakua*, our guardian. For some people it could be

Pele or one of the Hawaiian gods. Could be an ancestor, or an animal spirit."

Sunny touched the dolphin tattoo on her foot. "But what does that have to do with getting ready for something important in my life?"

"Spirits can help us with that. When the dog came to you in the village, it was a sign. The spirit world is trying to reach you, Sunny."

"Why me?"

Marie puffed on her cigarette. The tip flared in the dim light. A frog called for a mate, its croak sounding like the rat-tat-tat of a wind-up toy.

After a while, Marie spoke. "Don't know why you. It's for you to find out. The spirits want to help, but they won't unless you ask."

"What about the hallucinations? Am I supposed to believe that I actually flashed into a body I had centuries ago? When people talk about experiencing a past life, it seems like something cooked up in their imagination. Everyone always claims they were Cleopatra or Napoleon."

"What does it matter if it's imagination, a memory in our bones, another life, if we get wisdom?" Marie asked.

"Let's say I believe that I've lived a past life, and knowing about it could somehow change this life. And I believe that a spirit wants to help me. What am I actually supposed to do about all of that?"

Marie crushed her cigarette out in a coffee can on top of the icebox. "Everybody wants to do something. Sometimes, it requires do nothing, just be."

Frustrated by her fruitless attempts to find logic in fuzzy answers, Sunny wanted to jump up, thank the old woman for her hospitality, grab Lani, and head for home. She forced herself to sit back in her chair. She didn't want to appear rude. "Just be? I was just being at the village and got shoved into a time warp. How did that happen?"

Marie chuckled. "The past, present, future. All mixed up, yeah?"

"Einstein," Lani said. "Time isn't linear. When we grapple with things in this life, we're working on healing the past and on what will happen in the future."

"Are we talking Twilight Zone here?" Sunny asked.

Marie and Lani didn't answer.

"Okay, okay. I don't mean to be disrespectful." Sunny brought the coffee mug to her lips, inhaled the nutty aroma, took a sip. "Say I truly believed I've had a past life here. How do I avoid getting jerked between time zones? Let me tell you, it's no fun carnival ride."

"Gotta get quiet," Marie said. "Go deep inside to the silence and you will hear answers to all your questions."

"About the only quiet time I have is the drive to work."

"Quiet as in meditation, sitting in silence, shutting out the busy-ness." Lani's words pricked Sunny like a needle.

"'*Ae*. In the silence, your '*aumākua* speak to you. Our ancestors possessed wisdom and powers that were lost to us. Listen and you'll learn these things."

"Voices?" Sunny asked.

"Could be. Mostly the answer just comes into your mind, but you'll know you didn't think of it yourself."

"Sometimes the answer comes days later," Lani added.

"'*Ae*. At the moment you need it. The answer comes when you're heart is open," Marie said softly.

"If I go back to the village, will that hallucination thing happen again?"

"Your past life is there in the '*āina*." Better to prepare yourself in the silence and then claim that life."

The warm night air surrounded her like a shawl, but Sunny shivered. "How do I do that?"

Marie's voice dropped into the cadence of an eerie chant. "Be still. Empty your mind of all thoughts. Breathe deeply." She sucked in a deep breath and blew it out in a long, loud ha sound. "Breath is life. It connects us to the spirit world. Four deep breaths and find your center. Open your heart. Ask your '*aumākua* to guide you back to that ancient time, to show you what you must learn. Be still. The spirits will do the rest." The chant faded away on the breeze.

A whisper of fear and a scream of skepticism vied for attention in Sunny's mind. She pushed the fear away and rose from her chair. "Right now, there's so much going on at work. Maybe in a few months I'll be able to take a meditation class, try some breath work." She slipped on her sandals and carefully moved around the sleeping hound. "Marie, thank you for your time."

As she stood before Lani and Marie, Sunny sensed the abruptness of her actions. They sat motionless in their chairs, watching her, patrons riveted in the darkness of a movie theater.

Slowly, Marie rose. She took Sunny's hands in both of hers. "Whatever happens, remember your *'aumākua* are there for you." She gave Sunny's hands a squeeze. "There's someone in your life now who was with you before, in ancient Hawai'i. This person can be your friend or your enemy."

Chicken skin rippled across Sunny's back. "Goodbye, Marie. Thanks again."

They were silent as the car bumped out to the main road. Sunny wondered if her friend was angry. "Lani, if I had the time to get back into tai chi, maybe I could get the hang of what you and Marie talked about."

"Life never gets un-busy. The trick is to find quiet in the middle of the chaos."

"I know. You're right. It's just that . . ."

The dashboard lights illuminated Lani's smile. She patted Sunny's knee. "Not to worry, girlfriend. Someday you'll be ready."

Sunny lay in bed, two cats plastered around her feet. She closed her eyes as the conversation with Lani and Marie replayed in her mind. A twinge of guilt made her sigh. They were right about time for slowing down. She needed to take better care of herself, build in some stress relief. In fact, maybe that's all her hallucinations amounted to—stress overload.

She turned on the lamp, grabbed a pen and pad, and scribbled a note about signing up for yoga classes. She glanced at the cats. Keko— Hawaiian for monkey—sat up and licked her long, striped tail. Skipper, twenty-one pounds of sleek, black panther, stretched and patted her foot with his paw. She flicked off the light and turned on her side. The cats reshuffled and nestled along her back and legs.

David Kaneko popped into Sunny's head. He'd mentioned heart transplants. Maybe the twenty percent cuts were going to get him a transplant program. Damn it. She needed to get to sleep.

Sunny flipped over on her back, and the cats scrambled off the bed. She kicked off the covers. Maybe if she did some of that breathing Marie talked about she could relax. She took four deep breaths. Four more. Her fingers started to tingle. Jeez. Hyperventilating. She stared at the ceiling for a long time, concentrating on the smoke detector's tiny green light until she couldn't keep her eyes open. With a giant yawn, she turned on her side and drifted off.

❀ ❀ ❀

A young girl bursts through the door of the long house. She searches the circle of council members with wild eyes and finds me. "Mahana, we need your help. My mother will not stop bleeding. I am afraid she will die."

Her mother, Poemiti, delivered a big, healthy baby girl last night. We must see her at once. I signal to Tanemao as I rise from the mat. Tiare holds my arm to steady me. I look around the circle. "Thank you, my sisters and brothers, for your wisdom this day."

Tanemao and I follow the girl across the village. My legs refuse to move faster, so I send Tanemao ahead. "Make sure there are enough mats under Poemiti's legs so her feet are higher than her head. Bring a bowl of rain water." Tanemao breaks into a run.

I stop at my *fare* to fetch my pack, healing supplies wrapped in pure white *tapa* cloth. When I arrive at the birthing house, Poemiti's auntie clutches my hands and pulls me inside. Her wrinkled face is wet with tears. "Mahana, I have done everything I can think to do. The blood is still gushing."

I kneel beside Poemiti, my stiff knees complaining. I think I must be getting too old for this work. The thought flys away as I take Poemiti's hand in both of mine. Already, I am concentrating on pouring *mana*, the life force, into her being. Her skin is clammy, and her face is as pale as the *tapa* of my pack. I place my hand on her forehead and lean down to whisper in her ear. "Poemiti, it is Mahana. We ask that your spirit remain with us. Your daughters need you."

Placing my ear on her chest, I hear that her heart is beating very fast. I press down on her abdomen. Her womb feels large and mushy. The organ tightens like a fist under my firm massage. Poemiti cries out. Her whole body shudders. She stares at me, pupils dilated with fear. I squeeze her hand. "Stay with us, dear one. We are going to help you." She closes her eyes. A single tear runs across her cheek.

Auntie has packed Poemiti's birth canal with *tapa* cloth dipped in *'awa* to slow the bleeding and relieve the pain. The poultice is soaked with blood. Sending Tanemao to gather fresh *ti* leaves, I unwrap my pack. I offer a silent prayer, asking my *'aumakua*, the dolphin, to be with me.

When I have placed the four sacred objects around Poemiti—at her feet, her head, and on each side—I pour fresh rain water from a bowl into a large seashell containing a small amount of sea salt. I swirl the mixture and ask *Akua* to fill me with *mana* so that I may heal Poemiti. I smooth the salt water on her face, arms, chest, abdomen, and legs with my fingers. My touch seems to ease her trembling. Her womb has become boggy again. I massage and press hard until Poemiti moans and her womb clamps down, slowing the bleeding.

Tanemao returns with the *ti* leaves. I direct him to rinse them in the fresh rainwater and score them with my bone knife. He and auntie slowly bend Poemiti's knees and open her legs. Gently, I pack her birth canal with the leaves and a new *tapa* poultice. Tanemao and auntie straighten her legs, propping them up on a pile of *hala* mats as I massage her womb. We cover her with a soft *tapa* sheet.

Removing the gourd rattle from my pack, I sit crossed-legged at Poemiti's side. I breathe deeply, filling my chest until I feel great pressure, and release the air with a loud ha sound. Enormous waves of *mana* flow in with each breath. My whole body begins to tingle and grow warm. I shake the rattle over Poemiti's feet, head, and sides. A chant rises from my belly into my throat and grows louder as I shake the rattle over her womb. I send out fervent prayers to the spirits of wind, fire, water, and earth to be here with us. I call to Poemiti's guardian spirits to protect her.

With my eyes closed, I see bright light the color of the *ti* leaves, swirling and spiraling from the air around me into the top of my head. The light fills my head, my chest, pours into my belly, streams out into my arms and legs. My body vibrates with the emerald glow. My limbs sting as if assaulted by wind-driven sand. The rattle drops from my hand. I breathe deeply and allow the light to grow and pulsate. When I sense that I am nearly bursting with the illumination, I place one hand on Poemiti's womb and the other on her chest. I chant the words—"Your light through me, your light to Poemiti"—over and over. The swirling iridescence flows from my legs and torso, from my head, through my arms and fingertips to fill every space in her body with healing essence.

The last swirls of emerald light pour from me. I slump forward, drained. I feel Tanemao's strong hands on my back. He has been behind me the entire time, adding his *mana* to the power I have drawn from the spirit world. I sense auntie's hand on top of mine. Seated opposite me, she has helped me hold the power around Poemiti. She whispers close to my ear, "Feel her womb. Look at her face." With my eyes still closed, I press my hand on her belly. The womb is a tight ball. I glance up, sweat streaming down my face. Poemiti is looking at us with serene eyes. Her limbs are relaxed, and her pallor has turned to a faint blush.

I slip my arm under her shoulders and hold her close, thanking *Akua* and the spirits for healing our beloved Poemiti. "You rest now."

Poemiti nods and closes her eyes.

Food helps us regain our strength after the hard work of healing. Tanemao and I wash down bites of baked fish with coconut milk and finish our meal with banana and juicy *'ōhelo* berries. The dim light in my *fare* is soothing. A cool breeze off the river wafts in through the doorway. We doze a while. I dream of a woman who is trying to save a child. I cannot see her face. Just as she turns toward me, Tanemao is patting my arm.

"Mahana, may I go down to the river?"

His face is full of pleading. I want to send him on his way and return to my vision. But we must review the ritual we have just performed for Poemiti.

We sit facing each other, my pack between us. "Now, my fine apprentice, what is the most important thing for a healer to remember, no matter what the physical problem may be?"

His earnest eyes are riveted on mine. "We are to consider what the body needs and, at the same time, attend to the spirit."

Tanemao excels in discerning the signs of illness in the body and determining the remedy to be applied. I expect him to easily answer my next questions. "What happened to Poemiti? What was the treatment?"

His answers come back swiftly and accurately. The womb did not naturally tighten to stop the bleeding after childbirth. Rapid heart beat and pale, damp skin were the signs that she had lost a lot of blood. Bleeding is checked by a property in *ti* leaves. Elevating Poemiti's legs helped the blood flow around the vital organs.

Attending to the spirit is another matter. Tanemao shows more skepticism than reverence for this aspect of healing. First, I review a basic principle. "There is an unending source of *mana* everywhere—in the air, on the waves of the ocean, in plants and animals. We increase this life force in ourselves simply by breathing deeply. Also by being quiet and communing with the world around us. Before you can heal someone, you must increase your own *mana*."

Tanemao nods emphatically. "I understand the part about breathing deeply. The practice makes me feel more clear-headed so I can focus on what is making the person sick."

"You are missing the most important point. Breath increases *mana*. The reason I have taught you to breathe deeply and place your hands on my back during a ritual is so that you will add your life force to mine. Together, we gathered more power to focus on Poemiti's healing."

My apprentice shrugs. "What about the chanting and the rattle?"

I groan inwardly. I'm trying to teach this young man about being patient while he constantly tries my patience. "We will discuss that in a moment. After you have attended to the immediate physical needs, you must prepare a sacred space to do your work." I open my pack and take out the items one by one. "Begin by placing these four sacred objects around the sick person and calling in the spirits of the elements."

I hold up a large white feather from a sea bird. "This represents the wind, breath, *hā*." I tap my finger to my forehead. "The feather is also the symbol of our thinking self."

A black seedpod looks insignificant lying on the white *tapa*. "This kernel represents fire, *ahi*, and our spiritual self. The oil from this humble *kukui* nut lights our way in the darkness. We increase *mana* by seeing light in our mind's eye."

"Seeing light?"

"Yes. By imagining bright light we give the *mana* form. Healing light is the color of the lush jungle. We imagine it filling every fiber of the sick person."

Tanemao raises his eyebrow, but I go on. Turning over a fist-sized oval shell in my hands, I point out the two sides. The top is brown-speckled and smooth. "The shell represents water, *kai*, and symbolizes our feeling self. We increase the life force by cultivating joy, gratitude, and love. Our celebrations and feasts give us the chance to do that." I smile. Our last feast went on for days. At the end, not many of us felt much energy. "Maybe sometimes we cultivate too much joy."

Tanemao harrumphs. He is not one for our frequent festivities.

I display the underside of the shell, two ridged edges fold into the middle, resembling a woman's secret place. "The shell also represents *vahine*, woman. The ocean is our mother."

From the bottom of my pack, I lift a hefty stone, oblong with one flat end so that it stands upright. "The stone represents our physical self and earth, *honua*. When we are keenly aware of the beauty around us, our *mana* increases. It is also the symbol for *tane*, man." I place the shell and the stone next to each other. "With these two objects we also honor the sacredness of *vahine* and *tane*. Power comes in the equal joining of women and men." A wave of love swells in me as I think of the *mana* that comes from my joining with Tiare.

Holding up a *ti* leaf packet of sea salt and a scalloped seashell, I finish this part of the lesson. "We complete the sacred space by blessing the person with salt and water. The mixture must be made with fresh rainwater caught in gourds, as it is pure and not contaminated by touching the earth."

Tanemao is making an effort to be attentive. Yet, he cannot hide eyes that wander to look out the doorway and hands that fidget with a bone knife. He sighs. "You were going to tell me about the chanting and rattling."

"We create *mana loa* through our chants, through rattling and drumming, through dancing." I shake the rattle over my head. "The movements and sounds call the spirits in, building the life force all around us and increasing our personal *mana*."

I hold out the rattle to Tanemao. He accepts it, turns it over in his hand, and quickly replaces it in the pack. "Must I learn the chants?"

"If you are to take my place one day as the healer for our clan, you must learn every aspect of healing."

Another sigh. "What else?"

"You must also call in the sick person's *'aumakua*—the divine spark in each of us, the higher self, an ancestor protector. The *'aumakua* is all of these." Tanemao is frowning, so I remind him of his *'aumakua*. "Your protector is the shark, the most powerful guardian."

"Because I was the first to be born under the Fin of *Mao*. That is why my mother named me Tanemao, shark man."

"Yes. If I need to heal an illness in you, I must call on *Mao*. In order to be a healer, you must call on *Mao* to assist you."

Tanemao nods. His eyes snap wide open. "If we can heal like this then why do people still pass on? No one should ever die. My mother and father . . ."

"Ultimately, the spirit chooses to stay or go."

Tanemao rubs his face, shakes his head.

"That does not mean they wanted to leave you."

"Pah!"

I draw in a breath and let it out slowly. Ever since his parents crossed the rainbow, I have loved this young man as my own son. He must be given time. I want him to succeed.

I grasp his forearms. "That is enough for today. We will go over the gathering and pouring out of *mana* another time."

Tanemao's face brightens, the sun emerging from a dark cloud. He helps me up, and we walk outside. "Mahana, have you thought of how we will respond to the Tauati raiders?"

"The meeting tonight is time enough to ponder that."

"I still say we must be prepared for a battle."

We face each other. Meeting the fire in his eyes with a steady gaze, I remind him, "The Anuanua came here wearing the mantle of peace. War is not our way."

Tanemao steps back, and a reflection of light makes me squint. The symbol of his *'aumakua*, a large shark tooth dangling from a cord around his neck gleams in the sun. Backing away from me, he holds out his hands, palms upward. The fire still flares in his eyes. "Teacher, maybe it is time to change our way."

Before I can respond, he turns and jogs toward the river.

Six

Sunny hunched at her desk rereading a memo from David Kaneko. She wanted to wad up the paper and slam dunk it into the trash can. Instead, she propped her forehead in one hand. The touch of her cold skin to her eyes felt good. An hour nap would feel even better.

"Weight of the world?"

Sunny looked up to see Lani standing in the doorway. "Only about 180 pounds."

"Let's see. Too heavy for Katherine Nakamura. Definitely too light for your landlord."

"Kaneko."

Lani took Sunny's lab coat off the hook on the back of the door and tossed it across the desk. "Let's go for a walk."

The sun's warmth felt delicious after the chill of the surgical suite. Sunny turned her face up to the bright rays. "Now he wants to read the angiography films in the OR instead of down in x-ray. That's how they do it in Houston." They strolled in the gardens as she continued. "Not such a bad idea. The kicker is he suggested we use the pre-op rooms for the equipment stations. Everything we discussed about patient care went in his ear and got lost in a black hole."

"Why do you let him push your buttons? Can't you figure out a cubby hole for his equipment and just go on doing for patients what we've always done?"

"It's just that after my last meeting with him I thought there was a chance he'd get with the program."

They stopped at the day care center. Children chased each other around the yard and performed monkey routines on the jungle gym.

Sunny laughed to see a blonde girl pumping a swing as high as she could, a dare-devil gleam on her cherub face. "Enough gnashing of teeth. Anything exciting happening in your life?"

Lani's smile lit up. "Does a blind date with possibilities count?"

"Do tell."

"I met him in a bar."

Sunny groaned. "This can't be good."

"It's not like that. Do you know Jeff Bishop? He's one of the physical therapists in the UM Works clinic. We both served on the ethics committee last year."

"I thought this was a blind date."

"Let me finish, please."

"Okay, okay."

"Jeff introduced me to his brother."

"So what's he like?"

"He's a big guy. Used to play football. Now he sings and plays guitar in a band. Pete's incredibly sweet."

"Sounds like you're falling." The little blonde girl jumped off the swing in mid-air, landed on her knees, and popped up with a shout to a kid across the yard. "And what else?"

"He has a seven-year-old son."

"Could be tough being a stepmom."

"Sunny, I just met him. I'm going to take it one step at a time. For now, can't I have a little fun?"

"You're right. It's been awhile."

"Look who's talking. When are you going to get back out there?"

"I don't know. I think I've given up on finding someone. Maybe I'm too picky. Most of the time it feels like getting back in the dating scene would just complicate my life. Besides, I can't stand the small talk."

The fact was she couldn't stand another disaster like the last one. She'd fallen hard for a charming surgeon right after nursing school. Though she heard vague rumors, she clung to his declarations of love for years. If the rumors were true, she told herself, he'd changed. The engagement ring sparkled on her finger less than a month when she found him in a utility closet, entwined in the arms of a woman from housekeeping, surrounded by mops and jugs of cleaning solutions.

Her heart felt as if he'd wielded his scalpel and neatly excised two of the four chambers. The pain intensified when the news hit the hospital gossip mill. Everyone took the opportunity to give her the details of his escapades. The OR director reminded her that most cutters couldn't keep it in their pants. She felt like a fool, wallowed for months. Over time, she developed rock solid resolve to avoid surgeons and any other serious entanglements for that matter.

Sunny saw a boy collecting blocks scattered around the yard. He wore glasses and a perfectly clean outfit. She nudged Lani and pointed to the kid. They watched him build an intricate tower. A dark-eyed girl with a solemn face tried to add blocks to the structure. The boy grabbed the blocks and turned his back to the girl. "There's the next David Kaneko."

Lani laughed. They meandered on and stopped at a bench by a reflecting pool. "You know, Mr. Right isn't going to show up out of the blue."

Sunny stared at the giant orange and white fish circling in the pool. She leaned over to swirl her fingers in the cool water. The fish darted away. "Yeah. Yeah. These days I don't have the energy to track him down."

"You do look tired. What's going on?"

"Ever since our trek out to Marie's my dreams have been crazy. That same old man treating a dying woman. A bunch of people dressed in nothing but loin cloths having a meeting. I wake up feeling wrung out." Sunny looked directly at Lani to catch a hint of an answer before she asked the question. "Am I losing my mind?"

Lani gave Sunny a comforting hug. "No. You're not losing your sanity." She grasped Sunny's shoulders. "I envy you. *I ka nui*, as my *tūtū* used to say. This is huge, my friend. You're tapping into another level of energy, of consciousness."

"I just want a good night's sleep. Maybe I'll contact Steve Winship like you said. Get him to give me a sleeping pill."

"Better plan a couple hours for a complete psych eval." Lani bent down to dip her hand in the pool. The fish crowded around, brushing her fingers and opening their mouths wide. "You could just go with these dreams. Write down your impressions. Maybe you'll discover their meaning."

Sunny watched the fish, glittering like jewels in the sunlit water, drift toward the shade of the water lilies. She felt more like burying her head under a pillow than tackling dream analysis. One more thing to add to her list.

"Okay, I heard that deep sigh." Lani popped off the bench. "Let's try a different therapy. Pete's band is playing at The Wall on Friday. I guarantee an evening of dancing and little parasol drinks will take your mind off your troubles."

Sunny got up, and they headed back to the OR. She linked her arm in Lani's. "What would I do without you to pry me out of my rut?"

"Be a workaholic hanging with her cats."

Sunny winced. Maybe Lani was right. She just needed to get out more. Maybe then the dreams would go away.

The band finished their first set. At a front table, Sunny and Lani joined in the cheering and applause. Saturday night revelers jammed every inch of the bar at The Wall and spilled out onto the beach.

The lead singer placed his electric guitar in its stand and came over. Tall and muscular, he easily outweighed the average football lineman. Dark hair, hanging loose to his shoulders, light brown skin, and tattoos encircling his upper arms in geometric patterns gave him the look of a Hawaiian warrior. But his angelic, tenor voice and twinkling eyes made it hard for Sunny to imagine him in any battle.

Lani perched on the edge of her chair. "Pete Keola Bishop meet Sunny Lyon."

Pete reached across the table and gently clasped Sunny's hand. "Heard a lot about you. Glad you came out tonight." He pulled up a chair and took a sip of Lani's beer. He grinned. "Good crowd. You think?"

Sunny raised a beer bottle salute. "You have this place rockin'."

"I knew you'd love them," Lani said.

"How long have you played together?" Sunny asked.

"Couple of us fooled around with music in high school. This band's been together about nine years."

Sunny glanced around the room. "Looks like you have quite a following."

"They play clubs all over the islands, and they've cut three CDs." Lani held Pete's hand.

Pete nodded. "We're supposed to have number four out in a few months. Hard to round these guys up and get 'em in the studio. Hooey." The chuckle and impish grin softened his intimidating size and endeared him to Sunny.

She watched Lani and Pete gaze at each other, their eyes shining, and felt as if she were intruding on a very private moment. She couldn't get over how quickly their romance had bloomed.

Sunny noticed a couple standing near their table. "Pete, I think they're trying to get your attention."

He looked over his shoulder and gave the two a slight wave. "Gotta go. Good to meet you, Sunny. Leilani, don't wait up. Gonna be a late one." Pete leaned in and gave Lani a lingering kiss.

When he was gone, Sunny squeezed Lani's arm. "He calls you Leilani. This is more serious than I thought."

A blush crept up Lani's neck. "It's so nice to hear him say it. My grandmother was the only person who called me Leilani."

Sunny watched Pete make his way to the bar, greeting his fans with *shaka*—the Hawaiian hang loose, thumb-and-pinky wave. He signed his autograph for two shapely women clad in bikinis and hugged his buddies. "Popular guy, Lani. He gets a lot of attention."

Lani shook her head. "I'm not worried. It comes with the territory, and Pete's had his fill of groupies. Having a kid makes him a little more serious than some of the other guys in the band."

"It's a big responsibility. What about the boy's mother?"

They were practically yelling at each other over the din of the crowd. "Let's go out on the beach." Lani led the way through a wall of flowered shirts and halter-tops.

Sunny caught sight of Pete engaged in an intense conversation with the man who'd been waiting near their table. Pete's serious expression contrasted with the easy smile Sunny had seen moments ago. The crowd closed around her. She pushed through, excusing herself along the way.

The fresh air felt invigorating. Sunny took a seat by Lani on the low sea wall in front of the club. "You were going to tell me about Pete's ex-wife."

Lani shook her head. "They were never married. I think Kai was a love child. Pete and Sonia get along fairly well, enough to share time with Kai."

"Why did they break up?"

"A couple of reasons. Sonia hated sharing Pete with the band and the fans. And they fought constantly about his political activities. She thought it robbed even more time from their relationship and Kai."

Sunny picked a loose pebble off the wall and tossed it toward the water. It plopped on the sand, just out of wave's reach. "Political activities?"

"The sovereignty movement."

Sunny nodded. She was aware of the movement, even felt sympathetic toward it. She'd spent time at the Bishop museum learning the extent to which Captain Cook's 1778 arrival in the islands had sparked the decimation of the native population. Hawaiians were overwhelmed by disease, evicted from their lands, and forced to give up their language and most of their traditions. Now, many suffered from high rates of poverty and lack of education. The ER nurses at UM came face to face with the impact of those statistics every day. Sunny couldn't blame the Hawaiians for wanting to reclaim what they'd lost. "How involved is he?"

"That man who was waiting for Pete near our table is one of the leaders in Hawaiian Freedom. The band plays at all of their events."

"Didn't they organize the demonstration at the Maui airport a couple months ago?"

Lani handed Sunny a pebble. "Pete was there. So far the rallies have been peaceful but everyone thinks that as the sovereignty issue heats up, there could be trouble."

Sunny winged the stone. It landed in the foamy surf. "If Sonia had a hard time putting up with Pete's commitment to the band and his political activities, how are you going to deal with those things?"

"I don't know." Lani sighed. "It's been so long since I've felt like this, since someone was this crazy for me. I'm taking it one day at a time."

They were quiet for awhile. Lani pitched a pebble so it skipped across a swell. "There's just one thing."

Sunny had a hunch about the one thing. Since her mastectomy, Lani had fallen for only one man, a Navy pilot. He'd swept her off her feet literally and figuratively by taking her up in a bi-plane on weekends. He'd made her feel beautiful until their relationship turned intimate. "What's that?"

"Same old worry. What if the big love scene happens and Pete gets all grossed out?"

Sunny slipped her arm across Lani's shoulders, gave her a hug. "No way. You're gorgeous, and he's smitten."

"Damn. I dread that first encounter. Bra comes off, he looks away."

"Hey. I'm telling you. You and Pete are going to be the love match of the century." Sunny gave Lani a nudge. "Sounds like the band is starting up. Go back in there and protect your interests."

Lani hopped off the wall. "Thanks for the pep talk, girl friend. I'm going to stop worrying about the future and just enjoy the now." Her frown relaxed into a giant grin. "Let's do some dancing."

"You go ahead. I'll join you in a bit." Sunny watched her friend jog back through the crowd. She picked another loose pebble off the sea wall and rolled it between her fingers. The waves tumbled and frothed on the sand. Beyond the surf, ocean and sky merged into deep black.

The band launched into a rousing number. The crowd sang the words to the activist anthem—"living in a sovereign land"—over and over. A twinge of worry pricked her. She hoped Pete wasn't playing Lani along with his guitar. Even if his intentions were sincere, how much security could he, with his musician lifestyle and radical politics, offer? And what about that big love scene? Lani certainly didn't need any more pain in her life. Sunny threw the pebble hard, and it disappeared into the darkness.

She eased off the wall and made her way back to the front table. Some of the crowd had joined the band on stage, chanting the chorus and dancing with their arms raised high. In the middle of the group, Lani clapped her hands and sang along. Pete stepped back from the microphone to play a soaring riff on his guitar. The two of them beamed, their eyes locked on each other, as if they were the only ones on the stage.

Seven

Sunny buttoned her pajama top and stood in front of the bathroom sink, ears still ringing from the noise and music at The Wall. She pressed a warm wash cloth over her eyes and saw Pete and Lani on the stage, lost in their own world. What would it be like to be giddy in love again? It might never happen. She stared in the mirror, eyes narrowed. That wouldn't be the end of the world. After all, she had a rich life with work and friends and diving. Still . . . She touched the wash cloth to her cheek, leaned into its warm caress. To have a man look at you like Pete gazed at Lani . . .

She braced her hands on the sink, opened her eyes wide. White shot with red lines around a field of blue. Mini star spangled banners. If she didn't start getting more sleep, she was going to have to invest in a case of Visine drops.

Her image blurred, like a close-up on a television with snowy reception. Sunny blinked. Her reflection stared back at her in sharp clarity. She turned on the cold water, splashed her face, glanced in the mirror. Her dripping image wavered then disappeared in mist creeping across the glass. She rubbed the mirror with a towel but the cloudiness remained. She was looking through a window at thick swirling fog.

Sunny studied the mist, trying to discern a pattern. Gradually, a shape emerged. The face of the old man. Eyes dark and serene. Smooth skin a rich mahogany. Mahana. His name was Mahana.

Sudden dizziness made her slump down on the edge of the bath tub. Damn. Maybe the alcohol had triggered it this time. But she'd had only a couple of beers, and that was hours ago. She leaned forward, eyes shut tight, waiting for the spinning sensation to pass. What now? Maybe if she could make it to the bed she'd fall asleep. Damn, this was a royal pain in the ass. Lani had suggested she go with these spells, see what happens. Easy for her to say.

The air around her felt humid as if she'd just stepped out of the shower. Childish laughter chimed somewhere in the distance. Sunny straightened and opened her eyes, squinting at what seemed like the slanting rays of a setting sun. A hand squeezed her arm.

❁   ❁   ❁

Tiare and I walk on the river's edge after our evening meal. The water makes a soft rushing sound. The air is heavy and still, laden with the coming storm.

"How is Poemiti?" Tiare asks.

"The bleeding has stopped. She is sipping broth and nursing her baby."

"You are still troubled."

"Poemiti is out of danger. It is Tanemao who concerns me."

"What is the matter?"

"If our lessons involve discerning an illness, preparing treatments, he excels. When I teach him how to invoke the spirits for help in performing those tasks, he loses interest."

"Does he blame the great spirit *Akua* for the loss of his mother and father?"

"He refuses to discuss that."

"Maybe you should try one more time to draw him out."

"Maybe I should begin the teaching with Mareva. She is more thoughtful and eager to understand everything about healing."

"You could work with both of them at the same time. They could teach each other."

"Oh *vahine*, I am too old for such a challenge."

Tiare laughs as we sit on a flat rock at the river's edge. She wraps her arm around my waist. "My love, you have more vitality than many of the young men in our village."

I smooth a strand of hair back from her face. "When I am with you, I am their age."

Dark storm clouds gathering on the horizon are tinged with the fire of sunset. The laughter of children rings across the village as families draw together to watch the changing skies. I slide my arm across Tiare's shoulders, and she leans into me.

The light fades to pearl gray. Tiare breaks our stillness. "I, too, am worried about Tanemao."

"This morning's council meeting . . ."

"Yes. We are facing the first test of our commitment to live peacefully with others who are not of our clan. Tanemao's call to make weapons made me realize our biggest challenge may come from within."

I think of the ways we've dealt with disagreements and ill will amongst our people. Everyone involved in the dispute comes to council for peacemaking. We talk, sometimes through the setting and rising of the sun, for as long as it takes. Payment for wrong-doing such as the giving of a gift, forgiveness, banishment for a short time all work to remind us that we are one in spirit and love.

Tiare interrupts my musings. "Maybe others think the same as Tanemao. What will convince them that we must not take up weapons?"

"Remembering the horrors we left behind in Tahiti."

"Not so easy for the young people. They have not experienced those horrors first hand."

"We will find a way to convince them." I gently rub the back of Tiare's neck. "You are wise and patient. I have no doubt that you will lead us to right action with the people of Tauati."

She turns to me. "Mahana, the meaning of your name—sunlight—is what you are to me, my precious one." She glances skyward, then taps a finger on her forehead. "Whether the clouds are up there or in my head, you shine them away."

I wonder at the great blessing this woman is to me. The lines of age disappear in a smile as soft as the first light of dawn. Her eyes are darker and deeper than a pool at the bottom of a waterfall. I touch my forehead to hers. Our noses meet and we breathe deeply. Her scent is the sweet-spicy perfume of delicate 'awapuhi blossoms. She presses her cheek to mine and whispers, "Do you think we'll have enough strength for hauti after our meeting with Aimata and Omo?"

I chuckle. "I remember a time when we never had to be concerned about that. If not tonight, we have the morning."

We hold each other close, listening to the birds twitter as they find shelter from the coming storm. The air is pungent with the smoke of torches just lit and the aroma of cooking fires. A fish leaps out of the water; ever-widening circles ripple to the shore.

The long house looms like a cave around Tiare, Aimata, Omo, and me. The light of *kukui* oil lamps flickers on the thatched walls. We sit in a circle around one of the lamps. In the shadows, the *tatau* designs on Omo's face meld into a single dark swath across his nose and cheeks. He places the four sacred objects around the oil lamp. We clasp hands and breathe together, sucking in great drafts of air through our noses and blowing out through our mouths. My whole body tingles. My mind is as alert as when I study the ocean's surface to catch just the right fish.

Omo intones a chant, calling in the spirits of the wind in the east, of fire in the south, water in the west, and earth in the north. His voice grows thunderous and quavers as he calls in the spirits of our ancestors. Each of us silently asks our personal *'aumakua* to be with us. The chant softens. Omo raises his arms, "We thank you *Akua* for being with us. Help us to be wise and courageous this day." We sit quietly. The last words of the chant echo in my mind.

Tiare speaks first. "We are one with *Akua*. Let us work together for the good of all people. The issue at hand is how to respond to the raiding parties from Tauati."

Aimata leans forward. "The raiding parties are becoming a threat to our safety."

"Let us ask the questions." Tiare picks up the feather, symbol of the air and the mind. "What knowledge do we need?"

Aimata's answer is immediate. "We need to know if they have warriors and how they will move against us." She crosses her arms over her expansive breasts.

Omo allows a moment of respectful silence before he speaks. "Are they planning to move against us? We don't know that. We need to learn why they are observing us."

"How?" Aimata asks.

Tiare gestures with palms upraised. "Why don't we send our own observation party to Tauati?"

I picture our people landing the canoe on a beach there. "We should be prepared to do more than observe. Our emissaries must be ready to talk with whoever comes to meet them, ask them what they want from us and how we can help them."

Aimata is shaking her head before I finish speaking. "They could slaughter our emissaries."

I feel the tension in her statement simmering in our circle. I remain quiet for a few breaths and then speak slowly. "Aimata, that is a distinct possibility, a frightening one. Our people will go there shielded by *mana loa*. We must hold to the belief that this will be their ultimate protection."

Omo adds, "We cannot go there in fear, ready to fight. There would be no chance to make a peaceful encounter."

Aimata ponders Omo's words as she runs her fingers through her close-cropped hair. "I know what you say is truth. The Anuanua came here to live in a new way and we must keep that vow."

I look down, closing my eyes, feeling the tension subside. I am grateful that the people around this circle possess great respect for one another. Trust makes it easier to put aside one's own stance.

"The first step in our plan will be to send emissaries to Tauati to learn of their intentions and to offer our hands in peace." Tiare's look seeks a response from everyone. We each nod agreement.

In his palm, Omo cradles the *kukui* nut, symbol of fire and spirit. "What can we do to bring more light to this situation? How can we create good relations with the people of Tauati?"

After a few moments, Omo offers an answer that reflects his role as spiritual leader for the village. "Before we try to make any connection, we must be sure that we have done everything possible to be aligned with *Akua*. I say the first step is to perform the sacred *ori*. In this way, we will ensure the highest level of life force. Their people will recognize in our emissaries the light of honesty and peaceful intention."

Tiare notes for our circle that this new first step requires the entire village to make ready for a night of ritual dance and chanting followed by feasting.

I pick up the cowry shell, symbol of water and emotions, symbol of *vahine*. I admire the gleam of the polished surface. Turning it over gently, I run my finger across the ridged folds. "The *ori* will imbue us with refreshed gratitude for what we have and a willingness to show compassion to the people of Tauati. In what other ways can we show compassion?"

The generous aspect of Aimata's otherwise tough nature shines. "Let our emissaries take with them gifts of food, plants, and implements. In this way, we show them that they do not have to steal from us. We will freely share what we have." She paused, tapping her finger on her chin. "Mahana, you and Tanemao could offer healing treatments. Maybe they need help with their sick and dying."

"An excellent idea that will serve them and us. I cannot think of a better learning experience for Tanemao."

Tiare goes back over the steps we have determined so far. "The first thing we do is set the time for *ori*. In three to four days, Omo?"

"Yes. The moon is waxing and will be full in five days. This is the perfect time to form a relationship."

"After that our emissaries will sail to Tauati with gifts and the offering of healing work. They will seek to understand the people there and begin a mutual relationship. Are we agreed?" We all signal our assent.

Aimata lifts the standing stone, symbol of earth, the body, and *tane*. "How can we ensure a solid foundation for the future?"

Omo draws in a huge breath. "This is the most important question. We must care for this land and each other so that in seven generations there will still be peace and abundance."

This responsibility weighs heavy. We know that if we do not live in harmony with the world around us—nature and people—there will be irreparable damage. But discerning the right actions to take now for a time we cannot even imagine is an enormous challenge.

Holding out her hands, Tiare asks for the cowry shell and the standing stone. She places them side by side in front of her. "Woman and man, creating generations to come. The joining of our clan with theirs could ensure peace and prosperity. We could begin by welcoming a group of their young people to live with us, learn our ways as we learn theirs. In turn, we could send some of our youth to live there. Maybe one day there would be marriages between our peoples, babies that will carry a deep connection to both islands."

Aimata's breath hisses between her teeth. She sits as erect as the standing stone. "No. Our own situation is still too new, too fragile. It is one thing to trade with other clans and to help. It is quite another to encourage such a merging. We will lose ourselves. We came from Tahiti to create a new way of life. We must not endanger that."

Apprehension bubbles out of Aimata. This time, I sense it is important for us to let it boil in our circle. I offer another perspective. "Inevitably, if we are trading with another clan, relationships will occur. Friendships will bloom. People will share love."

Aimata picks up the standing stone. "And some people will grow to hate each other. Loyalty to one's own clan is easy." Her voice rises. "That loyalty only leads to hostility and war."

Omo shakes his head. "That is one path we all could take. Another possibility is that the clans would coexist in peace, settling differences before they become harmful disputes."

I feel my own tension rise. "Would it not be better to create a peaceful coexistence than leave it to chance?"

Aimata turns the standing stone over and over in her hands. She clenches the muscles in her jaw. Her dark, wide-set eyes lock with mine. "I believe that we should keep to our own community and protect our ways."

The silence bespeaks our impasse. Finally, Tiare says, "Aimata offers a valid concern. We do not know what reaching out to the people of Tauati will bring. Let us take more time to consider how to answer the last question about the future."

Aimata's relief is palpable. She sets the stone on the *hala* mat. "We can each ponder the question and discuss it again."

Tiare nods. "When we bring our plan to the council tomorrow, we can open the question to all of them."

I admire our safety leader's fortitude. "Thank you, Aimata, for causing us to think harder on this question. In this matter, we must travel together like water flowing in one direction."

Omo nods his agreement, hair undulating around his face like a wild headdress.

We join hands and draw in deep breaths, replacing the *mana* we have spent in our deliberations. Omo chants to release the spirits from our circle.

After a moment of silence, Aimata issues an amiable command. "Everyone get plenty of sleep. We have busy days ahead of us."

Omo's laugh is nearly a roar. "It's hard to get any sleep these nights with my son's snoring. Mahana, do you have a cure?"

Tiare and I glance at each other. She puts a hand to her mouth to cover a smile. Omo's raucous snoring is heard in nearly every corner of our village.

Tiare and I stroll back to our *fare*, torches lighting our way. The village is hushed, children sleeping, here and there someone sitting in a doorway. The lyrical notes of a nose flute dance on the breeze.

Tiare sighs. "This has been a long day."

"A fruitful one, my love. We have a new baby, a healthy mother, and a plan for relations with the people of Tauati."

"Mahana, we need to canoe down the river to rest at the ocean. Soon."

I smile. Those days refreshed us as we played on the beach, swam in the ocean, and slept in each other's arms in the shade. At night, we crouched on the rocks, Tiare holding a torch out over the water. The sea swirled thick with fish, and I cast my net wide. We feasted and loved each other until dawn found us exhausted. "It's a long way to paddle back up river."

Tiare cooed, "*Auwē*, what sadness. We would have to stay by the sea, eating and basking in the sun."

I stop on the path and face her. "I would comb your hair and massage every part of you with fragrant oil."

She slips her arms around my waist, and I hold her close. I feel her whole body against mine. Heat rises in my loins. I think my desire for *hauti* with Tiare is as strong as when we first joined so long ago. I run my hands through the hair at the back of her neck. Her hands slide from my back to my hips, pulling me even closer. She moves her hips against me. I want to take her here, on the grass, half way to our *fare*.

Cool water dropping on my bare skin jars my senses. Tiare looks skyward. "Do you think the spirits are trying to quench our passion?"

"They must know it is not possible." The raindrops are falling faster and harder now. We laugh and turn our faces up to let the water splash in our mouths.

Brilliant light flashes around us. The sky rumbles like the pounding of a thousand drums. Tiare's eyes are wide. "Oh Mahana, it is not wise to challenge the great ones." Her face blossoms into a smile, and she giggles like a little girl. "Let's hurry before they try to drown us."

Just as we reach our *fare*, the spirits turn their giant gourd of water upside down. Rain pours from the heavens.

We light a small *kukui* oil lamp and sit facing each other. Palm frond mats covered with many layers of *tapa* cushion us. I take up a soft cloth and begin to dry Tiare's shoulders and arms. She takes the cloth from my hands, sets it aside. "Let us imagine we have just had a swim in the ocean."

I cup her face in my hands. The light plays across her skin, reflecting the raindrops on her forehead and nose. "You are so lovely, my flower." She closes her eyes, her thick lashes sparkling with tiny beads of water. I caress her forehead and cheeks. Her breath quickens. Gliding my tongue along her chin and neck, I taste sweet rainwater and the salty tang of her skin. I gather strands of her hair and rub my face in the fragrant cloud.

Tiare opens her eyes to gaze at me. The only time I see this look—as if all at once she would cuddle me and eat me alive—is when we make love. I surrender to her touch. She strokes my hair back from my forehead and shoulders and smoothes the raindrops from my face. She nips at my cheeks and mouth. I close my eyes as I feel her warm breath and soft tongue on my ear. Tiare caresses the sagging flesh of my chest and arms as if I am still hard-muscled and strong. She murmurs, "Powerful *tane,* you are mine." My spirit soars.

We take a moment to catch our breath. My eyes fill with the sight of her skin, golden in the lamplight. My fingertips stroke the delicate turtle designs that sweep across her breasts. I caress the soft fullness of her belly above her *tapa* wrap. When I reach underneath her wrap to fondle her secret place, she utters a deep moan. Her body trembles. Mine answers with a hard jolt.

My ancient joints ache for relief, and I straighten my legs in front of me. Never taking her eyes from mine, Tiare straddles me. The skin of her thighs feels hot against my hips. She strokes my back and chest. Leaning forward, she gently teases my nipple with her teeth. My belly tenses with the sensation.

Tiare frees me from my loincloth. Her grasp is firm, urgent. I feel my *ule* move with its own life force in her hand. She rises up and guides me inside her. I gasp as I am enveloped in her heat. She moves her hips in slow circles. Leaning back on my hands, I drink in the sight of Tiare taking her pleasure. Her eyes are closed. Her mouth is open, her breath coming in shallow panting.

She changes the circling to rise up slowly and down. The exquisite sensation is nearly unbearable. I tip my head back as a groan rises in my throat, "Oh, *vahine*." I raise my hips to go deeper inside her, and my release comes in shuddering waves. Tiare utters a cry. I feel the rhythmic contractions of her body and wrap my arms tightly around her.

For a long time, we cling to each other, shivering and rocking. My pounding heart slows. I become aware of distant thunder and the torrent drenching the world outside. I whisper against Tiare's ear, "Try as they might, my love, they cannot put out our fire."

With a throaty laugh, Tiare leans over to extinguish the lamp. She sighs and settles on her side into the layers of *tapa*. I curl around her, my chest against her back, my hand on her belly. With my face nestled in the curve of her neck, I listen to her breathing deepen. I draw in her scent and thank *Akua* for my wondrous woman.

Eight

The Cabriolet shuddered as Sunny downshifted and zipped into a parking space at the Center. Monday morning traffic jammed the streets. She'd spent the entire drive mulling over the most recent chapter of Mahana's life to flood her brain. A blush warmed her all over when she remembered the love making. Maybe it was a message from her psyche about being starved for good sex. She moved the shift knob to neutral and set the parking brake. She didn't have time for a blind date let alone a passionate affair.

Sunny hurried through the front entrance and stopped just inside the doors. Something was different. The lobby seemed cavernous. Her breath caught in her chest. The aquarium was gone. In its place, slouched a row of lime green chairs. She waved to the attendant at the registration desk. "What happened?"

The older woman seemed on the verge of tears. "Don't know. They must have carted it off over the weekend. That's not the only change out here." She pointed to a telephone on the counter. "There's a plan afoot to eliminate the receptionists and have visitors call the operator for information."

Sunny shook her head and dashed for the stairs. What the hell was going on? Jack would probably know. Instead of answers, a barrage of questions awaited her arrival in surgery.

"Sunny, did you get a chance to talk to Purchasing about that new microscope?"

"Have we set up block scheduling for Dr. Chu so she can stay in the same room for all of her cases?"

"Finance called about the revised budget numbers. Are they ready?"

The staff surrounded Sunny. "The budget report's ready to go to Finance. The microscope has been ordered and will be here next week. As for Dr. Chu's block scheduling, she doesn't have enough volume to tie up a room all day. Who knows what happened to the aquarium?"

"I think you're about to find out," Jack said. "There's an emergency management meeting in fifteen minutes. Auditorium."

Sunny turned around and headed back out the double doors.

Most of the managers were already seated at the conference tables. Up front, Darwin, Katherine, and the entire board sat behind the podium. Everyone spoke in hushed tones as they waited. Sunny glanced up at the mural of Māui dragging the island chain out of the ocean. This morning, his struggle seemed a portent of things to come.

Someone flicked a switch, and Māui's act of creation disappeared behind a huge screen that dropped down from the ceiling. Just as Darwin stepped up to the podium, David Kaneko slipped into a chair beside Katherine. Sunny's gut lurched. Darwin's outside expert.

Darwin clicked through slides updating UM's dire financial situation. The twenty-percent budget cut would not be enough to keep UM from going under.

The director of Information Systems stood up. "Darwin, if you want to cut anyone else on my team, you can start with me."

"Goes for me too." The director of Perinatal Services folded her arms on the table. Others murmured agreement.

"Hold on everyone," Darwin said. He adjusted his gold-wire glasses. A nervous smile creased the corners of his mouth. "We're about to unveil an innovative plan that will enable us to maintain our core business. Later this afternoon there'll be a press conference to announce the merger of UM with Comstock Health System."

The auditorium rang with stunned silence. The board members and Katherine shifted in their chairs. David looked relaxed. Sunny's jaw froze in open disbelief.

"CHS is located in Houston, Texas." Darwin clicked through slides bulleted with information about the mainland corporation. "I'm certain this partnership will be a great benefit to the people of the state of

Hawai'i. I want to thank our board and Katherine for fully supporting this venture."

Sunny stared at Katherine. The administrator never once looked up.

Darwin gestured toward David Kaneko. "And I especially want to thank Dr. Kaneko for contributing his insight and expertise in putting this plan together." Kaneko gave a slight nod.

The IS director slammed his chair against the table. "This is pure bullshit." He stormed out of the room, tie flapping over his shoulder. Everyone talked at once.

Darwin tapped the microphone with the slide clicker. "You're all welcome to attend the press conference. This meeting is adjourned."

❀   ❀   ❀

Sunny caught up with Kaneko halfway down the corridor outside the auditorium. "What the hell just happened in there?"

He turned, his look of surprise hardening into a stare. "I'd say the kick-off of a good business plan."

"And I'd say the end of UM as we know it." Her shout echoed down the hallway.

"Let's take this outside."

Sunny pushed in front of him through the glass door leading to a garden area. Passing up a bench in the shade, she stood in the full sun and squared herself to face him. "You've been maneuvering this since the day you arrived."

He shrugged his shoulders and headed for the bench. "Board's decision."

"And you just happened to have the insight and expertise they needed."

Kaneko propped one foot on the bench and leaned forward on his knee. "CHS will save this place."

"At what cost?" He didn't answer. "These giant health care corporations take excellent care of the profit margin. Never mind patients and staff."

He practically lounged in the shade.

"Did you even consider the cost?"

"Cutting programs like massage therapy, hospice, preoperative teaching, and preventative health classes is not a great loss. A one percent margin means you get back to the core business."

"You never took time to understand our core business."

"The board redefined that to essential clinical services."

Sunny threw her hands in the air. "Right. Let's forget our mission to take care of whole people and create a healthy community." No doubt, they faced a tremendous financial crisis. But she was unable to fathom why the board hadn't chosen to work with Katherine and the managers to come up with solutions. The move to sell UM to a mainland corporation seemed so radical. "What's in this for Darwin Chang and the board? For you?"

"UM continues to operate and so do I."

"There's more to it than that."

David let out a hearty laugh, looking up to the sky and shaking his head. "You make it sound like there's an evil plot unfolding."

"You just don't get it. This is about wholesale abandonment of a better way to provide health care."

"I really think you're making too much of this."

"When a company like CHS acquires a hospital, the first things that happen are massive budget cuts, layoffs, and a total change in the culture of the organization. The emphasis isn't on quality care. It's on improving the bottom line. In the short term, the financial picture improves. Over the long haul, the drastic cuts make it impossible to meet the standards of care. We could even lose our accreditation."

"You needn't explain CHS acquisitions to me. My experience is that operations will be more efficient and more cost effective."

"Your experience?"

"My practice in Texas included doing surgery at a CHS facility two days a week. They certainly never lost their accreditation. And their patients received good care."

Sunny's mind scrambled to absorb what she'd just heard. "You pretty much delivered UM to CHS."

"I brought Darwin Chang a good option."

Sunny turned away, pressing the palm of her hand to her forehead, still unable to grasp how everything had moved so quickly. She whirled around. "What's your payoff for leading this charge?"

David arched an eyebrow. "If you don't like what's going on, I suggest you talk with Katherine Nakamura. Talk with Darwin."

"You bet I will. I'm not going to let this happen without a fight."

"Go for it." David headed back inside.

Sunny collapsed on the bench, knees and hands shaking. Her body sagged. She needed to fight a whole system. Katherine, a staunch champion of UM's care model, had abstained while Darwin presided over a sell-out. Katherine was the one person Sunny thought she could count on to defend UM. Were there other managers and employees who'd join her in the battle?

She started the long walk back to her office. If she rocked the boat, she could lose her job, be responsible for others losing their jobs. Maybe it was time for her to move on, work at a bookstore or a gourmet coffee shop. If she tightened her budget, she might even be able to make ends meet.

Back at her desk, Sunny noticed the photo she'd taken of a lemon yellow seahorse in the waters off Bora Bora. Maybe she could get a crew job on a dive boat. The pay sucked but the underwater benefits couldn't be beat. She leaned back in her chair and closed her eyes.

The phone's shrill warble made her jump. "Sunny, this is Katherine Nakamura. Can you come to my office?"

Katherine waved Sunny in as she shot rapid-fire responses into a telephone receiver. Sunny glanced around the room. Paintings of nineteenth century Hawaiian women, hefty and gorgeous, adorned the walls. A fresh bouquet from Katherine's garden always graced the oval conference table. Today, a striking arrangement of calla lilies soared above the satin wood surface. The bookcase held numerous plaques and awards presented to Katherine over the years for her contributions to community service projects.

Katherine plunked the receiver down and came around the desk to hug Sunny. "Thanks for coming over." The administrator looked stiffly professional in a petite suit and chunky gold earrings. She led the way to a couch and low table set with carafes, cups, and fresh fruit. "I know you were really upset at the end of the meeting this morning. I thought we should talk."

Sunny sat beside Katherine and accepted a mug of coffee. "Everyone was upset. What's going on? We were asked to cut twenty percent. Three weeks later the sale of UM is announced."

"Given our current situation, the merger seemed prudent. Darwin Chang has been in discussions with the CHS president for a couple of months. CHS pressured us for a decision."

Sunny shifted her position to look directly at Katherine. "Are you in favor of this?"

"There aren't any other options."

"Do you support this take over?"

"I do not," Katherine said softly.

"Then how can the board do this?"

"Remember, Sunny, I serve at their pleasure. They didn't consult me."

"I suspected that might be the case when Darwin called the meeting during your vacation."

"We talked on the phone. He said they would only present the quarterly figures to give everyone a heads-up. They were going to let the managers know that a planning retreat would be scheduled to address the issues."

"Retreat hell. They gave us a three-prong screwing."

Katherine shook her head. "When I got back, a letter of intent had already been signed."

"So, what's David Kaneko's story?"

"The official line is that he served as interim vice president of medical affairs for CHS and got heavily involved in their business planning. My guess is that even though Dr. Kaneko moved to the islands, he and Vance Turner, the CEO of Comstock Health System, remained close." Katherine stirred cream and sugar in her coffee. "When Darwin started looking around for an infusion of capital, Kaneko introduced him to Turner."

"What did Turner promise our brilliant heart surgeon?"

"My guess is an executive position in exchange for convincing Darwin and the board to strike a deal."

Sunny poured herself more coffee. "The pay off for Darwin and the board?"

"Now Darwin is in line to be board president for a much larger corporation. They'll all be paid a generous stipend to continue serving on UM's board. Who knows? Maybe some of the trustees are hoping for business connections on the mainland. One thing for sure, this plan is not about improving health care on O'ahu."

Sunny grasped Katherine's arm. "So, we fight it."

"I can't."

"What? You've worked harder than any of us to keep the dream of UM alive."

Katherine placed her full cup on the table. "Darwin and I went round and round when I got back. We started at calm discussion, escalated to hours of arguing, degenerated into my pleadings, and ended with his ultimatum. I can be a good soldier or look for another hospital."

"God, Katherine, I'm sorry. This is horrible for you."

"I honestly don't know what I'm going to do. My retirement isn't far off. I'd be crazy to leave now. Hell, maybe I won't even have to worry about making a choice. They probably promised my position to Kaneko." Katherine shrugged. "Maybe it won't turn out as badly as we fear."

"Unlikely."

"What'll you do?"

Sunny shook her head. "Bide my time. Fight. Leave. Quit health care. Damn, I don't know either."

Sunny left Katherine's office and wandered through the medical-surgical unit, trying to soak up all the things she loved about UM. A *mele* floated out of the speakers overhead. She smiled. Every time a baby was born at UM, the lullaby wafted through the hallways. Once, a woman whose mother lay dying of cancer told Sunny that the music gave her great comfort. Knowing that a new life had just come into the world somehow made it easier to let her mother go.

Sunny stopped at the nurse's station. Angela Garlasa, the unit manager huddled with a young nurse. Angela put her hand on the girl's shoulder. "Rena, you're looking a little stressed out."

Rena plunked a pile of charts on the desk. "I've been with Mr. Nance for the past twenty minutes. He was pretty worried about his lab tests. But now, I'm short on time to finish these notes."

Angela pulled out a chair. "Take a load off. How's Mr. Nance, now?"

The young nurse relaxed in the chair. "More calm. I promised we'd contact his doctor as soon as the lab tests come in."

"Good work. You go ahead and do your charting. I'll answer the call lights."

"Thanks, Angela."

Angela replaced a chart in the revolving rack and came over to Sunny. "How about that meeting this morning?" They moved to the far side of the station.

"I'm still trying to take it all in," Sunny said.

"Feels like we just got the rug pulled out from under us."

"Or we're still on the rug, and it's flying into an abyss."

Angela leaned against the counter. "If we feel that way, how will we be able to sell this to our staff?"

"Attend Snake Oil Sales 101?"

"The trend all over the country is to replace registered nurses with vocational nurses and aides. If CHS goes that route, our RNs will spend most of their time managing a team rather than giving complete care to their patients."

"Team nursing was the model back in the seventies."

"Yeah, but back then patients weren't as sick. Treatments weren't as complicated. The RNs had time to spend with patients and their families. Hell, someone could be in the hospital for a week with low back strain."

Sunny nodded. "My father."

"Now, the patients who used to spend days in ICU are on the regular units. RNs are performing procedures that only physicians used to do. But the bean counters don't understand why having registered nurses giving the care is so critical." Angela lowered her voice. "I have a friend who works in a hospital in Phoenix where they're touting team nursing as the new efficient, economical structure. The big sales pitch is that the RNs are finally doing what we're meant to do—manage other caregivers, consult with physicians, create care plans. God forbid we empty a bedpan or give a back rub. She says it's been total disaster."

"Why?"

"They're running around like crazed chickens trying to keep track of the non-professional staff. Patients wait for hours to speak to an RN. IVs run dry. Medication dosages are late. She discovered that one of the aides had been recording false blood pressure readings on the charts. When it came time to check vital signs, the chick took an extra coffee break."

"Jeez. Do you know if CHS uses team nursing?"

"I'm making it my business to find out." Angela tapped the counter in time to her words. "Things are going to change radically, Sunny. We have to figure out a way to fight this."

"I've been wrestling with that one myself."

A patient call light, accompanied by a soft chime, flashed over a door in the hallway.

"I have to go." Angela squeezed Sunny's shoulder. "Let's keep this conversation going."

Sunny scanned the counter and noticed a large scrapbook. She leafed through the pages covered with photos and glowing notes from people and their families who'd received care from Angela and her staff. One note simply stated, "Thanks for letting us cook mom's favorite dishes in your kitchen!" Intangibles that couldn't be itemized in a financial report. She closed the scrapbook. UM was in danger of losing its soul.

Nine

The glass of iced tea felt cool against her forehead, a contrast to the sticky warmth of the lounge chair beneath her. Sunny took a long drink of the tea. The mellow notes of Pete's guitar floated out of the CD player. She relaxed into the sweet scent of the plumeria trees, thankful for this place of refuge. After making sure the evening and night shifts were adequately staffed, Sunny had fled the Center for the solitude of her *lānai*. She couldn't bear to be anywhere near the press conference, the Darwin Chang and David Kaneko road show. She needed time to think, come up with a plan.

Sunny heard a low feline growl and scanned the yard for Skipper. She could barely make out his black form hunkered underneath a bush. Probably stalking a bug. The glare on the lawn made Sunny blink, her eyes watering. The grass wavered and for a brief instant, transformed into a garden plot with broad-leaf plants standing in rows. She closed her eyes.

Her pulse quickened. This time she wasn't going to let the dream sideswipe her. Lani told her to go with it. She drew in deep breaths and concentrated hard on the scene materializing before her eyes.

Tanemao and I have been collecting plants to restock our healing supplies. The baskets we carry grow heavier with each step as we make our way back from the jungle. The sun bakes our skin, and sweat pours off our bodies.

On the outskirts of the village, bright green *taro* patches shimmer in the heat waves. The patches are bordered by walls of perfectly fitted stones from the river. Workers stoop in shallow water to harvest the mature corms. They call and wave to us.

We stop for a drink of water from a calabash offered by one of the workers, an older man with a broad belly. He inquires about this morning's council meeting.

"We approved a plan to make contact with the people of Tauati," I say to Temana. I do not add that the council struggled all morning to come to agreement. Tiare dared not broach the subject of inviting their youth to live with us in exchange with our young people. "We'll need a basket of your best plants to offer them."

Our farmers tend the fields with great reverence. These shoots are the children of the *taro* we brought from Tahiti.

"Mahana, I will prepare them myself."

"The council is sending us to Tauati to heal their sick." Tanemao stands with his hands on his hips.

Temana gives a slight nod. "Then I wish you a safe journey."

We continue our trek. On the kind of sweltering afternoon in which nearly everyone would be resting, yearning for the cool air of evening, our village is a whirl of activity.

Tanemao drops his basket and breaks into an easy run toward the river where men and women are working in the shade. He halts and walks back to me, eyes downcast. "Teacher, can we check the progress on the canoes?"

"Go."

Aito greets us with a snaggle tooth grin nested in his beard. His dark skin is etched with wrinkles. The master canoe builder beckons us to a large *koa* trunk taking the shape of a sleek ocean vessel. "Mahana, look at this beauty. Very solid wood." His rough, scarred hands lovingly caress the hollowed-out log. "Lea be praised."

I think of Lea and smile. The goddess of canoe builders takes the form of the tiny *'elepaio* bird to accompany the men in their forest search for the perfect *koa* trunk. After they have felled the tree, the builders wait for *'elepaio* to perch on the log. If she hops around poking for spiders and beetles hiding in the bark, the men leave the log to rot and go in search of a new tree. If *'elepaio* whistles and chirps, running from one end of the log to the other, the builders know the tree will make an excellent canoe.

"Aito, will it be ready for the voyage to Tauati?"

"If we have to work day and night."

Tanemao and I watch the workers surrounding the new canoe. They carve the wood with heavy stone adzes and sharp seashells. Repeated smoothing with jagged coral and sharkskin accomplishes the final finish. Two wooden spars, 'iako, are lashed to the hull with sennet cords. Attached to the ends of the 'iako is the ama, a long, slender float made of light wiliwili wood. This outrigger gives the canoe balance and stability. Our expert canoe builders determine the length and size of the canoe parts according to the waters to be navigated. Unlike the big, double-hull, double-outrigger vessel on which we traveled in the open ocean from Tahiti, this more maneuverable canoe will excel in the choppy waters of the channel between the islands.

I see Aimata, towering over a group of young women and men as they walk the perimeter of our village. She is probably explaining one of the decisions we made this morning. Some council members wondered what would happen if a Tauati raiding party observes our preparations or the night of ceremony and feasting. Would they fear we are preparing for war? We determined that if our lookouts spot a raiding party, we will attempt to make contact with them and offer the hand of friendship.

In a grove of uru trees, Omo directs the ori dancers in their practice. He is seated crossed-legged, a folded piece of tapa on the grass in front of him. As he chants, he keeps a steady, two-stroke beat on the ipu heke by first slapping the side of the hollowed-out gourd, and then pounding the gourd drum down on the tapa on the ground. His wild hair sways in time to the beat.

"Why does Omo make them go through the same lines over and over?" Tanemao asks. "They know the steps."

"The dancers must understand the meaning of the movements. Every move must be precise." I watch them reposition their feet before Omo begins the line of chant again. "Dancing the ori is a sacred calling."

Tanemao raises an eyebrow. "I would sooner be called to wade in the taro fields."

At my fare, Tanemao and I sort the plants we have collected. Some will be dried and others steeped in hot water to make solutions. Tanemao squats in front of a basket, picking out large ti leaves and smoothing them into a neat pile. He keeps up a steady conversation about the coming voyage.

"The council is wise to send us with the emissaries. We most likely have treatments the people of Tauati have yet to discover. But I think it is a grave mistake to go there unarmed. They may attack us as soon as we land on their beach." He throws the basket aside. "We should spend the days before the voyage making a store of weapons."

My jaw clenches with irritation until my teeth ache, but I continue placing tiny purple flowers on mats to dry.

"Mahana, we should not have ignored their raiding parties for so long."

I open my mouth wide to relax my jaws. I'm ready to send Tanemao to wade in the *taro* fields. From birth he, like every child in our village, heard the chants of our history. He listened late into the night as our elders told stories of the journey from Tahiti. Why does he not understand? Bloodshed drove us to endure a long passage across treacherous seas in order to live without killing.

I set aside the healing supplies and motion Tanemao to a shady place near my *fare*. He frowns, not knowing why I have interrupted our work. I look directly into his eyes. "I want to tell you why the Anuanua left the island of Raiatea in Tahiti."

The beads of water sparkled in the sunlight as we splashed each other in the shallow water of the lagoon. My uncle, a big man like Omo, scooped me up, whirled me around, and tossed me back in the water. I laughed until my sides ached. After a short time for play, he grew serious, saying in a growling voice, "Boy, it is time we return to your lessons." That day, I learned how to make an octopus lure. Other days, I practiced knocking over coconut targets using his stone thrower.

I adored my uncle. He was a strong, greatly revered warrior in our king's elite guard. Pride puffed out my scrawny chest whenever I walked beside him. Since my father had been in frail health for many years, his brother undertook my upbringing to manhood. My uncle's lessons were strict. He demanded my best effort. I worked hard because I wanted more than anything to make him proud of me. There would always be time to play chase and search for wondrous things like tiny eggs in the bird nests along the cliffs.

My uncle and our warriors sailed off in canoes whenever another island threatened aggression. Mostly these skirmishes were small, with men returning wounded, rarely killed. But, I often heard the elders talking about the kingdom of Bora Bora, how the ruler there wished to subdue all of the other islands. Mother's face would line with worry. My only concern was the quick return of my uncle for our next lesson and play time.

My mother served as the healer for our people. Whereas the royal court commanded respect and reverence, she was accorded these because of her devotion to our people. Many a night I lay near my father in our *fare* waiting for her to return from caring for a seriously ill child or a woman in labor. She would place her hand on my cheek. "Child, why are you still awake?"

"Did you take the pain away, mother?"

"The spirits took the pain away." She whispered in my ear. "Go to sleep. Tomorrow you can show me what you have learned from your uncle."

I often told my mother funny stories I heard from the other boys to make her laugh. She gathered me in her arms and told me how I brightened her life. When I came of age, and it was time to choose a name, she suggested Mahana. The *ioa* seemed fitting. As I learned her healing skills, I sought to bring light and hope to my people.

Tiare's father served in the royal court as an advisor on matters of justice and daily life. With him at the king's side, the people could count on fair judgments when disputes arose. Tiare's mother had died a few years after giving birth to her only child. Devastated by the loss, her father never took another wife. The women of our village, including my mother, helped raise Tiare. As children, Tiare and I were siblings and friends. Later, we became mates—an outcome our parents always had in mind. But I am getting ahead of myself.

Just before my rite of passage into manhood, something happened that changed our lives forever.

A young priest ascended to the position of chief priest at the vast temple complex called Taputapuatea. He proclaimed a new and all-powerful god. This god had visited the chief priest in a vision and warned that Bora Bora would conquer Raiatea unless our people worshipped only Oro.

The king of Bora Bora had escalated his attacks on all the other islands. The skirmishes turned into fierce battles. The sickening sight of our canoes returning filled with dead and dying men became a regular occurrence. Tiare's father and my mother urged our king to attempt negotiations with Bora Bora. Our king feared losing his island and quickly agreed to the first ceremonial tribute to Oro.

At the appointed time, all our people gathered near the center of the complex where a new *marae* would be dedicated to Oro. On this day, the corner stones would be dropped into deep holes already excavated. Drumbeats reverberated around us. The king, dressed in his finest robes, knelt before the chief priest who chanted to the heavens. To my child's ears this chanting sounded wrathful, threatening. I squeezed my mother's hand and peeked around her to see my uncle's face, a solemn mask.

The drumbeats quickened. Assistant priests brought forward four men. I recognized one of the men, a petty thief who had been condemned to slave labor in the fields. The prisoners were led to the cornerstone holes. Three priests gathered behind each of them. The chief priest's chanting became more strident. The drums beat even faster. I glanced up at my mother and saw her face draw into a frown.

The chief priest shouted Oro's name three times, and the drumming ended abruptly. The prisoners bent down to shove the cornerstones into place. The task seemed impossible to me. Behind each prisoner, a priest raised a bone knife to the sky and swiftly brought it down, slashing across the throat of the condemned man before him. Blood gushed down the chests of the prisoners. Red droplets spattered the robes of the priests. I heard gasps and cries all around me. My mother pinned me to her side. The three priests at each corner heaved their prisoner into the hole. They strained and grunted as they toppled the huge cornerstone into the opening. The four stones landed with dull thuds.

The drums pounded again as the chief priest chanted praises to Oro. In the crowd, people cried out in disbelief. I buried my face against my mother's arm. She shouted over the din to my uncle, her voice wavering with fear. "Why has this happened?" The emotion in her tone scared me more than the sight of the murdered prisoners.

The chief priest raised his arms to quiet the people. He pronounced that Oro was pleased with the offering and the creation of a new *marae*. Our warriors would now be assured success in the battle with Bora Bora. The king bowed low to the chief priest.

For days after the ceremony, the elders huddled and talked in hushed tones about what had happened. Their furtive glances searched for eavesdroppers—members of the royal court or assistants to the priests. Some of the younger children acted out the chanting and slashing of throats until their parents scolded them and dragged them home.

One night when everyone thought I slept, I listened as my parents, my uncle, and Tiare's father tried to make sense out of what had happened.

"It could be that the priests elected the chief priest not knowing that he planned to invoke a supreme god who requires human sacrifice," my father mused.

"He claims that Oro communicates with him through visions. Who would dare cross a holy man for fear of the dark god's wrath?" Tiare's father asked.

My uncle snorted. "Dark god. I do not believe it. This so-called holy man saw a chance to use shock and fear to gain power over our king and safeguard his own position. Our gods have never been vengeful."

I heard pleading in my father's voice. "Then why would the other priests allow this to happen? Surely our people will not let this stand, even if the king shrinks from the chief priest."

"Brother, fear is a great weapon. The chief priest's new religion will keep us in line while inspiring dread in Bora Bora's king and his forces. Our warriors will easily win battles and overtake all the other islands, reinforcing the power of having Oro on our side."

Tiare's father sighed. "Maybe it won't be so grim. Those prisoners committed crimes against their own people. Though the measure was extreme, they deserved punishment."

"I do not favor killing as punishment," my uncle muttered.

"Let us hope there will be no more killings at the *marae*," Tiare's father said.

"If Oro desires more offerings, maybe the priests will choose only criminals," my father said, pleading turned to hopefulness in his tone.

My mother's voice trembled with anger. I imagined her standing in their midst. "What are all of you talking about? We have always shunned killing unless it happens in defense of our island. Not another person's life should be taken. Oro be damned! It is a god created in the mind of a power-hungry madman."

The men acknowledged the truth of her words. A time of deep sighs and silence passed. My uncle spoke slowly. "If there is any indication that what happened at Taputapuatea will be repeated, I will press the king to bring the chief priest under control."

"You must be careful," Tiare's father said.

My uncle harrumphed himself off the mat. "The king still rules Raiatea. He will listen to his elite warriors and advisors."

The human sacrifices continued. At first, the chief priest said the offerings were necessary to protect our warriors in battle. He selected more criminals to fall to priestly knives, their blood spilled on the new altar. When the chief priest announced that Oro required the offering of innocent lives to imbue our warriors with the power to conquer the other islands, my uncle flew into a rage. He went immediately to the king, refusing to fight a war of aggression and demanding that the sacrifices be stopped. The king told my uncle that he needed time to think. We waited anxiously for his response.

My mother and I returned from collecting ferns one evening near dark. Father lay on his mat. He said a messenger from the king made rounds in the village that afternoon. "When the moon shines directly overhead, everyone must be at the new *marae*." We sat in the doorway of our *fare* watching the moon rise slowly behind a fringe of palm trees. My parents held each other close and wondered in low voices about the king's order.

As the moon inched to a place above our heads, mother and I made our way to Taputapuatea. The light cast eerie shadows across the path. Others walked before and behind us, silent or speaking quietly. Straight ahead of us, I glimpsed the brilliance of many torches surrounding the *marae*. The pounding of drums grew louder.

Sorrowful wails echoed back along the procession as the first villagers entered the open area of the temple complex. The wails exploded into high-pitched keening. I wanted to turn and run back up the path. My mother clutched my hand and pulled me forward. Some of the people behind us rushed ahead. We heard their shrieks. What fresh horror awaited us?

My heart filled with dread. I stopped, my feet rooted on the path. My mother wrapped her arm around my shoulders. "We must see with our own eyes what has been committed in the name of Oro." As we neared the end of the path, a sour smell engulfed us.

Directly in front of us stretched the broad stone base of the *marae,* inlaid shells gleaming in the torchlight. Drummers stood at one end pounding a slow, steady beat. At the other end on a raised platform the priests flanked the altar. In front of the altar, the chief priest raised his arms to the sky. His feathered headdress glowed fiery red. In front of him, sat the king surrounded by members of the royal court. I strained for a glimpse of my uncle and Tiare's father.

Screams of terror resounded across the temple complex as people fell to the ground. Beside me, mother collapsed to her knees. The low cry that started in her throat became a shriek of agony as she tore at her hair. What could cause such anguish?

I glanced upward from the people on the platform. Strange shapes hung in the trees surrounding the *marae.* Like overripe fruit, the bodies of eight men dangled from the high branches, their chests and bellies split open. Dark liquid ran down their legs and dripped from their toes into carefully placed calabashes.

I moved in a trance from tree to tree staring at the faces of the dead men. They were not criminals but beloved members of our village— husbands, fathers, craftsmen, and warriors. Nearly stumbling on a gourd full of blood, I paused at a trunk off to the side of the altar. The sour-sweet stench filled my nostrils and caused my stomach to heave. My head rang with cries of mourning. My eyes moved slowly up the legs of the body. The jagged flesh of the torso gaped open, the dark maw shiny with oozing liquid. The neck crooked forward over the circle of rope. The face looked serene, as if the man slept. I recognized the bushy eyebrows and long, fine nose.

I reached up to touch the foot of my beloved uncle, remembering in a flash the patient lessons, the laughter, the strong arms lifting me high in the air—all of it sacrificed to a strange new god called Oro. A rage I never felt before or since flooded my being. I turned toward the platform, fixed my stare on the chief priest. I wanted to do to him what he did to my uncle. It didn't matter that I had no knife. I would do it with my bare hands. I screamed my vengeance and started running toward the altar. Suddenly, massive arms from behind wrapped around my chest. My feet left the ground. A deep voice whispered, "No. You will only suffer your uncle's fate."

Tiare's father held me in the shadows until my breathing slowed and I went limp. "We must find your mother."

As we searched the crowd, a growing realization that nothing would ever be the same for my family overwhelmed me. I saw women writhing in anguish, men pounding their chests, bewildered babies whimpering. Cries and incessant drumbeats filled my ears. Over the cacophony, the chief priest shouted praises to Oro.

We found my mother frantically searching for me. Sobbing, she pulled me to her. Tiare's father put his arms around us saying we must hurry back to our *fare*. After he saw us safely there, he went home and returned with Tiare. Until dawn, my parents and Tiare's father wept for my uncle and tried to fathom what had happened.

The sun peeked through the trees. The mourning subsided. My mother spoke in a husky voice. "The king will never stand against these sacrifices. He fears the chief priest will murder him too. War with Bora Bora will escalate to battles with all the islands. We must find a new home."

I heard not even breathing in the silence. The idea of finding a new home could barely be comprehended. Though our people have made many voyages on the sea, it would be impossible to leave Raiatea any time soon. A voyage required much preparation.

"We will have to make our way to the center of the island," Tiare's father said.

My father moaned. I knew why. The interior of the island is a more fearful place than the ocean. *Tupapau*—fierce ghosts—live in the dense jungle. Anyone foolish enough to venture into the interior would not come out alive.

"No *tupapau* could be more terrifying than Oro," my mother said.

The next night, twenty-seven of us slipped out of the village and made our way to the place where the Apoomau meets the sea. We carried our heavy bundles along the river away from the coastal plain. The river narrowed into a gurgling stream flowing out of an old volcanic crater ringed with jagged peaks lush with vegetation. We began our new life in the rainforest at the center of that crater, safe from the madness of Oro.

We called ourselves Anuanua—the rainbow clan—because we believe that when we die, our feet are set upon the rainbow. The name symbolized our death to the ways of Raiatea and the promise of a better life. Many rainbows arced across our little valley. We had all we needed—fish, fruit, taro plants brought from the village, and fresh water. We never encountered one *tupapau*.

Two challenges filled every waking moment. The first was to build a double-hull canoe worthy of taking us far across the ocean. The second was to create a new society based on reverence for human life, one that shunned killing of any kind. Before Oro, we had always been a people of compassion and harmony. We vowed that nothing would ever get in the way of those beliefs, not even defense of our village if it required taking the lives of others.

Mother and Tiare's father became our leaders. The elders honored the great spirit, *Akua*, and the spirits in nature. In turn, those loving spirits helped us through our struggle. The elders formed the council, and the council created the four questions we always consider whenever a decision is needed. Those questions about knowledge, light, compassion, and the future have helped us live the promise of peace.

For generations, seafaring parties had struck out in search of the heavenly homeland, Havaiki. A few returned to tell of fabled islands to the north, a land of glistening white peaks and liquid fire running into the sea. One of the elders had been navigator on such a voyage. He still possessed knowledge of winds and ocean currents. His skills in following the stars and the golden sea birds that headed north every year remained sharp. When out on the ocean, he could smell land, taste it in the sea water, and see it in a lagoon's turquoise reflection on the clouds. He felt sure he could find Havaiki again.

The start of our great voyage is forever etched in my mind.

Everyone clutched bundles of food, tools, plants—taro, coconut, bananas, breadfruit—and pigs and chickens. Another young man and I carried my father. Tiare walked beside my mother. Last to arrive, Tiare's father carried a bundle of pure white *tapa*. I noticed his stately bearing for the first time. He had become the keeper of our sacred objects, the symbols of *Akua*. People parted to give him a place in the center of our group.

He paused to gaze at us, each one in turn. Then he turned his face to the night sky. Raising his arms to the starry firmament, he chanted, "*Akua*, great spirit, guide our voyage. Give us courage. Give us wisdom. Grant our safety. Help us to take care of each other as we find our heavenly homeland." The circle began to chant with him. He lowered his arms. Our chanting faded away on the wind. Only the sound of water lapping on the riverbank broke the stillness. He smiled and shouted, "Loved ones, we go to Havaiki!"

All at once, bundles, animals, children, women, and my father were loaded onto the platform secured between the hulls of the massive canoe. The men pushed it away from the bank and leaped into the twin hulls. Digging into the water with large paddles, they propelled the canoe down river.

We glided silently into the lagoon, heading out to the breaking waves and open sea. The torches of Taputapuatea came into view. My skin felt icy. Tears blurred my sight, and I squeezed my eyes shut. I gulped the fresh sea air, trying to remember my uncle's booming laughter.

The open ocean was calm. We settled in, resting against supply bundles, at first too excited to sleep. Tiare and I gazed in awe at the starry sky, made all the more brilliant by the dark ocean that surrounded us. I tried to imagine the sight of liquid fire pouring into the sea and wondered what other amazing things awaited us.

The hulls sliced through the water, and paddling never ceased as the men worked in shifts to keep the gigantic canoe moving. As soon as the wind came up, they stowed their paddles and hoisted the single, triangular sail made of woven *hala*. For more than thirty sunsets, they took turns sailing the canoe and keeping watch. The shark spirit *Mao* pointed the way toward Le'a, the zenith star of Havaiki.

Ten

"At first, it was like watching scenes from a movie. The last few times, I've been looking through the old man's eyes." Sunny matched Lani's strides in an easy jog through Kapi'olani Park as she described her recent dreams. "It's just . . . so weird."

"I think it's because you were Mahana."

Sunny downed a slug of water and scanned the action in the park. Under a canopy of banyan trees, a group of seniors practiced the slow movements of tai chi. Families gathered around tables, their Saturday picnics filling the air with the aroma of barbecue. If only her life were filled with these simple pleasures rather than some kind of psychic chaos.

"I woke up in a cold sweat after seeing the bloody ceremony at the temple. Listen, my friend. You haven't lived until you've experienced sex as a man."

Lani laughed. "I want to hear every little detail."

"Never mind."

"I'm sorry. This is serious." Lani slowed their pace to a brisk walk. "Let's try to figure out why this is happening. How could it connect to what's going on in your life right now?"

"Hmm." Sunny wiped away a line of perspiration trickling down her cheek. "The old man was getting ready to do battle with his enemies, and UM's in a battle with a bunch of Texans. I don't think stone-throwers are going to be our weapon of choice."

"Sarcasm isn't going to help us analyze this. From what you described, Mahana wasn't getting ready to do battle. His clan wanted to keep the peace. How were they able to do that? Maybe you're going to find out how to solve this crisis at UM."

"Listen to you. You're talking like all of those things I've been dreaming about really happened."

"What if the connection is about Mahana's healing powers? Something related to complementary healing at UM? Maybe you're going to come up with a new therapy."

"Jeez, Lani. UM's situation being connected to a prehistoric tribe that we don't even know existed is a colossal stretch."

Lani shrugged. "Skimmer bug."

Up ahead, a man hunkered down beside a little girl along the path. The two seemed to be examining a colorful object on the ground. "Lani, is that—"

"David Kaneko."

"I'm out of here."

Kaneko stood up and glanced in their direction. Lani waved. "Too late."

The little girl held up a red, yellow, and blue kite, the string tail covered with polka dot bows. She patted Kaneko's leg. "Uncle David, can we fly it now?"

"You bet, sweetie." Kaneko lifted her up in one arm. "First, I want you to meet some ladies who work with me."

Sunny kept her distance as Lani offered her hand to the girl. "My name is Lani. This is my friend, Sunny. What's your name?"

"Kimmy." Ebony hair with perfectly straight bangs framed the little girl's solemn face. "Today's my birthday." She pursed her rosebud mouth and held up five fingers spread wide.

Kaneko kissed the top of his niece's head. His smile, dark eyes dancing, was stunning. Sunny couldn't believe this was the same person she'd tangled with at the Center.

"My family's commandeered that whole picnic area. Want to join us for a piece of cake?"

Sunny glanced over at tables festooned with purple balloons and mounds of brightly wrapped packages. "Thanks, Dr. Kaneko. Nice of you to offer, but we need to finish our circuit. Happy birthday, Kimmy."

Kaneko set Kimmy on her feet. "Are you ready to launch this high flyer?" He started to run backwards, holding the kite over his head. "Come on, Kimmy. We have to run fast."

Lani waved as the little girl trailed after Kaneko. "Happy birthday."

Sunny started back along the jogging path. "Did we just see Dr. David Kaneko or was that his good twin?"

"Get him out of scrubs, and he's a different man."

"He's probably jubilant over his victory at UM."

"Did you notice the dark circles under Kimmy's eyes?" Lani picked up the pace. "She was breathing hard even before she started running."

"She looked more like three than five. Maybe she was a preemie."

When they reached the field where Pete was coaching a football team of second grade boys, they flopped down on a blanket. Sunny pulled off her tennis shoes and watched the action. Pete crouched low, surrounded by players leaning in to hear his instructions. Then he rose out of the huddle, arms spread wide as he directed the boys to positions on the field. His long hair gleamed the color of dark chocolate. Hard muscles strained the sleeves of his shirt. Pete Bishop was a big man with moves surprisingly fluid. Handsome too.

As the boys fanned out across the grass, they all yelled, "Pass it to me, Pete! Pass it to me!"

Pete took a few steps back and launched the football in a high arc, shouting, "Tony, get under it. Kai give him some room."

Tony, a wiry kid with shaggy blond hair, snagged the ball, tucked it under his arm, and raced to the far side of the field. He spiked the ball on the ground and swaggered a touchdown dance. The other kids jumped up and down around him, pounding his back and slapping high fives.

"*Hele mai.*" Pete called them back into the huddle. "You guys know the drill. Ten laps around the field." The huddle responded with groans and grumbling. "*E kulikuli.* No complaining You guys gotta be in shape when the season starts."

The boys started their run around the field. Pete jogged over to where Sunny and Lani lounged on a blanket. He eased himself down between them and toweled off his face and arms. "Hooey. I'm proud of how hard these little guys work."

"They look good, coach," Sunny said.

Lani gently nudged Pete's arm. "You look pretty good out there yourself."

He draped the towel around his neck. "My plan is working, Sunny."

"Plan?"

"I knew Lani would fall hard when she saw me, all sweaty and outta breath, running around with a bunch of kids." Pete grinned.

Lani leaned against his shoulder. "Too late. You had me the first time I saw you, all sweaty and out of breath, at The Wall."

Pete put his hand under Lani's chin and kissed her cheek. The look of adoration on his face made Sunny blush. She turned away, fumbled with the ice chest, retrieved three bottles of water.

Pete took a long drink. "Sunny, you coming to the rally next weekend?"

"If everything stays quiet in the OR, I'll be there."

"We gotta be sure she gets right up front so she won't miss any of the speeches," Pete said.

"Did Hawaiian Freedom finally decide to include the band?" Lani asked.

Pete nodded and emptied his water bottle.

"How long are you scheduled to play?"

"Only thirty minutes. Gotta watch the time. People want to hang around. The cops get nervous. Nervous cops and fired up *kanaka* be big trouble."

Lani entwined her slim fingers with Pete's fleshy ones. "Everything will be fine. It's just a chance for people to come together peacefully and let their voices be heard."

"You and Sunny leave before the band starts. Get outta there in case things get wild."

Sunny took a sip of water. "We don't want to miss your performance."

"Better to come dance with us at The Wall."

Pete had grown serious with the same intensity Sunny glimpsed at The Wall. Was he trying to protect Lani from the risky side of his politics?

Twelve boys thundered down on them. Pete got up on his haunches and opened the ice chest. "You guys done with laps already?"

The boys all jabbered at once, grabbing water bottles and pieces of fruit.

Pete hugged three boys in each arm, gathering them in like a mother hen. "Okay. Remember practice on Tuesday after school. Gonna hand out jerseys, so be there."

A new discussion erupted about jersey numbers as the boys jostled to be first to dive into Lani's peanut butter cookies. After consuming most of the food, they resorted to pouring water over their heads and pelting each other with ice.

Pete interrupted the action. "Hey guys, practice is *pau*. See you on Tuesday. Keep up the hard work. You gonna be in the Hula Bowl someday."

Exclamations about throwing the baddest passes and making at least fifty touchdowns echoed across the field. Pete gathered the equipment into a canvas bag while Kai tossed the football into the air and ran under it for a catch.

"Hey, Dad. Go out for a long one."

Pete sprinted down field and turned as Kai, tall and stocky for his age, let go of a low, spiraling pass and started running. Pete caught the ball and ducked down as Kai, in a flying tackle, landed on his dad's broad back. They tussled over the ball, rolling around on the grass and giggling.

Kai jumped up, waving the ball over his head with both hands. "I got you."

Pete grabbed his son in a bear hug. "You sure did. Come on, buddy. Your momma's gonna be here." They sprinted toward Sunny and Lani, huge grins on their faces.

Lani gave Kai a high five. "Good practice."

"Thanks. Did you see that pass? Wasn't it great?"

"You've got some arm there," Lani said. Kai bent his elbow, pumping up a small round biceps. Lani pressed her fingers on the muscle and whistled. "I'll be sure not to get into an arm wrestling match with you."

Kai's face lit up with pride. "Are you going to come to our games?"

"You bet. But you'll have to teach me something about football. I don't even know all the positions."

"I can tell you all about football. I know a lot about the game. Isn't that right, Dad?"

Pete put his arm around Kai. "Sure do."

They heard a car horn and turned to see a woman waving out the moon roof of a red BMW. Pete hugged his son. "Don't keep your mom waiting. See you at practice."

Kai kissed his dad's cheek and ran to the car.

"Kai's a great kid," Sunny said.

"Thanks. Wish I could spend more time with him."

They sat on the grass, Sunny opposite Lani and Pete. "Does Kai's mom have a problem with that?'

"She's married to a rich record producer at Mountain Apple. They take big vacations. Always off island." Pete pushed a hand through his hair. "I'm working all the time."

Lani reached up to touch Pete's cheek. "Kai couldn't have a better father."

Pete brought Lani's hand to his lips in a caress so tender Sunny's heart ached. Lani wrapped her arms around his neck, pulling him close. Her baseball cap tumbled to the ground.

Sunny got to her feet, her voice a whisper. "Don't mind me. I'm just going to take a little walk." She tiptoed away, a grin on her face. They were such love birds. And Kai seemed delighted with Lani. She'd be a great step-mom.

Sunny strolled the jogging path, pondering Lani's question about how the dreams might be connected to events at UM. Why was it so hard for her to entertain the idea of being on this planet in other places and centuries? Maybe because that would point to a part of herself powerful enough to influence what happened here and now, a part over which she had no control.

She remembered the story of Taylor Caldwell whose books she'd read voraciously in high school. Some people swore Caldwell had lived past lives. The scenes in her books about ancient Rome and Victorian England were so realistic, it was as if she'd actually been in the haunts and lives of her characters. Though the famous author submitted herself to sessions of hypnosis in which she described many past lifetimes, she remained a skeptic until her death. Sunny could relate to Caldwell's stubborn denial.

But why was she suddenly having such vivid dreams? Why did she dream she was a man? That had never happened before. The action and conversations were so real and familiar, as if . . .

Sunny stopped in the middle of the path. What had Marie said? Even dreams conjured by imagination could offer wisdom. If she stopped getting hung up on the origin of the dreams . . . Lani was right. Maybe there was some idea, some strategy, hell, some magic she could use to turn things around at UM.

She wandered over to a bench in the banyan grove. Dark leaves the size of saucers clustered on the branches of the ancient trees. Leaves. Mahana and his apprentice had been working with leaves and plants in her last dream. They'd been talking about the history of their clan. Sunny lay on her back on the bench and gazed at the dappled arches above until creeping drowsiness fogged her brain and weighed heavy on her eyes.

I finish my story about our people and realize that Tanemao has barely moved, his gaze riveted on my face. I rest my hand on his shoulder. "Now you know why we will never arm ourselves against the people of Tauati. The murder of my uncle and my all-consuming desire to exact revenge on the chief priest taught me an important lesson. We must be vigilant for peace, my son. We are all just a breath away from violence."

Tanemao stares into the distance. I cannot read his expression or know if he accepts what I say. His eyes narrow. "What will we do if the people of Tauati do not have the same desire for peace? What if they are like the chief priest at Taputapuatea and desire only power?"

"The importance of those questions lies in how our actions will influence the answers. Think of the sacred stone at the center of our village. The stone has been carved into a perfect circle to represent the circle of life that encompasses everything—people, plants, animals, the sky, the ocean, our ancestors. Whatever we do within that circle touches everything else."

"I understand that. If we arm ourselves with many weapons and strong warriors, all others will fear our might and dare not attack us. There will be peace."

I answer with more questions for him to ponder. "What is the risk of a relationship built on fear? What if the others make more weapons and train many more warriors?"

Tanemao sighs. "What is our protection when someone does not have friendship in his heart?"

"A hole has been cut into the center of the sacred stone to represent the light of *Akua* and the *mana* all around and within us. When we live close to that center, we have all the protection we need." I place my hand on Tanemao's chest. "Compassion here—in our hearts—is our weapon. It fills the circle causing others to choose peace over power."

Tanemao nods but frustration still lines his face. The struggle for peace can spark a war within a man.

"My son, we have all grappled with these very questions. Be open. You will know the answers in your heart." I embrace him but I feel no response.

My love for Tanemao overflows. I fervently wish to ease his mind. Holding him by the arms, I tease, "Besides, if we spend all our time making weapons, there would be no time for feasting and celebrations and our lovely Anuanua women."

This attempt to turn our thoughts to lighter visions thuds like a coconut falling on sand. Tanemao just shakes his head and returns to sorting plants.

Eleven

High anticipation charged the air at the downtown Honolulu rally. Sunny scanned the crowd and estimated close to three thousand people in a kaleidoscope of flowered shirts, tank tops and jean cutoffs, straw hats, traditional *kapa* cloth robes, and *lei*. Food vendor carts lined the perimeter of the grounds. Booths displayed books, posters, tee shirts, and informational exhibits related to Hawaiian sovereignty. The Royal Hawaiian Band, dressed in white with cranberry sashes, played on a temporary stage.

The first five rows of folding chairs in front of the stage were reserved for respected elders, the *kūpuna*. Sunny and Lani sat on the grass off to the side, legs stretched out, basking in the sun. They sucked on pineapple shave-ice.

Behind the stage, the gray stone edifice of 'Iolani Palace—the hawk of heaven—soared over the colorful scene. Sunny let her gaze sweep from the front entrance to the cupola. Men and women dressed in traditional native attire stood on the wide steps. They were flanked by scarlet-feathered *kāhili*, the tall wreath-like standards of the royal court. Nine arches, supported by ornate Corinthian columns, graced the façade on the first floor, with nine more on the second floor. Above the cupola, the Hawai'i state flag flew upside down.

Sunny leaned toward Lani. "What's with the flag?"

"That symbolizes the sovereignty movement."

Sunny remembered that 'Iolani had encompassed the majesty of kings and queens for only a decade. In 1893, American businessmen illegally seized control of the independent nation and imprisoned Queen

Lili'uokalani. Now, the palace served as an enduring reminder of all the Hawaiians lost.

The band finished playing. Sunny sat up straight and crossed her legs yoga-style. "What goes on at one of these rallies?"

"Chanting, *hula*, speeches, entertainment. Mostly this rally is to educate people about the sovereignty movement, build solidarity so that legislators will listen to what Hawaiians want."

"Seems like there's not much agreement on that. The newspaper says some people want reparation. Money and land." Sunny waved a flyer someone had handed her. "This group wants independence from the United States. They want to go back to the monarchy."

"Some want to go all the way back to the days before the *ali'i*." Lani took a slurp of shave ice and frowned. "The issues are complex. How can stolen lands be returned to native people? Who's considered native? Can Hawai'i truly be independent, not just politically but economically as well?" She looked directly at Sunny. "There's one thing I do believe. The *kanaka maoli*, people who trace their lineage back to the time before outsiders came here, deserve the right to govern themselves."

"Sounds like the American Indian reservations."

"That's one of the proposals on the table."

Sunny bit off a large chunk of ice. She winced at the cold sliding down her throat, making the spot between her eyes throb. Waiting for the pain to subside, she formulated her next question. "What about the people who say the movement is racist?"

"How do they put it? I think it goes something like 'the future of the state shouldn't be based on the desires of a small minority who claim ancestral rights.' The oppressors' perfectly logical rationale." Lani dumped the rest of her ice on the grass and crumpled the paper cone.

"You know a lot about this movement. I don't think I've ever seen you so fired up about something."

Lani's gentle countenance returned with a smile. "Pete's influence. He really got me thinking about the issues."

Sunny looked around at the crowd. "At The Wall you said people were worried about violence at these rallies."

"So far, it's only been people getting in each other's faces, a few shoving matches."

"Seems pretty mellow today."

Lani gave Sunny a hug. "Not to worry. This is like a big *ohana* party."

A tall, slender man stepped to the microphone on stage and asked everyone to join in *pule*. His deep voice resonated over the hushed crowd. The Hawaiian prayer struck a chord deep within Sunny, the same feeling that welled up when she leaned into her mother's embrace after a long absence from home.

Next came the *kumu oli*. His chant, soft at first, rose to a booming cadence. On the last line, he faced the crowd and raised his arms to the sky. The crowd responded with enthusiastic applause.

Students from the Kamehameha School quickly took their places on stage to perform *kahiko hula*. Dressed in *kī* leaf skirts and white shell *lei*, the dancers kept time to the beat of an *ipu heke*. Their hand and arm motions portrayed waves in the ocean and the powerful strokes of the canoe paddler. They stamped their feet, intense concentration on their faces.

Sunny glanced at the people around her and saw expressions of joy and pride. She sensed a powerful connection between the chanters, drummers, dancers, and their audience, the same kind of connection she felt when she was working with the team in the OR. She folded her arms against the twinge of sadness in her chest. This day would not be ruined in worry about UM.

The crowd cheered as the dancers bent low in a solemn bow and exited the stage. Sunny looked over at Lani and shouted, "This is amazing."

"We've just gotten started!"

The crowd settled back into their seats. Lani tugged at Sunny's arm. "Pete's here."

Sunny looked in the direction of Lani's wave and saw the band members gathered at the far corner of the palace.

Pete motioned for them to come over. He gave Lani a kiss and bear-hugged Sunny. "Glad you could come. How's it so far?"

"This feels like a combination of the World Series opener and a visit from the Pope."

Pete laughed. "Check out the booths. You gonna get into some rousing conversations."

Sunny grinned and shook her head. "I'm just here to listen and learn."

Pete slipped his arm around Lani's waist, pulling her close. "You two leave before Keoni introduces us."

"Right," Sunny said. "I like the idea of beating the traffic."

Lani looked up at Pete. "Call me when you get home?" He nodded.

Pete reached out to Sunny, kissed her cheek. "You and Leilani pick a weekend to get together at my place. My barbecue is *'ono*."

"You're on. I'll bring the beer." Sunny gave a quick salute and headed for their spot in front of the stage.

Looking back, she saw Lani and Pete in an embrace. Lani's arms were wrapped around his massive waist, head on his chest, waterfall of black hair covering her face. Pete kissed the crown of her head. He tilted his face skyward, eyes closed, as if in a prayer of thanksgiving. Sunny breathed a long sigh and smiled.

"Who's Keoni?" Sunny asked as Lani sat beside her on the grass.

"Keoni Punahele. He's the president of Hawaiian Freedom. He'll give the last speech today. If we go over to their booth, I might be able to introduce you to him."

They turned their attention to the first speaker. An older man, brown as a *kukui* nut and wearing only a tan *kapa* cloth wrapped around his waist, stepped up to the microphone. Sunny stared at him. He reminded her of Mahana.

The man raised a huge conch shell to his lips and blew three long blasts. A sound, haunting as a horn calling out in thick fog, echoed over the palace grounds. "*Ua mau ke ea o ka 'āina i ka pono*. The life of the land is preserved in righteousness. King Kamehameha the Third gave us these words. This day, this movement is about turning a wrong into a right. It is about returning to the Hawaiians what rightfully belongs to us." He uttered a brittle laugh. "These words are the state motto. But this state and the federal government have refused to make things right." He paused as murmurs of agreement spread through the audience like a swell on the ocean. He raised the conch shell high above his head. "I call on our governor and the president of the United States to make things right." The swell transformed into a pounding wave of cheers and applause. The crowd began to chant, "Make it right! Make it right!" The man dropped his arms and bowed his head. The crowd chanted even louder.

Lani jumped to her feet, chanting and punching her fist into the air. Sunny stood up slowly. She looked around. She was really an intruder in this place. Maybe she should slink away and wait in the car.

Lani glanced at Sunny. She threw her arm across Sunny's shoulders, gave her a squeeze. "I can't hear you!"

Sunny joined in the chant.

While the next presenter tried to quiet the audience, Lani suggested they take a stroll around the grounds. They stopped at a cart to purchase lemonade and made their way to the Hawaiian Freedom booth. Lani stood on her toes, peering around the people jammed in front of the displays. "I don't see Keoni."

"That's okay. Maybe we can catch him later." Sunny turned and collided with a gaunt man bulling his way through the crowd. She raised her eyes from his chest to his head. Gray hair flying out as if he'd stuck a knife in an outlet, mouth a grim slash in skin the color of putty. His look of frozen anger paralyzed her. He pushed ahead, his brown backpack nearly knocking her sideways. Lemonade and ice sloshed to the ground.

The man elbowed Lani out of the way and shouted at the woman staffing the booth. "Where's Keoni?"

The woman just shrugged, palms turned upward. He growled something unintelligible and side-swiped Lani as he plowed back through crowd.

Lani grabbed Sunny's arm to regain her balance. "How rude."

"Do you know who he is?"

"I've never seen him before."

"Something tells me he's not here to thank Hawaiian Freedom for a great rally."

Lani went back to the woman in the booth. "Please let Keoni know that a tall man wearing a huge backpack is looking for him. He seems really upset."

The woman nodded and began talking into a two-way radio.

"That pissed off *haole* needs to catch a little of the *aloha* flowing around here," Sunny said as they walked away.

Back in front of the stage, they watched another *hula hālau* perform. Two speakers followed. One called for all military forces based in Hawai'i to be withdrawn. The other suggested that people protest the overthrow of the monarchy by refusing to pay state and federal taxes.

The speeches faded into background noise. Sunny searched the crowd over and over, looking for the man. She thought he'd surely stand out—scowling expression, white, long-sleeved shirt, and dark jeans—in the middle of smiling faces and bright-colored island wear. She noticed police cruisers and a couple of ambulances parked on the streets around the palace. As she scanned the mass of people again, she picked out police officers stationed at the edges of the crowd. She figured they'd probably recognize someone who might cause trouble.

Lani nudged her gently. "Hey, are you okay?"

"Fine. What's up next?"

Someone at the microphone announced, "We're going to take a fifteen-minute break while we get ready for our last speech and . . ." The announcer beamed and paused for effect. "The Sons of O'ahu!" The crowd erupted into enthusiastic cheers and whistles.

As people headed for the vendor carts, Sunny got up off the grass. "Ready to go?"

Lani stood. "Sunny, we can't miss Keoni's speech. I want to hear—"

"Didn't Pete say we should leave before they start playing?"

"Just one song."

"Lani . . ."

"Oh come on. This is the most exciting part."

Sunny shook her head.

"Don't give me stink eye. Pete will never know we're out here. I promise we'll leave after the first song."

"Okay . . . But, I think I'm going to have to let Pete know about this streak of anarchy I see developing."

Lani howled. "Don't you dare."

"Or what?"

"Or I'll get Marie to put a curse on you."

"You got me. My mouth is sealed."

"I'm joking. Marie doesn't do black magic." They went back to lounging on the lawn. "Sunny, I've been thinking. Maybe you should visit her. She might be able to help you sort out your dreams."

"I don't know. Her warning about someone in my life being my friend or my enemy. It's hard to believe that soothsayer stuff." Sunny looked up at the palace facade, the columns standing like soldiers at attention. She couldn't go on trying to ignore the dreams. "Maybe you could help me figure out what the dreams mean if we really took some time to piece it all together." Maybe then the disturbing scenes would go away.

"Let's get together some evening this week. We can do some breathing exercises, quiet meditation, and see what comes up."

"Thanks, girlfriend." Sunny scanned the people around them. "What do you think happened to that nut with the backpack?"

"Keoni probably calmed the guy down. He's good at handling tense situations."

As if on Lani's cue, the president of Hawaiian Freedom stepped to the microphone. "*Aloha nui loa*! I'm Keoni Punahele!" The crowd cheered, everyone standing, some with children perched on their shoulders. "Greetings and love to all my brothers and sisters."

The cheering got louder. Pete and the other band members had taken their places behind Keoni. They yelled and whistled along with the audience.

"You all know how I feel," Keoni shouted. "We Hawaiians have a right to be free!"

People began to chant in unison. "Freedom, freedom, freedom."

Sunny saw Pete scanning the crowd in front of the stage. His gaze stopped just past Sunny's left shoulder. He'd spotted Lani. With a barely detectable wag of his index finger, he gave her a stern look. Lani blew him a kiss. Pete made a motion as if to catch the kiss and pressed his hand to his heart. He smiled and mouthed, "Go."

As Sunny watched their exchange, she sensed jostling in the crowd off to her right When she turned in that direction, she saw nothing that seemed out of the ordinary.

Up on the stage, Keoni waved his hands in an effort to bring the noise level down. "We've talked story all day. It's time for some fun." The audience answered with more cheering. Keoni turned slightly and motioned to the band with an outstretched arm. "Please welcome The Sons of O'ahu!" The crowd roared as the drummer started a loud, steady beat on the base drum.

A bang like the sound of a giant cherry bomb caused people to shout and scatter. A second explosion followed. Not able to see what was happening in the crowd, Sunny looked back toward the stage.

It seemed as though someone pushed the slow motion button on the remote control. Keoni lurched backward, legs collapsing and bright red blossoming on his pastel shirt. With a look of bewilderment on his face, Pete dropped his guitar and wrapped his arms around Keoni's torso. He lowered the wounded man to the floor. Pete's face twisted in a grimace. His arms were covered with blood.

Another loud bang exploded closer to Sunny. The people in front of her threw themselves to the ground.

An invisible finger pressed pause on the remote. A freeze frame wavered in Sunny's view. The man with the backpack stood in front of the stage, legs spread wide in a combat stance, hands wrapped around a revolver. Pete was looking down, pressing his hands on Keoni's chest. Sunny tried to cry out a warning. Robbed of breath, limbs encased in wet cement, she could only watch in silent horror.

Pete looked up, got to his feet. With his eyes fixed on the gunman, he took a couple of steps back. The man raised the revolver slightly. Sunny squeezed her eyes shut and prayed for a miracle to stop the action.

Seconds elapsed. Sunny opened her eyes to see the gunman turn his back to the stage. As she ducked down, she glimpsed the vacant look in his eyes, the iron set of his jaw. He fired two shots into the crowd, shoved the gun in his mouth, and pulled the trigger.

The remote control clicked on fast forward. People were screaming and running in every direction. Sunny sprang up. Where was Lani? She'd been right there. As she pushed her way through the surging crowd, she glanced up at the stage. Pete, a look of sheer panic on his face, jumped down from the platform. With his eyes riveted on the ground not far from Sunny, he plunged forward.

Sunny snapped around to look in the direction he was headed. She saw a crumple of peach flowers on white silk. Long black hair fanned out over the grass as if arranged for a shampoo commercial. Slender arms and legs splayed out like the limbs of a rag doll. As she ran, Sunny could hear herself screaming her friend's name.

They knelt on opposite sides of Lani who lay face down. A gaping wound on her back streamed blood. Sunny's heart pounded in her ears, but the steely calm of the operating room took over. She called Lani's name and with a steady hand felt for a pulse in her neck. Sunny looked up at Pete, caught the anguish in his eyes. "She's got a good pulse. Help me turn her over. We need to make sure she can breathe. Slowly now."

Pete's big hands shook as, together, they gently eased Lani onto her back. Sunny carefully tilted Lani's chin up and watched her chest for a moment. She placed her cheek near Lani's nose and mouth. "Pete, give me your shirt and then roll her toward you a little." He quickly stripped off his flowered shirt and eased Lani over, one hand cradling her head, the other cupping her hip. Sunny stuffed the shirt against the flowing wound. "Okay, back down. Real easy."

Sunny grasped Pete's arm. "Her breathing is very shallow. We need the paramedics right now."

Pete nodded, bolted up, and shouted for people to get out of his way.

As she watched him sprint toward the ambulance, Sunny became aware of the chaos around her. People cried out names, trying to connect with loved ones they'd lost in the panic. Someone behind her screamed for the paramedics. She glanced back and saw three men lifting Keoni off the stage. Police officers, talking on their radios, pushed their way toward the front of the palace. They yelled at onlookers to get away from the gunman's body.

Sunny turned back to Lani. The pulse in her neck seemed thready, her breathing more ragged, skin ashen and cold. "Come on, come on," she muttered, urging Pete and the paramedics to hurry. CPR, two breaths to five chest compressions. Or was it one breath? It didn't matter. Lani was going to be alright.

Sunny slipped her arms around Lani's shoulders and whispered near her ear, "Stay with me, girl. Pete's getting help. You stay with me, Lani. Stay with me."

Twelve

Ku'ulei Williamson, the *kumu oli*, took her place in front of the bonfire on Makua Beach. A *maile lei* of emerald leaves draped her shoulders. Dark, wavy hair cascaded below her waist. "We are here to honor the life and spirit of our beloved Leilani Alamea Lewis. We call to our *'aumākua* to be here with us, to help us in our sorrow."

In a deep voice, she began to chant, matching the words with graceful movement. She bent low and swept her hand in a curve along the sand. "*Honua*. Mother earth. Pele, come. Ground and support us as we honor our precious one." She gestured to the sunset sky. "*Hā*. Misty air, fragrant wind, breath of life. *Pueo,* come. Lift us up as we honor our precious one." Turning, she stretched her arms out to the ocean. "*Kai*. Cooling waters, gentle rains. *Manō,* come. Purify us as we honor our precious one."

Sunny stared at the ocean. Far out beyond the breakers, a small yacht bobbed on the swells. She folded her arms across her waist. Her muscles ached from holding in the giant hollow space that seemed to have replaced all her internal organs. If she let go, the hollow space would swallow her whole.

Facing the fire, Ku'ulei spread her arms out at her sides. "*Ahi*. Roaring flames, red-hot embers. *Mo'o*, come. Help us to accept change as we honor our precious one." She turned back to the gathering. Closing her eyes and lifting her face to the sky she chanted, "*'I'o*. Divine spirit, be with us as we honor Leilani."

The hiss of the logs on the fire reminded Sunny of the ventilator at Lani's bedside, the phalanx of monitors beeping out of time. She and Lani had sworn over drinks at The Wall they'd never be at the mercy of the machinery they manipulated every day in surgery. Lani kept the oath. All of her organs simply shut down.

The strains of a melody brought Sunny back to the wide arc of people around the fire. She saw familiar faces—nurses, surgeons, anesthesiologists, staff from all over the Center, and friends. Pete played his guitar softly, firelight reflecting on his tears. Pete in the ICU. She watched as he warmed Lani's cold feet with his big hands, kissed each of her toes, gently caressed her legs, the only places on her body not taped, bandaged, or jabbed with a tube. He sang a sweet love song close to Lani's ear.

Sunny jammed her fists into her abdomen and looked up at the stars twinkling in a maroon sky. The splendor seemed to mock their grief.

Ku'ulei spoke. "I invite all of you to come up and share your memories of Leilani."

People came forward to talk about their good times with Lani and how she had touched them. A high school pal remembered how Lani had patiently tutored him through algebra. "I made her crazy with all my questions but she never gave up on me." Grace Pukui talked about Lani's skill and reassuring presence in the operating room. Someone told the story of how Lani got hooked on line-dancing. Many recalled her courage during the cancer treatments.

Sunny could barely focus on the words being spoken. The plants in Lani's apartment needed watering. Someone needed to cancel her gym membership. Lani's position in the OR needed to be filled. Oh, God. Why couldn't she remember what was special about their friendship?

Silence floated on the wind, and Sunny sensed people waiting for her to speak. She stared at the sand. She'd practiced a speech, one designed to buoy everyone and pay tribute to the pure sunshine of Lani's spirit. Tears welled up, frozen shards stabbing her eyes and cutting away the inspiring eulogy. "I miss her."

Ku'ulei rocked Sunny in a long embrace. With her arm still across Sunny's shoulders, she addressed the gathering. "Leilani wanted her ashes to be scattered in the sea. In a few moments, we'll hear the call of the conch shell. That will be the signal for the boat to go farther out. Her loved ones—brothers Steven and John and her *tūtū*, Marie—will place a broken *lei* on the water. They'll pour her ashes out to stream down into the arms of Kanaloa, spirit of the ocean."

Sunny moved away from the fire to stand at the edge of the gathering. She longed for her brain to shut down, but it just kept reviewing the endless details of all that had happened, trying to fathom the unfathomable. Why did Lani stay against everyone's wishes? She should have dragged her friend to the car. Why hadn't they arrested the lunatic who'd been harassing Hawaiian Freedom for months? Why? Why?

Ku'ulei passed a basket to the person standing nearest her. "Here on the beach, we'll pay tribute to Leilani with fire." She held up a small flower. "As the basket comes around, please take a *hau* blossom. To our ancestors *hau* was sacred, representing the precious spark of life. Your flower opened yellow this morning. It turned orange this afternoon. Now it's dark orange and beginning to close. Its delicate beauty lasts only a few hours, just as we are in this life a short time. The fire represents transformation. When we cast our blossoms into the fire, we release Leilani's spirit to soar far and wide, to soar home to *Akua*, to soar high in pure love."

Ku'ulei threw her flower into the blaze and murmured a prayer. "As you come up to offer your flowers, we'll chant a farewell to Leilani." The long, mournful wail of the conch shell sounded.

They came forward to say goodbye. Some paused in front of the fire in quiet meditation before surrendering their blossom to the flames. Others dropped their flowers on the hot coals at the edge and moved quickly away. Quiet chanting swelled to a rich chorus as more and more voices added their farewell. *Aloha, aloha pua makamae, a hui hou.* Love and farewell, farewell precious flower, until we meet again.

Sunny stood in front of the fire, rigid, crushing the velvet *hau* petals. Warm hands enfolded her fist. Ku'ulei gently coaxed her fingers open. Sunny watched the blossom flutter onto the glowing coals. For an instant the flower burst into brilliant color and then quickly withered to ash.

The sign for Kauhale O Waimea appeared in the headlights. Sunny cranked the wheel and gunned the engine. The car hurtled down the gravel road, bounced off lava boulders at the hairpin turns, and skidded to a stop in the parking area. She jumped out, slamming the door so hard the whole car rocked. "What is it? What is it with this insane, frigging world? People get offended and just blow each other away.

That fixes it. Let's all go to our corners and get our guns ready for one great battle."

Running like someone late for the last train, she reached the middle of the village gasping for breath. She turned slowly in the center of the clearing, arms raised, panting, shouting. "Okay, goddamn it . . . I'm here . . . you're supposed to be here . . . where's the goddamned help?" Her head pounded in a vice of fury. Sunny scanned the edges of the clearing and screamed, "What? No friendly dog to lead me to the promised land? No fiery Pele to make it all better? Where the hell are you now, Mahana?"

Her arms windmilled the air as she paced. "That's what I thought," she yelled. "Let the mortals just screw each other over. Tear up this world until there's nothing good left." She stopped to gulp air. Marie's face floated before her. "Old woman, you promised the spirits would help us." She let out a harsh laugh. "There aren't enough benevolent spirits in the universe to make a dent in the mess we've created." The answering silence infuriated her.

She ran down to the bank of the river and roared into the dark water. "Where are the fucking night marchers? Why don't you help me? Come on, come on. Let's get revenge on all the bastards that make this world a sorry-ass place to be." Gasping for breath, rage pounding like a drum, she collapsed to her knees and shrieked to the night sky, "It's a goddamned sorry-ass place to be!" Her voice echoed down the canyon. She slumped forward, forehead grinding into the sand, arms clutching her stomach. A low moan rose up from her gut as she rocked back and forth. "Lani, I'm so sorry. I'm so sorry. So sorry."

After a long time, Sunny shivered in the cool wind. Her lungs and throat burned. She pushed herself to her feet. Grains of sand on her forehead sprinkled down onto her eyelids and cheeks. She absently brushed them away and trudged back to the car. Her hands shook as she turned the key in the ignition, put the car in gear, and inched along the gravel track.

Back out on the highway, Sunny clung to the steering wheel and stared straight ahead. Her body felt drained, mind shut down in a red throb. The car lugged along in third gear as she followed the road east, then south along the windward coast. In a stretch of dense foliage, dull remembrance nudged her to veer into a rutted lane. A chicken flapped into the beam of her headlights. She jammed on the brakes. The front bumper of her car grazed the back end of the rusty station wagon.

Sunny heard the dog whine a faint greeting and a rocking chair creak. She saw the amber glow of a cigarette in the dark. "*E ho'i i ka pili.* Come here to me."

Sunny stood in front of the rocker sensing the arms reaching out to her. She dropped to her knees and buried her head against Marie's bosom. Warm hands smoothed her back and neck.

Violent sobs shook her body. The frozen tears melted and poured out, soaking Marie's gown and plastering Sunny's hair to her face. She rocked and moaned and gasped for breath as she caved into the giant hollow space at her core. She slumped down until her head rested on Marie's legs. Marie's strong arms supported her body while she wept— wept for Lani, for herself, for the whole sorry-ass world.

Thirteen

Floating on the edge of sleep, Sunny listened to the hard rain. Her limbs felt waterlogged. All the muscles in her abdomen and chest ached as if she'd crunched a thousand sit-ups. The skin on her face felt drawn, eyelids gritty.

Shadows in the stormy light took shape. A wicker chair stood in the corner and a chest of drawers on one wall. A lacy-fern-patterned quilt covered the bed. Across from the foot of the bed hung a portrait of a stately Hawaiian woman, wavy hair flowing around her face and shoulders, eyes dark and piercing.

Sunny struggled to recognize her surroundings. She studied the portrait. The woman resembled Marie. Like the downpour outside the window, dim memories of the past twenty-four hours flooded through her. Sunny didn't know how long she had cried in Marie's arms. How had she ended up in this bed? Events and emotions seemed to be recorded less in her mind and more in every fiber of her body. Her heart felt literally broken, in need of a plaster cast.

At the sound of soft tapping, the door creaked open. Marie came in carrying a tray. She placed coffee, fresh fruit, and a glass of water on the nightstand and sat on the edge of the bed. They embraced. The scents of tobacco and orange blossoms enveloped Sunny.

Marie picked up the plate of fruit. "You need to eat."

"I think the water is about all I can handle right now. Besides, I've imposed on you long enough. Thanks for taking me in last night."

The old woman, a glint of moisture on her cheek, looked down. "Good that you were here."

"I'm so thoughtless. You've lost her too."

Marie cried softly. She fished a tissue out of her pocket and blew her nose. "*Auwē*. My precious *keiki*. She's with her *tūtū* now." Marie dabbed at her eyes and stuffed the tissue back in her pocket.

Sunny held Marie's hand for a long time and listened to the rain. Memories floated in—crouching behind a waterfall with Lani, shouting to each other over the roar. They'd hiked for an hour, sliding in the mud, hanging onto branches, and laughing until they were panting for breath. A touch on Sunny's cheek brought her back to the room.

"You eat, rest. Plenty time to talk." Marie gave Sunny a hug and closed the door quietly.

Sunny curled into the depths of the bed. The tears overflowing her eyes and heart matched the steady cascade outside the window.

She found Marie rocking on the *lānai* and sat in the wicker chair next to her. The storm had diminished to a light shower. The yard, surrounded by dripping emerald foliage, looked like a jungle pond. The air, so laden with moisture one could almost cup a handful, smelled of rich earth. Frogs croaked a chorus under the house.

Sunny tried to summon the energy to formulate a plan. She grappled for a first step and wondered at the stubborn blankness of her mind. She'd always been one to hit adversity head-on, action being her favorite prescription for frustration or sadness.

"What you thinking, Sunny?"

"I should go into work. Sundays are usually pretty quiet in the OR. It would give me a chance to make sure everything's ready for this week."

"Can you take time off?"

"I probably have eight or ten weeks vacation saved up." Sunny leaned forward, propped her elbows on her knees. "What would I do staying home?"

Marie didn't respond.

"There are big problems brewing at UM." A faint voice nagged at her to get up, get on with it, go back and fight like hell. Lani wouldn't want her to wallow. But she felt immobilized, incapable of heeding the call.

Raindrops pattered on leaves. A patch of blue in the sky opened wide, and sunlight streamed out of the dark clouds. A rainbow shimmered over the yard, bands of color so vibrant they seemed rock solid.

The Anuanua. Mahana's clan believed that when someone died they walked over the rainbow. Fresh tears coursed down Sunny's cheeks. "Marie, you and Lani have both said my dreams are about spirits trying to assist me, give me the chance to learn something." Marie held out a tissue. Sunny pressed it to her face. "Why didn't they help me keep Lani from dying?"

Marie didn't answer. She rubbed Sunny's back.

"Lani and I were going to spend some time figuring out the meaning of the dreams. She wanted me to come back to you, but I . . ."

"You scared. Sometimes we think it's better not to know all there is to know."

"I think if I had known Mahana's whole story, maybe Lani would still be here."

"Maybe."

Sunny stared at the gray clouds where the rainbow had disappeared. "Mahana and his people were trying to live peacefully with their neighbors. His apprentice wanted to get ready for battle." She rubbed her face with both hands. "I don't know what happened to them. The dreams stopped two weeks ago."

"You can invite them to come to you."

A chill replaced the aching in Sunny's chest. She'd seen too much violence and pain for one life, let alone two.

Marie took Sunny's hand in both of hers. "When you ready."

The low rumble of thunder filled the quiet between them. The clouds turned a dark slate as the breeze picked up. Marie pushed herself out of the rocker. "Let's eat."

Sunny devoured eggs scrambled with Spam lunch meat, fruit, and toasted Hawaiian sweet bread. She sipped dark coffee, savoring the nutty aroma as she watched Marie eat.

The old woman wielded a fork and knife with hands as wrinkled as an elephant's trunk, fingernails stained nicotine yellow. She rolled her food around in her mouth, gumming until it was soft enough to swallow. A small chunk of egg rested on her ample bosom. Small child, road-worn truck driver, wise sage. Sunny wanted to bask in this woman's comforting presence and never go back to her own world.

Marie wiped her chin with a paper napkin, spied the crumbs on her chest, and laughed. "When you get old, most of your food ends up outta your mouth." She started to collect the plates.

Sunny touched Marie's arm. "You rest. I'll have this tidied up in no time." She washed and rinsed the dishes, stacking them in the wooden rack on the counter.

A brilliant flash lit up the windows, followed by an instant crack and rumble and the drumming of a downpour.

"Hina's busy," Marie said.

"Hina?"

"Hawaiian moon goddess. Expert *kapa* maker. Up in the sky, Hina spreads her sheets of *kapa* to dry in the sun. Puts big stones on the corners to hold the sheets in place. Wind blows them off, and we hear thunder." Marie made a swirling motion with her hands. "Boom! Hina hurries to fold up her *kapa* so it won't get wet. The cloth is so white, it reflects the rays of the sun. That's the lightening."

"Do her tears make the rain?"

"Could be. Jealous husband sent Hina away to live on the moon."

Sunny placed the frying pan on the stove and returned to the table. "Sounds like a jerk."

"If Hina hadn't gone to live in the sky, we wouldn't have the beauty of storms."

"So much in life seems to be like that. Both good and bad." Another clap of thunder sounded. Tears burned behind Sunny's eyes. "What good could possibly come from Lani's death?"

Marie wiped her eyes with the heels of her hands.

"Lani believed everything happens for a reason." Sunny's words ended in a squeaky sob. Tears overflowed, made her nose run.

"You here."

"Just like her." Sunny laughed, mopped her face with a napkin. "Takes the big powder and forces me to figure out the mysteries of life. Guess I shouldn't disappoint her." She sighed, her chest heavy from crying. "What do I need to do?"

"Do nothing. Just be." Marie rose from her chair and held out her hand. She led Sunny back to the bedroom guarded by the stately *wahine*.

Sunny settled on the bed. Marie placed candles around the room. She lit a bowl of *kiawe* incense, the woody scent permeating the air. She sprinkled water from a seashell around the bed, gently touching wet fingertips to Sunny's forehead, the hollow of her neck, chest, and belly. "The spirits know you're here but they *kōkua*—help us—only if we ask."

Sunny nodded.

Marie stroked Sunny's forehead and cheeks and gently placed a hand over her eyes. Her touch felt warm and soothing. "I'll be right here while you journey. Your *'aumākua* will protect you." Marie stroked Sunny's arms and pressed her hand lightly on Sunny's chest. "Just listen to my voice. Let all your thoughts and worries go." Marie pressed her hand on Sunny's abdomen. "Take deep belly breaths and empty your mind."

Voice and touch enveloped Sunny. In waves of deep breaths, the rubber band tension of muscles all over her body slowly released. Thoughts floated away like tiny boats on a slow current.

Marie stroked Sunny's legs and feet. "Breathe deep and ask the spirits for their help."

A prayer flowed into Sunny's mind. "Please show me what I need to know." As she concentrated on the prayer, Marie's words faded into a soft chant. For a time, she drifted between the words of the prayer and the cadence of Marie's voice.

The chant grew louder, more commanding. "Breathe in the *mana*, the power that's all around us. Breathe in the *mana*."

A tingling sensation started in Sunny's belly and spread through her legs and arms, up into her neck and face. She pushed a twinge of panic away by blowing out a deep breath.

"See the *mana* as a ball of light deep inside you."

In her mind's eye, Sunny saw a brilliant spark at her core grow into a golden ball that infused her whole being. The ball expanded, radiating out in great shimmering arcs.

The chanting intensified, flooding the room, her ears, her mind. "The *mana* grows. The light fills this room. This *hale*. Grows bigger still. The light flows in a glowing river to your village."

Sunny watched the light pour out of the room, through the house, out into the jungle, along valleys, and over cliffs.

The chanting dropped to a whisper at her ear. "Let yourself go. Sail on that river of light. Fly to your people."

Sunny felt herself rise on the crest of a giant wave. Physical sensations disappeared as her consciousness exploded in a brilliant fountain. Gliding on the shining river, she watched the arcs of light swirl and stream into the village. The glowing river filled each hut, swathed the plants in luminescence, and flooded the clearing.

Our home is ablaze in light. Near the river, a great bonfire burns. Torches brighten the village paths and surround the clearing. The sacred stone in the center of the clearing is decorated with *lei* of ferns and seashells and ringed with *kukui* lamps. Only on such a special night, a night that prepares us to reach out to the people of Tauati, would we be so extravagant with wood and oil.

Four days of hard work fill my sight. The canoes, awaiting Omo's blessing, are arranged in perfect rows on the river bank. Their hulls gleam in the firelight. At the long house, *ti* leaves and mats are mounded with fruit, *poi*, baked fish and pig, roasted chicken, yams, and squash. Calabashes are full of water and *'awa*. Drummers and dancers watch for Omo's signal. Everyone, dressed in their finest yellow *tapa* decorated with intricate fern patterns, anticipates the call to the circle. I feel child-like excitement tingle in my old man's body. The drums have not sounded, and already the *mana* is rising.

Tiare steps in front of the sacred stone and raises her arms to the sky. A drummer pounds out four slow beats on the *pahu*. The other drummers join in on the next four beats and continue in the slow rhythm of the heart. In quiet reverence, everyone enters the circle to sit facing Tiare, our elders in front. Only Aimata and the lookouts posted around the village are absent. When everyone is in place, the drumming ceases.

Omo stands next to Tiare and begins the ceremony with a chant. "Oh wise ancestors we call you to be with us." He sprinkles the gathering with cleansing salt water as he chants. All beseech their own ancestors and protector spirits to come. The clearing is filled with voices calling out.

Omo's voice rises above the others. "Oh spirits of wind and fire, of water and earth, we call you to our circle. Spirits of the east and south, of the west and north, hear our call." As he chants, Omo moves around the clearing, lighting a torch in each of the directions. Tiare holds up the sacred objects, each in turn—feather, *kukui* nut, seashell, and standing rock—then places them at the foot of the sacred stone.

"*Akua*, with humble hearts we ask you to be with us." Omo moves to the front and stretches his arms to the sky. The gathering is hushed.

Tiare holds up a large *koa* bowl brimming with samples of every food prepared for the feast. She chants in a clear voice, "*Akua*, we offer you all that we have in gratitude for your presence."

Omo, still reaching up to the sky, calls out, "Oh great *Akua*, fill us with your light. Fill us with your love. Fill us with your *mana*." Tiare joins him, and they chant the words over and over. We raise our arms to the sky. One by one, voices begin to call out the words. As the chanting grows louder, we rise to our feet and move side to side in unison.

The bright lights of torches and lamps fill my eyes. The chanting fills my head. For a brief moment, I am back at Taputapuatea. I see the blood dripping from bodies hanging in trees and hear the chief priest screaming to Oro. My muscles grow taut and start to quiver. What if we cannot prevent that violence from coming here? My gaze focuses on Tiare's serene countenance. The chanting wraps around me like a reassuring embrace. I breathe in the *mana* so palpable in the air, utterly grateful for the loving spirits in this gathering.

Four loud drumbeats signal the end of the chant. Tiare and Omo step off to the side as we sit on the grass. The dancers take their places at the front. The men wear yellow *malo*—loincloths—and red *tapa* sashes. The women are covered from waist to feet in *ti* leaf skirts. White shell *lei* encircle the ankles, wrists, necks, and heads of all the dancers. Their stance is erect and proud, faces stern.

Four slow beats. One of the dancers calls out the first line of the chant. The *pahu* starts a steady two stroke beat—pah, pah-pah, pah, pah-pah—as Omo chants a commemoration of our voyage from Raiatea. His voice sounds sonorous and commanding. The dancers stamp their feet, crouch low, rise up, turning from front to side and back again. Their arms and hands express the search for guiding stars, the motion of the canoe on giant waves, the swirling of the winds. Pounding and stamping and resonating chant mesmerize the gathering. Just when it seems the spell will never end, Omo's voice breaks, a dancer calls out the last line, and the *pahu* sounds four beats. The dancers, crouched low on powerful leg muscles, move slowly off to the side. Everyone jumps up, shouting praises and appreciation.

The dancing continues with the men portraying the search for the perfect tree to carve into a canoe. The gathering roars with laughter at the dancer who hops around like *'elepaio*. The women come to the front to dance a tribute to *Mao*, the shark spirit who protects our village. As the drum pounds and the chanting grows louder, people join in, matching their steps to those of the dancers. Sheer joy overflows in the circle. Tiare and I clasp hands and stamp our feet.

When Omo senses the flow of *mana* reaching a peak, he signals the drums to stop. We hear him call out to *Akua*, see him turn to face the sacred stone. Our arms open wide, palms turned to the heavens. "*Akua*, thank you for filling us with your light. Thank you for filling us with your power. Help us to go to the people of Tauati with love in our hearts. Help us to go unafraid. Help us to go in peace." We bow our heads low and murmur the same prayer.

On Omo's signal, the drums start a more frenzied beat. He shouts, "Let us beseech *Akua* to bless our canoes." Cries of assent answer his call as everyone moves toward the river. I look around for Tanemao. Children skip by, their parents rushing to catch up. The elders follow close behind. Tiare, Omo, and the dancers have gone ahead to prepare the blessing ceremony. Maybe Tanemao is with them.

I start across the clearing, basking in the joy that permeates the air. At the sacred stone, a strange sensation halts me—cool water running along my leg. I reach down. My skin feels dry. When I take another step, everything in my sight whirls like a waterspout over the ocean. I close my eyes to stop the spinning.

I sink to my knees and collapse against the stone. My hands rest on the base, a huge, flat rock buried in the ground. Sights and sounds swirl through my mind. Tanemao, arms stretched forth, exhorts a gathering. I cannot hear his words over the cheers and cries of the people. His image wavers into the shape of *Mao*. The shark circles and circles in a tranquil bay, sunlight glinting on the tip of its fin.

I feel no fear. This vision must point to Tanemao's destiny. My heart quickens. One day, he will be a leader for our people

The vision of *Mao* gradually fades. I feel warm hands on my arms. I hear a soft voice. "Mahana, my beloved, are you all right?"

I open my eyes to see the lovely face of my Tiare. The warm glow of torchlight frames her head. She sits beside me, enfolds me in her arms. My body is limp with exhaustion, and I gladly lean against her. She strokes my cheek. "Was it a vision?"

"Tanemao. Have you seen him tonight?"

"Just before the ceremony, he was talking with Aimata."

"The vision . . . Tiare, we need not worry about Tanemao."

Tiare presses her smooth palm to my cheek. "You must talk with him soon."

When strength finally returns to my limbs, Tiare and I join the others who have begun feasting. They crowd around us, wondering if their healer needs healing. When they learn I have had a vision, they nod in relief. They know of my visions, how they leave me weak, that when the time is right I will share the revelation.

Families and friends fill their bellies with the fruits of their labors. Laughter fills the air as they talk story and watch the children play. Cups of *'awa* are passed around. Everyone relaxes to enjoy the spontaneous drumming and dancing. We roar as Omo and his mate strut the steps of a lovemaking chant. On the last line, he sweeps her up in his arms and carries her toward the jungle. She breaks free and pulls him back to go on dancing. Other couples join in. Tiare and I chuckle, predicting this night will bring our village a precious baby or two.

The celebration draws to a close as families drift off to their *fare*, couples murmur in the shadows, and the elders discuss the morning voyage. Omo reaches out to Tiare and me. Embracing us both at once, he speaks from his heart. "I feel sure our visit to Tauati will be a success. We go with the *mana* of great *Akua* and the powerful compassion of the Anuanua."

I clasp hands with Omo. "Old friend, your chanting lifts—" My praise for him is interrupted by shouts of alarm.

Aimata and the lookouts emerge from the dark jungle. They carry a sagging form. We hurry to meet them. I realize it is Tanemao. Aimata gasps for breath. "Mahana, I fear he has been mortally wounded."

"Get him into the long house. Tiare, bring my pack." I support Tanemao's head as we cross the clearing. I pray to *Akua*, to Tanemao's *'aumakua, Mao.* Give him strength. Help us save him. My life for his.

Omo sweeps away the leavings from the feast with one motion of his arm, and we gently place Tanemao on the mats. One look at his belly tells me that Aimata may be right. Blood gushes from a gaping wound. Pressing my fist into the jagged hole to staunch the flow, I look up at Aimata. "What happened?"

"We found him down river at the edge of the *taro* fields. He may have encountered a Tauati raiding party." Aimata holds out her hand. "This was lying beside him." I recognize Tanemao's bone knife.

Tiare returns with my pack. She pulls out folds of clean *tapa* and presses them into Tanemao's wound. Omo begins a chant as he splashes pure rain water on my hands and sprinkles Tanemao's body. I continue to call on *Mao* as I unwrap a packet of bone needles, select one, and with shaking hands, thread it with *olonā* fiber.

Tanemao moans and looks up at me with watery eyes. He whispers, and I bend low to hear what he is saying. "I am sorry, teacher. I wanted to protect our village."

"Tanemao, that doesn't matter now. You must drink." I watch as Aimata holds a bowl of *'awa* to his lips. My jaw is clenched tight. I struggle to deepen my breathing. The potent liquid will barely touch the pain of a wound so great.

Aimata moves behind Tanemao's head, places firm hands on his shoulders. Others restrain his arms and legs. I kneel at his side, hands positioned over his wound. On my signal, Tiare removes the *tapa* bandage. With one hand I press the edges of the wound together as I puncture the ragged flesh with the needle. So much blood wells up, I can no longer see the tissue I am trying to sew. Tiare presses again with the *tapa*. The cloth is soaked with blood. She pulls it away. I dive into the wound with my needle, trying to wrap a few stitches before the wound floods once more.

Tanemao cries out. Be strong, my boy. Just a little longer.

Tiare compresses the wound with fresh *tapa*, lifts it so that I can work my needle until it is drowned in blood, holds pressure again. The edges of the wound come together but the blood continues to flow. We place a poultice against Tanemao's belly and gently lift him to wrap lengths of *tapa* tightly around his torso.

Tiare and I place the sacred objects around Tanemao—feather, *kukui* nut, sea shell, and standing stone. I give Omo my gourd rattle. He has been chanting quietly and now lifts his voice to boom in the long house as he shakes the rattle.

I place one hand on Tanemao's torso, the other on his forehead, and suck in deep breaths all the way down to my belly. Green light swirls into my head—all the healing *mana* in the air, the earth, the plants around us. I continue to breathe as the *mana* builds in my body, though I feel Tanemao shivering under my hands. When every part of my being is filled with the healing power, I blow a great breath across his body, see the green light flowing from my body into his, pray, "Your light through me. Your light to heal Tanemao." I pray and send forth the light for countless breaths.

The last vibrations of *mana* leave my body. I look at Tiare. Her eyes meet mine. Tears well up and spill onto her cheeks. I take Aimata's place behind Tanemao's head. Omo helps me lift his shoulders onto my lap. The *tapa* wrap is completely soaked with blood. A sweet-sour smell fills the long house, my nostrils. The sickening smell from my childhood.

Tanemao opens his eyes, draws in a ragged breath. "They came tonight."

"Shhh, my son. You must rest."

Pain sends a spasm through his body, and he cries out. "I thought they might attack the gathering. We weren't ready for them." He bends his legs, trying to push himself up for an easier breath. Omo helps him lean against my chest. I wrap my arms around his shoulders and place my cheek against the side of his head.

I want to take his burden so he can be in peace. "Go on, Tanemao. Tell me everything."

"I know we were supposed to welcome them but . . . I was afraid they would take advantage of the celebration." Tanemao's breath gurgles in his throat.

I whisper in his ear. "Did they strike you first?"

His body trembles violently. His hands clench my arms. "No, no. They started toward the village. I . . . " Tanemao grips me so hard my arms ache. "I only wanted to distract them. As they passed by me, I stabbed the last man in the leg. I thought that would give me time. Time to run to the clearing and warn everyone." The pain makes him cry out again. He finishes through clenched teeth. "I could not get away." His dark eyes are wide, desperate. "Did they come?"

"No. They must have returned to Tauati."

"I have put everyone . . . in danger."

I feel his life ebbing away, his spirit slipping back to *Akua*. "All will be well. Now, you must rest."

The trembling is violent, his limbs quaking. Tanemao's words rush out on a last, bubbling breath. "Mahana, I am sorry." His grip releases, and his arms fall to his chest. The light in his eyes fades.

As Omo begins the chant to help Tanemao cross the rainbow, cries of *auwē*—the sound of mourning—fill the long house.

I whisper in Tanemao's ear, "You are well loved by your people. I love you."

My arms rock his limp body, once so strong and determined. My tears drop on his forehead. Tanemao, why has your spirit chosen to leave us? The vision in the clearing. I was certain you would take my place as the healer for our people. How could I have been so wrong, failed you so completely?

I clutch Tanemao to me. Grief washes through my whole being. And another stronger sensation. Fear. The violence we left behind has followed us here. The warriors of Tauati will return, no longer skulking in the dark, but overwhelming our village in the light of day. I look down at Tanemao's chest. Dark spirals, symbols of the Anuanua, stand out against flesh the color of bones left to dry in the sun. The shark tooth pendant rests in the hollow of his neck. Its gleaming surface is smeared with blood.

Fourteen

Sunny wakened to the roar of torrential rain pounding on the tin roof above her. Her arms ached as if she'd been paddling a canoe for hours. She looked down at her chest, half-expecting to see a wash of blood.

Marie stroked Sunny's arm. "I'm here."

Sunny curled on her side, gripped Marie's hand between both of hers. "Mahana's apprentice was killed. It was like being with Lani when she . . ." A flash of Lani's bruised face, breathing tube protruding from her mouth, tape anchoring it in place and distorting the smooth skin of her cheek, hit her like a fist to the stomach, robbed her lungs of air. She sat up to catch her breath and felt Marie's strong arms wrap around her.

"Lotta things on your mind. We'll have plenty time to talk, yeah? You rest."

Sunny shuddered at the sticky feeling on her skin, the sour taste in her mouth. "Marie, would you mind if I take a shower?"

Marie hoisted herself off the edge of the bed and shuffled over to the dresser. She pulled out a blue *mu'umu'u* splashed with red hibiscus flowers. "You wear this while I wash your clothes."

"You've done too much already."

"*A 'ole pilikia.* No problem."

Hot water streamed over her shoulders and back, soothed her aching arms. Sunny scrubbed every inch of her skin with soap. She let the water run on her head, into her mouth, swished and spit it out. Grief hunched in a dark recess of her mind. Grief for Mahana's loss. Grief for the loss of her best friend. She'd heard it a million times. You take it one day at a time, put one foot in front of the other. She couldn't even make one foot shuffle into a first step. One day seemed like months of paralyzing sorrow.

She slipped into the *mu'umu'u* and wandered out to the kitchen where Marie stirred milk into a steaming cup of coffee. A forlorn piece of toast from breakfast beckoned her. She polished it off in three bites.

"Journey work takes lotta energy," Marie said.

"Sounds like the rain stopped." Sunny absently brushed the crumbs from her hands and drifted through the front room toward the *lānai*, her mind wrapped in a fog. She sat in the wicker chair by the old icebox. Marie's hound got up from the far end of the *lānai* and plunked down against Sunny's feet. She scratched his bony head. The dog oozed into a full length stretch. She envied his total surrender to sleep.

Yellow finches flitted in the dripping, emerald foliage around the yard. Their hops created tiny rain showers, drops glittering in the sunshine. Chickens strutted in zigzag patterns feasting on the night crawlers flooded out of the ground. Funny how life rolled on even though she felt as if hers had come to a standstill.

The screen door creaked open. Marie plopped in her cane rocker beside Sunny and lit a Camel filter. "How you feel?"

"Like I've been crying for weeks."

"You have. Maybe not your eyes alla time. For sure your soul."

Sunny studied the pattern of flowers on the *mu'umu'u*, the bright colors a loud contrast to her pale skin. "Marie, why would an ancient Hawaiian healer come back as a white woman?"

"Many have had the privilege of living in *aloha*. They needed to get pushed out of the nest, like baby birds. Share that *aloha* with the rest of the world. *Alo* means presence. *Hā* means breath. Hawaiians believe that breath is connection to *Akua*. Breath is the presence of the divine. More and more people live in that connection, live the true spirit of *aloha*, we'll have peace, no more killing."

Sunny shook her head. How could she share something that she didn't even have for herself? There must be others who'd do a much better job at spreading *aloha*. Hell, Lani should have been the one.

Marie tamped her cigarette out in the can on top of the icebox and leaned forward as if to push herself up. She froze on the edge of her chair, head hanging low. "Sunny, don't think about why you. Think about what and how."

"What and how?"

"*Hele*."

Sunny followed Marie down the wooden steps and around to the back of the bungalow. A rustic gazebo made of bamboo poles and thatched palm fronds sheltered a wide area in the middle of the yard. Tools, gourd pots, mats, and what looked to Sunny like curly wood shavings littered the shady area. "What's all this?"

"I'm going to teach you Hina's craft Some people call it *tapa*. Hawaiians say *kapa*." Marie pointed to a pandanus mat. "Sit." She ran her hands through the wood shavings. "Bark of breadfruit tree. In olden days would've been the mulberry, *wauke*. Hard to get now." She held up a large scalloped shell and a sharp piece of stone. "We scrape away the soft inner bark and soak it in those pots over there. Sea water for two weeks to clean and soften."

With the shell, Marie demonstrated the scraping process and handed Sunny the stone. Sunny gripped one end of a piece of bark. She scraped downward with the stone. The soft pulp lifted, curled. The rough part of the wood scratched her knuckles. Her hand slipped, and she grazed her leg with the stone. The abrasion stung like a carpet burn. After working only a couple of strips, her fingers started to ache. "I guess it takes some time to get the hang of this."

"'*Ae*. Many years." Marie gathered up the pulpy ropes of inner bark, dunked them in a large ceramic pot. Then she moved to another seawater pot. She removed pieces of bark, lighter in color than the ones they'd been scraping, and laid them on a large stone resembling an anvil.

Sunny remembered the *kapa* making demonstration at Kauhale O Waimea on living history day. "This is when you beat the bark into cloth."

"'*Ae*." Marie handed Sunny a smooth wooden beater. It looked like a baseball bat for a one year old. Her voice lifted into a sing-song lilt. "Lots more work before it's cloth." She nodded for Sunny to begin pounding.

Sunny knew she lacked the correct technique when Marie took the beater from her and gave the pulpy mass a series of hard whacks. The bark started to spread out into a smooth strip. Marie handed her the beater. Sunny imitated her strokes. She stopped to examine the mass. "Looks pretty flat, huh?"

Marie just shook her head, waved a hand for Sunny to keep going.

After a while, Sunny's arms and upper back ached. "I need a break."

Marie inspected Sunny's strips. "*Maika'i*. We'll put these strips in the sun to dry and bleach." She poured two cups of fresh water from an insulated jug and handed one to Sunny. "Rest."

Sunny rubbed the muscles in her right shoulder and arm. "How did you learn this skill?"

"Passed down on my mother's side. When I was a little girl, my *tūtū* gave me a beater specially made for me."

"Mahana and his clan wore yellow *kapa* decorated with a fern pattern."

"Tell me about Mahana.'

"He cared deeply about his people, about their commitment to peace. He used breath and green light and . . . Energy. Some kind of energy to heal. Mahana loved celebrations." Sunny's words came out in a rush. "Tanemao was like his son. Mahana so wanted him to get the hang of the Anuanua's ways. But the guy was a rebel." Her pulse quickened. "And Mahana adored Tiare." She remembered their conversation the night they made love. "Marie, Mahana means sunlight."

Marie smiled.

"A thousand years. The same name."

They were quiet for a while. Sunny waved away a mosquito buzzing near her cheek. She still didn't have the answers to the what and how. Was she supposed to take a course in complementary medicine? Quit working in the OR and start a massage therapy practice? The mosquito landed on her arm. She slapped it and flicked the carcass off her skin. The way things were going at UM, she might have to do just that.

"Sunny, was there anyone in Mahana's life who's in your life now?"

"Tanemao and David Kaneko. They are so much alike. Tunnel vision. My way or no way. Incredibly frustrating personalities. They both possess excellent technical ability. You can't find a better cardiac surgeon than Kaneko. Is he back after a thousand years?"

"He may still have lessons to learn. In each lifetime we get a chance to do work that brings us closer to the divine."

Sunny drew a curl of dry bark through her fingers, feeling the rough texture. She pondered the man of long ago and the man who could spark her fury now. "It's strange. Tanemao was a skeptic questioning the beliefs of his people. A fish out of water. But David is right in the mainstream, skeptical of anything that isn't totally concrete."

"Each needing a teacher." Marie motioned Sunny over to another set of pots. "When the strips are dry, we soak them in fresh water for one week."

Sunny wrinkled her nose at the odor emanating from the pots. "Whew. Smells rotten."

"Fermented. Makes *kapa* stronger." Marie handed Sunny a different beater, rectangular, the sides grooved with a diamond pattern. "We put two strips together and pound. Keep overlapping strips and pounding until we have a piece of cloth."

Sunny gave the wet bark a couple whacks. The rancid smell made her lean back and take a breath. The Anuanua must have worked hard just to clothe themselves. She moved closer to the anvil and wielded the beater vigorously, determined to turn out a piece of *kapa* even if it measured a mere two inches.

They talked and took turns pounding. Marie asked, "Did you see Lani?"

Sunny added a strip and pounded the edges. "Mahana's mate, Tiare, was like Lani—soft spoken, patient, wise." But what did it matter? She needed her friend in this life time, right now. Sunny stopped pounding and looked directly at Marie. "This past life thing . . . the whole idea is so far-fetched."

"Lots of things we can't explain. How do young sea turtles find their way across hundreds of miles of ocean to their breeding grounds?"

Sunny tapped the beater against her palm. She'd read an article in a dive magazine on that amazing bit of marine biology. "Scientists think they follow an energy grid that surrounds the earth."

"Could be. Could be they know because they've been there before, in the bodies of their ancestors."

Sunny turned the beater over and over in her hand, studying the diamond pattern.

"Our spirit, our energy never goes away. Just takes a different form." Marie gently lifted the beater from Sunny's hand. "Past, present, future. All connected, just like the diamonds in this pattern."

"Seems like that energy is a river through time."

"*'Ae*. Each of us floats on that river. We can paddle our canoe upstream to see ourselves in the past. We can glide downstream to see ourselves in the future."

"Have you seen the next version of yourself?"

"*'Ae*."

Sunny, reluctant to probe for fear it would seem disrespectful, waited for Marie to say more.

The old woman silently inspected the *kapa*. She carefully lifted the twelve-inch square of cloth and placed it on a drying rack. "After the *kapa* bleaches in the sun, it'll be ready to decorate." Marie handed her a piece that had been through the final drying process. "Hold this up to the light. You can see the diamond pattern from the wood beater."

Sunny examined the square. "Like a watermark on stationary."

"*'Ae*. In olden days, clans each had their special imprint."

"This is tedious, back-breaking work."

Marie nodded. "A sacred honor."

Sunny pressed the sturdy *kapa* between her fingers. "I don't know how Mahana's story ended, if the Anuanua were able to keep the peace with their neighbors."

"When you most need the answers to your questions, they will come."

Marie lined up three jars filled with different-colored liquids. She poured a little from each jar into separate bowls. "Plant dyes used to decorate the *kapa*. Boiled *noni* root makes yellow. Brown comes from *kukui* nuts. Mangrove root gives red." Marie held up a crude brush made out of a dried pandanus fruit. "We brush or stamp the designs on the cloth. Same dyes can be used to color a whole piece of cloth. My ancestors made black *kapa* by soaking it in the mud of *kalo* patches."

Sunny ran her finger over the fuzzy brush end of the round, shriveled fruit. "*Taro* fields?"

Marie clucked her tongue as she stirred the liquid in the bowls. "You learning, girl." She selected a carved wood block out of a box, dipped it in brown dye, and pressed it down on the *kapa* square. "Getting the lessons of Mahana's life is like making a perfect piece of *kapa*. You must be willing to do the tedious, smelly work. Do it with patience and love." She held out the cloth. The edge of the *kapa* glowed with lacy ferns–the Anuanua motif. "*Ua pili māua.* We are all connected."

Sunny stared at the *kapa*.

With a deep groan, Marie hauled herself off the mat. She motioned for Sunny to follow and trudged back to the bungalow. In the living room, on a small table lay a piece of *kapa*. She handed the red rectangle to Sunny.

The cloth was covered with an intricate pattern of brown chevrons and solid black lines. "This is exquisite," Sunny said. "It must have taken you many hours."

"Lani made this *kapa*. I want you to have it."

Tears clouded Sunny's vision. "We lost her too soon."

Marie wrapped her arm around Sunny's shoulders. "Each one of us comes to this life to do certain things. When those things are *pau*, our spirit may choose to go home."

Sunny toted the bags from her car into Marie's kitchen. Wanting to repay Marie in some small way, she'd decided to grocery shop for dinner. Besides, she needed a break from their mind-bending focus on the intersection of her life and Mahana's.

"Look at all this." Marie beamed. "We gonna feast."

"I'll do the cooking so you can take it easy."

"Gonna spoil me."

Sunny whipped up a simple meal of fried rice with bits of sausage, steamed long beans, and papaya slices. After they ate, she cleaned up the kitchen and carried two bottles of beer out to the *lānai*.

Marie set a plate of dinner scraps in front of the old hound and plopped in her rocker. She took a swig of beer and lit a cigarette. "Hooey. I'm full as those fat hens."

The chickens huddled in the bushes around the yard, nesting for the night. Shades of peach and pearl gray streaked the eastern sky as the sun slipped past the mountains behind Marie's bungalow. A breeze ruffled the fur on the dog's back, tickled the skin on Sunny's arms.

"Marie, I'm going home tonight."

"You can stay."

"I feel welcome here. But I have a lot to think about. The what and how."

"Most important thing. Take time every day to be quiet. Breathe. Listen to your inner voice. Be open to your *'aumākua*. Let Mahana speak to you."

Sunny squeezed Marie's hand. "Thank you so much for helping me sort this all out."

"*'Ae. Mālama pono a hui hou.*"

"What do those words mean?"

"Take care of yourself until we're together again."

"I'll be back, Marie. I need to decorate that piece of *kapa* we made."

"It'll be waiting for you." Tears glinted in Marie's eyes. She placed her hand on Sunny's cheek. "Don't be scared. You have everything you need to handle what will come."

Fifteen

Sunshine slanted across Sunny's bed. She pushed herself into a long cat stretch and headed for the kitchen. Munching a bagel, she carried a cup of coffee to her desk. Jack wasn't expecting her in the OR until early afternoon. She wanted to use this time alone to analyze her dreams of Mahana and the discussions with Marie.

Skipper arched his sleek ebony body across the entire writing surface of the desk. Keko curled up in Sunny's lap. Slowly pulling a writing tablet out from under Skipper, Sunny laughed when he didn't move. "I missed you guys too." She scratched Keko behind one ear and searched for a pencil.

Sunny kept thinking about Marie's last piece of advice. "You have everything you need to handle what will come." What was coming? Was there something in Mahana's life that would help her keep Kaneko and his posse from slashing all that was good at UM? She stared at the blank paper. Maybe if she wrote down everything she could remember about Mahana and his people, an answer would emerge.

Sunny started with Mahana's treatment of the hemorrhaging woman. She tried to capture every detail of the ritual—the chant, the sacred objects, the shimmering light. After an hour, she'd covered six pages with recollections and impressions. She leaned back in her chair. Keko looked up with sleepy blue eyes. "Hey, princess." Sunny stroked Keko's snow leopard fur and reviewed the pages.

The four questions the Anuanua used to plan their strategy for relations with their neighbors seemed familiar to Sunny. She remembered every word with sharp clarity, as if she'd been asking those questions for years. What knowledge do we need? What can we do to bring more light to this situation? How can we show compassion? How can we ensure a solid foundation for the future? She reasoned that the Anuanua asked these questions in much the same way the UM staff constantly checked the criteria for patient care—factors such as safety, accuracy, and emotional support. The criteria maintained their goal of excellent care. Mahana's questions were designed to guarantee the goal of peace.

Sunny stroked Skipper's panther-like head. She wondered what bringing more light entailed. It probably didn't mean shedding more light on a situation. They already had a question about gaining knowledge. The man named Omo had related bringing more light to fostering good relations with the neighboring island. Maybe it meant simply doing the right thing.

What if UM considered these questions and the impact of the merger? Maybe the execs would realize things wouldn't change for the better on their current course. That wasn't going to happen, not with Kaneko, Darwin, and the Texans. Sunny groaned, tossed her pencil on the desk. She was never going to figure out what her dreams meant. The what and how. She might be Mahana reincarnated, but she sure didn't possess his wisdom, let alone his *mana*. Marie's words rolled around in her head. "The answers will come. Just take time to breathe and be quiet."

Sunny positioned her feet flat on the floor, straightened in her chair, and took a couple of deep belly breaths. She closed her eyes, pictured Mahana's face, took two more breaths, blowing the air out her pursed lips. Concentrate. What if she shared the questions with Katherine? They might be able to wangle a meeting with the board. Stop thinking. Concentrate on Mahana. Deep breath. Let the thoughts float away on tiny boats. If it's boats, don't you need to imagine some water? Damn. She resettled in her chair, took two more breaths, focused on Mahana's deep set eyes.

She jumped at the shrill warble of her beeper. Jack wouldn't be paging her unless something major had come up. She dialed the direct line. "Jack, this is Sunny."

"I need you to come in." Jack sounded out of breath. "We have an emergency. Kaneko's going ballistic. I'll fill you in when you get here."

"On my way." Sunny jumped up, dumping a yowling Keko to the floor. "So what's up with Kaneko?" she asked Skipper as she grabbed her purse. He blinked and licked a paw. She gave his tail a tweak. "You have the con, buddy. Lord knows when I'll be back."

⊕   ⊕   ⊕

Sunny heard the tirade as soon as the automatic doors whooshed open into the surgical suite. She recognized Kaneko's voice and felt an instant churn in her stomach.

David Kaneko, face flushed, had Jack backed into a corner of the scheduling office. "We need to get this case started. Now!"

Jack's rigid posture let Sunny know the supervisor struggled to control his anger. "Dr. Kaneko, we're calling—"

"I don't want to hear any goddamn excuses." Kaneko grabbed Jack's shirt, crumpling the material in his fist. "Do you understand what I'm saying? We can't wait another hour."

Jack clamped his hand on Kaneko's arm, forcefully disengaging the surgeon's grip on his shirt. Raising a fist, Jack took a step forward as if to throw a punch.

Sunny stepped between the two men. "Excuse me. What's the problem here?"

Kaneko turned his wrath on Sunny, the deep cleft in his chin punctuating a sneer. "I'll tell you what the problem is. We need to do an emergency case, and there's no staff available." The volume and pitch of his ranting rattled the office window.

They stood in a face-off. Sunny took in his angry, waiting stare, glanced at his chest. For an instant, she felt as if she'd just downed two shots of vodka on an empty stomach. Suspended on a fine gold chain and centered in the v-neck of Kaneko's scrub shirt, a polished shark's tooth gleamed. She gripped the counter to halt the dizzy sensation.

"Did you hear me, Ms. Lyon?" He emphasized Ms. with a condescending tone. "Ms. Lyon?"

Sunny blinked, took a deep breath. "Dr. Kaneko, we can't solve anything when you're yelling. Can we please discuss this calmly?"

"There's nothing to discuss. The staff should be here when we need them."

"We're running all ten rooms," Jack growled. "The first-call people are already here doing an aneurysm repair. There aren't any second-call people. We axed them to save money."

Kaneko pounded the countertop and glared at Sunny. "You need to get off your ass and get a surgical team in here now."

"Dr. Kaneko, your abusive behavior is preventing us from finding a way to get this case started." Sunny folded her arms. "Stop it now, or I'll hold you responsible for the delay."

Kaneko leaned forward, his face inches away from Sunny's, his voice menacing. "What's delaying this case is your inept management."

Feeling rage rise in her like an elevator rigged with a jet engine, she placed both her hands squarely on the surgeon's chest and pushed him backward. "You'll have your surgical team." She gestured with her thumb toward the door behind her. "Now get the hell out of here!"

Silence swelled in the room and flooded the corridor. Sunny's brain registered the incredulity frozen on Jack's face, the muscles bulging at Kaneko's jaw line, and the shock of her own behavior. She clenched her hands to control the trembling.

Behind her, Mike Jansen's steady voice broke the stillness. "David, Sunny and Grace will take care of this. Let's go get a cup of coffee." The anesthesiologist grasped Kaneko's arm.

Kaneko slammed his fist on the countertop again. "Goddamn it."

Mike kept his hand on Kaneko. "Come on. Let them do their jobs." As he guided the surgeon out of the office, Mike glanced back at Sunny. His expression said, "Better get this settled, or there'll be hell to pay."

Grace Pukui squeezed past the two men into the office. Sunny figured Kaneko had already gone to the chief of surgery to complain about the situation. Grace had arrived to light some fires. "Sunny, how soon can I get started?"

"This is your case? I thought Kaneko was the surgeon. What's going on?"

Jack tugged his shirt down, smoothing out a fistful of wrinkles. "Kaneko's niece has an atrial septal defect. The echocardiogram and a neurological consultation indicate emboli."

Sunny remembered the little girl running after Kaneko in the park, the dark crescents under her eyes. Young children could experience a sudden crisis related to a hole in the wall between the chambers of the heart. The opening, sometimes undetected for years, caused blood to flow in the wrong direction. The turbulence of that flow, in rare instances, triggered the formation of clots.

Grace said in a calm voice, "We need to get Kimberly into the OR as soon as possible."

Those tiny pieces of thickened blood could travel from the heart through arteries up to the brain, causing a stroke. Sunny turned to Jack. "What about people who have the day off?"

"No one's answering the phone."

Sunny stepped out into the hallway and studied the day's schedule on the white board. Grace and Jack stood on either side of her. "How soon will we have a cardiac scrub nurse freed up?"

Jack pointed to the details on the board for rooms five and seven. "It's neck and neck between the aneurysm and the coronary artery bypass in five. Both scrubs are going to need a quick break before another long procedure."

Sunny turned to Grace. "Do you have an assistant lined up?"

Grace nodded. "And Mike for anesthesia."

"What about the perfusionists?"

Jack paused, brushing a hand across his crew cut. "One of the perfusionists in five can set up the pump."

"Okay. I'll scrub in to set the case. Jack, you open the packs for me. When one of those scrubs is available, I'll circulate."

Grace headed out of the suite, calling over her shoulder, "Thanks, Sunny. I'll let the family know."

Sunny tossed her purse in her locker, hung up her street clothes, and pulled on scrub pants and shirt. She covered her hair with a cloth cap and slipped into her rubber clogs. As she straightened out the ties on a paper mask, she strode briskly down the corridor, mentally ticking off the special sutures and instruments Grace would need. She glanced through the window of the operating room door and saw Jack racing around opening packs of sterile supplies.

The splash of warm water streaming into the scrub sink drenched her arms and settled her heart rate. She unwrapped a plastic scrub brush, pumped clear pink soap from the dispenser onto the bristles. As she scrubbed each finger, she thought about the confrontation with Kaneko in the scheduling office. The ferocity of her response alarmed Sunny. She couldn't recall ever losing her cool like that. In all her years spent in operating rooms, no surgeon had ever rattled her so much. Why Kaneko?

She remembered the blood-smeared shark tooth in the hollow of Tanemao's neck. Sunny shook her head and concentrated on her hands. She scrubbed her palms. If she and Kaneko really were connected by a past life, that could explain the strange effect he had on her. She moved the brush in circular strokes on the backs of her hands and up each forearm to the elbow. Dropping the brush in the sink, she rinsed away the lather. She held her hands up at chest level so the water dripped off her elbows and pushed open the operating room door with her shoulder, thankful that she wouldn't have to deal with Kaneko again for hours.

The cold air of the operating room soothed her as she carefully dried her hands and arms with a sterile towel and donned a gown. Jack fastened the ties at the back of the gown as Sunny snapped on latex gloves. He pointed to a large metal basin. "I put all your blades, sutures, cautery, and suction tubing in there. Let me know when you're ready, and I'll pour your solutions. I'm going to call Pediatric ICU to see if the staff is ready to bring the patient down to surgery."

Sunny rested her hands on the big steel instrument table and sighed. The room seemed reassuringly familiar and yet, surreal. Lani would never again be here with her. She remembered her friend's dark eyes smiling over the surgical mask, the way a wisp of Lani's long hair always escaped the bouffant cap at the back of her neck, the calming effect she had on surgeons like Kaneko. Sunny blinked tears away and reached for a large tray of instruments.

The energy level in the room surged as team members hustled to prepare for the case. The perfusionist moved the heart-lung machine, festooned with plastic bags of solutions and metal clamps, into place across the room. Mike checked the tubing and valves on his anesthesia machine. He popped open vials of medication, drawing up solutions into syringes and labeling them with color-coded tags. "David's a real hothead, isn't he?

Jack tucked the leads for a variety of monitoring equipment under the mattress of the operating table, within easy reach when the time came to place them on Kimberly's body. "Shouting matches are the routine when he's here, even when it's not about his niece."

Grace entered the room. She slapped the patient's x-rays up on the view box. "I just talked with David. He's calmed down. Apparently, his niece has been having problems with respiratory infections. She's had episodes of shortness of breath and tachycardia. The confusion, blurry vision, and slurred speech started this morning. I think David feels badly that he didn't make sure she saw a pediatric cardiologist sooner."

Sunny mounted tiny curved needles onto delicate titanium holders, carefully straightening out the curves in suture finer than a human hair. The exacting task couldn't keep her from feeling a twinge of self-reproof. Had she been too hard on Kaneko? No. It was her job to set a limit on tantrums in the OR. But guilt could easily turn into rage. She'd been dealing with that same metamorphosis ever since the rally.

Jack stood in front of her table with a clipboard. "Ready?"

His voice jarred Sunny out of the now all too familiar litany of ways she could have saved Lani's life. "What?" She noticed the clipboard. "Oh, ready."

They counted instruments, suture needles, scalpel blades, and sponges. Then Jack left to bring Kaneko's niece to the operating room.

With her hands wrapped in a sterile towel, Sunny watched the perfusionist tap air out of yards of clear plastic tubing as the heart-lung machine circulated bright red blood. Her eyes scanned the room. Cabinets with glass doors held neatly arranged solution bottles and clear plastic packages. On Mike's anesthesia machine a rainbow of fluorescent lines streamed across monitor screens. Precise rows of clamps, scissors, forceps, and carefully placed bundles of towels and sterile drapes covered the instrument table. The perfect orderliness of the operating room had always given Sunny a sense of security and control.

She stared at the diffused white outline of the heart on the chest x-ray and pondered the out of control shift in her life. A deranged man, trying to get revenge at a rally had taken her friend's life in a frenzy of gunfire. Her clashes with Kaneko had escalated from differences in point of view to rapid-fire accusations and physical confrontation. Words floated up from the past, Mahana's words. "We are all just a breath away from violence."

The heavy door creaked open, and the scrub tech from room five came in, hand outstretched for a sterile towel. With a build resembling a giant redwood trunk and a deep Louisiana drawl, Damon exuded a relaxed air that even the worst surgical nightmares couldn't shake. The male surgeons especially liked working with him because he could discuss every sport, rattling off all the latest standings and player statistics. Sunny liked Damon because he could keep up with any surgeon, getting them what they wanted when they wanted it. "David's out front quizzing Grace on how she's fixing to do the repair."

Sunny held up a sterile gown, and Damon slipped his dark-brown-tree-branch arms into the sleeves. "Sounds like our man. And Grace?"

Damon jammed hands as wide as the broadest sycamore leaf into gloves Sunny stretched open. "Amazing Grace." He chuckled. "Gave him a step-by-step explanation."

Sunny pulled off her gown and gloves. She fastened the ties on Damon's gown. "I just hope this goes without a hitch."

"A doc's relative?" Damon snorted. "Anything that can go wrong will most certainly go wrong."

The door slammed open as Mike and Jack guided the gurney into the room. Nearly hidden by blankets and portable monitoring equipment, the little girl lay very still. Her brown eyes, fringed with thick lashes, opened wide when Sunny took her hand. "Hi, Kimberly. Are you doing okay?"

The girl shook her head. "My name's Kimmy." She sounded tipsy, words running together. She closed her eyes, clutched a frayed cloth bunny to her chest. Her eyes snapped open and she twisted on the gurney to stare around the room. "Uncle David?"

Sunny stroked Kimmy's forehead. "Honey, he's waiting for you right outside. You'll see him as soon as you get out of surgery."

The little girl gave her a stoic nod.

Sunny disconnected monitor leads and untangled intravenous tubing. "Kimmy, we're going to move you over to this big table. Just put your arms around my neck." Sunny scooped up the little girl, and Jack slid the gurney away. She gently placed Kimmy on the operating table.

Mike adjusted a small foam pillow under Kimmy's head. He wrapped a child-sized cuff around her arm to measure her blood pressure. "Pretty soon you're going to get real sleepy."

Kimmy's eyes narrowed as she looked up at Mike. "No more shots."

Mike held up a length of IV tubing. "That's right. I'm going to put the medicine right in here." He attached a syringe to the line and slowly injected the drug. Mike rested his hand against one side of the little girl's head and spoke softly by her ear. "When you wake up you'll be all better. You're heart will be just like new, and soon you'll feel really great."

"Would you like to listen to some music? Little Mermaid?" Sunny asked.

Kimmy blinked, her eyes large and bleary. She nodded in slow motion.

Sunny adjusted a small headset against the little girl's ears. Kimmy yawned and gradually relaxed her grip on the bunny. Mike tipped her chin up, placing a mask over her nose and mouth to assist her breathing.

The team gathered around the little girl. Grace and Sunny held her small hands. The perfusionists came to the foot of the table, gently resting their hands on her legs. Damon and Grace's assistant stood behind Sunny. They paused for a moment. Grace looked around the circle at each face. "Each one of us is blessed with the skills to help heal this child. Each one of us is an important part of this team." Grace caught Sunny's eye and winked.

Sunny nodded. "Let's give Kimmy and each other our best."

"Right on," Damon whispered and turned back to his instrument table.

Grace and the second surgeon went out to the scrub sinks. Sunny assisted Mike as he slipped a breathing tube into Kimmy's trachea. She inserted a catheter in the child's bladder, wrapped a cautery-grounding pad around her thigh, and tucked her thin arms securely down at her sides. She washed the skin on Kimmy's torso with orange iodine solution. Damon covered the little body with sterile towels and drapes until the only part exposed was a rectangle around her sternum.

The atmosphere, normally buoyed with humorous conversation and the beat of soft rock, remained subdued. Grace possessed a command of nearly as much sports trivia as Damon, but she was quiet as they adjusted overhead lamps and clipped suction tubing and cautery to the drapes. Only the hushed strains of Brahms filled the room.

Grace and her assistant, with Damon slapping one instrument after another into their hands, made the incision and split Kimmy's sternum with a small saw blade. After opening the pericardial sack around the heart, Grace inserted a cannula into the tiny aorta and two more into the vena cavae, vessels carrying deoxygenated blood to the lungs and back to the heart.

"Let's go on bypass," Grace directed.

Gradually, the heart-lung machine took over the work of circulating blood through Kimmy's body. A chilled drug solution injected directly into the aorta and icy saline poured into the chest cavity stopped the beating of her heart.

Grace made an incision in the right atrium. Gently holding back the tissue with tiny retractors, she examined the hole in the septum. "There are still a few clots in here." She carefully removed the clumps of coagulated blood with tweezer-like forceps. "The opening in the septum is four centimeters."

Grace fashioned a patch for the hole using a section of tissue removed from the pericardium. With the same delicate stitches a tailor uses to fashion a fine piece of silk, she sewed the patch in place. As she tacked down the last centimeter, she said, "The patch is almost in. We'll have the atrium sutured in five minutes. Let's start warming."

The heart-lung machine warmed the circulating blood and, along with a heating pad underneath Kimmy, elevated her body temperature. As her temperature neared normal, the child's heart stirred, first in erratic spasms, and then gradually in rhythmic contractions. With the concentration and composure of a tightrope walker, Grace closed the incision in the atrium of the beating heart—a feat akin to crossing the high wire in a strong wind.

"Mike, are you ready?" Grace asked.

Mike stood up behind the sterile screen at Kimmy's head and looked at Grace. "It's a go on my end."

Grace directed the perfusionist. "Decrease pump flow."

Mike kept an eye on all the monitors around him. "Blood pressure is falling. I need dobutamine and dopamine drips."

"Getting them ready now." Sunny prepared the medications to elevate Kimmy's blood pressure. The child's heart wasn't strong enough to take over the work of circulating the blood. If they couldn't wean her off the heart-lung machine, they would lose her.

The click and whir of the heart-lung machine replaced all conversation as they waited for the blood pressure to rise. Grace never rushed the process. The surgeon wanted to give Kimmy's heart every opportunity to take over.

Sunny hurried around the room, carrying drugs to Mike, opening sterile supplies for Damon, and attending to reams of paperwork. She thought how impossible it would be to tell David his niece had died on the operating table. She groaned inwardly when she heard Grace's next order.

"Give me the paddles."

Damon handed Grace two paddles that looked like giant metal lollypops. He passed the cables attached to the ends of the paddles to Sunny. Moving the defibrillator closer to the operating table, Sunny plugged the cables in and set the voltage level. "Ready."

Grace placed the flat, round ends directly against the sides of the heart. She pushed the button on each paddle simultaneously to deliver the electrical current. Watching closely for the quivering movement of the heart to convert to a steady beat, she removed the paddles. After a few moments, Grace announced, "We've got a good rhythm. Let's try coming off bypass."

Sunny stood beside Mike. They both peered over the sterile screen down into Kimmy's chest. Her heart, looking dark pink and healthy, pumped with strong contractions. Grace directed the perfusionist to slowly turn the pump down until it stopped. As the perfusionist announced the decreasing flow of the heart-lung machine, the heart spasmed until it resembled a bag of undulating worms.

Grace sighed. "Pump back up." She grabbed the paddles. "Defib." She pushed the buttons. Kimmy's heart jogged into a normal rhythm. Grace looked up at Mike. "Let's start a lidocaine drip."

As Sunny moved to prepare the medication to reduce the sensitivity of the heart, Jack came into the room. "David's ready to barge in. What do you want me to tell him."

Sunny stood next to Jack. "First we had problems with her pressure. Now she keeps fibrillating."

Grace moved away from the operating table and stretched her back, keeping her gaze riveted on Kimmy's chest. "Tell him we're getting ready to come off bypass. Don't let him come back here."

"Will do." Jack rushed out of the room.

Grace stepped back to the operating table. "I want to give her a couple of minutes." While they waited, Grace gently checked around the heart for bleeding. Finally she said, "Okay, we have a strong, regular beat." She signaled to the perfusionist to turn the pump down.

"Three's a charm," Mike muttered. As the heart-lung machine slowed to off, he kept an eye on cardiac rhythm and blood pressure.

"Come on, girl," Sunny urged silently. "You can do it."

When Kimmy's heart kept up a steady, powerful beat, Grace moved into high gear. "Okay, let's finish up and get her to Peds ICU."

For the next half-hour, the team flew through the final movements of the surgical ballet. The surgeons rapidly closed the chest. Damon and Sunny recounted all sponges and suture needles. Sunny readied the equipment they needed for transport. Mike continued to monitor rhythm and pressure to make sure the child remained stable. They removed the sterile drapes, applied dressings to the chest incision, covered Kimmy with a gown and warm blankets, and carefully transferred her into an ICU bed. Grabbing the paperwork, Sunny followed Mike and Grace as they rolled the bed out of the operating room.

Sunny saw Kaneko and Jack talking in the corridor. Kaneko rushed toward them. He looked worn out, more like an anxious uncle than a cocky surgeon. As she helped Mike steer the bed toward the elevator, Grace gave Kaneko a quick report. "The next few hours are going to be dicey."

Sixteen

Fourteen hours later, on anvil-like feet, Sunny trudged up three flights of stairs to Peds ICU. Her legs ached and her temples throbbed. During the night, they'd rushed Kimmy back to surgery twice for bleeding. The failure of the body's clotting mechanism had caused repeated hemorrhaging. After one last check on Kimmy's status, Sunny planned to catch a few hours of sleep at home.

At the nurse's station, she sank into a chair and waited for the unit supervisor to finish her telephone conversation. She stared at the array of monitors on the wall, prayed for good news. The bright lines and blips endlessly marching across the screens threatened to lull her into a stupor.

Tara rolled her chair next to Sunny. With curly red hair and a freckled nose, she looked more like an aging Orphan Annie than a twenty-five-year veteran of intensive care units. In her brusque Aussie twang, Tara never minced words. "She's circling the drain, Sunny."

"More bleeding?"

Tara flipped the pages in Kimmy's chart. "That seems to be under control for the moment. We're keeping her on the lidocaine drip because we've had to defibrillate twice."

"Doesn't her heart just need time to calm down?"

"Sometimes that's the case. But that's not the worst of it. We're concerned about her neurological function. The child's showing signs of paralysis on her right side."

Sunny frowned. "A clot could have broken off before we cross-clamped the aorta."

Tara closed the chart. "That could have caused a stroke." She shook her head. "There's not much margin for risk with these little tykes. The blood pressure drops, and the brain doesn't get enough oxygen." Tara tossed the chart on the desk and stood. "Hell, the combination of drugs and transfusions can cause neurological deficits."

Sunny rose from her chair thinking about the grim implications—the life-long challenge of living with a disability, life as a vegetable, death. "Have you seen Kaneko?"

Tara motioned to the room across the hall. "He's in there. Kimmy's parents went to get something to eat."

Sunny paused in the doorway. Kimmy, barely visible in a nest of tubes and wires, looked as frail as a baby bird. Kaneko leaned forward in a chair by the bed. Rumpled hair, dark creases under his eyes, and a day's growth of beard made him look much older than forty.

Sunny spoke softly. "Hi."

He looked surprised to see her. "You're still here." His voice sounded as if he'd been yelling at a basketball game. Sunny wondered if he'd been yelling at the ICU nurses.

"I wanted to check on Kimmy before I headed home."

Kaneko pushed back the chair and moved around to the foot of the bed. "Thank you for all the time you put in today." He sounded sincere.

Sunny walked to the bed and stood directly in front of him. For an instant, she flashed on her hands flat against his chest pushing him backwards. Every part of her winced. She gently touched his shoulder. "David, I'm so sorry."

He glanced at her hand, and she quickly moved it away. "So am I." He turned toward the window. The sky glowed with the first blush of dawn.

Sunny wished she could somehow ease his misery. "It's not your fault."

He turned back, face devoid of expression, took up his post by the bed.

Sunny rested her hand on the bedrail. "Why don't you go home. Get something to eat, a shower, some sleep. I'll stay here. We'll call you if anything changes."

He arched an eyebrow. "I appreciate your offer. I need to be here." The return of his usual arrogant tone dismissed her.

Sunny shrugged, turned to leave. She looked back and saw David slumped in the chair. He seemed focused on somewhere other than a place in the room. It must have been wrenching for him to come face to face with his own helplessness. Sadness formed a lump in her throat as she started the long walk back to her office.

She closed the door and aimlessly shuffled the piles on her desk. With her grief over Lani's death still fresh, Sunny felt David's agony in her bones. She couldn't stand to watch another young life slip away.

She leaned back in her chair. A few minutes of quiet was all she needed to think more clearly. She closed her eyes, yawned, relaxed against the weight of exhaustion. The scene of Mahana healing the hemorrhaging woman reeled out against her eyelids. Green light shimmered around the images. Mahana's voice intoned a prayer to *Akua*.

The day dream vanished as quickly as it had come, leaving Sunny's mind in a sprint. She popped up, searched the metal filing cabinet beside her desk, and retrieved an article torn from a nursing journal. She scanned the pages. A study on distance healing revealed that patients who were prayed for by people they didn't know had lower complication rates. She twisted the paperclip. Mahana's ritual included much more than prayer and no study to back it up.

Sunny bit her lip. Attempting a healing ritual to save Kimmy's life required a giant leap of faith. She didn't know if she had the conviction or the courage. Would David and his family be able to suspend their total reliance on cardiac medicine? She rubbed her gritty eyes, feeling the assault of twenty-four sleepless hours. At this point, what did they have to lose? They'd run out of conventional options. Maybe Kimmy was the reason for all of her dreams of Mahana. She flipped through her Rolodex cards and dialed Marie.

Marie listened to the details of the situation and agreed to help. Sunny needed to find a way to get her to the Center. She turned the Rolodex, found another number, dialed the first three digits, and hung up the telephone. Only a few days had passed since she'd seen him, overwhelmed by sorrow. That image shifted into one of him embracing the woman he adored, a halo of sunlight illuminating her waterfall of dark hair. Lani would urge her to make the call.

His voice sounded raspy. "Hey."

"Pete, this is Sunny. How are you?"

"Missing her bad."

"Me too." A long silence made Sunny think the line had gone dead. "Have you been spending time with Kai?"

"He's away at football camp."

Silence. Sunny cleared her throat. "Anything doing with the band?"

"Nope."

Sunny leaned forward, resting her elbows on the desk. She cradled her forehead in one hand. Grief and small talk didn't mix. "I have a favor to ask of you." He didn't respond. She forced herself to continue. "There's a very sick little girl here at UM. We've done everything possible, and it looks like she's not going to make it. I called Marie for help. Would you be willing to bring her to the Center?"

"Sunny, I . . ." His voice faded, as if he'd put down the receiver.

"You wouldn't have to stay." More silence. "Please. I can't think of anyone else to call."

He let out a sigh. "Okay, we'll be there in an hour."

"I'll meet you in the lobby. Pete, thanks."

"No big thing." He clicked off.

"Hang on, Kimmy," she whispered. "You stay alive, little girl."

Sunny scoured her surroundings for objects like the ones Mahana used in his ritual. In the courtyard, she found a finch's golden feather to symbolize air. She grabbed a seashell off her bookcase to represent water and feminine energy. Digging in her purse, she came up with a book of matches to symbolize fire. An advertisement on the cover caught her eye—Hit The Wall. Sunny smiled, thinking of how she and Lani had sipped beer there and pondered the complexities of life. Girl, you're probably having a good laugh. Your skeptical friend is finally giving all you believed to be real and powerful a go.

She looked at the three objects on her desk and wondered what she could use to represent earth and masculine energy. There wasn't time to find an oblong, standing stone. She remembered the plants in the surgery waiting area and hurried down the hall. A small pot in the corner of the room held an anthurium. Protruding out from red heart-shaped leaves, the yellow flower spikes looked like tiny penises.

After gathering all the objects into a large metal basin on her desk, Sunny went up to Peds ICU. Kimmy's condition hadn't improved. She peeked in the door of the child's room. Betty sat erect in a chair at the bedside, stroking her daughter's arm. Mark, Kimmy's father, stood on the other side of the bed. His hand fidgeted with a corner of the sheet. David leaned against the wall, staring out the window. Despair hung like fog in the room.

Sunny checked her watch, let Tara know about her plan, and headed for the main lobby. She scanned the people coming and going. Marie and Pete hadn't arrived. She took a seat facing the front doors, tapped her fingers on the chair. A strange mix of excitement and dread swirled in her gut. What if David and his family wanted no part of a healing ritual? What did she actually need to do for the procedure? What if their effort was in vain? What if word got out about what went on in Peds ICU? She remembered the uproar over a Laotian family in a California hospital where she worked. They came into the pediatrics department with a priest and a live chicken to heal their baby. The infection control nurse went nuts.

She spied the scar on the tile floor where the base of the aquarium had been removed. If the family wanted a healing ritual for Kimmy, damn anyone who'd try to get in their way. UM was a place where all kinds of life-saving therapies should happen.

Sunny looked up and saw Marie and Pete coming through the front doors. Marie wore a woven pandanus hat squashed down on the crown of her head and a brown canvas bag slung over one shoulder. Her *mu'umu'u*, green ferns on a white background, billowed around her. She hugged a carved drum to her chest. Pete walked beside Marie. His dark hair, flowing past his shoulders, lifted in the breeze. Together, they towered over almost everyone else in the lobby, both in stature and countenance.

Sunny hurried to meet them. "Thank you so much for coming." She hugged Marie, drum and all.

The old woman flashed a broad smile filled with perfect, white teeth. Sunny kissed her cheek.

"How's it, my *keiki*?" Marie asked.

"Better, now that you're here."

Sunny turned to Pete. His brown shirt and khaki shorts hung loosely on him, his robust frame noticeably diminished. Pete's face, covered with a full growth of dark beard, looked drawn. The twinkle in his eyes had disappeared. The geometric tattoos on the golden skin of his upper arms were the only reminders of the musician she'd met at The Wall.

Pete leaned down to hug her. "Sunny, good to see you."

Her heart ached to see him in such a miserable state. "I'll take Marie home so you can go."

Marie touched Pete's shoulder. "He'll stay. We need this big *kanaka*."

Sunny led them to a small waiting room off the lobby. Pete took the drum from Marie and carefully placed it in the corner of the room. Sunny moved three chairs into a tight circle. "Kimmy's uncle is Dr. David Kaneko. There's a strong possibility that he'll reject the idea of a healing ritual."

Pete leaned forward, resting his arms on his thighs. "Could make a surgeon feel like a failure."

Marie took off her sun hat. Her silvered hair tumbled around her face. "This man needs to know it's not his fault. It's about the work of spirit together with his medicine."

Sunny nodded emphatically.

Marie looked directly into Sunny's eyes. "You truly believe that?"

"Yes, but . . . Yes, I do."

Marie talked Sunny and Pete through the steps of the ritual, making clear what each of them needed to do. Sunny listened hard. She wished she'd remembered to bring pen and paper.

Marie asked them to link hands. Drawing in a deep breath, she murmured a prayer, "*Akua*, walk with us. Help us to bring love and healing to this precious *keiki* and her *'ohana*. We are family, each other's *'ohana* on this earth. *Mahalo*." Marie slowly rose from her chair, spreading her big arms wide. Sunny and Pete stood, and the three of them embraced.

Sunny wanted to take in the words of Marie's prayer, relax into the arms of these powerful friends. But her muscles tensed. Her mind struggled to remember all the details of the ritual.

Marie placed her hands on Sunny's cheeks. "Your spirit will remember."

Sunny asked Marie and Pete to wait in the hallway outside Kimmy's room. The scene hadn't changed. Except now David sat in a chair in the corner, staring at the floor.

"Excuse me," Sunny said softly. Mother, father, and uncle all looked up at once, jarred out of their weary vigil. "Could I please have a moment with you? There's someone I'd like you to meet. Someone who might be able to help Kimmy."

David jumped up. "I'll handle this."

Betty, a frown deeply creasing the lines between her eyebrows, rose from her chair. "Hello, Sunny. David, I think Mark and I need to hear this too." She grabbed her husband's hand. "Come on, Mark."

Tara stepped in to watch Kimmy as the family followed Sunny out into the corridor. She introduced them to Marie and Pete, noticed David's familiar arch of the eyebrow. This wasn't going to be easy.

They gathered in the care conference room, everyone settling in chairs around the table except David. Sunny patted the chair next to her. "You can sit here if you like."

He folded his arms and leaned back against the wall.

Sunny stared at David, decided to ignore him. She'd gotten to know Betty and Mark during the many times she'd come out of the OR to give them updates on their daughter. Now, she would focus on them, just as she would attend to the parents of any sick child in her care. "You both know we want to do everything we can for Kimmy—"

"We're losing her." Betty covered her face with her hands.

Mark put his arm around her shoulders. "Please don't . . ."

Betty glared at him, tears streaming down her round face, dripping off her chin. "Mark, our little girl is dying."

Sunny stood up and came around the table to sit beside her. "Marie can help us bring healing energy to Kimmy."

Betty wiped her cheeks with a handkerchief. "How?"

Marie rose and shuffled slowly to the other side of the room. Sunny offered her chair, and Marie plopped down. She swiveled until she sat knee to knee with Betty. Taking the mother's hands into her grandmother hands, she spoke softly, "It's like saying a prayer for your little *keiki*. Only we are all together, all around her, all praying at one time. Doing that brings in the *mana*, the life force, to heal Kimmy."

David leaned toward them, bracing himself with his hands on the table. "Now wait a minute—"

Betty held up one hand to silence her brother-in-law while she clung to Marie with the other.

Mark adjusted his thick glasses and cleared his throat. "Do we have to believe in what you do?"

Marie smiled, compassion welling in her eyes. "No, no. You only have to concentrate on your love for your daughter."

Marie briefly described what Betty and Mark would see and hear during the ritual. She assured them that nothing would harm Kimmy. She paused and invited their questions.

Before the parents could respond, David slammed his hand on the table. "This just creates false hope that my niece will make a miraculous recovery."

Sunny glanced at Pete. He caught her look and moved around to stand by David. "Dr. Kaneko, what else do we have but hope?"

Betty looked up at her husband, desperation in her eyes. "I want to do this, Mark."

Marie cautioned them in a firm voice. "There's no guarantee that Kimmy will get better. Like all the other treatments, this can help. The rest is left to spirit."

David let out a huge sigh. "This is so much voodoo."

Mark, his jaw set, stood up. "Please, David. We appreciate everything you've done, what all the doctors and nurses have done." He paused to choke back a sob, tears rimming his eyes. "We want Marie's help. If you can't support us, maybe you should go."

David looked stunned. He pushed past Pete and out the door.

Mark turned to Marie. "Please come and meet our little girl."

They followed Betty and Mark to Kimmy's room. Panic seized Sunny's throat, left her breathless. These parents were counting on her to help. What in hell made her think she could pull off an ancient healing ceremony? She stopped Marie in the corridor. "I can't go in there," she whispered. "I don't know what I'm doing."

Marie enfolded Sunny in her arms. "Mahana knows."

The warmth of Marie's embrace and the sound of the old man's name—her name—loosened the grip on Sunny's throat. She breathed in

Marie's calm, blew out her fear. She had to trust that when she entered Kimmy's room, Mahana's wisdom would come with her.

They gathered around Kimmy. Tara stepped out and closed the door. Betty and Mark stood on the far side of the bed, hope and fear mingled on their faces. Sunny and Pete took their places across from them. Pete held the basin with Sunny's collection of objects.

Marie positioned herself at the foot of the bed and set the drum on a low stand. She moved her hands in a circular motion on the head of the drum four times, pounded out four slow beats. "*Akua*, we are here only for the highest good for this *keiki* and her *'ohana*." Her voice filled the room with an otherworldly resonance. "Come. Be with us to bring healing to Kimmy." She pounded four more beats and nodded to Sunny.

Sunny set the potted anthurium at Kimmy's feet. "Spirits of earth, be here now." She put the book of matches on the pillow above Kimmy's head. "Spirits of fire, be here now." Betty and Mark watched every move. Sunny prayed silently—please help me to help them. Placing the seashell at Kimmy's left side, she said, "Spirits of water, be here now." She laid the feather along Kimmy's right side. "Spirits of air, be here now."

Marie held up a *koa* bowl filled with clear liquid. "This is water from the sea to bless and cleanse us for our work here." She sprinkled Sunny with the salt water and gave her a hug. "*Aloha*," she said softly. "When we say *aloha*, we say, 'I share the breath of life with you. I see the divine in you.'"

Sunny took the bowl and sprinkled a few drops on Marie's shoulders, touched a few to her long hair. "*Aloha*, Marie." She did the same for Pete. When they embraced, he whispered in her ear, "You're doing fine."

Marie bestowed the blessing on Betty whose face threatened to dissolve in a fresh torrent of tears. Mark removed his glasses and closed his eyes to receive Marie's *aloha*.

Sunny reached out for the bowl. She sprinkled a few drops around Kimmy's head. With her fingertips, she touched the sea water to Kimmy's chest and arms. She flicked a few drops along her legs and feet. She gently pressed her wet fingers to the little girl's forehead.

Dark lashes brushing pale cheeks gave Kimmy the look of a porcelain doll. "*Aloha*, Kimmy. We ask your spirit to stay with us."

Betty erupted into sobs. Mark held her close until she regained her composure and nodded. "I'm okay. Please go on."

Sunny heard the slow creak of the door opening behind her and the soft squish of rubber soles on the tile floor. She looked over her shoulder to see David standing just inside the room, his body stiffly at attention, hands jammed in the pockets of his lab coat, a look composed of granite.

Mark held out his hand. David eased in beside Mark. They embraced.

Holding the bowl of ocean water, Marie turned to David. He swayed backward as though she held a bowl of hissing centipedes.

"It's okay, brother," Mark said.

Marie placed her hand, fingertips wet with drops, on his neck and then on his forehead. "*Aloha*, David."

It was almost as if Marie's touch dismantled an invisible shield around the surgeon. Sunny thought David might collapse on the bed. Emotion flooded his face like water raging over the top of a dam. Relief, fear, despair, bewilderment—Sunny could only guess what feelings threatened to overcome him. The clenched-jaw expression of anger he'd worn for hours was gone.

Sunny nodded a greeting to David and turned her attention back to Kimmy. She lay very still. An endotracheal tube protruded from her rosebud mouth, ventilator causing her chest to rise and fall. Sunny listened to the rhythmic sigh of the breathing machine, remembered the hemorrhaging woman, heard Mahana calling to the woman's guardian spirit. She looked at David. "Let me have your pendant."

"What?"

"The shark tooth."

He unclasped the gold chain and held it out to Sunny. The white triangle of saw tooth ridges gleamed. Sunny gently placed it on Kimmy's chest. "*Mao*, spirit of the ocean we ask you to protect this child."

Marie's fingers tapped feathery beats on the edge of the drum. "*Ua pili māua.* We are all connected. We are one in *Akua*." She rested her hand on the small, blanketed feet in front of her. "Place your hands on Kimmy."

Mark and Betty touched Kimmy's head and arms. David enfold his niece's small hand in both of his and bent to kiss the tiny fingertips. The gesture wrenched Sunny's heart. She placed her hand on Kimmy's thigh and closed her eyes.

Marie took a slow breath. "Breathe deeply. Breathe in the *mana* all around us."

Sunny drew in as much air as she could and blew it out gently through her lips. As she took another breath and another, she could hear the others doing the same. Soon, their breathing synchronized.

Marie began a steady beat. "Now breathe easy. Close your eyes. Clear your mind. Let your thoughts float away like boats on a river. Just let them float away." She lowered her voice. "See Kimmy when she's well. Playing on the grass at home. Skipping along the sidewalk. Her skin is rosy. Big smile on her face. She's healthy."

Sunny pictured Kimmy on a swing, arcing higher and higher, her delighted giggles floating on the air like iridescent bubbles catching the sunlight.

Marie continued drumming. "Focus on your vision of Kimmy. Let the energy and love you feel flow through your hands to her body." She intoned a chant, the melodic sound weaving around them like a warm breeze.

Fear needled Sunny. She couldn't feel anything flowing through her hands. The image of Kimmy started to fade. She struggled to hang on to it, but it evaporated. Trust. Start again. Mahana, please. Just listen. Drumbeats and ancient Hawaiian words swirled a cocoon around Sunny, blocking out the chatter in her brain, conjuring up an image of Kimmy swinging as high as the treetops.

Sunny felt a tightening in her belly. Her breathing began to come in deep gasps. Each breath filled her with heat that radiated from her chest, out to her arms and legs, flooded her neck and face and head. The sound of a rattle joined the drumbeat. Sunny took up the chant, but in her ears Mahana's voice called out the words. Her mind's eye let go of the vision of Kimmy and turned inward.

At her core, a smoldering spark began to glow. As it grew, it flared a rich green. The ball of emerald light exploded in her body, flooding her whole being. She had the physical sensation of water flowing through every fiber. The light flashed green to her hands and feet and gushed up through the crown of her head. Powerful hands imprinted warmth on her back. She felt a surge of energy. Green light radiated into blinding brilliance.

Without opening her eyes, Sunny stretched out her arms and pressed her hands to Kimmy's torso and legs. She didn't know if she actually uttered the words or heard them in her mind. "Your light through me. Your light to heal this precious one." She watched the light flow through her hands into Kimmy's body. The glow spiraled in the little girl's chest, surged into her legs and feet, arms and hands, flowed into her neck and head. The bed shimmered in an emerald vortex. Light swirled in the room.

As the last tendrils of green sparked from her fingertips, Sunny's muscles trembled. Her legs felt like gelatin. Perspiration trickled down her back, beaded her forehead. She swayed a little and felt Pete's grip on her shoulders, helping her to stay upright. "Thank you, Mahana," she whispered.

The drumming slowed to a stop. Marie pounded out four distinct beats. "We thank you, great *Akua*, for being with us. We thank you for your healing *mana*. *Mahalo nui loa*."

Sunny hesitated to open her eyes. Had she imagined what just happened? What had the others seen? How was Kimmy? She focused on Marie's face. The old woman nodded.

Sunny looked at the little girl. Nothing had changed. Kimmy lay still and pale. She glanced at Betty and Mark and David. They weren't acting like they'd witnessed anything disturbing or strange. She sensed only one difference. A profound peace permeated the room.

Without asking if their daughter would be well, Mark and Betty murmured their thanks to Marie. Out in the corridor, David shook Pete's hand. When he approached Marie, the old woman held out her arms. To Sunny's surprise, David allowed himself to be enfolded in Marie's bear hug.

David stood in front of Sunny. "I don't believe anything's changed, but it was moving to imagine Kimmy healthy again." His eyes welled with tears. "Thank you."

Sunny, without a thought, hugged David. He held her tight. She felt tingling creep up her neck to the top of her head. When they parted, she noticed a flush on David's cheeks.

Sunny turned to Pete. "You had my back."

"And Leilani had mine. She was with us, Sunny."

"That girl wouldn't have missed this for anything."

They embraced.

"Leilani always said she wanted the three of us to spend more time together," Pete said. "Never thought it would be like this."

Sunny linked her arm with Marie's as they walked toward the elevators. "Thank you, dear *tūtū*. I owe you so much."

"You were a good friend to Lani. Payment enough."

"Will Kimmy recover?"

"Can't know for sure. Kimmy's spirit will make the choice to stay or go."

"There's so much I don't understand. I have so many questions—"

Marie hugged Sunny. "Enough for now. It's time for you to rest."

Seventeen

I stare at the cache of knives my apprentice has hastily crafted, flex my fingers to calm myself. "Tanemao, you have not heard anything I told you."

Tanemao fingers the handle of a crude bone knife. "What harm can come if we are prepared to defend ourselves?"

"Have you finished sorting and soaking the plants we collected?"

"No . . . I—"

"I entrusted you with the healing skills. Now, you have abandoned our work to make weapons."

"It doesn't necessarily mean we will use them." Tanemao squats down to bundle the knives in *tapa*. "They will serve as a warning, a deterrent."

"Our history means little to you. The power of spirit and the force of fist are never in one body at the same time."

He says nothing.

My mind travels back to Raiatea, swirls with images of flesh torn and bleeding. Shrieks of terror fill the air as women and children run through the trees, searching in vain for places to hide. I grab Tanemao's shoulders, shake him. "Your actions endanger our people."

Still, he does not speak.

"Go away," I scream. I push him backwards. A puff of dust rises where his shoulders and back strike the ground. There is disbelief on his face. "I will no longer instruct you."

"But, why?"

"You cannot be healer and killer at the same time."

He shakes his head.

"You will have to find other work to do for our clan." I kick the bundle of knives away from him. "Not making weapons."

"No, teacher, please." He pushes himself up to kneel in front of me, reaches out, eyes pleading. "I want to become a healer. I will try harder. I swear it."

My heart feels as cold as an ancient lava flow deep in the shade of the jungle. The shark tooth glints on Tanemao's chest. I want to rip the cord from his neck. "You are not worthy to master the sacred healing practices."

He covers his eyes, moves his hands to the top of his head, tears at his hair.

I turn my back, walk away.

In front of my *fare,* I slump to the grass, my body shaking. Great *Akua*, what have I done? I want to grab my hurtful words out of the air and stuff them back in my mouth. Why did I not show him compassion? How could my spirit be so weak?

I will give Tanemao another chance. We will talk before the ceremony tonight, before we sail to Tauati. My head is hurting, and the grass is so warm. I lie in the sun, wait for the shaking and pain to pass. Just a little rest, Tanemao, and I will find you.

Sunny pressed her hand against an ache in her forehead, wrestled out of comatose sleep to find the ringing telephone. She picked up the receiver. "Hello?"

"Sunny, this is David Kaneko."

"David?"

"I'm sorry I woke you."

"I'm used to it. How's Kimmy?"

"We just took her off critical status."

Sunny pushed herself up on the pillows. "That's so good to hear."

"She's breathing on her own." He paused, cleared his throat. "May I come over?"

"What?"

"I know I'm sounding strange, but I want to talk with you in person."

"Now?"

"Would an hour give you enough time?"

Sunny hesitated. She stared at the clock, trying to determine if 6:00 meant morning or evening. P.M. It felt more like midnight. She didn't have the energy to spar with David. "I have time tomorrow—"

"It's important."

A flash of her dream—pushing Tanemao hard, his pleading as he knelt on the ground—flared in her brain, burned away the last groggy strands of sleep. "Do you need directions?"

"See you at eight o'clock."

Sunny burrowed under the covers, jostling the cats until they abandoned the bed. Her mind reeled. The healing ritual. She'd been overtaken by a strange presence, somehow used as a conduit for powerful energy. Kimmy was doing better. She wanted to read every page of the girl's chart to understand how her condition had changed. In her gut, she knew those pages wouldn't answer any of her questions.

Sunny tossed off the covers and perched on the side of the bed. She needed a shower and some food to help her body catch up with her racing mind. The food might even relieve her dull headache. The curious dream. Mahana sent Tanemao away. Did he give up on his apprentice too soon? Maybe Mahana never had another chance to talk with Tanemao before the young man died.

She zipped through the shower, slipped on shorts and a green-striped top. In a way, she was looking forward to seeing David. She'd certainly seen a completely different side of him in Kimmy's room. Sunny remember David's meltdown at Marie's touch and smiled. The granite must have had a few hairline cracks. She pictured him holding his niece's hand in both of his, his slender thumb pressing each tiny fingernail in turn. It had been astonishing to witness his softer side.

Sunny toweled her wet curls into submission and put on her favorite earrings. The green stones sparkled in the lights around her vanity mirror, transporting her back to Kimmy's bedside and the emerald light radiating from her own body. Sunny felt certain that healing energy had flowed from her, from everyone in the room, into the little girl. But what if Kimmy's improvement was just a coincidence or delayed effect of treatment? Maybe Grace had tried a different medication. Sunny looked in the mirror, wagged a finger at her image. "Let it be."

❀ ❀ ❀

David stood there with a large paper bag in one arm and a bottle of wine in the other. He looked as if he expected her to greet him with an embrace and a kiss, as if they'd been lovers for a long time and this was their usual middle-of-the-week evening together. He handed her the bottle of wine. "Peace offering?"

Sunny laughed. "More like beware of Greeks bearing gifts. Come in."

He stepped out of his loafers and followed her to the kitchen. He glanced around the room. "I like the white with just a touch of operating-room green."

"Home away from home. Thanks for bringing all this food."

David lined up the containers on the counter as Sunny searched for a corkscrew. She opened the cabinet, brought out two wine glasses, and placed them next to the bottle of zinfandel.

"Spoons and forks?"

"The drawer in front of you." She popped the cork and poured the wine. "David, what happened with Kimmy? Is she responding?"

He paused, spoon full of marinated mushrooms in mid-air. "She's doing much better. I promise to tell you everything. Let's eat first."

Sunny frowned. "Do you always have to be in charge?"

"It's the captain of the ship thing." He waved the spoon, mushrooms teetering precariously. "Plate."

She took two plates off the shelf and handed him one with the same snap she used to hand up forceps during a procedure. "Haven't you heard, Dr. Kaneko? The surgeon as captain of the ship is definitely passé. Besides we're in my kitchen, not the OR."

He scooped out mounds of spinach salad, tabouli, and fruit dusted with coconut. "So, do I have your pardon for, what did you call it, abusive behavior?"

"If you promise no more Al Pacino tirades."

"Deal." He hefted the plates and headed toward the table.

Sunny wedged the wine bottle in one elbow and grabbed silverware, napkins, and the wine glasses. "Let's go out on the *lānai*. Bring the bread."

"Yes, madam director." David tucked the baguette under his arm and retrieved the plates. He followed her through the living room.

They settled into thick-cushioned wicker chairs on either side of a round glass table. Sunny looked out over the garden drowsing peacefully in the soft evening air. "This is my favorite time of day."

A cricket chirped to welcome the coming darkness. Yellow plumeria blossoms drifted from the canopy of trees onto the grass, filling the air with heavy perfume. An anvil-shaped cloud on the horizon flared with the last fiery tints of the sunset.

David lifted his glass. "To watching a sunset instead of a cardiac monitor."

Sunny clinked her glass to his. "And sipping wine instead of rancid coffee." She flicked her napkin into her lap. "I'm starving."

They ate in silence, replenishing bodies that had functioned for hours on petrified bagels and cream cheese. Sunny wondered about David's change in demeanor, his unusual charm. What was on his mind? She dabbed her mouth with the napkin. "Tell me what happened with your niece."

"About an hour after you left the Center, Mark paged me. He met me outside Kimmy's room, looking so agitated I thought he'd finally lost it."

Sunny scooted to the edge of her chair. "And?"

"Kimmy was conscious, trying to pull out the endotracheal tube."

"How were her vital signs?"

"Normal sinus rhythm. We shut off the lidocaine drip and extubated. So far, no more episodes of fibrillation."

"Bleeding?"

"Clear drainage coming through the chest tubes. All the bleeders sealed off."

Sunny paused, hesitant to ask her next question. "Signs of stroke?"

"Just weakness on her left side. The neurologist believes she'll regain full function with therapy."

She sat back in her chair. The possibility that the healing ritual saved Kimmy's life overwhelmed her as much as if she'd gotten news that Lani had been sighted at the grocery store. Sunny stared at her hands in her lap, remembered the sparks flying from her fingertips. "That's wonderful. Betty and Mark must be ecstatic. You must be."

David nodded, raising his face to the sky.

Sunny looked up too. Deep ebony chased the dusty blue of twilight.

She lit a plump candle in the center of the table. The light flickered patterns between them and illuminated David's face. When he looked at her, his eyes shimmered with tears. "I thought we'd lose her."

"I know."

David refilled his wine glass and gestured with the bottle toward hers. When she shook her head, he sat back in his chair. He took a long taste of the zin. "What happened in that room? What did you and Marie do?"

"When all else fails, try prayer?"

"Come on, Sunny. That wasn't simply a prayer service."

"What do you mean?"

"Apart from the drumming and chanting, there was a . . . buzz in the room. No . . ." David set his glass on the table, stared at the candle. "It was like when I was a kid. I'd rub a balloon against my head and hold it next to my arm. The static electricity made the hairs stand up. Like that." His words tumbled out. "A charge in the air. An energy. As if we were all holding hands and the first person in line stuck a finger in an electrical outlet. It felt like a current welding us together, to Kimmy." He raised his hands in frustration. "Am I making any sense?"

Sunny studied the rim of her wine glass. The crystal etching sparkled in the candlelight. She wanted to tell him everything, start from the beginning when the flash of her life as Mahana left her confused and skeptical, explain how the dreams just kept coming, propelling her back to an ancient time. She wished she could describe her experience of Mahana's life and ask David to help her figure out the implications of the Anuanua's strange powers. But remembrance of her battles with David over UM quenched that desire instantly. She didn't know if she could trust him.

"Sunny?"

She rubbed her face with both hands. "David, I don't know what happened. I've been learning about energy work, studying with Marie. The theory is that we can summon energy from the world around us, from within ourselves, and transfer it to someone who needs healing."

"Is this energy supposed to reverse the breakdown of all the biological processes?"

"I don't know."

"You must want to know the reason for Kimmy's turnaround."

Sunny shook her head slowly. "I want to stop craving a scientific explanation for everything. Why does positive visualization help people overcome cancer? Hell, we can't explain why beta-blockers keep people from dying after a heart attack. But we know they do."

"They say if you're in medicine long enough, you'll see a miracle or two. I've seen some amazing recoveries, the most stunning this morning. I've always believed that research should supply the how and why."

"Does that mean we wait for science to catch up?"

"Do no harm."

"I worried about that. When you called, I dreaded hearing that Kimmy was having more problems. Or worse."

"She's alive, and no one has a clue why."

Sunny watched David's pensive face and remembered how Tanemao struggled to understand the intangible. The connection filled her with a surge of affection. "What would you say if I told you that the ritual we used comes from the ancient Hawaiians?"

"How did you find out about it?"

"The spiritual practices have been passed to people living today by their ancestors."

"Spiritual practices or superstitions? The Hawaiians I know, including some of my relatives, believe in all sorts of myths. My uncle won't drive over the Nuuanu Pali at night for fear of being attacked by the ghosts of King Kamehameha's great battle there."

"Maybe the superstitions and myths point to powers humans once possessed and lost."

"What you're saying is, by amping up a kind of bio-energy and laying our hands on someone, we have the power to stop hemorrhage, cure arrhythmia. Damn. Wipe out cancer."

"I don't rule out any of those possibilities."

"Reminds me of a movie my brother rented for Kimmy's birthday party. This little alien revived a dead plant by touching it."

"It's not that simple. I think the ability to use energy for healing requires as much conviction as our reliance on beta-blockers."

He paused, staring at the candle again. "I can't put blind faith in folk medicine."

"David, I'm sorry I don't have the answers you want."

He didn't respond.

She spoke softly. "What does it matter if we don't have an explanation? Isn't the important thing the fact that we had a chance to do something for Kimmy, and she's going to be well?"

"Just be grateful for the miracle."

"Yes."

His eyes searched hers. "I don't think you're telling me everything."

Sunny didn't answer. She was still trying to fathom this new, more friendly version of the hot shot surgeon. And why did she suddenly feel like the modern day Mahana with David as her skeptical apprentice?

"Thanks for being there," David said.

Sunny gave a slight nod.

"There's one other way I'd like to say thank you."

"David, why are you being so hospitable?" Sunny smiled to soften her candor. "This isn't like you. It's making me a little nervous."

He winced. "Guess I deserve that. Let's say I've finally learned what all savvy first year residents know. Stay on the good side of nurses. They can save your ass."

Sunny laughed.

David held up his hand. "But let me finish. I've heard you're a scuba maniac. Is that so?"

"Oops, the secret's out. I'm truly a compressed air freak."

"Want to go diving some time?"

Sunny pondered the surprising invitation.

"Could improve physician-nurse relations," David said.

"Dive site?"

"I'll pick a thriller."

"No long surface swims."

David raised his hand in a pledge. "Anchor over the site. Drop straight down to eighty feet."

"We're on."

"Good. I'll call you for a calendar check." He rose from his chair. "I want to look in on Kimmy." Sunny started to get up. "Stay there. I'll let myself out."

She snapped a military salute. "Aye, aye, captain. Thanks for dinner."

Instead of turning to leave, David stood looking at her, a slight smile curving the perfect bow of his lips. Candlelight played on the high arch of his cheekbones and deepened the shadow in the cleft of his chin. Sunny felt the inexplicable urge to feel the softness of his mouth against hers. She blew out the candle. "Goodnight, David."

He disappeared through the French door.

Sunny started to collect the dishes. She picked up David's glass, remembered the unabashed appreciation in his eyes. She swirled the last bit of wine around in the goblet and raised it to her lips.

Eighteen

Sunny leaned into the wind and water spraying up over the bow. In front of her, dark blue swells stretched all the way to the western horizon. A school of flying fish popped up from the deep to skim across the water and disappear. She shouted over the engine roar. "Did you see them?"

David perched in the helm seat of the Boston Whaler, one hand on the engine, the other on the wheel, tropical shirt flapping behind him. He grinned. Sunny remembered Pete's expression. "Island boy *to da max*."

She hadn't expected to hear from David after the evening on her *lānai*. He called several days later to schedule the dive trip, and she didn't think twice. In the past five weeks, she'd lost her best friend, discovered herself as an old man, and learned about the demise of UM. She longed for the ocean's comforting embrace.

The sea shifted from cobalt to turquoise. David pointed to an orange mooring buoy just ahead. He nosed the boat up to the dive-site marker. Sunny scrambled out onto the bow pulpit and leaned over the deck rail. With a grappling hook, she snagged the marker and clipped it to a rope attached to the boat.

"Good work." David stopped the engines, rummaged inside a storage locker under the starboard lounge. He pulled out a dive flag attached to a metal rod and jammed it into a bracket on the hull.

Sunny climbed over the low windshield back onto the helm deck. She turned a slow three-sixty. To the north, frothy clouds bunched over Kaua'i. A mile east, the coast of O'ahu and the jagged Ko'olau Mountains meandered to the horizon. She thought of Lani. That girl had loved being out on the water, watching the panorama of clouds and light over the islands.

David draped his shirt over the steering wheel. "Welcome to Turtle Reef."

She caught herself studying his lean torso. Smooth skin the shade of coffee with extra cream. Sunlight burnishing the definition of muscles in his chest and arms. She tugged on her wetsuit. "Good choice, captain. I've been meaning to check out this dive site." She cinched a weight belt low on her hips. "How did you get interested in diving?"

"I wanted to be a marine biologist. Mom wasn't having any of that."

"What do you mean?"

"She had two sons—one to manage the family business and the other to become a doctor. I sure didn't want to be stuck running a neighborhood market. So, along with all the science and math, I took every scuba diving class the school system offered." He rubbed the inside of his scuba mask with defogging solution. "What about you?"

"I read an article about treasure hunting and pictured myself discovering gold coins in the wreck of a Spanish galleon."

David opened a gate in the stern, revealing a swim platform. "Not many ships from the Armada out here."

"My most exciting find so far was a pile of beer bottles in an old row boat."

He laughed.

They checked their equipment, making sure the dive computers displayed correct information and the regulators breathed freely. "Did your parents want a nurse in the family?" he asked.

"They did give me a nurse's kit when I was little. Mainly, I think they just wanted me to be happy."

"Are they here in Honolulu?"

"California. I see them a couple times a year. I miss them. My mom still gives me her new age advice on the telephone."

"New age?"

"Last week, she told me I should rely on radical trust."

They sat on the starboard bench, snapped on fins, adjusted their masks. He gestured toward the stern. "Let's see how you do with mom's suggestion."

Sunny shuffled to the edge of the swim platform and tucked her regulator in her mouth. With a giant stride, she splashed down into the water.

She floated on the swells, watching David get ready for his entry. His meticulous preparation reminded her of a tee shirt worn by a dive master known for being a stickler on safety. It asked IS THERE A HYPHEN IN ANAL RETENTIVE? At least he wouldn't be one of those sand-kicking, reef-wrecking, swim-like-a-bat-out-of-hell idiots.

David splashed in, kicked over to her, and pointed a thumb down. They released the air in their BC jackets and drifted to the bottom.

A veil of bubbles swathed Sunny's face. Her vision cleared to reveal valleys of star coral and ridges of volcanic rock. The sound of her breathing filled her ears. She checked her dive computer—fifty feet, sixty feet.

At eighty feet and inches above the ocean floor, Sunny floated in a sitting position, legs crossed tailor style. She felt the familiar adrenalin rush as she gazed up at the bullet shape of the boat. In the crystal blue water, the craft looked to be only a few feet away and seemed a world apart.

David hovered in front of her, signed okay. She returned the signal to indicate she felt fine. They skimmed along the sand toward the coral reef, Sunny swimming a little behind him. He kept his arms folded across his abdomen, as slow kicks sent him gliding through the water. Her eyes followed the line of his slim hips and runner's thighs. Perfect form.

He beckoned her to a large outcropping of coral. A black and white fish charged out like an attack dog. David pointed to a gelatinous clutch of eggs anchored to the coral. In the slow motion of underwater gestures, he pounded his chest with his fists. This male fish is guarding his young.

Sunny cradled her arms, swayed as if rocking a baby, then turned her palms up. Where's mom?

His eyes laughed as he made a dancing motion with his hand across the coral. She's out playing around.

She nodded and flashed the hang loose sign.

They cruised along the reef. Something moved just ahead. An octopus stretched spiraling tentacles across a footstool of rock. Sunny looked over at David and realized he'd been keeping her in his line of sight. Excellent. She didn't have to worry about clanging her tank with her knife handle if something out of the ordinary happened.

He moved next to her. The light brown covering on the octopus, rough and horny to match the ocean floor, turned smooth and dark. The master of camouflage disappeared into a crevice. David nodded and clapped his hands. Nice find!

He pointed to his computer and then at her. How much air in your tank?

She flashed five fingers twice. 1000 psi.

He flashed back five, five, and two. 1200 psi. It figured. He would be the Zen master and use less air. She watched him cruise along the reef. He was a different person under water. Funny, attentive. Hell, maybe they needed to keep a tank of compressed air in the surgeons' locker room.

David placed one hand on top of the other and wiggled his thumbs. Turtle. Thirty feet away, green sea turtles floated in the water and rested on the coral. Schools of black and neon-blue fish, bustled about the turtles, cleaning the algae off their shells. Sunny counted ten patrons in line at the underwater salon. She watched a turtle rise to the surface for air, her eyes riveted on its sunlit silhouette.

Sunny felt David's shoulder touching hers. She squeezed his arm. Their eyes met, and she winked her appreciation.

David checked his dive computer and held a thumb up. Sunny returned the signal. Forty minutes had seemed more like five. She watched the sandy bottom grow more distant, feeling the twinge of longing that always jabbed her at the end of a dive. They swam to the boat, hoisted themselves up the ladder, and shucked off their equipment. "Awesome dive," Sunny said. "I rarely see that many critters at one site."

"Always happens when you go with a wanna-be marine biologist." David pointed to a corner of the stern. "Fresh water shower over there. I'll set out some grub." He slid open the companionway door and disappeared into the cabin below.

Sunny peeled off the wetsuit, adjusted her bikini, and basked in the warm shower. She tried to sort out the jumble in her brain, the tightness in her gut. There was no denying she felt attracted to David. And he seemed attracted to her. That probably had something to do with the way they came together over Kimmy. Maybe the past life thing. But she hadn't forgotten his part in the UM situation, how he'd blown her off after the merger announcement.

David appeared in the companionway. "Ice water or soda?"

She saw his gaze sweep from her head to her feet. He smiled. Heat radiated in her neck and face. "Ice water."

"We'll have margaritas after the next dive. Come on down."

She covered her bathing suit with a pareau and followed him down the teakwood steps. Rich pecan cabinets held a television, music system, and double berth. Sunny stroked the soft leather of the dinette. "Ocean-going luxury."

"I'm leasing her until I decide if I want to plunk down a bundle for the right to have a name painted on the stern."

"That would be?"

"Haven't given it much thought. Something like Cut and Run?"

She laughed. "Only if you're a surgeon with lapsed malpractice."

David took a wedge of brie sprinkled with almonds out of the microwave and added crackers to the plate. He lifted a colander of plump, red strawberries and green grapes out of the stainless steel sink. "There's a salad in there."

She opened the refrigerator and spied the bottles of orange crème soda, Corona beer, and drink mixers. The bottom shelf held a container of lemons and limes and jars of green and black olives. "Wow. Did you stock this puppy?"

"The outfit at the marina does that."

Sunny's mouth dropped open when she peeked in the freezer. "Haagen-Dazs ice cream bars. That does it. You'll have to pry me out of here. I think my refrigerator contains a half-eaten sandwich and a can of cat food."

"Aha. Now, I know the way to your heart."

"Much easier than going through the sternum."

They carried lunch up top. David extended a canvas cover across the helm deck for shade, and they sat opposite each other on the lounges.

Sunny popped a strawberry in her mouth, leaned back, savored the tart sweetness. "Food always seems like an extravagant pleasure after a dive."

"You're a good diver."

"Thanks. I was thinking the same about you."

They traded dive stories, topping each other in the you-won't-believe-this category, like the young whale that rested its head on the swim platform. Sunny sensed them both avoiding any discussion about work and UM.

When they finished lunch, she stretched out on the lounge, closed her eyes, smiled inside. David considered her a competent diver. Exactly what attracted him to a woman? She hadn't heard any rumors linking him with someone. An uninvolved surgeon was about as rare as one who wore a shark tooth. She was probably a cool blonde with honey brown eyes and a Texas drawl. Maybe she even worked for CHS.

A seagull screeched overhead. She opened her eyes to see David looking at her as if studying a puzzle. "What?"

"Seems like I knew you before UM. That night at your place, I wracked my brain to think of when."

"They say we all have a double somewhere."

"Not your physical features. It's how you enjoy your surroundings. It was the way you watched the sunset and declared it your favorite time of day. I swear I've heard you say that before."

Sunny's pulse quickened. She sat up, stared at the ocean. A vision of Tanemao walking with Mahana floated on the swells. "How long have you had these symptoms, doctor?"

"At Kimmy's bedside, during the . . . ritual . . . when I looked at you, it was like looking at someone else, but someone I recognized."

"Déjà vu?"

He shook his head.

She swallowed hard. "Maybe we knew each other in a past life."

He tossed a strawberry stem over the rail. "I don't believe in that jazz. Whatever's going on, I just want to you to go back to being the insufferable OR director."

Sunny glanced around the cockpit. "Where did I put my whip?"

They laughed. David leaned forward, his elbows resting on his knees. If she did the same, their foreheads would be touching. Maybe she could tell him about Mahana and Tanemao through some kind of mind meld.

"I haven't been able to stop thinking about our conversation," he said.

"Say more."

"Kimmy's doing well. She'll be discharged tomorrow. When I think of how it might have turned out . . ." He shook his head. "Mark and Betty, my parents . . ."

"I can't imagine the agony of losing a child."

"The point is my niece is alive, and we don't know why."

Sunny stared at her feet. There was a good chance that what she was about to say would end their idyllic day. But she couldn't resist making a point. "I know you don't want to hear this, David. But, we won't figure out why Kimmy's alive if we lose UM's complementary medicine program."

He leaned back on the lounge, arms spread wide on the rail, one foot propped up. "The UM budget is in the toilet. I want money for research, new technology, advanced surgical techniques. CHS has deep pockets."

"If there's a chance in hell to figure out what saved Kimmy, it won't be with CHS running the show."

"Here we go again. How do you know that?"

"We didn't have enough staff to cover her surgery. Why do you think CHS has deep pockets? They cut to the bone."

He just looked at her.

Sunny leaned back on the lounge, took a deep breath to blow away the mushroom cloud of irritation blooming inside her. "I admire your desire to provide the very best surgical care. I want that too. We need to work on all of the above."

"Without money?" David raised an eyebrow. "What do you propose we do about the budget?"

"That's a major concern. I won't deny that. But a deal with the devil isn't the remedy."

"Damn it, Sunny. CHS isn't the evil empire."

Sunny bit the inside of her lip. She needed to back off. Hammering on his resistance wasn't going to change his thinking.

David stared into the distance.

The rocking motion of the boat calmed her. She checked her watch. "We've been out of the water for ninety minutes. What about the next dive?"

Lines of frustration on his face smoothed into a slight smile. "Koko Wall."

A short cruise north brought them to the mooring buoy over a dark stretch of ocean. As they tugged on their gear, he reviewed the dive plan. "There's a network of lava tubes and caves here. We'll go out along the reef, come down the wall about sixty feet, and work our way back to the boat. The drop-off here is about 350, so keep your eyes open for the big pelagics. Rays and sharks."

Sea life on the reef resembled the palette of an artist wild for color. Brilliant turquoise parrotfish with beak-like mouths nibbled algae. Belted wrasse darted among the rocks, sporting orange, periwinkle, green, and powder blue stripes. A bandit angelfish, looking like a raccoon, touched its mouth to Sunny's mask. She laughed and shooed away the fish lips.

The wall looked like a complex of large and small condominiums. Sunny shined her flashlight in a hollow and spied an orange spiny lobster waving a tentacle. In the condo next door, her flashlight revealed a conger eel, white body writhing. It charged forward, flashing needle-sharp teeth. She jerked back. The eel slithered out into open water and disappeared into another crevice.

Tapping Sunny's arm, David pointed down. They kicked away from the wall and hovered over the deep blue abyss. Her eyes strained to see something, anything, in the infinite void. Her heart pounded in her ears as she sucked air from the regulator. She checked her computer to make sure they hadn't dropped lower than sixty feet and fought the urge to kick madly back to the wall.

David held out his hands, and she clasped them. They stretched out like skydivers suspended in liquid space. Sunny took a deep breath and watched their bubbles rise in glittering columns. Her body relaxed, pulse slowed. She wasn't in danger of drifting endlessly without an endless supply of air. Strange. Drifting was the way she felt most of the time these days. David's firm grip steadied her, gave her the freedom to enjoy the magic around them. She needed to find that kind of anchor in her life topside.

A manta ray with wingspan twice David's height soared out of the chasm, arcing over their heads. On its ghost-white underside, black markings formed a perfect W. Sunny and David moved apart, shifting to watch the ray fly over the reef to feed.

David motioned for her to follow. Cruising along the wall, they came to an opening large enough for two people to pass through. He held up his hand, signaling her to wait. She watched him slip through the mouth of the cave until the tips of his fins disappeared. After a minute, he came out. He reached out to Sunny, and she took his hand.

The tunnel-like entrance opened into a large sea cavern. A white tip reef shark circled in a shaft of sunlight filtering through a hole in the top of the cavern. Sunny hesitated. She knew they wouldn't be able to back out of the cave fast enough. David tightened his hold on her hand and pulled her up next to him. He flashed the okay sign.

They watched the torpedo-shaped body spiral in the shimmering water, its tail undulating in slow strokes. The gills, diagonal slashes along the side, pulsed. Sunny estimated the shark's length at five feet and reminded herself that its diet consisted of octopus and fish, not humans. David linked his arm through hers.

The shark drifted toward them. The dorsal fin loomed dark gray, white tip glinting in the sunlight. Its mouth hung open, a wide gash filled with hundreds of razor-sharp triangles. The shark glided closer. Sunny flinched. David tightened his arm around hers, snugging her close to his side.

The shark slowed and turned. Its eye fixed a vacant bead on them. Sunny held her breath so her bubbles wouldn't startle the shark. She looked at David. His regulator had stopped discharging bubbles. He seemed to be in a stare-down with the creature. She tugged his right arm with both hands. He remained face-to-face with the shark, locked in a kind of trance.

He reached out with his left hand. His fingertips stroked the side above the gills. The shark seemed to lean into his touch. Sunny stared, feeling as if she were watching a Hindu mystic kiss a cobra. David caressed the flank with his whole hand. The shark turned toward his outstretched arm. Sunny tugged harder on his right arm. David hovered in the water, transfixed. She released her grip, fumbled for the knife strapped to her ankle, and braced herself to stab a dark eye. Suddenly, the powerful tail slashed sideways, and the shark darted into a dark recess at the back of the cave.

❀   ❀   ❀

On the boat, they shrugged out of their BCs. Sunny unzipped her wetsuit. "What happened down there?"

David didn't answer.

He stowed the air tanks in the brackets along the port rail and tossed his BC into the rinse barrel in the stern. He stuffed his mask, snorkel, and regulator into his dive bag. Sunny wondered what was going through his mind. He sat on the starboard bench and stared at his hands, rubbed them together as if to verify the sensation of touch.

She sat beside him. "Are you okay?"

"This is going to sound insane." David combed his hands through his hair. "I felt completely calm. Like that shark somehow knew me. I needed to touch him." He shook his head. "You must think I'm narced."

"Rapture of the deep? There's not enough nitrogen in your blood." She touched the shark tooth on the gold chain around his neck.

"My dad gave it to me when I graduated from college. A reminder to hang tough in med school."

"It belongs to you in more ways than you can imagine."

"What?"

"Now it's your turn to think I'm crazy." She paused. "It feels risky to tell you this."

"Go on."

"A long time ago, you lived a life here in Hawai'i as a man named Tanemao."

He frowned.

"Shark man. That's what Tanemao means. Your protector is *Mao*."

David looked as if she'd told him he'd grown a set of gills.

"We were both in that life."

"I knew there was something you weren't telling me."

"You'd have figured me for a flake."

"I wouldn't call you that. But—"

"My mind still has a hard time wrapping around it."

"Sunny, you expect me to believe—"

"You may have just connected with your *'aumakua*."

"You expect me to believe that we lived another life together."

"The ritual for Kimmy came from that life."

"I thought that was Marie."

"She helped me understand it, believe in its power."

David stood and closed the gate in the stern. He kept his back to her.

Sunny shaded her eyes to look at the horizon. The afternoon trade winds whipped the ocean into marching rows of white caps. She felt hot, but not from the sun. She hugged her arms across her abdomen. "I don't blame you for thinking that what I've told you is bizarre." She stood, steadied herself against the rocking of the boat. "It's getting late. Do you want to head in?"

"Good idea." He turned toward her. "No." He touched her shoulder. His hand felt cool on her burning skin. "Not yet. Look, I . . . I need some time."

"I know."

"It's just that all of this is so far off my radar screen."

She nodded.

"Let's stay for a while. We can have those margaritas."

"I need one," Sunny muttered.

David swung down into the galley. Sunny went back to the lounge in the helm. She rubbed her forehead. The ancient past, the present push-pull, the future of UM. A day out on the water, and they weren't able to escape any of the time zones.

He held a frosty drink in each hand. "Let's go sit on the bow. Makes you feel like you're on a tiny raft in the middle of the ocean."

"Terrific. I hate being adrift."

They sat side by side, backs against the windshield. David sucked on a slice of lime and tossed it in the water. "Operating on people doesn't allow much room for niggling doubt. I've had a good measure of that lately."

"About?"

"For starters, the whole thing with my niece. Why didn't I get a pediatric guy to look at Kimmy as soon as I suspected there was something wrong?"

"What made you hesitate?"

"I have an older sister. She tries to run everyone else's life. Gives me this hair-trigger reaction, so I try to stay out of all of it."

"Families make us do strange things."

"If I'd gotten more involved . . ."

"Stop blaming yourself. You know there's a high probability the outcome would have been the same."

He nodded and took a swallow of margarita. "Then there's the merger."

Sunny sipped her drink, waited for him to go on.

"It's easier for me to talk about research and budgets than things like past lives and what happened with Kimmy."

"Believe me, David. I understand that."

"On one hand, I think it's better to have UM as part of a thriving corporation than not at all. On the other, I'm starting to see your point. We could lose the UM that saved my niece."

"So, what do we do?"

"I don't know."

When she returned to work after staying with Marie, Sunny had tried in vain to learn the status of the deal with CHS. "Do you know what's happening with the merger?"

He shook his head.

"Could you ask Darwin Chang to delay so we have time to work on the money issue?"

"It's been nearly two months since the decision was made. I'm sure the ink's drying on the paper."

"One telephone call?"

"I'd need to talk with the CHS exec as well. Vance Turner doesn't like retreat." He drained his glass, stared out at the ocean.

"You're the only person they'd listen to."

He sighed. "Okay. I can't promise anything."

"Thank you."

"I owe you one."

The boat rocked on the white caps, sea spray whipping across the bow. Sunny thought about how the day had unfolded. David's openness surprised her more than the shark encounter. Maybe there was a lot they both needed to learn from each other.

Sunny finished her drink. "Any other niggling doubts?"

He laughed. "Yeah. My strange affinity for sharks."

"You know what I think."

David stood. "It's getting rough out here. We should head in." They climbed back onto the helm deck. "Want to drive?"

"Sure."

Sunny kept a steady hand on the wheel as the Whaler skimmed across the water, the bow leaping up over the waves. David sat across from her. She looked at him and couldn't tell what brewed behind his dark glasses.

A pod of spinner dolphins, taking turns leaping out of the water, kept pace alongside the boat. She slowed the engines to stop. The dolphins circled, diving down on the starboard side and popping up at port. Their smiley faces and soaring bodies radiated exuberance. Sunny moved to the aft deck, watched until the last sleek acrobat disappeared below the waves.

David stood in front of her. "You're grinning."

"I love those guys."

"That explains the tattoo on your foot. How long have you had this strange affinity for dolphins, madam director?"

She thought of Mahana summoning his 'aumakua. "For as long as I can remember."

He gently grasped her shoulders. Sunny watched his dark eyes explore her face. He smoothed a curl behind her ear. The warmth emanating from his body, the touch of his fingertips, the sound of his breathing made her feel as if she were drifting back down to eighty feet. She wanted to call a time out but she couldn't speak.

David ran his finger from her ear, along her jaw line. His mouth barely brushed hers. She took his hand from her face, held it tight, pressed her lips against his.

They drew apart, Sunny's astonishment mirrored on David's face. "We should go," she whispered.

Slipping his arms around her waist, he pulled her to him, teased her lips with light kisses. She wound her arms around his neck, felt the tingle of every vertical inch of her body jammed against his. His hands moved up her spine to cradle the back of her head and entwine his fingers in her hair. He pressed his mouth hard on hers, parting her lips with his tongue. She shivered. Eighty feet and going deeper.

Overwhelming fear of falling into an abyss came flooding back, setting off a Klaxon alarm in her brain. Passion too quick with a surgeon she hardly knew. She'd been in over her head once before and nearly drowned. Sunny eased out of their embrace, one hand resting on David's chest, the other gripping the deck rail.

He lifted her hand from his chest to his lips. "Let's go. You drive."

Sunny climbed into the helm seat of the Boston Whaler. She gripped the wheel and gunned the engine, speeding toward the harbor and fleeing from her past.

Nineteen

Skyscrapers twinkled in the picture windows of David's living room. Sunny heard the clink of glassware as he poured a bottle of wine. After their dive trip, she vowed to avoid further social encounters. But his office nurse called the OR to request that Sunny meet him at his home. He had important information to share, a matter he didn't want to discuss at the Center. Her gut churned with anticipation and dread. It had to be about the merger.

"Would you like some cheese and fruit? Crackers?" he called from the kitchen.

"I'll pass. I had a fish sandwich before I left the Center."

"I heard those were dangerous." He handed her a glass of red wine, sat beside her on the white leather couch.

"Not if you get them to leave off the secret sauce." Sunny held up her glass. "Do we have something to toast?"

David set his glass on the coffee table. "I had a meeting with Darwin Chang yesterday. Vance Turner showed up. Just happened to be in town, brought his family over from Houston for vacation." He sighed. "It would have been much easier to convince Darwin to delay the merger. Then he and I could have tackled Vance."

"What did you say?"

"I decided to try for the best of both worlds. I told them the board needed to take another look at funding the programs slated to be cut and made the point that the complementary healing practices offered at UM aren't available anywhere else in the islands."

"And?"

"Darwin repeated his mantra of paring down to essential services. He says the programs are of questionable value and a drain on the profit margin."

"What did Vance say?"

"I suggested that we think about the future, that people are beginning to pay out of pocket for options that insurance doesn't cover. Hypnosis for pain management, acupressure. We should look at ways to make money as well as cutting costs. Comstock Health System could tap into a gold mine here. Vance said there are no funds to keep the programs running even in the short term."

Sunny put down her wine glass without taking a sip. "Damn. Why can't these people figure out some creative financing?"

"Part of the original merger deal was a pool of money for cardiac research at UM. I suggested we earmark a portion of those funds for a complementary medicine department on the basis that UM could lead the way in researching outcomes of the therapies offered. It actually makes sense if those therapies complement what we're doing in cardiology and surgery. Outcomes like reduced need for pain medication." David pushed his hand through his hair. "Hell, I even fed them some of their own fancy language. Create a foundation for the research of advanced techniques in care targeted to promote wellness."

Sunny turned to face David. "You've really been thinking about a workable strategy. Thank you. Thank you for offering up the money they promised you for research."

"Before you shower me with gratitude, listen to the rest of the story." David went over to a desk near the windows. He handed her a page of bright white stationary topped with the Comstock logo, an eagle with wings spread in flight.

Dear Dr. Kaneko,

It was a pleasure to meet with you and Darwin Chang about the partnership between CHS and UM. I'm excited about the opportunities a merger of two excellent health care corporations will bring to the community of Honolulu. This letter outlines the decisions we discussed.

In the next three months, we will begin a trial of coronary artery bypass procedures without the heart-lung pump. The candidates will be strictly screened so as to maintain a low mortality rate. Patients who qualify for that type of surgery as well as for other high risk cardiac procedures will be sent to Houston. It is preferable that these surgeries be performed in a facility where advanced procedures are done on a regular basis. Of course, UM will continue to do the bread-and-butter surgeries such as routine bypasses and adult valves.

I hope you will consider our request to return to Houston to lead our cardiac research program. We need your talent and willingness to test new procedures. Though we initially indicated that such a program would be established at UM, we now believe that growing one healthy cardiac program is far better than duplicating efforts in two facilities.
Sincerely,
Vance Turner, CEO

Sunny glanced at David, scanned the letter again. "They're planning to decimate UM's cardiac program."

"Patients will see CHS physicians for the pre-surgery workup and stay in Houston for immediate post-surgical recovery." David took the letter from Sunny, sailed it across the room. "Betty and Mark would have had to find a cheap hotel room or apartment there. Meanwhile, their corner market would have gone belly-up. Pure bullshit."

"Did you tell them about Kimmy's recovery?"

He nodded. "Darwin made a crack about voodoo medicine."

"I'm so sorry, David."

"It was like listening to myself." He retrieved the letter and returned it to the desk. "Damn. I should have seen this coming. This is what happens when physicians without their own attorneys try to strike business deals. Texas verbal contract, good buddy."

Sunny reached for her wine glass, took a long swallow, the fatigue of defeat descending on her like chain mail. "Are you considering the Houston offer?"

David lounged beside Sunny, propping his bare foot on the edge of the glass coffee table. "In the early years, I could hardly believe my good fortune in getting a position with DeBakey. I didn't think I'd ever come back to O'ahu except to check on my parents."

"What changed?"

"I got tired of the assembly-line atmosphere. Small fish, big pond. I knew I'd have a long wait to lead a research project."

"Sounds like CHS wants to give you that opportunity."

"Yeah. 4,000 miles away. I've begun to appreciate being home. Besides, I don't want to give them the satisfaction of leading me around by the nose."

"I'm sorry it turned out this way."

"Thanks for not saying I told you so."

"Listen. I want you to get how much I appreciate your taking them on even though I am the insufferable OR director."

"Who called you that?" He ran one finger along her arm, down her hand to the tip of her middle finger. A tingling wake followed his touch.

She shrugged.

He laced his fingers with hers. "You were right. Things are going to get worse at UM."

"And there's not a thing we can do about it." Sunny extricated her hand and unfolded herself from the couch. "I need ice water."

"Refrigerator door." He followed Sunny to the kitchen and sat on a barstool at the counter.

She leaned against the sink. "Look at that view. You can wash dishes and never take your eyes off Waikīkī."

David swiveled on the barstool to look out the windows. "I like being up here by the university. My parents are just down the hill in Makiki." He turned back to Sunny. "This place is a lease like the boat. Maybe I've never believed I was coming back for good."

"Did you save your cowboy hat?"

David groaned, rubbed the late evening stubble on his chin. "Are you giving up on UM?"

"I've run out of ideas. Katherine has caved. If they wouldn't listen to you, they sure aren't going to pay attention to me. Mostly, I've been thinking it's time to move on. I don't want to help dismantle UM."

David grabbed his keys off the counter. "Let's walk."

The road climbed past palatial homes, stands of eucalyptus trees, and university buildings. Sunny walked backwards up the hill, arms outstretched. "All of Honolulu at our feet."

David joined her promenade-in-reverse and picked up the pace to a jog. "This is the way Mick Jagger gets in shape for a concert tour."

She ratcheted up the tempo. "I didn't think you'd have an inkling about the Rolling Stones."

"In-flight magazine."

Sunny turned and dashed up the hill. He matched her strides as they raced to the crest. At the top, they leaned over, hands on knees, sucking air. "Guess we're not doing a concert tour any time soon," Sunny gasped.

David pointed to a gravel track meandering off to the right. "A little farther up there's a park."

They settled on the grass at the edge of a small promontory overlooking Mānoa, the neighborhood slumbering against the backdrop of city lights. Fine mist and the fragrance of eucalyptus filled the valley at the foot of the steep Ko'olau range. Birds, heading for their roosts, called to each other as they winged up the canyon.

Sunny stretched out her legs. She chided herself for going on a walk with David instead of going home. But it was just a walk. They needed a chance to shake off the grim news from Darwin and Vance Turner. She leaned back on her hands, inhaled the moist air, watched a plane's blinking lights move across the skyline. She'd make sure they stayed grounded.

David tied suture knots in a long blade of grass. "I hate to see you leave UM."

"Me too. Maybe there's something else waiting for me."

"Something left over from that other lifetime?"

Sunny smiled. It was strange and pleasing to hear him talk about past lives and complementary medicine.

"Tell me about Tanemao."

"Are you sure you want to know? I don't want you freaking out and charging back down that hill."

He laughed. "I promise to be in total control of myself at all times." In the light of a half-moon, the same intense expression he wore in the OR settled on his face. "I want to know."

Sunny hesitated. How was she supposed to share an experience that defied words? On the boat, he said he didn't believe in such things.

Now, he sat quietly, completely focused on her. She swallowed against the dryness in her mouth.

She told him about the hot afternoon in Kauhale O Waimea when she first saw Mahana, how the dreams of ancient Hawai'i just kept coming even though she tried to ignore them. She talked about how the events at UM and Lani's death drove her to Marie. Here she paused, a sob ambushing her throat. David gave her time to go on, didn't pat her hand and coo. She regained her composure, described Mahana and the Anuanua, explained Tanemao's apprenticeship and the ritual to save the hemorrhaging woman.

"Sounds like what you did for Kimmy."

Sunny nodded.

"So, Tanemao was learning to be a healer."

"He excelled at diagnosis and treatments, but didn't give much credence to the spiritual aspect."

"Maybe he was afraid."

"Tanemao definitely lived in fear." Sunny told David about the threat from the neighboring island and Tanemao's pleas to prepare for war. She described how Mahana and the council planned a peaceful solution by discussing a series of questions, the night of feasting and dancing. When she came to the part about Tanemao's clash with the raiding party, she fell silent.

"What happened?"

Sunny stared at the distant lights. A glowing river took her back to a place filled with weeping. She saw blood flowing from Tanemao's abdomen, his body shaking violently. Her arms held him close to ease his wracking pain. A rush of sorrow made her lightheaded. She pressed her palms to her temples, felt a sudden flash of anger. "You were killed. You couldn't accept the possibility that we didn't need to fight." Her voice rose to a shrill octave. "You took things into your own hands and died for nothing!" The sound of her words echoing in the valley and the shock on David's face jerked her into the present. She covered her face with her hands. "Jeez. I'm sorry."

"Sunny, it's okay." The tenderness in his voice, his touch on her shoulder, made her look up. "You were back there. I could see it in your eyes and hear it in your voice."

"Some days I feel like I'm going crazy. Maybe my mind fabricated this whole thing."

"Sounds too real. You couldn't have made this up." He squeezed her arm. "Tell me the rest. What happened to the Anuanua? Did the warriors come back?"

"I don't know. I haven't seen that part." The shark tooth glinted on David's chest, evoking a memory of her last dream. "Mahana sent Tanemao away, stripped him of his apprenticeship. In a way, Mahana's rejection may have caused Tanemao's death."

David knotted another blade of grass. He chewed on the slender leaf. "What makes you think I was Tanemao?"

She had to ponder the question, think back to how his identity had first dawned on her. "When Marie asked me if anyone in Mahana's life was in this life, I just knew. Sort of like the feeling you get when you see a celebrity on the street. You say to yourself—wow, that's him." She took the blade of grass from him and slid the knots through her fingertips. "Seems like you and I have been in the same sort of struggle for a couple of lifetimes."

"And you thought I needed saving, like Tanemao?"

Sunny's gut twisted. "You make me sound like a television evangelist." She handed back his knotted stem. "I just thought if there was a chance that you'd recognize the power of body, mind and spirit . . ."

"We'd make a good team."

"We might be able to save UM."

"And now that Darwin and Vance aren't going for it?"

"Marie talked about learning the lesson of my past life."

"Have you figured that out?"

"I've always believed that when you make up your mind to do something, you can pull it off. Inherited that from my mom. She doesn't know the meaning of surrender." Sunny shifted her position, looked up at the sky. "I think there are times when we have to let go, let people be who they are, do what they do." She sighed. "Who knows. Maybe some things play out in a way we'd never choose and then turn out better than we could ever imagine."

"It's not time to throw in the towel, Sunny."

"On you or UM?"

"Both."

Maybe he was right. A slight breeze wafted up the valley, swirling the misty air. Sunny shivered.

"Chilly?"

"A little." She checked her watch. "After midnight. You aren't going to get much sleep."

"Neither are you. Or are you planning to take the day off, madam director?"

"No, sir. I have to get back to the piles on my desk."

"I guess we should call it a night." He stood. She took his outstretched hand and pulled herself up. They paused, hands still clasped, eyes in a visual grip. Sunny fought the urge to lean forward and kiss him. She looked away, turned to go.

On the walk home, she kept her hands in her pockets. "Thanks for listening to my tale."

"It's my story too."

Halfway down the hill, David led her on a shortcut through the campus. They followed a creek to a grove of blue gum trees and ferns. In the center of the grove, a massive volcanic rock rose from a ring of *ti* plants.

Sunny could just decipher the words etched into the dark monolith. "Pull hard at the *ti* roots and you will live. Is that some kind of warning to keep up with gardening chores?"

David laughed. "Hawaiian proverb." He bent down to stroke a broad leaf. "The roots of the *ti* are huge. The saying means that if you're strong and have courage, you'll survive."

"I'm amazed that after a drinking binge, the college kids don't take it as a license to test their brawn and rip up a few plants." She circled the rock, looking up at the silver and shadow in the trees.

"My study group used to come here," he said.

She ended her circle in front of him. "And you were reminded to be strong and courageous in those horrendous classes like calculus and physics."

"Actually, I needed the courage for composition and creative writing. I could never find my muse."

"I think I'd always find my muse here. This place is like an enchanted forest guarded by fierce *menehune*."

"That's what amazes me about you."

"What?"

"You always look for the magic."

They stood facing each other. For the second time that night, she saw the total focus of his attention on her. The light in his eyes made her think of molten rock bubbling up to the rim of a crater. She reached up to stroke his cheek, touch her fingertip to the perfect bow of his lips. He opened his mouth and caressed her finger with his tongue. When he drew her finger in, a ribbon of lava flowed along her arm, across her chest, and oozed down to tighten the muscles in her belly. Her brain chanted a warning. Her body screamed to kindle a fire long banked. She moved her hand to the back of his neck and kissed him hard.

David wrapped his arms around her waist, snugging her against his chest. His hands slid down to her hips and pulled her closer. She tilted her head back as he traced the curve of her neck with kisses. The brightness of the moon made it seem as if they were standing on a stage. She moved her hands to his chest, leaned away.

He raised his face, looked into hers, then glanced around the clearing. Grasping her elbow, he propelled her toward the trees.

Like teenagers racing the curfew clock, they stumbled through the ferns, into the shelter of blue gums. The air hung thick with the scent of moist earth. Sunny backed into the shadows, pulling David toward her until her spine rested against a massive trunk. The rough bark scratched her skin, triggered the chant. What was he thinking of her blatant lust?

David ran his fingers through her hair and gently pinned her head to the trunk. He covered her mouth with his. She closed her eyes, tasted a grassy sweetness, felt dizzy from the pressure of his hands on her head. All thoughts, like shards of glass, liquefied in the molten stream rising within her.

Sunny flicked her tongue along his neck and nipped the fine skin over his collarbone. She breathed in the scent of spicy soap. Her breasts tingled as he teased her nipples through the fabric of her dress. She kneaded the taut muscles in his back, moved lower to squeeze and pull his hips against her, sensed his hardness. The pressure of his body robbed her of breath, made her feel as if she would be forever fused between him and the ancient tree.

David kissed her again, merging his tongue with hers. He lifted her skirt and slid his hand along her thigh. Now, she saw the bubbling crater behind her own eyes, red lava fountaining high. She willed him to reach higher, deeper. Suddenly, he took his hand away, smoothed her skirt. "Do you hear that?"

Sunny held her breath to listen. "Someone's whistling." She felt a little disoriented, braced herself against the tree. "I can just see the headlines tomorrow. Heart surgeon and operating room nurse caught in lewd act on university campus."

David gave her a quick peck on the mouth and edged out of the trees to scan the area. He returned to the shadows. "Whoever it was is gone. Probably security making the rounds." He grabbed her hand. "Let's get out of here."

They charged down the valley road to the house. The warning chant in Sunny's brain started up again. What was she thinking? She wasn't. She'd completely lost control. Saved by the whistle. Time to run like the wind.

He unlocked the front door, led her into the foyer, and took her in his arms. "You should stay. By the time you get home, you'll have to turn around and leave for work."

Over his shoulder, Sunny glimpsed a painting on the wall. Disjointed, Picasso-like bodies tumbled across the canvas. She moved out of his embrace, took his hands. "I think I'll go."

"Are you sure?"

The light in his eyes, lava simmering just below the surface, threatened her resolve. She looked down. "Thanks, David, for all you've done, for this evening." She squeezed his hands, ducked into the kitchen for her purse.

At the front door, he kissed her forehead. "See you tomorrow, Sunny."

"Bright and early." She winced at her too chipper tone. At the car, she looked back.

Lit by the glow of the foyer, he stood in the doorway, lifting his hand in a slight wave.

Twenty

Damon handed Sunny a sterile towel off the back table and shook his head. David must be in a sour mood, she thought. She dried her arms, donned a gown, and snapped on gloves.

She'd been avoiding David for a week, escaping into her office when she saw him in the corridor, ignoring the note he stuck on her computer monitor. He left a message on her home answering machine. She played it three times, started dialing his number, hung up the phone. Easier to hit the erase button. She wanted to keep it just friends but she didn't know how.

The circulator fastened the ties at the back of Sunny's gown. "Things have been a little edgy in here."

"What's going on, Jill?"

"This guy's heart is like wet tissue paper. They've had to use felt pledgets to keep the Prolene suture from pulling through."

Sunny adjusted the gloves around her fingers. She listened to the click and whir of the pump. She'd do her job, engage in professional conversation only, and get back to her office.

"Do we have someone to hold the heart?" David glanced up over his magnifying lenses.

"Sunny's here," Jill said.

David's eyes lingered on Sunny, but she couldn't read his look. "I need you up here."

She eased in at the head of the table, between David and the drapes blocking out the anesthesiologist. Mike Jansen was back there, staying low out of the vortex of tension.

"I have to do three anastamoses."

"Okay." By the time he had the third vein-graft sewn onto the heart, her arm would feel like wood.

David gently tipped the heart up. He laid a wet lap sponge across the surface of the back side. "I need your left hand." Sunny positioned her arm up over the chest, her hand poised in the air. David placed his hand on top of hers to guide her fingers into position on the heart. His touch felt warm and firm. A knot tightened in her stomach. He pressed lightly on her hand. "Do you have it?"

"Yes." Sunny leaned her hip into the operating table. She tried to focus on something other than the fact that David's arm rested against her.

Dr. Carl Calhoun, David's assistant on the opposite side of the table, supported the vein on the fingers of one hand. His other hand applied traction to the suture. A tall man, sporting bushy white eyebrows over black marble eyes, Carl loved to gossip about hospital politics. "Did anyone here go to the big celebration yesterday?"

"Yeah, I went," Damon said in his smooth bayou drawl. "They had some mighty good cake."

"Who was there?" Jill asked.

Damon handed Carl the suture scissors. "All of the high mucky-mucks. That dude from Texas, Turner. And Katherine. She looked worn out."

David tied the last knot, and Carl clipped the suture as he continued talking. "The way they're touting this merger, you'd think Superman came to save Honolulu."

David handed the suture and needle holder back to Damon. He grasped Sunny's wrist. "I need you to pull the heart a little toward you. That's it. How are you doing?"

"Fine." He leaned toward her. The pressure of his arm near her breast trapped a breath in her throat. She concentrated on the weight of the powerful muscle beneath her hand, the bulk of the heart against her fingers.

"Let's have the vein," David said. He trimmed one end and pierced it with an eyelash-size suture needle.

Carl returned to the merger conversation. "I'm wondering why CHS wanted a facility over here."

Damon squeezed sterile saline out of a fresh lap sponge and placed it on the field, close to the open chest cavity. "Pacific rim presence."

"First O'ahu, then Japan." Carl nodded his massive head. "Maybe they'll pour some big bucks into this place."

Sunny saw David glance over his magnifiers, heard irritation in his voice. "Carl, loosen up on the suture."

Jill chimed in. "The scuttlebutt is just the opposite. Slash and burn. A bunch of people are brushing up their resumes."

"Damn it." David shifted against Sunny, raised his voice. "People, I'm having trouble concentrating. Continue this discussion when we're out of here. Carl, let go of the suture. We have a knot."

Jill shrugged and returned to her paperwork. Damon busied himself arranging instruments. David carefully untangled the knot and draped the suture over Carl's fingers. "Let's try this again."

Sunny transferred her weight from one foot to the other, wiggling her toes to relieve the cramp in her calf. Frozen in position, her arm ached. She tried to ignore the pain by making a plan to remind the staff to keep OR conversation to a minimum.

Her fingers started to burn and tingle. Sunny drew in a couple of deep breaths and studied the side of David's face. A dark rectangle of sideburn edged out below the hem of his cap. At his jaw line, the muscles clenched and released as if he were chewing gum. Hidden by the surgical mask, the cleft of his chin stood out clearly in her mind. Sunny closed her eyes, pictured his smile. She remembered their day of incredible diving, the night above Mānoa. Heaviness swelled in her chest. She opened her eyes wide and stared at the clock on the wall.

"Sunny." The snarl in his voice snapped her to attention. "Your fingers are slipping. I'm going to tear the artery if you don't keep the frigging heart retracted."

"I'm sorry. My hand is numb."

He set the needle holder down. His voice softened. "I've got the heart. You can let go. Let's try your other hand."

Sunny flexed her stiff fingers and stretched the muscles in her shoulders. He tilted his head down to look at her over the magnifiers. She saw a flicker of something in his eyes. Disappointment? Sadness?

"I'm just about finished with this anastamosis. We have one more." David repositioned the heart. This time, his touch on her hand felt hard, mechanical.

Sunny concentrated on the heart beneath her fingers, willing her attention away from her own.

⊛   ⊛   ⊛

Sunny climbed the stairs to surgical services on the third floor. She'd hurried out of the department before David's case finished, spent some time checking charts in medical records. She hoped he was up in ICU or already back in his office.

As she reached for the knob on the stairwell exit, the door whooshed open. David nearly tackled her. "Sunny."

For a fraction of a second, she considered rushing past, hunched over like a ball carrier headed for the end zone. Instead, she stepped back. "How'd the rest of your case go?"

"Fine. Thanks for scrubbing in."

She nodded.

"Why haven't you returned any of my messages?"

"I've been completely jammed. The general surgery schedule is maxed out, and we're still short staffed."

"That's not it." He closed the door and took a step toward her. "What's going on, Sunny? I want to see you again."

Acutely aware of the tight space and the flight of stairs falling away behind her, she grasped the handrail. She glanced up at the dull white walls soaring to the floors above. What was she supposed to say? Once burned, twice shy? "David, I don't think it would work between us."

He frowned. "Why not?"

"We're a cliché. The surgeon and the nurse. Happens on every television medical show."

The lines in his face softened. He brushed a wisp of hair back from her cheek. "What are you afraid of?"

"Nothing. I'm just being realistic. Those stories rarely have happy endings."

"This isn't about another hospital frat boy looking for a fling."

She stared at the whorls in the rough concrete landing.

"What's the problem?"

"We work together. We've become friends. Let's leave it there."

"I don't want to leave it there." He reached out for her.

She moved toward the door, but he blocked her way. "I can't talk about this right now."

"When?"

"I have to go." She started back down the stairs.

"I'm leaving for Houston in two weeks."

Sunny paused, but her heart kept going, dropping all the way to the ground floor. "You took the research position."

"Cardiac case volume has been down. The group won't have any problem covering for me until they find another surgeon."

"Have you told Grace?"

"Yesterday."

"What did she say?"

"She doesn't like it, but she's letting me out of our partnership agreement."

The heat in the stairwell surged inside her. "I thought you said it wasn't time to throw in the towel."

"I'm not letting them give this research program to someone else."

"I'm confused. You want us to be more than friends, and you're not even going to be around? Wait." She took one step up. "I get it. Hospital frat boy looking for a little something to remember on a lonely night in the lone star state."

"Whoa. How in the hell did you come to that conclusion? You're way off. No, wait." His eyes narrowed. "I'm the one that's way off."

"What's that supposed to mean?"

"I thought we'd started something real. I was going to ask you to come with me."

What did he think? She'd jump at the chance to start over in Texas? "That's rich, David. Create your perfect little plan and expect everyone else to go along."

His eyes widened in a glare. "Shit. There's no talking to you." He brushed past her, took the stairs down two at a time. His lab coat flapped behind him as he rounded the landing. He paused on the next flight, looking up at her. "You never gave me a chance to present my plan for your modification, madam director."

She stared down at him. The arch of his eyebrow, his cool stance, hands stuffed in pockets, infuriated her. "You mean the first mate missed a chance to salute and shout aye, aye captain."

He shook his head and disappeared below.

"Damn you!" Her words ricocheted all the way to the top floor.

Sunny ran as hard as she could along the beach, arms pumping, toes digging into the sand. Running was better than screaming, better than thinking. She pushed toward Diamond Head as she dodged kids building sand castles and a dog chasing seagulls. She ran until her lungs burned and she had to lean over gulping air, the surf splashing around her legs. A cramp in her side ached. She sloshed in the low tide until the pain started to fade and pivoted for the return sprint.

In her car, she slugged down half a bottle of water and toweled the sweat off her face. She tilted the seat back, draped the towel over her eyes. She'd been on a roller coaster ride with David. Adversaries, dive buddies, cohorts in an effort to save UM, almost lovers. Teacher and apprentice from another lifetime. They'd ended it in the stairwell before there was a chance to simply be friends.

Mahana. What did he do when Tanemao was gone? Did he ever forgive himself for the young man's death?

She remembered sitting beside Tanemao, wishing he was still alive.

In the deep of the night, sorrow mixes with apprehension. In our hearts, we long to stay with Tanemao and pay him the honor he deserves for diligently caring for our sick. In our heads, we know we must prepare for what may lie ahead.

We wrap Tanemao's body in pure white *tapa* and place him in his *fare*. Strands of fragrant *maile* vine and the sacred objects surround him. A single *kukui* lamp, carefully tended by one of the young men, burns at his feet. At his head, we set a calabash of *'awa*. Omo sprinkles everything with salt water as he intones the rainbow chant. When he is finished, I place a *lei* of bright yellow and red bird feathers on Tanemao's chest. In his serene face I see the young boy who followed me everywhere, asking endless questions. My belly wrenches with a moan rising from the depths of my being.

Except for the little children, everyone in the village is awake. Tiare calls the council to the long house. Many others wait restlessly outside. All the council members begin talking at once, some nearly shouting their concerns. I picture the opening in the middle of the sacred stone. In times like this, it is so easy to forget we must first be in the light of *Akua*.

Tiare raises her hands for silence. "Let us breathe in the *mana* all around us. Let us ask *Akua* to be with us in our time of sorrow and need."

People settle in their places, join hands, and breathe deeply. Gradually, the comforting sense of connection to each other and to the spirit world returns.

Aimata speaks first. "Maybe Tanemao was right. If the people of Tauati send warriors, we should be ready to defend our village." Others express their agreement and wonder aloud how we can quickly prepare a defense.

Tiare lets the conversation flow around the circle for a time and then stands. "My sisters and brothers, we face the first test of our commitment to live peacefully with others. Would we so easily shrink from that commitment? We are torn with the loss of Tanemao. Let us not seek to bind our broken hearts with weapons and battle plans."

The long house is quiet as the council ponders Tiare's rebuke. I feel the struggle raging within each person. It seems as if our commitment is suspended in the air over the center of our circle. Will we just blow it away with the cold breath of fear or reach out to embrace it?

Tiare sits beside me. I take her hand. I look around at drawn faces. "When Tanemao died in my arms, he whispered his repentance for his aggression and for bringing harm to our village. Let us not dishonor him by acting in a way that Tanemao came to regret. Let us find the courage to keep our commitment to peace."

The members begin to murmur and nod. Omo responds to this shift. "Each of us must look within ourselves to be sure we are filled with as much light and compassion as possible. If just one has a whisper of fear or revenge in the heart, our *mana* will be weak. We must spend the rest of this night in prayer for light."

This time Aimata stands. "The lookouts and I will gather all of our people at the sacred stone." Tiare nods. We leave the long house in a solemn line.

In the chaos, neglected torches and lamps have gone out. The clearing is bathed in bright moonlight and surrounded by deep shadows. We sit shoulder to shoulder on the grass. A few children, wide-eyed, huddle against their parents.

Omo's soft-spoken words float out over the gathering. "We each are born with a perfect bowl of light. As we grow and learn, the light in our bowl grows too. Our *mana* increases. But if we put stones in our bowl—stones of fear, anger, hate, revenge, envy, selfishness—the light in our bowl will diminish and die. This night, each of us must look into our bowl of light. If you see stones there, turn your bowl over so they will fall out, so fear and anger will leave your heart. Imagine the glowing light of *Akua* pouring out of the heavens to fill your bowl. Let that light flood your whole being and fill your heart with compassion. Ask your ancestors and protector spirits to help us. Beseech the great spirit *Akua* to be with us."

Hour upon hour we concentrate on what is in our bowls and whisper prayers. Our ceremony—the dancing and chanting to build *mana*—has transformed into solitary rituals of mind and heart. Each one feels the weight of responsibility to the clan. We know we must add our own *mana* and compassion to the whole so we may live in peace.

The brilliant moon dims as the first pink streaks of light paint the sky over the Fin of *Mao*. The twittering of birds grows into raucous chirping to greet the sun. As I look at the Anuanua bowed in prayer, I know at this moment the people of Tauati are coming across the water.

"Hey, lady, are you okay?"

Sunny felt someone tapping her arm. She pulled the towel from her eyes and squinted at the girl standing beside her car. The teenager had a silver ring in her nose that anchored a fine silver chain stretching from a silver ring in her left ear. Her brows were knitted in concern. Sunny sat up. "I'm fine."

"Cool." The girl hopped on a skateboard and skittered across the parking lot.

Sunny closed her eyes. A glowing bowl shimmered in her mind. What did it mean? What did the spirits want her to understand this time?

She straightened her seat, started the car, and headed for the east side of the island.

Twenty-one

She sat in a chair beside Marie. The hound flopped down in front of them. A glossy-feathered hen, followed by a line of chicks, strutted out of the bushes to peck in the red dirt.

"I miss my Lani," Marie said.

"Me too. I've really needed to talk to her." Sunny smiled. "The velvet hammer. She could call me on my crap and make it seem like a compliment."

They sat quietly, the cane rocker creaking counterpoint to the dog's snoring. Clouds, passing across the sun, traced a shifting filigree of light and shadow on the grass. Sunny closed her eyes. The breeze brushed her cheek like the touch of fingertips. Was that Lani? Her eyes burned. Moments of sorrow came and went like brief squalls. She'd learned to wait for their passing, letting herself flow with the emotion.

Marie reached in her pocket and handed over a tissue.

Sunny wiped her face, blew her nose. "Everything seems to be going sideways."

Marie nodded and rocked.

"A big mainland corporation took over UM. We're starting to treat sick people like bodies on a conveyor belt. Remember David Kaneko?"

"*'Ae.*"

"David helped engineer the merger. After Kimmy's healing ritual, he started to regret that move, even tried to stop the execs from axing our complementary healing services."

"Student listened to the teacher, yeah?"

"His willingness to ask questions when he's always the one with the answers amazed me."

"So, instead of an enemy, he's a friend."

"If there was a chance for friendship, I blew that. We spent some time together. It got intimate real quick. I got scared and didn't respond to any of his calls or notes. Today, he let me know he's going back to Texas. We argued. I said some things that were unfair, mean."

"You can always apologize."

Sunny nodded. "I need to talk with him before he leaves." She rubbed her face, let out a huge sigh. "Everything's so screwed up, Marie."

"What you going to do?"

"Maybe take a vacation. Look for another job."

The old woman swayed in her rocker. Sunny extended her bare foot to rub the hound's bony side. Out in the yard, two chickens squawked and flapped their wings at each other.

"After I had the argument with David, I had another dream about Mahana. The Anuanua were getting ready to meet the warriors from the neighbor island. Some ceremony about bowls and stones."

Marie stopped rocking. "Bowl of light."

"That's it. What do you think the dream means?"

"What does it mean to you?"

"You always answer my question with more questions."

Marie lit a cigarette, puffed and inhaled the white cloud. "'*Ae*."

"The Anuanua came to Hawai'i to escape the bloodshed in their homeland. But they weren't just giving up and running away. They weren't cowards. They were courageous enough to choose a different life."

"And what does that mean for you now?"

"I don't know. Choose something different for my life?"

The old woman stubbed out her cigarette and hauled herself up from the rocker. "Come on. Take me to the market."

"What?"

"Need more cigarettes."

"I'd take you for anything else but that."

Marie propped her hands on her hips. "You gotta let me have my one naughty pleasure."

"Smoking is bad for you, Marie."

She crushed on her wide brim hat. "Lived a long life. What's the use of stopping now? Come on, Sunny."

"Okay. Okay. I'll take you."

Marie, bosom nearly brushing the dashboard, sat regally in the passenger seat of the Cabriolet, one arm propped on the window ledge, the other resting across the back of the driver's seat. Her head would have bumped the convertible top if Sunny hadn't put it down.

They joined the line of cars snaking along the road. Locals honked and flashed shaka as they passed each other. Beach-goers lugged ice chests, umbrellas, bags of food, and small children as they darted across the road to the county park.

At the park entrance, an old man sat in a sagging beach chair. His white hair and beard shown in stark contrast with his nut brown skin. He wore a faded red shirt. The rest of his attire was hidden by a sign balanced on his bare feet and resting against his knees. The uneven block letters spelled out GIVE US OUR LAND. A bunch of teenagers two cars ahead screamed obscenities at the old man. One of them pitched a giant-size drink cup. The container hit the old man's shoulder in an explosion of ice and amber liquid. Soda dripped off the side of his face and arm, tracing dark streaks on his shirt. He remained still, expressionless, eyes looking straight ahead.

When Sunny's car inched past the old man, Marie waved to him. "*Ey, brah.*" He responded with a slight nod.

"Who's that?" Sunny asked.

"Ben Mahi. Been there every weekend for years. Sometimes one of his kids sits with him. They must be in their forties now."

"The sign?"

"Hawaiians were promised homestead lots eighty years ago. Ben and his family still waiting for theirs."

Sunny shook her head. How many times had she traveled this road for a weekend jaunt and didn't even notice him?

"Could die before he sees his land," Marie said.

"Why does he keep coming out, putting up with abuse from people like those idiots up ahead? Seems like he should have some peace in his old age."

"That is Ben's peace. Standing up for what's right."

Marie pointed to a clapboard building with a tin roof nestled between the boundary of the park and a narrow strip of beach. Faded ads for soft drinks, cigarettes, and beer covered the front of the rustic market. By the screen door, a hand-lettered sign announced fresh *'ōpakapaka*. A dented truck pulled out of one of the spaces in front of the store. In the bed of the pick-up, a scruffy brown dog guarded a jumble of fishing poles, nets, and buckets.

Sunny held the passenger door open for Marie. "I'll wait out here."

"Want anything?"

"No thanks." Sunny sat on a wooden bench near a path to the beach. She remembered Ben's stoic face. It took guts to demand justice decade after decade with no relief. Why hadn't he given in to anger or defeat?

She looked up to see a ball of sparkling ruby ice chips cradled in a paper cone. "Got you a treat," Marie said.

Sunny smiled. "Want to go out on the beach?"

"Sure."

Marie pushed her hat down on her head and leaned on Sunny's arm. A patch of shade under a pandanus tree beckoned to them.

Marie lit a cigarette and took a long draw. "Mahana had lotta fear."

Sunny crunched shave-ice, savored the cherry sweetness, and pondered Marie's statement. "He feared Tanemao would start a war all by himself. He was nearly right. But Tanemao's clash with the raiding party might never have happened if—"

"Acting out of fear and anger makes us miss opportunities."

"Mahana possessed that wisdom when it came to how the Anuanua should respond to people from another island. When it came to how he treated his apprentice . . ."

"Lose our head with the ones close to us."

"You think I'm missing an opportunity with David?" Sunny raised her eyebrows. "A mad, passionate affair?"

Marie let out a belly laugh that ended in a juicy cough. "Could be lotta fun," she rasped. "What you think? If you'd acted out of true *aloha*, what might have happened?"

"For one thing, I wouldn't have avoided David. If we'd had a chance to talk sooner, there wouldn't be this huge misunderstanding." Sunny shook her head. "When you've been burned, it's hard to trust someone's intentions."

"Hard to trust yourself. You gotta believe, whatever happens, you can handle it."

Sunny wasn't sure about that. In the stairwell, she'd gone off the deep end, stuck David in the broom closet with her fiancé. She'd jumped down his throat when he was just trying to have a conversation. "I really don't believe David's just looking for a fling."

"Then trust your gut. It'll be *pono* with him. It will be right."

Sunny took another nip of ice. She cared for David. His vulnerability had touched her heart. Yet, she'd let her fear push him away. "What if I take the risk, talk with him, and find out he doesn't want to have anything to do with me?"

"*Pono* isn't a guarantee you get what you want. It will be what it needs to be. You gotta trust. You gotta *chance 'em* and find out."

Sunny sucked on her shave-ice while Marie smoked. Mahana may have missed an opportunity to patch things up with Tanemao. She didn't intend to make the same mistake.

Marie crushed her cigarette out in the sand. "Why you all *pau* with the Center?"

"CHS is here to stay. There's nothing I can do to change what's happening."

"You sure?"

"I know where you're going with this, Marie. Mahana's curse. I'm giving up too soon."

The old woman lit another cigarette, pulled the brim of her hat lower to shade her face, stared toward the ocean. Sunny followed her gaze. High above the people splashing in the shimmering water, frigate birds hovered on the wind. Their v-shaped tails punctuated the sky.

"You know *kōlea*?" Marie asked.

"What's that?"

"The golden bird that led our ancestors here from Tahiti. That bird knew the way to the future. You are *kōlea*."

"What do you mean?"

"You have the privilege of seeing in the past how the future could be. Your calling is to lead people to that future."

Sunny turned toward Marie. The frozen ball plopped on the ground. Rivulets of cherry red seeped into the sand. She crumpled the paper cone in her fist. How could she be like a bird when she felt as useless as melting ice?

"You know what healing is possible," Marie said. "Healing flowed through your own hands. You know how Mahana's people prepared themselves to keep the peace. Gifts given to you."

"That doesn't mean I can do those things." She slumped against Marie. An elbow jabbed her side. The glare on Marie's face shocked her more than the hard nudge.

"How do you know if you don't try?" Marie's shout ended in a bout of coughing. She held up the cigarette. "You right, *keiki*. Bad for me."

Sunny gently eased the butt from Marie's fingers and crushed it out. "Does this mean you're going to stop?"

"When you stop running away, yeah?"

Sunny blew out a deep sigh. She longed to give back the so-called gifts, erase Mahana from her consciousness, and turn back the clock to the days of charging hard in the OR without much else to worry about. "Why me?"

"I don't know why you." The rumble of the surf and the din of beachgoers nearly drowned out Marie's quiet words. "Some Hawaiians would be very angry to hear a *haole* lived as one of our original ancestors. They'd say she has no right to this knowledge, these gifts."

The breeze off the ocean stiffened, lofting grains of sand to sting Sunny's legs. Marie's words stung even more. She loved everything Hawaiian, held a deep reverence for the culture, tried to show respect by working at Kauhale O Waimea. "Marie, I do not want to offend anyone. Believe me, I'd like to forget everything that's happened."

The old woman's voice rose. "This Hawaiian says that ancient time was your time. And now is your time. Don't turn your back. Don't be like so many others who've come to these islands and brushed aside what's sacred. Don't wish for it to be easy."

Sunny picked up a pebble half-buried in the sand and rubbed it with her thumb. It wasn't that she wanted it to be easy. She didn't know if she possessed the fortitude or patience to be the trillionth drop of water that finally made a crack in the stone. Like Mahana, she didn't give people much time to become believers. Marie's *kōlea* thing—showing the way to a future born out of wisdom from the past—paralyzed her.

"What's in your bowl, Sunny?"

"I'm scared."

"Sure you're scared. Mahana was scared."

"How do I find the guts to go on like Ben? I don't know if I have what it takes to be the only one standing."

"Ben has his *'ohana* just like Mahana had his people. You're not alone. This time, maybe even Tanemao will be there with you."

"But I don't even know if the Anuanua succeeded in what they chose to do. Maybe they were all slaughtered."

"Trust."

Rely on radical trust. Had Marie been talking to her mother? "Will you help me?"

"Why you think Lani brought us together?"

Sunny nodded. There had to be a reason for all the things that had happened over the past months. What was that reason? What would be the outcome? Not knowing was the toughest part.

"Think of it this way," Marie said. "You be like *kōlea*. Fly the way, with spirit under your wings. People see you and spread their wings. Then spirit can lift them up too."

"You make it sound so simple."

"It is."

"I'll make you a deal. I'll flap my wings like *kōlea*, and you'll get rid of those cancer sticks."

Marie let out a belly laugh. "'*Ae*."

Sunny felt the smoothness of the pebble in her palm. If she didn't try to save UM, she might never find peace. She tucked the pebble in her pocket, stood up, and offered Marie her arm. "Let's go in the market and get you some of that nicotine gum before you change your mind."

Marie laughed again and hefted herself off the sand.

Sunny gave herself completely to Marie's massive hug. She felt tingling course through her body, like the adrenalin rush of flying over an abyss eighty feet below the waves. "Thank you, Marie."

Out over the ocean, the frigates dipped and soared gracefully on the wind.

Twenty-two

In the crawl of traffic back to Honolulu, Sunny had plenty of time to think about what she could do for UM. CHS wasn't going away. She had to take up where David left off in his meeting with Darwin and Vance. If a big demand for UM's complementary medicine services could be demonstrated, the execs would have to listen. Like Mahana, she needed to rally a village.

Who could help her get the community involved? The individual would have to be acquainted with movers and shakers, linked to the grass roots public. She knew only one person with those kinds of connections. Right about now he might be setting up for a Friday night gig at The Wall.

Threading her way through the outside tables occupied by late-lunchers, Sunny smiled at the familiar sign by the lounge door. NO SHIRT, NO SHOES, NO PROBLEM. Cool darkness enveloped her. She gave her eyes a moment to adjust to the dim light. The air smelled of stale beer and ocean. A man with a steel gray crew cut and a gold hoop in his left earlobe polished beer mugs at the bar. He saw Sunny and called out, "Hi. The lounge doesn't open until seven. We can serve you food and drinks out on the patio."

Sunny climbed onto a battered barstool. "Thanks. I'm looking for Pete Bishop."

He nodded toward the stage at the far end of the room. "Just got here. They're out back unloading their gear."

She held out her hand. "I'm Sunny Lyon. You're the owner, right?"

He clasped her hand. "Gary Stone. I keep wanting to get a divorce from this baby, but I can't seem to walk away. Been together nearly twenty years. She got her name because I used to dive the wall out there. Gave that up when I ruptured an eardrum in a friendly boxing match."

"You must know how popular your place is with the UM crowd. Some weeks, I've been here almost every evening after work."

"Thanks for the business. Guess you medical types need the stress relief. You a friend of Pete's?"

Sunny nodded. "His girlfriend Lani was my best friend."

"I'm sorry. What a horrible deal that was. For a while, I didn't think Pete would bounce."

"How's he doing now?"

"His first night back he sounded ragged, but at that point I knew he'd be okay." Gary dunked more mugs in sudsy water in the sink below the bar and wiped his hands on his jeans. "Can I get you something to drink?"

"Soda water with a lime."

"Coming right up." He shoveled ice into a tall glass, dispensed the fizzy liquid, and fixed a lime wedge on the rim. "You work at UM?" He added a straw and slid the drink toward Sunny.

"Operating room. I don't know how much longer I'll be there. Things are changing, not for the better."

"That's too bad. The Center has a reputation for really good care."

Sunny squeezed the lime into the soda and took a long swallow. "Would it matter to people around here if they knew UM was going down hill?"

"Hell yes. Everyone I know knows someone—family member, friend—who goes there for therapy or classes. My brother gets biofeedback treatments at the Center."

"Would people speak up?"

"Maybe if they knew what they were losing."

"Hmm." She took another sip of her drink.

Gary glanced toward the stage. "Pete, someone's here to see you."

She swiveled around on the stool to see Pete setting down a guitar case and small amplifier. He looked up. A smile tweaked the corners of his mouth. "Ey, Sunny. What brings you here?" He came toward her, arms open wide. His full beard was gone, and he looked less haggard than on the day he brought Marie to the Center. They rocked together in a long embrace.

"It's good to see you back at The Wall," Sunny said.

The smile disappeared. His eyes were like deep pools of flat water. "It'll never be the same."

"Without Lani at the front table, it must seem like a huge hole in the middle of this room."

"Huge hole in my life."

Sunny nodded. She traced a pattern in the condensation on her glass. She knew the emptiness and couldn't think of anything to say.

Pete leaned on the bar. Gary pushed a bottle of beer in front of him. "Thanks, *brah*." He motioned to Sunny. "Let's go out back." As they walked by the van, the band members waved. "Donny, after you get your drums set up, catch a break. I'm gonna take care of the sound, yeah?" The drummer signaled a thumbs-up.

They sat side-by-side on the sea wall. Far out beyond the breakers, the ocean color alternated between turquoise and brooding slate as clouds sailed across the sun. Pete took a swig of beer and leaned forward, elbows on knees. "Leilani's been gone over a month, and I still see her lying on the grass at 'Iolani, in that hospital bed." Pete rubbed his face. "I want to remember her smile, Sunny."

"Me too." Sunny thought for a moment. "Do you have a photo of Lani?"

Pete shook his head. "We never got around to getting our picture taken. She didn't want to give me an old one."

Sunny searched her wallet and withdrew a snapshot taken at a staff party. The print radiated with Lani's laughter.

Pete set his beer on the wall and held the photo as if he were cupping a butterfly in his big hands. He stared at the picture, looked at Sunny. "You sure?"

"It's yours."

Pete tucked the picture in his shirt pocket, wiped his eyes with the heels of his hands. "Thanks," he whispered.

"How's Kai?"

"Getting to be number one tight end. Bugging me to start practice again."

"What's going on with the band?'

"Gotta get back in the studio. The guys count on me to lead the charge." Pete shook his head. "I go through every day like in a fog."

"Maybe it's enough right now just to play a few nights a week."

Pete didn't respond. The boom of the waves filled the silence between them. After a while, he took a deep breath, straightened up, slipped the mask of relaxed-island-boy back in place. "What's up, Sunny? Still going at it with that surgeon?"

"That's a long story better saved for a time when I can drink along with you. I'm here because I need your help again."

"You and Marie." He circled his finger in the air at the side of his head. "You two are just trying to make sure I don't go *pupule*."

"You bet. We don't want to lose you. Besides, you're the one with all the connections."

"Who do you want to meet?"

"I need to get a whole lot of people in the community together to give testimonials."

"You trying to get elected for public office?"

Sunny laughed. "I've already been elected by a unanimous vote of one to be a *kōlea*."

"Huh?"

"Marie."

"Ah." Pete held up his hands. "One *akamai wahine*. Very clever. So, why does she want you to be the bird of our ancestors?"

Sunny told Pete about the CHS merger and the resulting changes. "I figure if we can get people to say loud and clear what they expect from this not for profit, tax exempt, beholden to the community corporation, CHS will reconsider the budget cuts. A forum has to happen soon, before the disgruntled staff at UM gets complacent or bails."

Pete let out a long whistle. "Buggah of a task."

"Got any ideas?"

"I could reach all the activists groups pretty quick. Good coconut telegraph."

"What?"

"E-mail."

"I was thinking about a full page ad in the *Honolulu Advertiser*."

"Cost you plenty."

"I know a few docs who'd probably kick in."

Pete drained the last of his beer, twirled the bottle in his hands. "There's a couple of local rags that would run ads for sure."

"If we could get radio and television involved that would be even better."

"My brother's wife works for one of the TV stations. The one that has the reporter who does stories about helping little guys fight big companies."

"Take Action with Irene Pualoa."

"That's it. I'll talk to Jeff before we go on tonight."

"Great. I'll send you the copy for the newspaper ads so you can check to make sure it includes all the information people need. Once this hits the media, I think CHS will agree to hold a community forum. That's when we'll need the testimonials."

"They're gonna find out this isn't Texas, yeah?"

Sunny thought she caught a hint of the old sparkle in Pete's eyes. She squeezed his arm. No wonder Lani loved this man. Despite the darkness in his life, he didn't hesitate to offer help.

They sat quietly. An outrigger canoe sliced through the waves, the crew leaning hard on their paddles. She thought of Marie's comment. Some Hawaiians would resent Sunny being the one to bring ancient wisdom to the present. She worried that Pete felt that way. "Could we talk about one more thing?"

"Sure."

"When you came to the Center to help us with Kimmy's healing ritual, I told you about my experience of a past life here in the islands."

Pete nodded.

Sunny bit her lip. She dreaded offending him, searched for the right words. "I wouldn't blame you for resenting a *haole* who claimed to be one of your ancestors. It doesn't seem right. Most of the time I wish it hadn't happened. I would never want to . . ." She cringed at her own babbling.

He turned toward her and took her hand. "Sunny, we got enough enemies. We need everyone, no matter where they're from, willing to help the Hawaiian people. Most of the time white people will listen only to another white person anyway."

She clasped his hand in both of hers and breathed a sigh of relief.

"Doesn't mean it's gonna be easy for you. *Kōlea* journeyed thousands of miles."

"I keep thinking of Kimmy. If we can do that kind of healing for more people, it'll be worth the struggle."

Pete stared toward the ocean. When he looked at her, his eyes brimmed with tears. "Wish we could have done that for Leilani."

Details of the Monday morning cases filled nearly every white space on the giant schedule board. Sunny studied the column of surgeon names. David wasn't listed for any procedure. She'd left a couple of messages on his pager and one on his home phone the day before, with no response. She decided to ask Grace Pukui about him. The chief of surgery would be finished with a heart valve replacement in an hour.

At her desk, she made a list of tasks completed and pending for the community forum. On Sunday, she and Pete designed the ad for the newspaper. The message noted the programs and services to be discontinued and urged the public to contact UM by telephone, letter, and e-mail to express their concerns. They spent hours telephoning people for contributions toward the cost of the ad and needed just a few more donors. Pete's sister-in-law, Olina, secured a tentative agreement from Irene Pualoa for coverage in her regular television segment.

More calls needed to be made to assemble a core group of volunteers to prepare for the forum. Marie promised to work with those individuals on meditation for compassion and positive outcomes at the forum. Sunny planned to recruit people unafraid of the so-called touchy-feely stuff.

She flipped through her Rolodex, jotting down names and numbers. David's card popped up. Sunny put down her pen. Their scene in the stairwell replayed in her mind. He'd asked her to go with him to Texas. That had to mean he wasn't involved with anyone else. Unless he'd tossed out the idea to make her feel rotten for accusing him of frat boy behavior. She groaned. The cynic never disappeared for good.

Sunny picked up the cowry shell she'd used for Kimmy's healing ritual. Stirred by childhood fancy, she held the open side of the shell to her ear. A little ocean still rumbled in there. She studied the brown-speckled pattern, ran her finger across the porcelain-cool surface. The shell represented water, the flow of emotions. She had a chance to choose the emotion that drove her behavior. More than anything, she wanted to choose love over fear, distrust, and anger.

The chief of surgery appeared in the doorway. "Got a minute?"

"Absolutely, Grace. Please have a seat. I was going to catch you when you came out of room five." Sunny looked at her watch. "Guess I lost track of time. I've been trying to get a hold of David Kaneko with no luck. I didn't think he was leaving for a couple of weeks."

"That's why I stopped by to talk with you." Grace took off the paper cap and fluffed up her hair. "He decided to leave sooner. Wanted to find a place to live and meet his new staff. He's wasting no time with the research start-up."

A lump lodged in Sunny's chest. Just like Mahana, she might never get a chance to patch things up. "Were you surprised he resigned?"

"No. David seemed dissatisfied here. And yes. I thought CHS would give him money to do his work here. I was shocked they railroaded their ally back to Texas." Grace shook her head, ripped the paper mask from around her neck. "Just as well. He never really fit into our program."

Sunny turned the shell over in her hand. "Grace, did you know that he went to the execs and asked them not to cut our complementary medicine services?"

"No. What inspired him to do that?"

"I asked him for help. He cared enough to listen He went to bat for us even when he wasn't completely sold on all the non-mainstream things we embrace. Since his niece's recovery, he was starting to fit in."

"Amazing. Sad that none of that worked out, and now we're losing a good surgeon."

Sunny couldn't tell Grace how very sad his leaving made her feel. She put down the shell and glanced at her list. "If you have a couple more minutes, I'd like to tell you about a plan in the works to rescue UM."

Grace nodded and settled back in her chair.

Twenty-three

"Anyone have questions or concerns before Marie starts our meditation?" Sunny glanced around her living room where twenty-four people sat cross-legged on the floor, shoulder to shoulder on the sofas, and in their own folding chairs—activist leaders, managers and employees from the Center, Pete and a couple guys from the band, Jeff and Olina, and a few of Marie's friends from all along the coastal road, including old Ben in his rickety beach chair.

Olina, black hair pulled into a chignon at the nape of her neck, raised a perfectly manicured hand. "It's still hard to focus on the light. I start thinking about what happened at work or what I need to do when I leave here."

"'*Ae*. Connecting with spirit is hard. Takes practice. Remember when you learned how to drive?" Marie grinned and waggled her finger. "How many times did you make a wrong turn? Drive off the road?"

The room filled with laughter and nods of recognition.

"But if you hadn't left your driveway, you'd still be walking, yeah?"

When the laughter died down, Sunny added, "If your brain sends you thoughts about yesterday or tomorrow, just say thanks and let those thoughts float away like little boats on a river. Refocus on your bowl of light, even if it's only for a minute or two."

Marie nodded. "The more we're here in the present, the more we connect with spirit."

An employee from the Center raised his hand. His rectangular, dark-framed glasses gave him a professorial look. "Do you really believe imagining golden light will have an effect on the community forum tomorrow night?"

Sunny wished they had more time to prepare. The overwhelming response to the newspaper ad nearly shut down the patient advocacy office at UM. When Irene Pualoa aired a report on the impact of the merger, it didn't take long for Vance and Darwin to agree to the forum. This group had come together almost every night for the past two weeks to practice Mahana's bowl of light meditation. How often had she struggled with her own skepticism? She hoped they were ready.

"I do believe we'll have an impact," Sunny said. "Sometimes it's hard for me to hang onto that belief because there aren't any guarantees. It's not turn this key and the engine will start. We're trying to be human vessels for healing energy. We have to trust the universe to take care of the rest."

"What we have to lose if we focus on things like love?" Marie asked.

"No loss," Pete said quietly. "Gonna get peace inside our hearts no matter what happens."

Tara, the nurse from intensive care, intoned in her Aussie twang, "Serenity is not freedom from the storm, but peace within the storm. I read that somewhere. Guess we'll see how peaceful we can be in the storm."

"Maybe we shouldn't expect the forum to be a storm," Jeff said.

A heavy-set woman, wearing an acid green blouse, nudged Tara "Why imagine a challenge that might not materialize?"

"Good point," Tara said.

"On the other hand, it might be better if we're prepared for a raging debate," Olina said, glancing up at Jeff.

Others joined in the discussion offering their opinions on the best mindset for the meeting.

Sunny waited for the ripple of comments to fade. "We've already agreed to focus on one thing—holding light and compassion and the intention for peacemaking in the room. If we do that, the people of our community will feel safe enough to speak about their concerns, and the executives will open their hearts. You think we can we do that?"

Two people, then three more, nodded their heads. Gradually everyone in the room indicated their agreement.

"Okay, then." Sunny turned to Marie. "Shall we start?"

Marie began by asking everyone to take two big belly breaths, drawing the air all the way down to their *piko*. "Get comfortable and focus on your breathing. Breathe in through your nose and out through your mouth in a long ha sound." They synchronized their breathing for four ha breaths. She told them to imagine holding a beautiful bowl, the bowl they were given at birth, and take four more ha breaths. "First be sure no stones in that bowl. Then breathe golden light into it. See light rise up from your bowl and fill this room. See it join with light from all the other bowls around you."

Sunny concentrated on her bowl. The light expanded into a sparkling geyser, raining brilliant shards around her. The golden glow shimmered in the room and grew even brighter as others added more light.

"I'm gonna count to three, and we'll release this light of compassion and courage and wisdom into the world." Marie drew in a deep, audible breath. "*'Ekahi, 'elua, 'ekolu*. Send the light into the world. See it spinning up, up, high above us. Far above this *hale*, out into the night, carrying goodness to all who will receive it." She let a few quiet moments pass, then whispered, "*Mahalo nui loa*."

Sunny watched the light swirl into a brilliant whirlwind rising up to burst through the top of the house, great luminous clouds gathering and flying far beyond the horizon.

We gather on the river bank. This morning our emissaries would have boarded canoes amid cheers and prayers for a safe voyage to Tauati. Instead, fervent prayers plead for safety here on our own shore. We wait in sadness and uncertainty. Tanemao is gone. The canoes, festooned with *lei* of *maile* and colorful feathers, sit empty on the sand.

Aimata and her lookouts, breathing hard, rush out of the jungle. Tiare, Omo, and I meet them. Sweat sheens Aimata's massive body. "They have just entered the mouth of the river from the sea."

Tiare speaks in a low voice. "How many canoes?"

"Five."

"Warriors?

"Armed with spears and clubs."

"Who else did you see?"

"An older man with a feathered headdress rides in the bow of a canoe that is larger than the others."

"The chief," Omo says.

"Behind him stands a man short of stature and wearing many shells."

Omo rubs his chin. "He could be their priest."

"They are accompanied by a dozen young men." Aimata grasps Tiare's shoulder. "Nearly forty in all canoes."

"Keep watch, Aimata. Let us know when they are at the bend."

Aimata signals to her lookouts. As they disappear into the lush foliage that fringes the river, Tiare turns to us. "Omo, get everyone into position. Mahana, is everything ready?"

I nod as Omo hurries away. For a brief moment, the look of calm slips from Tiare's face. Her eyes speak of the panic that threatens to overwhelm us. I take her in my arms and whisper, "I know, my love. Being the leader at a time like this brings much doubt. Remember, your wisdom has brought us all this way and will not fail us now." I gently turn her away from the river. "Look at the Anuanua. Our people thrive. We live a good life."

"But, Mahana, what if they harm us? What if we have led our people to believe in a commitment that ultimately is their death sentence?"

"We've seen with our own eyes where the other path leads—a life we don't want to live anyway." I look into her eyes, willing her all the love and *mana* I can summon. "Tiare, whatever happens this day, we stand in the light of *Akua*. That is all that matters."

It is not long before the canoes of Tauati, full of grim faces, glide silently toward the bank. The men in the big canoe leap out and haul the vessel onto the sand. The smaller canoes follow. The chief steps out, black and blue feather headdress gleaming in the sun. His face is inscrutable. Even with a deep scar running across his cheek, he is a fine-looking man. The one we assume to be the priest steps out of the canoe. He is surprisingly agile under the weight of an immense shell cape that covers his entire torso. Shorter than the chief by two heads, he stays close to the ruler's side. Warriors quickly take places on either side of the two men. They hold in front of them clubs of wood and stone and spears with tips fashioned from sharpened shells and shark teeth. One grips a club that appears to be the great bone of the leg. The sight of this war party, something never seen on our shore, fills me with dread.

Omo, Aimata, Tiare, and I stand facing them. Even the sounds of the birds and the river are hushed. I glance back at the circle of our people. The children, puzzled by the strange-looking men, huddle quietly in the center. Mothers nestle sleeping infants. The adults and young people surround them, sitting cross-legged and calm. On the edge of the circle, our elders stand erect and proud. Everyone, eyes softly focused, concentrates on staying filled with the light of *Akua* and casting that light around the people of Tauati. I can feel their *mana* radiating against my back.

Tiare steps directly in front of the chief. His stony expression cracks into a frown. She speaks softly. "We welcome you to the home of the Anuanua."

The chief remains silent, but his eyes are open wide. I wonder if his reaction stems from being confronted by a woman or his inability to understand her words. He puffs himself up to his full height, closes the gap between them, and pounds his fist to his chest. I fight the urge to step in. The man's voice is high-pitched for such an enormous frame. "I am Hiro, chief of the Tauati people." Though the pronunciation differs somewhat, his Tahitian words are familiar.

Tiare bows her head in greeting, and then places her open hand on her chest. "I am Tiare of the Anuanua."

Hiro does not return the respectful bow. "One of your warriors wounded my man last night." A wave of his long arm directs our attention to the bodyguard nearest him. A jagged gash glows angry red on the young man's calf.

Tiare responds with a steady gaze and an upturned palm. "Not a warrior but a young man learning to be a healer. He reacted to one of your scouting parties."

"You cannot dishonor my people in this way." The chief reaches out as if to grab Tiare's wrist.

Aimata steps toward him. Instantly, the Tauati warriors leap forward, their weapons leveled at our heads.

Omo begins to intone a soft chant. I feel a surge of *mana* arise from our people. Staring hard at the chief and his priest, I imagine brilliant white light engulfing them. After a moment, Hiro's hand begins to tremble. He lowers his outstretched arm and steps back. Glaring, he signals his warriors to move away. I sense that he is struggling to fathom the power confronting him.

The Tauati priest fixes his attention on Omo who continues to chant. The priest frowns and cocks his head. Tiare turns to him. "The chant asks for the peace of *Akua*." His eyes narrow as if he is trying to discern a secret weapon in the words.

Omo's chant and waves of *mana* fill the silent space between us. Hiro clenches his fists, belligerence and wonder battling on his face. The priest keeps his eyes on Omo. Sunlight glints on his shell cape and the tips of the warriors' spears. The last line of the chant fades. I breathe in the scents of sweet *maile* vines, sour sweat, and the tang of fear. I breathe out my desire for peace. Hiro grabs a club from one of his warriors. His scowl deepens the scar on his cheek. My breath catches in my chest. I feel my belly tighten and concentrate on the *mana*. All of us are rooted in place like ancient *koa* trees. I close my eyes and imagine him dropping the club. A child's giggle breaks the stillness.

Hiro returns the club to his warrior and folds his arms across his chest. "You must pay us for your aggression."

I move beside Tiare. "Chief Hiro, let us first show you something." He does not respond. "As you can see, we are not armed. Please come with us." He looks to the priest who gives a slight nod. Hiro motions to his bodyguards and follows Tiare and me. Omo and Aimata remain behind, stationed between the Anuanua and the warriors from Tauati.

At the door of Tanemao's *fare*, I pause. "My apprentice was the one who injured your warrior."

We step inside, eyes adjusting to the dim glow of a *kukui* lamp. The acrid odor of burning lamp oil assaults my nostrils. Chief Hiro stares at the body shrouded in *tapa*.

I crouch low beside Tanemao and look up at Hiro. "Is this not payment enough?" I see a flicker in the chief's eyes.

After a long silence, Tiare speaks. "Chief Hiro, can we go to the long house?" He nods and pushes past her, through the doorway.

Before I leave the *fare*, I ask the young man attending Tanemao to fetch my pack, some *ti* leaves, and fresh water and bring them to the long house.

Tiare and I sit facing Hiro and his priest, Pao. Their bodyguards stand directly behind them, weapons ready. She offers the chief a cup of 'awa. He hesitates, accepts the cup, and takes a sip. Recognizing the taste, he sucks down the liquid. Tiare passes cups to Pao and me. No one speaks as we finish our drinks.

Breaking the silence, Tiare motions to the calabashes, *tapa* bundles, and wooden cages arranged neatly at one end of the long house. "Please accept these gifts as our welcome and symbol of our desire for peaceful relations with the people of Tauati."

I select a cage containing a handsome rooster and two plump hens and place it before Hiro. He eyes the birds and then nods his approval. "What else?"

If Tiare thinks the question rude, her face does not show it. "We offer you foodstuffs, *tapa* cloth decorated with Anuanua designs, fish hooks and lures, seeds for plants you may not have on Tauati, shell *lei*, and a pig."

Upon hearing of the pig, the hint of a smile tugs at the chief's lips. Then he frowns. "What do you want?"

"We want only peace, Chief Hiro. We want friendship with you and your people. We would welcome the chance to trade implements and knowledge with you." Tiare takes a deep breath. "We want you to join with us in a promise that there will be no bloodshed between our clans."

Pao speaks for the first time. "What if we don't make this promise?"

I sense the fear in their hearts, the distrust in their minds. Remembering there is powerful *mana* all around us, I draw in a chestful of air. I focus on filling my being with compassion. I picture us surrounded by the light that heals all destructive thoughts and feelings.

Tiare points to the bodyguard with the gash on his leg. "There will be more wounded, more dead like our Tanemao. We will lose loved ones and friends." Her tone grows passionate. "Never-ending war will bring unending grief." She leans forward locking eyes with Hiro. "At the very least, we will lose the great benefit of working together to help our islands grow and thrive."

The young attendant appears in the doorway with my pack. I signal him to come in and open the bundle of supplies. "Chief Hiro, let me treat that gash on your man's leg. If the wound does not heal properly, he will become gravely ill."

This time the chief does not look to the priest for his approval. He nods vigorously. I beckon the bodyguard to a mat beside my supplies. His eyes dart a look of uncertainty at the chief. The chief urges him to join me.

"Please lie on your belly so I can have a good look at your leg."

Hesitantly, he lays down his spear and stretches out on the mat. Looking back over his shoulder he never takes his eyes off what I am doing. I study his face and realize he is younger than I thought. I turn my attention to his wound. My heart is stricken to see the damage done by Tanemao's knife. For a moment, I am distracted by grief for Tanemao and for the harm he has caused. I shake my head, begin a silent chant for healing.

When I gently press on the edges of the wound, the young man flinches and draws in a sharp breath. His skin is flushed and hot. First I pour a copious amount of 'awa on the gash to lessen the pain. With fresh water and pieces of *tapa*, I clean the wound out. His body is taut but he does not cry out. From a small calabash, I pour the putrid smelling juice of *noni* fruit into the wound. He grunts a sound of disgust. Enduring the odor of vomit is a small price to pay for the liquid's extraordinary healing properties. I cover the wound with fresh *ti* leaves and wrap the leg in lengths of *tapa*.

I want to complete the treatment with a chant accompanied by my rattle and the sacred objects to call in the healing spirits. But I know not how the people of Tauati honor the spirit world. I do not want to endanger our fragile opportunity to build friendship with Hiro. My silent prayer will have to suffice. I hand the bodyguard a bundle of *noni* fruit, *ti* leaves, and *tapa* strips. "You must be certain to apply the juice of this fruit to your wound every morning and night. Change the *ti* leaves and *tapa* each time as well." He nods and accepts the bundle.

Hiro and Pao have been watching us intently. They look relieved when the young man leaps from the mat, takes up his weapon, and resumes his place behind the chief. Tiare smiles broadly and beckons me to sit beside her. "So, Chief Hiro, can we make a promise?"

The chief slowly removes his headdress, draws his shell and feather *lei* up over his head. He holds out the strands to Tiare. She slips them on and offers the chief her own *lei*. He places her gift around his neck and dons his headdress. Tiare extends her hand, palm up. Hiro places his hand, palm down, on hers.

I cover their hands with mine. We all look to Pao, waiting for him to extend his hand. Hiro directs him with a sharp motion of his head. The priest places his hand over ours, but his skin never touches mine.

Back at the river bank, the warriors load our gifts into their canoes. Without a farewell, Pao hurries to board the chief's vessel. Hiro nods to Tiare. Just before his bodyguards help him into his canoe, he turns to me and whispers, "Thank you for helping my son."

The men of Tauati, faces still as grim as when they landed on our shore, turn their canoes into the current and paddle toward the sea. We watch until they disappear around the bend. Aimata and the lookouts sprint toward the jungle to follow their course.

Omo blesses our people and sends them home to get food and rest, asking them to return to the sacred stone later in the evening. He sits with Tiare and me by the river. We go over every detail of our encounter with Hiro and Pao. We conclude there is a good chance for peace with Hiro. About Pao, we are not so certain.

Omo's great head sags with fatigue, but his smile glows as bright as a thousand torches. "We passed the first test of our commitment. *Akua* knew our courage and sent us much love and light." His smile suddenly fades. "If only Tanemao could have been with us." He struggles to his feet. "I am weary. I will see you tonight, my beloved ones." We watch him trudge away.

Tiare looks down and draws patterns in the sand with her finger. With my hand under her chin, I gently tilt her head up. Tears course down her cheeks.

I take her in my arms. My tears mingle with hers.

After a long time, Tiare wipes her eyes. "I think it is time we rest, Mahana. There is still much to do." She stands and reaches out to help me up.

"You go on, my love. I want to sit with Tanemao for a while."

Tiare nods and starts toward our *fare*. She comes back to stand before me. "Do you think we can make the peace last?"

I shrug. "Every encounter holds promise and threat. We must never stop believing in the promise." I gaze up at her. Beneath the lines of exhaustion, her face is more beautiful than ever. "Tiare, you were magnificent today."

She caresses my cheek. "You also."

As I watch Tiare walk away, I notice dark rain clouds billowing up the river valley. On the horizon, against a blackening sky, a rainbow shimmers. I imagine Tanemao walking there.

The soft light in Tanemao's *fare* envelops me. I nod to the young attendant, alert and solemn in the corner. "I'll stay for a while. You get something to eat."

I sit cross-legged at Tanemao's side and bow my head. My mind reels with all that has happened. My body feels beaten from lack of sleep and food. My spirit is nearly drained of *mana*. I can summon no more light.

As I look into Tanemao's handsome face, words tumble from my lips. "I am so sorry. I failed as your teacher, failed in my love for you. Please forgive me, Tanemao." I place my hand on his chest. "You were brave. You put yourself in danger to protect our people." The shark tooth, now polished, rests just below the hollow of his neck. "I thought the spirit of the shark had deserted you. But *Mao* was with you." Thoughts, words, pain keep bubbling up as I try to make sense of what happened. "Maybe we had to go this way. Maybe you had to do it so there would be a reason for Hiro and for us to make peace." A moan rises from my belly. "But if that is so, then must there always be death to have peace?" I hold my head in my hands. "Why did you have to leave us? You are so young, so full of promise. Your people need you. I need you." Tears fill my palms and run down my arms.

I press my hand to his forehead, my tears a final salt water blessing. "Thank you for giving us the gift of your life. Your feet are on the rainbow where there is only *Akua's* love."

Slumping forward, I moan and rock until there is nothing left to pour out. Great emptiness fills every part of my being.

A flash jolts my mind's eye. The face of a woman, skin the color of sun-dried bones, the flesh of one whose feet are set upon the rainbow. The eyes. They sparkle as if she is very much alive. Her eyes are round, the color of a clear sky, not like any I've ever seen. Are there people somewhere who look this way?

I feel no fear. Instead, I have the overwhelming sense that this woman and I are in some way a part of each other. How is that possible when we are so different?

I see her hand on the brow of a child with skin like mine. Somehow I am certain this woman with eyes like the sky is a healer. I feel the emanation of her *mana*, a river flowing through me. The water is warm. Floating on the comforting stream, I lie beside Tanemao. I concentrate on the woman's face and the face of the child and feel sure that this vision means we will make the peace last for many generations to come.

Sunny heard people murmuring to each other. She opened her eyes.

"Deep breath." Marie sat beside her on the sofa.

Sunny sucked in air, stretched, rubbed her eyes. She noticed all the empty chairs. Saw Pete in an armchair near the sofa. "Did everyone . . ."

"They thought you went deep meditation and tiptoed out," Pete said.

Sunny, now alert and remembering her dream, grasped Marie's hands. "They did it. The Anuanua kept the peace." She described the details of the meeting with the warriors of Tauati. "Do you think the dream is a message about the forum?" She shook her head. "Using light and energy was a way of life for the Anuanua. We've been practicing less than two weeks."

"Everyone has this knowing inside," Marie said. "Gonna call it forth. May not be big like Mahana's powerful force, but it'll be filled with enough spirit."

"*Ey*, we're standing on the shoulders of our ancestors," Pete said. "No chance for failure."

"But this could be our last shot for UM. They scheduled the forum on a Friday night. If we don't have enough people . . ."

Marie placed her hands on Sunny's shoulders. "It'll be what it needs to be. Maybe we just planting a few seeds. Get 'em?"

"Got it."

Twenty-four

A bubble of anxiety swelled in her gut. She stopped in the hallway to search the depths of her briefcase. The smooth stone she'd found on the beach felt cool against her fingers. Sunny tucked the stone in her blazer pocket. She grasped the handle of the door at the front of the auditorium and hesitated. How many people had come? She took a deep breath and walked in.

The crowd filled every seat, leaned against the walls, and spilled out four double-doors in the back. Patches of plum, rose, and teal marked the sections where UM staff in their bright-colored scrubs congregated. Sunny spotted Grace talking with Mike Jansen. Irene Pualoa and her camera crew huddled off to one side. The entire meditation group took up the last row.

Pete waved. Marie sat next to him, head bowed as is if in prayer. The seat on the other side of him was empty. He rested his arm across the back of the chair. Sunny imagined Lani sitting there, grinning, and signaling thumbs-up encouragement.

Old Ben sat in the front row. Sunny offered him her hand. "Thank you, Mr. Mahi for being here."

Ben grasped her hand in a gnarled grip and nodded. "*Aloha.*" He said the word like a blessing and smiled.

"*Aloha.*" Sunny pictured him stationed at the park entrance, his composure as cola from a hurled cup streamed down his face. She held his hand a moment longer, hoping for an infusion of his courage. Then she took a seat at the end of the row.

A side door opened. Darwin Chang led a large contingency to a long table at the front of the room. Sunny recognized Vance Turner from his photograph in the UM newsletter—suit jacket, expansive enough to cover two men, and a ruddy, cherubic face. Darwin and Vance took the center chairs at the table, each flanked by their respective executives. Katherine Nakamura, the lone woman, sat at the far end on Darwin's side. The men adjusted three table microphones, shuffled papers, and filled glasses with ice water from pitchers placed at perfectly spaced intervals. Vance pulled a mike toward him, tapping twice to check the sound.

"Good evening, ladies and gentlemen. Thanks, y'all, for coming. I'm Vance Turner, CEO of Comstock Health System." In Sunny's imagination, Vance's Texas drawl made his conservative suit disappear, replaced by a bolo tie around the flabby neck and a butter suede ten-gallon hat atop the balding head. "To my left here is Darwin Chang, chairman of the UM Board of Directors."

Vance and Darwin proceeded to introduce their own board members and officers. Sunny scanned the people at the VIP table. She glanced up at the mural of Māui pulling the island chain from the sea and imagined the demi-god dragging the executives up out of a pit.

"Let's get started by taking a look at the plans we have for UM. We have a few slides to show you." Vance looked back over his shoulder. "Can someone lower the screen?"

Sunny reached in her pocket, palmed the stone, and stood. "Excuse me, Mr. Turner. Our *kūpuna* would like to open this meeting with a blessing."

Vance stared at her as if she hadn't spoken a word of English. He quickly shifted gears with a broad smile. "Why, of course. That would be mighty fine." He lifted the cordless mike from its stand and held it out to her.

Sunny took the mike and turned to the crowd. "*Aloha*. My name is Sunny Lyon. I work here at UM. I want to introduce *kumu oli*, Ku'ulei Williamson who will lead us in prayer."

The woman who presided over Lani's memorial service rose from her chair and faced the gathering. She wore a black *mu'u mu'u*. A swath of red *kapa* was draped across the left shoulder and pinned at her right hip. A band of tiny cowry shells encircled her head, pearlescent against her dark hair. She embraced the whole room with outstretched arms. Her deep voice resonated with an otherworldly vibrato, filling the vast space with a sacred chant.

Chicken skin rippled on the back of Sunny's neck. A soft vibration surged around her as if a tremor had begun deep in the earth. She stole a glance at the VIP table. Had anyone else felt the hum? They sat at attention. No sign they'd experienced anything unusual. Ku'ulei finished the chant, and the crowd resounded with 'ae and amen.

Sunny handed the mike back to Vance who glanced over his shoulder again. "Now, can we have someone lower that screen?" He clicked through bullet-pointed slides detailing plans to enlarge the diagnostic imaging department at UM and to build a six-story parking garage. He emphasized the advanced care provided in Houston with photos of the buildings, care units, and staff. "This is just the beginning of the benefits CHS will bring to this community. Mr. Chang, would you like to add anything?" He pushed the mike toward Darwin.

In contrast to Vance's casual air, Darwin's posture was rigid, his expression a tight frown. He pushed a strand of limp gray hair from his forehead. "We're very proud of the partnership we've forged with CHS. Not only will we reap the benefits Mr. Turner talked about, but we'll also be able to provide excellent care for everyone on O'ahu, the outer islands, and indeed, the Pacific Rim."

Vance retrieved the mike. "All righty. We'd like to take questions from the audience. You'll notice there are standing microphones on either side of the room." He paused and looked toward one end of the front row, a frown narrowing his eyes. Irene Pualoa and her camera crew had moved into position and were filming. "I see we have the media with us tonight." He smiled. "Y'all give us some positive exposure now. As I was saying, if you'd please step up to one of those mikes to ask your question, everyone will be able to hear you."

Muted conversation rippled through the gathering. Sunny stared at the stone resting in her hand. A tiny pockmark in the smooth surface gave rise to a hairline crack. She closed her eyes. The deep earthquake hum grew stronger. Rather than hearing it, she felt it inside, against her skin, a vibrating cushion at her back. She visualized light rising in the room. The golden fog swirled into a warm cocoon, filling her with calm. Someone cleared his throat. Sunny opened her eyes.

A man who looked to be in his seventies, his frame wiry and yardstick straight, stood at the mike. He wore a tee shirt that identified him as THE ONLY PERSON WHO REALLY KNOWS WHAT'S GOING ON. He held up the newspaper ad. "Mr. Turner, why are you cutting all these services?"

"Please call me Vance. And your name, sir?"

"Jose Alvaro."

"Mr. Alvaro—"

"You can call me Joe. What about what it says here in the paper?"

"I'm assuming most of you have seen the ad?" Vance scanned the room. "Okay. Well, I think the ad is a bit misleading, Joe. CHS is definitely not opposed to those kinds of programs. Some people have benefited greatly from alternative care. Excuse me. I guess we're calling it complementary medicine now. Some day we may be able to provide a whole range of therapies throughout our system."

Darwin grabbed the mike. "The fact is we're in a very tight economic situation which requires us to cut back to our core services such as x-ray and surgery."

"But these are core services, Mr. Chang." A tiny woman with a pixie haircut stood on tiptoes at the mike across the room from Joe. "This kind of care helps people get better and saves lives."

Darwin started shaking his head before the woman finished her sentence. "That may be true in some instances. However, we've had to set priorities."

Murmurs in the crowd grew to loud conversations. Joe crumpled the newspaper ad in his fist and returned to his seat. The woman on tiptoes adjusted the microphone stand and planted herself squarely in front of it. "Mr. Chang, my name is Jeanie Victor. I'd like to tell you my story."

"We're here to take questions about the plans Mr. Turner shared with you." Darwin folded his arms in front of him. "There isn't time for unlimited discussion. "It's the end of a long week, and I'm sure everyone wants to get home at a decent hour. Are there any more questions?"

Conversations sounded angry. Sunny closed her eyes and drew in a deep breath. The meeting was already going sideways. Marie and Pete needed to pump up the volume of light. She squeezed her fist around the stone and left her seat to stand next to Jeanie Victor. "Vance,

Darwin." As she waited for the crowd to settle down, Sunny could feel the vibration again. It surged against her like a tide rolling from the back of the room. "At UM, we're here to serve the community. Please give the people who've come to this meeting a chance to tell you what they need."

Darwin's mouth tightened in a scowl. Vance put his hand over the mike and exchanged words with Darwin. Darwin sat back in his chair. Vance, flashing another cowboy grin, addressed the crowd. "We have a saying back home, folks. You can always tell a Texan, but you can't tell him much." He paused. The room was quiet. His smile faded. "Well, I want you to know I'm not that kind of Texan. I want you to go on and tell me what I need to hear. Please continue, Ms. Victor."

"A year ago, I was told I had only a couple of months to live. Ovarian cancer. The doctor across town was so cold and technical when he gave me the diagnosis. There was one thing he didn't give me—hope. I rushed to a university hospital on the mainland. I figured that was my best chance for survival. They said my only option was high dose chemotherapy, that it would probably make me very sick, and wouldn't do me much good. The staff treated me like I was already a corpse in the bed. I'm still alive because I came home to O'ahu, came to UM.

"My first night here, I cried for hours because I was so scared. A nurse stayed with me the whole time. The next day a team surrounded me. My doctors, nurses, therapists hugged me, answered my endless questions, gave me lots of options, and encouraged me to choose what's best for me. I've been on a regimen of herbs and fractionated dose chemo to prevent severe side effects. Through guided visualization my tumor is shrinking. My doctor thinks they'll be able to operate and get all the cancer out.

"My daughter went to her first prom last weekend . . ." The diminutive woman paused to clear her throat. A radiant smile lit up her face. "Janna looked so lovely. She wore the dress of her dreams. I was here to make that dress because of the care I've received at UM. Mr. Turner, Mr. Chang, you need to know there's no place on earth like UM. We are 'ohana, all the patients and their families and staff together. There is love and hope and healing here. Please don't cut those things in your budget."

Vance's tone was solemn. "Thank you, Ms. Victor. I'm mighty glad to hear your good news."

Darwin still sat with his arms crossed in front of him, his head tilted down as if he were studying his sleeve.

At the other mike, a young man with blonde, spiked hair leaned on a cane. An intricate tattoo of a lizard emerged from under his black shirt and crawled up his neck. Behind him, Gary Stone, the owner of The Wall, stood with his hands jammed in his pockets. "I'm Raymond Stone. Have you ever had such awful pain that you puke your guts out, bang your head against the wall, wish you were dead?"

Vance looked startled. "Well, son, I can't say that I have."

Raymond pointed at Darwin. "You?"

Darwin adjusted his gold wire-rim glasses, stared at the young man, and slowly shook his head.

"A lot of nights, that's how I felt. Used to ride a motorcycle. Had a freaky accident. Never dreamed there could be pain like that. I was takin' some heavy-duty painkillers. Now, I come here three days a week. They hook me up to this machine that's helpin' me learn how to relax the muscles. Biofeedback. I'm gettin' by on aspirin and not wishin' I was dead anymore."

People lined up at both mikes. Vance nodded and winked and said thank you to every person. Darwin gradually sat back in his chair, eyes riveted on the speakers, his jaw slack. At intervals, he rubbed his hand across his mouth or the back of his neck. Sunny closed her eyes and imagined him surrounded by brilliant golden light.

The last person to speak, a UM staff member in plum scrubs, stethoscope dangling out of one pocket, introduced herself. "Hi. I'm Sue Barton. When I worked at the big hospital across town, I rarely got to take a break. By the end of my shifts, I was frazzled, scared of making a mistake, frustrated because I had no time to be with the people who needed me. I'm the nurse who sat with Jeanie Victor that night. I felt honored to be with her. I've never worked any place where I had time to do that. I've completed a course UM offers, one that I tell every new staff member they should take as soon as they can—the sacred work of healing. The most important events of people's lives happen here—birth, death, struggles with serious illness, dealing with feelings of anger, guilt, fear, and even joy. Gentleman, we're doing sacred work here. Stop cutting our staff. Don't turn us into a factory line."

The room erupted into applause and loud cheers.

Darwin steepled his hands in front of him. He looked sad.

Vance motioned to quiet the audience. "Thanks to all of the folks who've shared their stories with us. I must say I've been touched. We need to ponder everything we've heard and get back to y'all real soon."

A hundred side conversations commenced. Sunny squeezed the stone so hard her fingernails dug into her palm. She returned to the mike. "Mr. Turner, we need your word tonight that you will support what we do and how we do it."

The conversations evaporated to a few whispers. Vance flashed another warm smile. "Now, Ms. Lyon, we can't move ahead until we've discussed this."

"I understand that. I have some questions we can use to begin the discussion right now."

The smile faded from the CEO's face. "Ms. Lyon, we don't have time. I think we need to let these good folk head on home."

A woman behind Sunny grumbled loudly. "Does he think we're stupid? He just wants to get his tail out of here without responding to anything we've said."

"Mr. Turner, why don't we ask our customers if they wish to stay and participate in planning for UM's future?"

Here and there, people called out. "We'll stay. You need to include us. This meeting isn't over."

Vance glared at her. "Ms. Lyon—"

Sunny felt waves of vibration hum in her bones. She held the Texan's stare.

A voice boomed from somewhere in the back of the room. "Vance, it looks like everyone wants to stay." Sunny's breath caught in her chest. She strained to see David striding up the aisle. He looked crisp and handsome in a close-fitting polo shirt and tailored slacks. Sunny blinked to make sure it wasn't another dream. The television camera crew followed him to the mike. He stood with his hands on his hips, one eyebrow arched. "Let's hear the questions."

Vance started to rise from his chair. Darwin placed a hand on the big man's forearm. They exchanged a few words. The CEO settled in his chair and nodded to Sunny.

Sunny glanced at her yellow tablet. "Are we in tune with our higher purpose?"

Katherine reached for the mike and stood up at one end of the VIP table. "I'd like to read UM's mission statement. 'We are an instrument of true *aloha*. We enhance the lives we touch by caring for the body, respecting the mind, and comforting the spirit. We offer a broad range of healing therapies to enhance the lives of the people who come to us. We are their *hoa hana*, their partners on the path to wellness. We reach out to promote the health of our community and never forget the importance of *'ohana*.'"

"Thank you, Katherine." Sunny looked at Vance and Darwin. "From what many people have said tonight, it sounds like we've been striving to fulfill our mission. We ask that you consider how the plans and changes you're bringing to UM will keep us aligned with our higher purpose."

"What's your next question, Ms. Lyon?" Vance asked.

"What guidance, knowledge, and insight do we need?"

Vance pointed to a hand waving across the room. "Sir, you have something to say."

Gary Stone walked to the mike. "I run a business. Granted, it's a tiny operation compared to UM, and we're not taking care of sick people. Although, sometimes I feel like a psychiatrist." A few regulars at The Wall chuckled. "You guys need to figure out how to get more money in order to keep these programs. What about asking the business community to ante up? We got some big resorts on this island. Maybe you could tap into government money. There's always enough of that for the military bases around here."

Sunny stepped back to give Sue Barton the mike. "I think we've seen the tip of the iceberg tonight. You should run a survey to find out how the services at UM fill the needs of this community, gather more data. Publish the results. I bet we'll have more clients knocking at our door than we can accommodate."

Vance motioned to Sunny.

"The next question is what actions will bring more light to this situation?"

Vance frowned. "What does that mean, Ms. Lyon?"

"I'd like to ask Marie Maikui Kealoha to answer your question. Marie would you come up?"

Pete helped Marie walk to the front. She paused a moment to catch her breath, then tapped her finger to the side of her head. "Mr. Turner, Mr. Chang, light comes from open minds." She placed her hand on her chest. "From open hearts. Light means being honest." She raised her fist. "Light means justice." She opened her arms wide. "Light means we be creative together to solve these problems." Marie's voice fell into a cadence as if she were delivering a chant. "Money. Why all this worry about money? Light is believing in abundance. Whatever we need is here for us." She took a deep breath. "Light is the energy for good that is all around us."

'Ae and right on and amen rippled across the room.

Darwin leaned toward the mike. "Thank you, Ms. Kealoha."

Marie put her arm around Sunny. "How can we show compassion? That's the next question. How you making sure there's *aloha* at UM, like it says in your mission statement?" Marie's words sounded more like a command than a question. She puffed herself up to her full height, took Pete's arm, and walked slowly back to her chair.

Darwin gestured to someone behind Sunny. She turned to see an old man, sparse tuffs of hair on his bald head, maneuvering a wheelchair forward. Gold wire-rim glasses perched on the end of his nose. Sunny stared at the likeness of an older Darwin. She lowered the mike to his level and moved aside.

"I am Franklin Chang. They took out my gallbladder last year." Franklin's voice trembled as he formed his words. "The people here treated me with respect. They wanted to give me a massage. Said, 'Oh, Mr. Chang, would you like to listen to some music?'" His shout came out raspy. "I don't care about those things." The audience was still. Sunny cringed. What point was he trying to make? His voice dropped to a near whisper. "They offered me those things. Made this ninety-year-old man feel like someone important. That is compassion to me."

Darwin slowly rose from the front table and made his way down the aisle. He bent low, his face inches from the old man's. "Uncle, what are you doing here?"

"Thought maybe you'd listen if I came with a bunch of people. Respect, nephew, it's about respect."

Darwin grasped the handles on the wheelchair and whisked the old man to the back of the auditorium.

Sunny adjusted the mike, looked into every face at the VIP table. "Franklin Chang's story reminds us how important it is to make decisions out of compassion for human beings rather than out of fear."

"Ms. Lyon, I think your logic is a little whomperjawed. No one here is afraid. We're just trying to make good business decisions. That's the best way to serve this community."

Katherine leaned forward to look directly at Vance. "When an entire board sees forsaking our mission as a solution to budget problems, that's a cowardly act, not a good business decision." The administrator sat back in her chair as if she were calculating the cost of her outburst. The enthusiastic applause from the crowd did nothing to ease her pained expression.

Vance ignored Katherine. "I trust we've covered all your questions, Ms. Lyon."

"There's one more. How can we ensure a solid foundation for future generations?"

Mark and Betty Kaneko came forward. Mark held Kimmy in his arms. Betty held the mike. "This is our daughter, Kimberly. It's her generation and those who come after her that we need to think about tonight."

"Hello, Kimberly." Vance's mouth turned up in a saccharine smile.

Betty tilted the mike toward her daughter. "Can you tell everyone how you got well?"

"Dr. Grace fixed my heart, but I still felt bad. I couldn't get out of bed. I felt so cold. My mommy and daddy and my Uncle David warmed me up." A smile beamed on Kimmy's face. She buried her head in Mark's shoulder.

Mark's voice sounded hoarse. "Our daughter is with us because of Ms. Lyon and Ms. Kealoha. They . . ." He shook his head, pressed his fingers to the bridge of his nose.

Betty hugged her husband and daughter, then turned to the executives. "They brought loving energy and healing touch to help Kimmy. The point is, that kind of healing should be as much a part of the way you take care of people as are pills and x-rays. It should be available for everyone here, for our children, our grandchildren, and our great grandchildren."

Applause broke out across the room as the family went back to their seats. Sunny waited for the noise to die down. "Mr. Turner, let's work together to find the resources to keep our commitments to this community. Can we do that?"

Before Vance could answer, Darwin spoke into the floor mike across from Sunny. "Mr. Turner, if you want UM to be part of CHS, you'll have to help us find the means to care for people our way."

A deafening roar erupted in the auditorium. Sunny looked back at rows and rows of people on their feet, cheering and clapping. Her chest felt too small to contain the elation swelling in her heart.

Vance stood, his face a tight mask. The noise gradually faded. He leaned down to the mike on the table in front of him. "I believe that would be a deal breaker, Mr. Chang." He buttoned his suit jacket and headed for the door.

Twenty-five

The CHS executives looked as if they'd just seen their CEO disappear in a column of smoke. They pushed back their chairs and hurried after him.

Still at the floor mike, Darwin said, "Folks, let's take a ten-minute break." The momentary hush in the crowd shifted into a din. Darwin moved to the front and huddled with the UM executives. After a few minutes, the group followed in the CHS wake. Irene and her camera crew stayed close behind them but were turned away at the door.

People milled in the aisles and talked in animated clusters. Sunny stood on tip-toes to catch sight of Marie. The old woman waved. Sunny raised her palms in a what-now gesture. Pete and Marie pushed through the crowd as Sunny edged toward them from the front.

Sunny called over the noise. "Got any suggestions?"

Marie pointed to the exit where Vance and Darwin had disappeared. They stepped out in the hall and heard Darwin shouting. "Katherine Nakamura is right. We promoted this wellness center and all these remarkable services. But when the going got tough, we looked for an easy way out. We were willing to change whatever we needed to change, cut whatever we needed to cut in order to obtain your financial backing."

"May I remind you the contracts have been signed, partner," Vance shouted back.

Marie squeezed Sunny's arm, moved in close. "We're here to hold the light," she whispered. "Breathe. Build the *mana*."

Sunny watched Marie draw in a deep breath and blow it out her mouth with a ha sound. Pete closed his eyes and did the same. Sunny felt a flush creeping up her neck and looked toward the clutch of administrators. They seemed unaware of the three interlopers a little way down the hall. She took a breath, but kept her eyes riveted on Vance and Darwin.

Katherine's voice resounded. "Vance, you see the strengths of UM as obstacles, the fluffy stuff that costs too much. We should be spending as much money on preventing illness and keeping people healthy as we spend on treating disease."

Vance turned his back on Katherine and shoved a finger in Darwin's face. "Can't spend money you don't have. You want us to save your ass, you get on board with our financial plan."

Darwin raised his hand, hesitated, drew it through his hair. He shoved his way to the edge of the group and stood with his arms folded, head bent.

"Breathe," Marie whispered.

Sunny closed her eyes and took a deep breath. A vision of Mahana facing the Tauati warriors flashed in her brain. She focused her mind's eye on a spark of white light, imagined it growing brighter. She took another deep breath and imagined it flooding the hallway, wrapping around everyone there.

"Hold on, gentleman," Katherine said. "Why don't we all take a breather?"

Sunny concentrated on the light, listening hard for a response.

Katherine continued. "I want us to think about the risk if we don't find a way to keep our commitments to this community."

Marie started a chant, the sound barely audible, the Hawaiian words unmistakable.

"I'll tell you what the risk is," UM's chief financial officer interjected. "The city revokes our not-for-profit charter, and we close."

"And the crowd in there will lead the charge," Katherine said.

"Shit. You people are acting like a bunch of gnats in a hailstorm." Vance paused for a long moment. "Hell. I'll play along."

Marie murmured, " *'Ae*."

"How're you going to make budget?" Vance asked. "CHS isn't backing a loser."

The group was quiet. Sunny breathed deeply and sent white light swirling around Vance and Darwin.

"I'll get the money." Darwin's voice rang out in the hallway. Sunny opened her eyes. Darwin stood facing Vance and Katherine. "Just give me five minutes to make a call."

Sunny squeezed Marie's shoulder, touched Pete's arm. When they opened their eyes, she motioned them into the auditorium. Most of the people had taken their seats. They chatted, quieted fussy children, kept their eyes on the exit that had swallowed all of the VIPs.

Pete pulled out three chairs at the end of a row. *"Ey, sistahs*, what you think?"

Marie shrugged. "No telling." She eased into a seat.

Vance's drawl echoed in Sunny's ears—hell, I'll play along. "At least we got them to take a step back." She twisted in her chair to glimpse David at the back of the room. He was holding Kimmy, laughing with Betty and Mark.

Darwin and Vance entered the auditorium followed by their entourage. They took their places at the front table in a museum-like atmosphere. Sunny searched Vance Turner's expression for an indication of good news.

Vance adjusted the microphone. "First of all, I'd like to thank y'all for staying this late. The community interest in UM is impressive. We've decided that for now we'll continue the services we've been talking about." Vance waited for the applause to die down.

Joe Alvaro, the first person to speak hours before, stood at the floor mike. He'd smoothed out the crumpled newspaper ad. Now he waved it high. "Do you mean these services won't go away?"

"That's what we mean, but—"

Darwin cut in. "UM needs to raise half of the money to keep those programs going in the short term. I'm pleased to announce that First Islands Bank will get us started with $100,000 over the next three years. I hope other corporations will realize our value to their employees and follow our lead. We'll be looking to all of you for ideas to secure the rest of the funds. I know we can do it. We owe it to our *keiki*. Thank you everyone."

With one last round of applause and cheers, the crowd poured out of the auditorium. Sunny felt like running laps around the room, shouting hallelujahs until someone needed to pull her off the ceiling. Instead, she watched the UM executives vacate their chairs, pausing to chat, grinning as if they'd just won the lottery. Darwin shook hands with Katherine who was smiling for the first time in recent memory. Vance's tight expression made Sunny think he couldn't wait to board the flight to Houston.

Sunny scanned the mass of people flowing into the aisles. Maybe David had left with Betty and Mark. She felt a tap on her shoulder and turned, hoping to see his face.

Darwin offered his hand. "Thank you for giving us the chance to make some different decisions."

Sunny shook his hand. Had he seen her in the hallway? "My pleasure. I appreciate your willingness to stand up for UM."

He nodded.

"May I ask what changed your mind?"

Darwin adjusted his glasses. "Getting reconnected with the people." The corner of his mouth quivered. "And my uncle. Before his surgery, he dreamed of his own death. He believes the staff here saved him."

"I'm glad Mr. Chang was with us tonight."

Darwin bowed his head slightly and turned away.

Sunny stared at the floor, rubbing the stone between her thumb and forefinger. She never expected the turnaround to be so huge. She'd gotten exactly what she wanted and could scarcely take it in. The urge to find a quiet corner made her head spin. A warm hand squeezed her arm.

"My precious girl, you flew the way, and they came with you." Marie crushed Sunny in a hug. "You are true *kōlea*."

Pete wrapped his immense arms around them both. "Powerful *wahine*."

Sunny smiled up at them. "I'm grateful to have your friendship. Thank you. *Mahalo nui loa*."

They embraced again. Then Pete took Marie's arm. "Come on, *Tūtū*. It's a long way to your *hale*."

She watched them walk slowly up the aisle. At the door, Marie turned and waved. Sunny raised her hand to return the wave and dropped the stone. She smiled. It lay on the floor, broken in two.

Twenty-six

Sunny sank into a chair in the back of the empty auditorium. She studied the two pieces of the stone, fitted them together, let them fall apart. Water dripping on a rock. More like a torrent of water pummeling a sand bar. Kimmy's healing had amazed her, but the impact of the power they'd just summoned drained her body and stunned her mind. She wanted to savor this moment, float in the wonder of pure magic and humbling miracles. If only Lani could have been there.

A chair clattered behind her. The janitors were probably anxious to start cleaning. She slipped the pieces of stone into her blazer pocket and started for the front row where she'd left her briefcase.

"You held their feet to the fire."

His voice sounded low, warm. Sunny's heart bounced against her ribs. She turned to see David straddling a chair, his arms folded across the backrest. The brilliance of his smile made her feel shaky. She swiveled a chair around to face him, mind racing to find words, and sat down. "I had a lot of help. Thanks for jumping in. When I asked them to consider our planning questions, I thought the curtain was coming down for sure."

"Wouldn't you love to know what happened when they all left the room?"

Sunny smiled.

David watched her with such intensity that she felt compelled to look away. For weeks, she'd longed for a chance to apologize, a chance to heal their past. Now, he sat right here in front of her. Her stomach tightened. *Chance 'em.* "Did you get any of my messages?"

"I did. Our last conversation—"

"I apologize for what happened. I know I've been acting crazy since that night at your house."

"You've had me baffled, to say the least."

"In the stairwell, I told you I wasn't afraid." She shook her head. "Not true." His expression was unreadable. She bit the inside of her lip. "Let's just say it's a once-burned-twice-shy thing."

David nodded slowly. "I figured. I'm not that guy, Sunny."

"I know." In the silence, she forced herself not to tap her fingers on the metal chair. "Anyway, I just wanted to let you know that I've enjoyed our time together very much. I'm disappointed you're leaving."

He tapped a rhythm on the back of his chair. "So, you're no longer avoiding me?"

"I really want us to be good friends."

He arched an eyebrow. "Would that include an occasional dinner?"

"Most definitely."

"Tomorrow night." David got out of the chair. "It'll be my last taste of fresh 'ahi before I head for longhorn country on Sunday."

Sunny stood. "We'll have to send you care packages by same-day air."

They laughed, faced each other, inches apart. "David, I appreciate all you've done for UM, for me."

"You're a courageous woman."

"Thanks."

He backed toward the door. "Shall I pick you up at seven?"

"No. I'll pick you up at six. I know a place where we can see a nice sunset. That is if you don't mind riding in an island wreck."

He tossed her a salute, turned to go. "I'm always up for an adventure."

"By the way, Grace said you were gone for good. Why did you come back?"

He faced her, a smile playing around his lips. "Let's just say it's a once-burned-absolutely-never-shy thing."

Fat raindrops, glittering in the late afternoon sun, dotted the windshield. Dark clouds loomed over the verdant folds of the Ko'olau Mountains. Sunny exited the freeway and steered the car toward the clouds. A rainbow arched in Mānoa Valley, vivid bands of cerulean, gold, and crimson suspended in mist. She parked in front of David's house and watched as the rainbow gradually disappeared in the shifting light.

Sunny bowed low when he answered the door. "Your limousine awaits."

David peered around her. "Hmm, vintage Cabriolet with just a hint of rust. Let's put the top down."

"We might get soaked."

He turned in the doorway. "Let me get my wetsuit."

She laughed and grabbed his hand. "Come on. We're going to miss the sunset."

Sunny shouted over the wind and the straining of the engine. "Tell me about Houston."

"It'll be two years max. My plan is to stay there long enough to get familiar with the CHS research protocols and run a trial study. Vance finally agreed to a beta site at UM."

Sunny turned on the windshield wipers. "Hmm, sounds familiar."

"This time I'll get it in writing, a formal contract. If not, I'll be begging Grace to let me back in the group by the end of the month."

"Have you lined up a place to live?"

"Corporate apartment near the hospital. If that gets old, I still have friends there who'll help me find a house."

Raindrops stabbed Sunny's face. Sadness stabbed her heart. There was no denying her feeling of loss. She drove across the city and headed east.

"Are we going back to your place?"

"You could say that." She glanced at David. The puzzled look on his face and his wind-tousled hair made her want to reach out and caress his cheek. She kept her hand wrapped around the shift knob.

"What about you? What are you going to do now?"

"Darwin asked me to be the director of a new complementary medicine department."

"Whoa! Good show, Sunny." He held up his hand for a high five. When they touched, he squeezed her hand, laced his fingers with hers.

"I'll have to be a quick study. Tapping the business sector for money, writing grants, research. I have no experience in those areas."

"Piece of cake for someone who handles pompous surgeons." His tight hold on her hand sent a ripple of warmth through her body.

Sunny moved her hand back to the gear knob and downshifted to turn off the highway. The sun slipped from behind the clouds to beam on the gravel road. She clicked off the windshield wipers.

In the parking area, they gathered the cooler, picnic basket, and blanket from the back seat. Sunny led David past the *hale* to the clearing. He set the cooler on the grass, his eyes wide, mouth open. He turned slowly, scanning the surroundings. "This is Mahana's village."

She knelt down and rubbed the rough rock, buried in the ground. "The massive round stone stood here. It marks the place where they held the ritual the night Tanemao was killed."

David hunkered down next to her, their knees almost touching. He stroked the rock as if it held the magic of a genie's lamp. "Show me the rest."

She suddenly felt awkward. Her voice dropped into tour guide cadence. "The *hale* are not the original buildings, of course. The long house over there is where they held their council meetings. The area by the river is pretty much the same. Although, the river ran much wider and deeper back then."

They walked down to the river bank. Gardenias spiced the air. A raucous call-and-response choir of mynahs swooped from tree to tree high above them. Slanting rays of the sun burnished the mountain rising over the village.

She pointed to the peak. "The Fin of *Mao*."

David stared up at the peak. She stood quietly beside him, waited. He walked a little way up river. She didn't follow. He needed time to grapple with the power of the place, the mystery of his own past.

Sunny spread out the blanket. She leaned back to watch the clouds bunch up behind the peak, gray puffs outlined in copper against a Botticelli blue sky. A sense of peace infused her. They'd closed the circle by coming home to Kauhale O Waimea. No matter what happened from now on, they'd accomplished more than she had imagined possible just a few short months ago.

David came back down the river's edge and sat opposite her on the blanket. "Thank you for bringing me here. It's funny. I grew up on

O'ahu. But I've never felt especially rooted to this island. Until now. This place . . . " He shook his head. "I don't know."

"It's not easy to put into words."

"Maybe I shouldn't thank you. Now it'll be even harder to get on that plane."

She popped the cork on the champagne. "You've waited a long time for this opportunity, David. It deserves a toast." He held the flutes while she poured. Raising her glass, she intoned, "To the next major breakthrough in cardiac surgery."

He clinked his glass to hers and took a sip. The wind in the palms rattled the silence between them. He put down his glass, a searching look in his dark eyes. "I don't want us to go our separate ways this time around."

Sunny tried to sort out the jumble of thoughts tumbling around in her head. He still wanted more than she felt ready to give. But then why did it feel like her heart was pleading with him to stay? "I can't go to Houston. I still have to figure out how to use Mahana's gift of healing. I need Marie for that."

"No, no. I wouldn't ask you to leave UM. You need to get things going before the big dogs change their minds."

She took his hand, turned it over to trace the lines in his palm. Beautiful hands, sensitive enough to handle the most delicate tissue, strong and steady enough to endure long hours reviving a dying heart. She stroked his fine-tapered fingers and shivered to remember the arcs of fire they'd sent through her body. It wasn't fair to ask him to wait. She closed his hand into a fist and cupped it in both of hers. "If we're meant to be together, it will happen."

He looked directly at her, eyes riveted, unblinking. "I've dated quite a few women. Had a girlfriend in Houston for a while. Until you, I never met anyone worth my time."

Sunny looked toward the river, tears stinging her eyes. Why couldn't she totally trust him, herself, this connection?

"This isn't the surgeon-nurse cliché. This is about two people who've been together a long, long time." He cupped her chin in his hand, leaned forward to kiss her, his lips lightly brushing hers. "There's no if, Sunny. We are meant to be together."

"David, you needed some time to understand us in our past. I need some time to get to know us now."

"You got it. We'll just ease into the present." He stood up. "Let's catch that sunset."

They walked down to the river's edge. He stood behind her, his arms around her waist. Fiery rays streaked the maroon sky. The storm clouds over the peak had cleared, replaced by a crescent moon. Sounds enveloped them—the splash of a fish capturing a twilight morsel, an owl hooting somewhere in the jungle upstream. She folded her arms across his, and they swayed to the soft rushing of water.

The wind coming up the valley from the sea cooled Sunny's skin. She leaned back into David's warmth. Mahana and Tiare had held each other in this very spot, dreaming about their canoe trips to the beach. "Marie says we can find ourselves, find each other, on a river through time."

He pointed toward the ocean. "So our future is just around that bend."

"Does it bother you that we can't see where the river ends?"

"Not at all."

She turned in his arms. The shark tooth gleamed on his chest. She fingered the rough surface. "Because no matter what, you hang tough?"

He shrugged. "No, because you won't be able to get rid of me this time, old man."

She laughed and tweaked the cleft in his chin. "There's hope for you yet, my fine apprentice."

They gathered up the gear and headed for the car. At the edge of the village, Sunny stopped to look back across the clearing. *Hale* floated in the blue veil of night. The surrounding jungle lay deep in shadow. She half-expected to see a white dog materialize in the bushes and lope toward her. She closed her eyes and whispered, "Thank you, Mahana." Looking up at the sky, she focused on a single, brilliant star, one brave enough to compete with the last glow of sunset. "Thanks for not giving up on me, girl friend."

When Sunny turned, she saw David waiting for her. She studied his face. He returned her gaze. They stood still, as if they were listening for a starting gun to the future. He arched an eyebrow and grinned. She let out a deep sigh and seized a head start in the race to the car.

GLOSSARY

HAWAIIAN - ENGLISH

A HUI HOU (ah hoo-ee hoh-oo) . . . Goodbye, see you later, until we meet again

A 'OLE PILIKIA (ah oh-leh pee-lee-kee-ah) . . . No problem, no trouble

'AE (eye) . . . Yes

AHI (ah-hee) . . . Fire

'AHI (ah-hee) . . . Yellow-fin tuna fish

'ĀINA (eye-nah) . . . Land, earth

AKAMAI (ah-kah-my) . . . Smart, clever

AKUA (ah-koo-ah) . . . God, goddess, divine, spirit

ALI'I (ah-lee-ee) . . . Royalty, chiefs, kings and queens

ALOHA (ah-lo-hah) . . . Love, greetings, compassion, spirit of love

ALOHA NUI LOA (ah-lo-hah noo-ee lo-ah) . . . Much love

AMA (ah-mah) . . . Outrigger float

'AUMAKUA (ow-mah-koo-ah) . . . Family god, deified ancestor, guardian spirit (Plural: 'AUMĀKUA)

AUWĒ! (ow-way) . . . Alas!

'AWA (ah-vah) . . . Tea from kava root, mildly narcotic

'AWAPUHI (ah-wah-poo-hee) . . . Wild ginger. Used for shampoo, lubricant for massage

CHANCE 'EM (chans em) . . . Take a chance, go for it, risk it (Pidgin-English)

E HO'I I KA PILI (eh hoh-ee ee kah pee-lee) . . . Come here to me

E KOMO MAI (eh koh-moh my) . . . Welcome! Come in. Come hither

E KULIKULI (eh koo-lee-koo-lee) . . . Hey! Be quiet!

E 'OLU 'OLU MĀLAMA PONO (eh oh-loo oh-loo mah-lah-mah poh-noh) . . . Please take care. Please be careful

'EKAHI, 'ELUA, 'EKOLU (eh-kah-hee, eh-loo-ah, eh-koh-loo) . . . One, two, three

'ELEPAIO (eh-lay-pie-oh) . . . Flycatcher bird

EY, BRAH (eh brah) . . . Hey, brother (Pidgin-English)

EY, SISTAH (eh sees-tah) . . . Hey, sister (Pidgin-English)

HĀ (hah) . . . Breath, life

HALA (hah-lah) . . . Pandanus tree. Leaves used to weave mats, sandals, canoe sails, fans, baskets LAU (lah-oo) means leaf

HALE (hah-leh) . . . House

HAOLE (how-leh) . . . Caucasian, white. One without breath

HAU (hah-oo) . . . Lowland tree with heart-shaped leaves and hibiscus-like flower

HELE MAI (heh-leh my) . . . Come here

HOA HANA (hoh-ah hah-nah) . . . Partner, colleague

HONUA (hoh-noo-ah) . . . Earth, world

HULA (hoo-lah) . . . Story-telling dance of Hawai'i

HULA HĀLAU (hoo-lah hah-lah-oo) . . . Hula school

'IAKO (ee-ah-koh) . . . Outrigger boom

'I'IWI (ee-ee-vee) . . . Scarlet Hawaiian honey creeper

I KA NUI (ee-kah-noo-ee) . . . This is big

'I'O (ee-oh) . . . Truth, true

'IOLANI (ee-oh-lah-nee) . . . Royal hawk

IPU HEKE (ee-poo heh-keh) . . . Gourd drum used for entertainment and celebration

KAHIKO HULA (kah-hee-koh hoo-lah) . . . Ancient form of hula

KĀHILI (kah-hee-lee) . . . Feather standard, symbolic of royalty

KAHUNA (kah-hoo-nah) . . . Seer, expert, keeper of secrets

KAI (kah-ee) . . . Sea, sea water

KALO (kah-lo) . . . Taro. A yam-like corm with large, green heart-shaped leaves

KANAKA (kah-nah-kah) . . . Hawaiian person (Plural: KĀNAKA)

KANAKA MAOLI (kah-nah-kah mah-oh-lee) . . . Descendant of people who lived in Hawai'i prior to 1778

KAPA (kah-pah) . . . Cloth made from pounded mulberry bark

KAPU (kah-poo) . . . Forbidden, sacred, keep out

KAUHALE (kah-oo-hah-leh) . . . Hamlet or settlement

KEIKI (kay-kee) . . . Child

KEKO (kay-koh) . . . Monkey

KĪ (kee) . . . Ti. Woody plant in the lily family. Used for wrapping food, cooking, hula skirts, lei, medicine, to ward off evil spirits

KIAWE (kee-ah-vay) . . . A tree from Peru, first planted in 1828 in Hawai'i

KOA (koh-ah) . . . Large, native tree

KŌKUA (koh-koo-ah) . . . Help, assistance, to help, helper

KŌLEA (koh-leh-ah) . . . Pacific golden plover, migratory bird

KUKUI (koo-koo-ee) . . . Candlenut tree. Nuts used for lamps, torches, oil, cooking, jewelry

KUMU OLI (koo-moo oh-lee) . . . Chant master

KUPUNA (koo-poo-nah) . . . Respected elder (Plural: KŪPUNA)

LĀNAI (lah-nigh) . . . Porch, veranda, balcony

LAU LAU (lah-oo lah-oo) . . . Pork wrapped in ti or banana leaves, and baked or steamed

LOMI LOMI (lo-mee lo-mee) . . . To knead, squeeze, traditional Hawaiian massage

LEI (leh-ee) . . . Flowered necklace, wreath for the neck

MAHALO (mah-hah-lo) . . . Thank you

MAHALO NUI LOA (mah-hah-lo noo-ee lo-ah) . . . Thank you very much

MAIKA'I (my-kah-ee) . . .Good, fine, well

MAILE (my-leh) . . . Native twining, fragrant vine with glossy leaves used for lei, used to scent kapa

MĀLA (mah-lah) . . . Garden

MALO (mah-lo) . . . Male's loincloth

MANA (mah-nah) . . . Divine power, spiritual essence

MANA LOA (mah-nah lo-ah) . . . Great power

MANŌ (mah-noh) . . . Shark

MELE (meh-leh) . . . Song, poem

MENEHUNE (meh-neh-hoo-neh) . . . Legendary race of small people

MO'O (moh-oh) . . . Lizard, dragon

MU'UMU'U (moo-oo-moo-oo) . . . Long, shapeless, Mother Hubbard dress

'OHANA (oh-hah-nah) . . . Family, kin group

'ŌHELO (oh-hel-oh) . . . Small shrub in the cranberry family

OLONĀ (oh-lo-nah) . . . Native shrub, bark used to make strong fiber strands, rope

'ONO (oh-no) . . . Delicious, savory, good

'ŌPAKAPAKA (oh-pah-ka-pah-ka) . . . Blue snapper

PAHU (pah-hoo) . . . Ceremonial drum, often carved from lower section of palm tree trunk and covered with a shark skin head

PALI (pah-lee) . . . Cliff

PAU (pow) . . . Finished, ended, all done

PIKO (pee-koh) . . . Navel, belly button

PILI (pee-lee) . . . Grass used for thatching

POI (poy) . . . Paste made of pounded, cooked taro corms

PONO (poh-noh) . . . Right, goodness, proper, correct

PUA (poo-ah) . . . Flower

PUEO (poo-eh-oh) . . . Owl

PULE (poo-leh) . . . Prayer

PUPULE (poo-poo-leh) . . . Crazy, insane

SHAKA (shah-kah) . . . Hawai'ian greeting by waving thumb and little finger, middle three fingers bent down. Hang loose

STINK EYE . . . Dirty look, frown, scowl

TO DA MAX (too dah macks) . . . Expression of boundless enthusiasm, no limit, knock yourself out (Pidgin-English)

TŪTŪ (too-too) . . . Grandmother, grandfather (informal)

UA PILI MĀUA (oo-ah pee-lee mah-oo-ah) . . . We are all connected

'UHANE (oo-hah-neh) . . . Spirit

'UKULELE (oo-koo-leh-leh) . . . Hawai'ian guitar. Leaping flea

ULE (oo-leh) . . . Penis

WAHINE (vah-hee-neh) . . . Woman, lady, wife

WAI (why) . . . Fresh water

WAIMEA (why-meh-ah) . . . reddish water

WAUKE (wah-oo-keh) . . . Paper mulberry tree. Bark used to make kapa

WILIWILI (wee-lee-wee-lee) . . . Hawai'ian tree. Wood close to the lightness of balsa. Used for canoe outriggers, surfboards, net floats

TAHITIAN - ENGLISH

FARE . . . House

HAUTI . . . Make love, play

IOA . . . Name

MAO . . . Shark

MARAE . . . Temple

NONI . . . Indian Mulberry. Source of dye, wood, medicine. Polynesian
cure-all

TAHUA ORI . . . Dance master

TANE . . . Man, husband

TAPA . . . Cloth made from the pounded bark of the paper mulberry

TARO . . . Starchy elephant-ear tuber, staple food of Pacific islanders

TATAU . . . Tattoo

TI . . . Plant in agave family. Used for cooling fever, treating coughs,
internal hemorrhage, inflamed tissue, infection

TUPAPAU . . . Ghost

URU . . . Breadfruit

VAHINE . . . Woman, wife

To order more copies of *River Through Time*, please visit www.riverthroughtime.com.

Printed in the United States
36964LVS00004B/109-510

9 781593 302917